INFEROS
EDGE

INFEROS EDGE

THE FALLEN PANTHEON

ALEJ McKINLEY

Andrade Hulse
PUBLISHING

Second Paperback Edition, 2022
Printed in the United States of America
Book Cover & Interior Design by Eight Little Pages
Asphodel City Map Illustrated by DayDayDraws

Library of Congress Cataloging-in-Publication Data
Names: McKinley, Alej, author.
Title: Inferos Edge / Alej McKinley
Description: Second edition.
Summary: Twenty-year-old Estephanie Carmel-Baumer Xiu moves to Asphodel City and helps a deceased crime boss find their killer, entrenching herself in the city's dark underworld and dangerous characters.
Identifiers: LCCN (print)| LCCN (ebook)
ISBN 0-9000000-0-0

For information contact:
Andrade Hulse Publishing, LLC

Para Mama y Papa—
Sé que no es tu gusto, pero igual te dedico este cuento porque es una prueba
física de que tus sacrificios no fueron hechos en vano.

To Mom and Dad—
I know it's not your taste, but I still dedicate this story to you because it's
physical proof that your sacrifices weren't made in vain.

TRIGGER WARNINGS

List of trigger warnings located behind Acknowledgments.

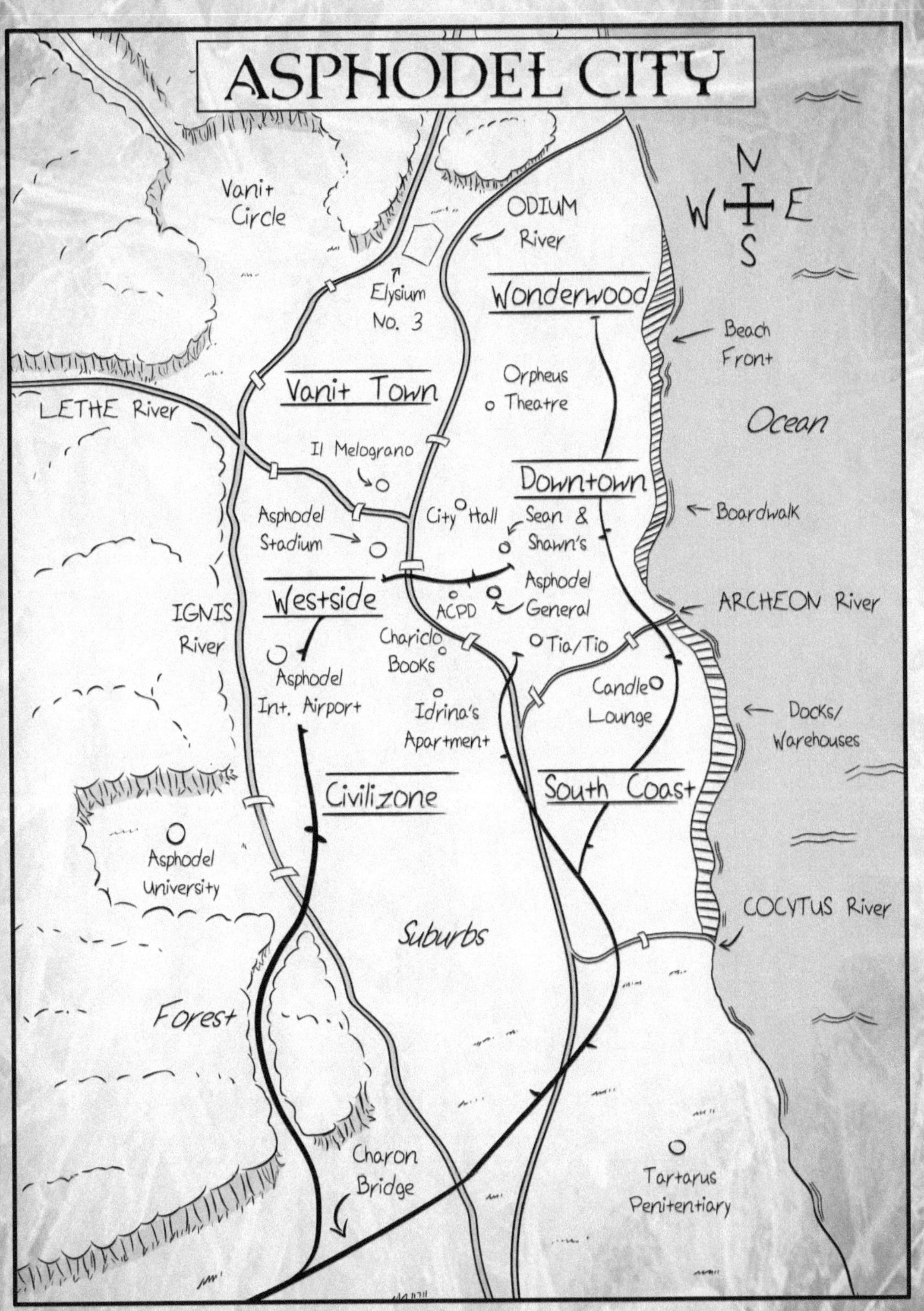

ASPHODEL CITY
N
W   E
S
Vanit Circle
ODIUM River
Wonderwood
Elysium No. 3
Beach Front
Vanit Town
Orpheus Theatre
Ocean
LETHE River
Il Melograno
Downtown
Asphodel Stadium
City Hall
Sean & Shawn's
Boardwalk
Westside
ACPD
Asphodel General
IGNIS River
Chariclo Books
Tia/Tio
ARCHEON River
Asphodel Int. Airport
Idrina's Apartment
Candle Lounge
Docks/ Warehouses
Civilizone
South Coast
Asphodel University
Suburbs
COCYTUS River
Forest
Charon Bridge
Tartarus Penitentiary

FALL

PREFACE

If someone had told me that I was the reincarnation of the Greek goddess Persephone, Queen of the Underworld, destined to confront my heart's desire while also being involved in the ultimate battle between life and death to save humanity in a year's time, I would have been relieved that of the two of us, I was the least crazy.

And *I'm* the one who can see dead people.

SEEING IS BELIEVING

WELL, well, well. It looks like someone finally gathered enough courage and audacity to murder Catalina Beatrice Patron.

If Catalina wasn't so incandescent with burning outrage, she would have approved the ballsy attitude. After all, there was nothing Catalina appreciated more than blunt honesty. She was an in-your-face type of gal, a real go-getter. Nothing stopped her from achieving whatever she wanted. A violent and permanent termination of her life at the Orpheus Theater Opera House in Asphodel City was clearly the only way to go for someone as accomplished and beautiful as her.

In fact, this assassination would have been the perfect ending for the untamable Catalina.

Except for one thing.

Her attacker shot her in the head while her back was turned.

The disrespect! No words, no dramatic confrontations, no blathering grievances. Whoever had come for her was a complete let down in more ways than one.

Catalina Patron couldn't fathom being murdered by some spineless shadow. If she was going to be gunned down at her favorite place, she was going to make damn sure it was a violent and dramatic murder that all of Asphodel City would talk about for *weeks*. She would have no less.

Thankfully for Catalina, the killer missed.

The bullet bounced off her caramel tresses, leaving behind a faint sting and the quiet hiss of a gun.

Quick as lightning, Catalina pulled out her own gun strapped to her thigh holster and whirled around. The bang was much louder this time, causing the audience and performance on stage below her balcony box to react in a panic. To her annoyance, she missed. Her killer was already racing out the door.

Catalina ran after him, but stopped outside her door when she saw her bodyguards. They were dead, slumped against the wall like broken marionettes. She double-checked their pulses to make sure they weren't breathing. She clenched her fist. Her anger doubled when she saw their guns still inside their holsters.

The assassin hadn't given her men honorable deaths.

Now this was extra personal.

Chaos descended as theater goers rushed to exit the building. Catalina knew she had ten minutes before the police arrived and her manhunt for the assassin ended. She took an extra gun from her men and stomped towards the door all the way down the hall that read *Employees Only*.

A ferocious scowl stayed plastered on her face.

With the distraction of her dead men, the assassin had earned himself plenty of time to escape by now, but something told Catalina that wasn't what he wanted. After all, why go through the effort to get to her here and now at Orpheus Theater if not to take her down once and for all? Sure there'd be plenty of opportunities later—get in line, buddy—but he had to know she would be a ravenous watchdog afterwards. Nothing short of death would stop her from hunting down the spineless coward. In fact, if she didn't find him tonight, her assassin would have exactly twenty-four hours to spend as a free man before she put a bullet between his eyes.

That was a Mad Dog Patrona guarantee. She never failed to find who she was looking for once she had her sights set. It's what made her such a valuable asset to the Erebus crime syndicate, after all.

Her heels clacked with each step down the empty, white stairwell. Instincts told her the assassin had gone to the first floor employee corridor leading to the offices and underground tunnel. She felt every inch the bringer of death as she burst through the doors, gun pointed as her caramel gaze scanned the halls.

She caught a few unsuspecting staff members staring at her in horror as she stalked past them. It took five minutes, but when she passed the set design warehouse door, Catalina paused. One of the metal doors was propped open by a tiny fraction. It was small enough that anyone else wouldn't have noticed, but big enough for Catalina to know that this was where her quarry wanted to die.

Both hands equipped, Catalina slammed open the door. She aimed both guns to her immediate left and right.

"Come out, *cobarde*. Bulletproof Betty wants to play now!"

Despite her Spanish accent, Catalina's words echoed crystal clear through the large room as the motion detector turned the lights on. Suddenly she could see various large prop pieces for different Broadway sets organized chaotically. And there, several feet in front of her stood the assassin dressed all in black with his face covered. He shot at her and hid behind a large armoire.

Catalina let the bullet bounce off her cheek before firing at his hiding place and rushing to it. She found him gone by the time she made it. She whirled around when another bullet whizzed by her neck.

"*Hijo de mier—*"Catalina fired at him with both guns and kept her barrage going, the exploding pops loud and damaging to fragile ears. It wasn't until she ran out of bullets that she discarded one of her guns and grabbed her backup magazine from the opposite thigh holster.

Blood wafted to her nose. Catalina knew in that instant one of her bullets nicked him somewhere. She grinned manically.

There would be no escaping her now.

Following the pained groaning and whimpering, Catalina kicked aside a grecian wall riddled with bullet holes her assassin had used as a shield and aimed low. Shock colored her face when she saw a recording device on the floor emitting those vulnerable sounds.

From behind a muscled arm grabbed her midsection tightly, trapping her arms. The cold muzzle of a gun was slammed into the base of her skull. He fired.

The ringing sound was louder this time. It echoed through her ears like a clash of cymbals. The stinging was more prominent as well. In that instant, Catalina knew her assassin was determined not to leave the warehouse until one of them died.

And to add insult to injury, he knew about her bulletproof weakness, though not exactly where it might be located.

A scarlet smirk curved her lips.

Catalina kicked back and jabbed her assailant in the gut. Whirling around, her sharpened fingers went for his throat, but he blocked it at the last second. Other foot ready, Catalina roundhouse kicked the hand holding the gun. The firearm went sailing through the air, clattering to a stop beside an old grandfather clock on the other side of the room.

"You've got guts, but guts alone can't kill me," she taunted, stepping forward just as her mysterious killer took a few steps back. He looked helpless and pathetic, backing up next to several tables holding styrofoam pillars. "Not so mighty without your gun, *verdad?*"

Suddenly he stood his ground, legs stiff and shoulders pushed back. Catalina arched a thin brow.

"Fight me the old fashioned way," he said, voice muffled, fists raised in a boxing stance.

A niggling sensation of familiarity came to her. Something about this guy was familiar to her. Had she met him before?

"Why should I?" Catalina aimed her gun at his forehead. "Seems to me you've been planning this encounter."

"One doesn't go up against *La Patrona* recklessly," he explained, hands raised.

So he did know me personally, she thought. She needed to unmask him quickly.

"Of course," she said, "but your actions are starting to smell *desperate*."

He stiffened.

Bingo.

"You're up to something and I'm in the way," she said, finger on the trigger. "Otherwise you wouldn't attack me without a hell's chance of winning. What's your goal here? Who are you? And how do you know about my bulletproof weakness?"

He lowered his hands. Too late.

Catalina failed to see his fingers pluck a taut rope next to his hip. A horrifying groan of metal came from behind her. She whirled around in time to see wires and ropes pulling a metal shelf filled with stage lights down from the ceiling. Catalina turned to run just as the assassin pulled a smaller gun from a strap at his ankle and aimed.

She felt the bullet first, the soft unmistakable hiss of a gun fired lost in the crescendo of the crash. Her wide gold choker flew from its place around her throat. The bloody dent on the inside and a few specks of blood was the only indication of its master's gruesome end.

Catalina flopped to the floor, hair sprawled messily. Only one winged eye peeked from beneath caramel strands. Her vision was fuzzy, coming in and out of focus as thick liquid stained her face. Black laced shoes stepped on her hair and a bony ankle sporting a boring, simple tattoo filled her vision.

"So much for Bulletproof Betty," he mocked. "I wish I could savor this moment, but I've got a lot to do and your precious Erebus to destroy. Rest in pieces, *bitch*."

He was gone.

Blood seeped past scarlet lips. Icy black smoke slowly surrounded her, making it difficult to breathe the last bit of air in her lungs. With each ticking second, a dark oppressive feeling overcame her. Her eyes dulled, her breathing reached its shallow end.

Silence.

I.

TO SETTLE IN SANITY

BEING EXPOSED to murder early in the morning on a peaceful October day was not something I enjoyed experiencing. If I was a pessimist, I would have taken the whole thing as a sign that my move to Asphodel City was going to be filled with nothing but misfortune and death.

Instead, I rolled my eyes.

I had been so focused on planting the roses my cousin Idrina wanted and the oriental lilies I favored, that when the decapitated ghostly body of a young woman phased through the floor of the balcony and my flower bed, I nearly shrieked in surprise.

The body flickered a few times, bluish gray smoke surrounding it like hot steam. I tried willing it away from my work space, but nothing happened. I sat back and sighed, my gardening mood suddenly ruined. Even on the seventh floor of Idrina's apartment, I was not safe.

At least this spirit was harmless, if not macabre-looking.

Other than the missing head and rope burn around the wrists and ankles, the body itself appeared to be athletically fit and well proportioned. If she had been alive, her skin would have been glowing and soft to the touch. Faint whiffs of perfume broke through the heavy scent of blood that clung to her. Even her clothes were tailored, sleek, new. An accountant? Lawyer? Socialite? Maybe a classy hooker? I was no expert on popular fashion brands, but if I had to hazard a guess, she was wearing Chanel maybe? Idrina would know, but there was no way I was telling her about the ghost floating in her balcony.

I nearly flinched when the body shifted sideways, neck stump facing me. The cut was eerily clean, the death blow cauterized. It raised many questions in my head, namely who murdered her because clearly a dame dressed like her with a wound like that couldn't have killed herself. After a few minutes, the transparent body jerked before a head materialized out of thin air right on her neck. Brown eyes blinked, puffy Botox injected lips opened and closed in shock. She was pretty, and terrified of her surroundings. A shriek escaped the woman before she exploded into a cloud of dark mist. A glowing purple butterfly emerged from its depths.

Uh-oh.

I rushed to my feet just as the air outside turned glacial. The spray bottle in my hand slipped, falling to the floor with a thud. I didn't bother picking it up. The roses and oriental lilies I half-planted could also wait. Right now, the safety of Idrina's apartment was imperative. I closed the sliding glass door just in time to see *him*.

Burngemear.

A nightmare made real, he materialized out of the blue, looming over the balcony like a terrifying giant shadow. If this had been my first time seeing him, I would have fainted straight away.

But it wasn't. I was five when I saw him for the first time. In a church, no less. He didn't appear *in* the church though, rather I traveled to *him* unintentionally. Same church, different realm.

But that's a story for another time.

Dressed in black robes, dark clouds at his hem, a skull with four large horns with thorns perched over his face, and small glowing butterflies fluttering to him from far and wide, Burngemear was a terrifying sight to behold. I had never heard him say anything in all my years of seeing him. Despite that however, he would stalk and stare at me. It had been so frequent and obsessive when I was younger. As time progressed and I grew older, I saw him less and less until it became once or twice a month, his presence always feeling like a magnetizing black hole.

The butterfly spirits around Burngemear never stood a chance. They fluttered eagerly into the darkness surrounding him, disappearing forever. The same happened to the ghost woman's butterfly spirit. She flew towards him and was swallowed up by the black clouds without hesitation. Just like that, the mysterious decapitated woman was gone as strangely as she had appeared.

I had hoped that would be the end of Burngemear, but he stayed where he was, ever the silent ominous shadow that never went away when I wanted him to. It's a good thing Idrina wasn't here right now.

"Phani?" called a feminine voice from the hallway. "Did you finish setting up your plants?"

Never mind.

Her footsteps became louder as she neared.

"Uh, yeah, for the most part," I answered, turning away from the balcony in time to see Idrina Glenda Rivera-Carmel Xiu enter the living room.

Idrina was a first cousin from my father's side of the family, complete with dark olive skin and silky black Mayan hair the Carmel Xiu's were famous for. It was weird to see her in person after twelve years. Upon receiving my AA and stressing out over what to do after graduation a few months ago, I initially hesitated in giving Idrina a call. We had been close as kids, but once she moved away, we kind of drifted apart.

She has grown so much from the gangly sixteen year old that I remember. She was still tall, a rare phenomenon for any Carmel-Xiu female, but now she had the added bonus of curves to fill her brand-name white blouse and khaki shorts. Even in a ponytail, her hair was enviously long and sleek, unlike my sleek dark pixie cut. If I didn't already know she was a resident cardiac surgeon at the Asphodel General Hospital, I would have thought she was an editorial model or an influencer on social media, at least.

Stories wove themselves through the family gossip vine that Idrina had changed drastically once she decided to pursue medicine. When she got the big promotion to move to Asphodel City, they say she turned into an ice queen and disdained anything related to her old life, even going so far as to force her parents to live in a small busted home while she stayed in a luxurious penthouse earning the big bucks.

While they were half right, everything else was exaggerated.

"Good, I can't wait to see what you planted. I've always wanted to put some flowers outside, but I never get around to it. Too busy," Idrina said with a smile, lips plump and red. She walked to the kitchen with light steps, never noticing the large, dark figure still floating outside her balcony.

"Of course," I replied with a nervous grin. "I'm just happy you're letting me indulge in my hobby. I don't mean to brag, but I'm pretty good at gardening."

Idrina giggled. It was a pleasant and familiar sound reminiscent of my childhood memories with her before she moved away. My smile became genuine.

Grateful for the distraction, I focused on Idrina as she dampened and rinsed the cloth she had used to clean the powder room in the kitchen sink.

I watched her over the white granite countertop as she made quick work of her task. No awkwardness showed in the movements of her body. Despite being older than me by seven years with little to nothing in common, Idrina was ever patient and graceful as she performed her role as host and gracious relative with aplomb. Not once did she come across put out or annoyed by my presence. I, on the other hand, was a jumpy, insecure mess whenever I started a conversation with her.

How I ended up plucking the courage to ask her if I could stay with her in Asphodel City for a few months, at least until I found a place of my own, was a miracle I still felt winded by.

I took deep discreet breaths in an attempt to calm myself when the floral scent of roses wafted in my direction. I glanced to my left and smiled at the lush bouquet of red roses sitting proudly in a crystal vase next to several framed pictures. There were tons of her parents, our grandparents from Guatemala, me when I was ten with my dad (which surprised me to be honest), some friends I didn't recognize, and most noticeable of all, a picture of her with her arms wrapped around a cute guy around her age with blond hair and twinkling blue eyes. By the look in their gazes as they stared at each other, he was obviously her current boyfriend.

But just to make sure...

"Who's that?" I asked, turning to Idrina.

Idrina looked up and smiled.

"That's Ryan, my boyfriend. You'll meet him when he gets here later. He's taking us out for dinner as a welcome to the city gesture."

I blinked in surprise. "He is? That's nice of him. He doesn't have to spend the money though. I would have been fine with a slice of pizza."

Idrina smiled at the sink fondly. "He's thoughtful that way. He sent me those roses yesterday, in fact. He can be a bit extravagant, but that's his love language apparently, so don't feel too weird about him treating you. He can afford it. Though if it makes you feel better, I told him to keep it casual."

I chuckled, moving away from the side table to approach her.

"Do you need any help cleaning up around here? I know you said you were fine, but I still want to help."

Idrina waved me away with her perfectly manicured hand.

"No, girl, trust me. I deep cleaned this place several days ago and gave it another quick pass yesterday morning. I'm only touching up the powder room since I found better guest towels at Woodingstone's for a bargain," she gushed. "I just need to take them out of the dryer in a few minutes."

"Woodingstone's?"

"It's like Target, but bigger, more expensive, tons of brand-name clothing and homeware decor. Not to mention, their prosciutto deli sandwiches are *to die for!*"

I blinked.

Current Idrina was such a contrast to the Idrina I grew up with. And yet, not really.

In fact, I still remembered a vivid image of Idrina playing in the mud with me after a dreary rain shower. Her colorful dress had been dulled brown, hair sticking every which way with a bright smile gracing her chubby cheeks. It was so rare a memory that I sometimes wonder if I'd dreamt it. The mischievous, muddy child of old was not the critical, professional bombshell standing before me.

It's amazing how time changes people.

Wrapped up in my thoughts, I missed half of Idrina's conversation.

"—for tonight, okay? It's got to be flawless, considering it's today of all days. Now enough about that," Idrina went on, unaware I hadn't been paying attention. "Now that you've officially moved in, what are your plans in Asphodel City?"

My mind blanked, the question catching me off-guard. Turmoil and anxiety began growing inside me with each passing second. Where do I start? What do I even say? As a jobless, broke, in debt, university major undecided, twenty-year old staring at a directionless future, I wasn't sure I was qualified to answer such a question with confidence.

I was grateful Idrina hadn't pressed for more details about why I wanted to live here when I first asked her for room and board. Still, knowing how gossipy the women in my family were, I knew it was only a matter of time before she started asking questions. Thus, her question wasn't surprising. However, even with mental preparation, I still blanked on an answer.

"I…I-I'll get a job," I stammered.

It was imperative I find one. I had bills and rent to pay for.

When Idrina let slip the monthly amount she owed on her apartment, I just knew it was code for "pay your share, Asphodel isn't cheap!" She made it clear early on I could take my time looking for a job though. It was thoughtful of her, but despite us being family, I couldn't take advantage of her kindness like that. I wanted to take my responsibilities seriously now that I was partially living on my own. I also didn't want to burden her while I took this break from academics to "discover" myself—my father's words, but he wasn't wrong.

I was a mess in almost all aspects of my life. The school loans I accumulated in the last two years became too much to ignore and I was at an impasse on what to study after receiving my Associates in Arts degree. My father wasn't aware that I owed a little over ten thousand grand plus interest. I may have fed him a fabricated story that I got a scholarship to prevent him paying for my tuition. He already pays for a mortgage, regular utility bills, insurance, monthly car payments, my exorbitant, ongoing medical bills, and he just recently suffered a knee injury at work that put him out of service for a while. I could tell he was frustrated with the lack of productivity and the mounting pile of debt on top of our daily expenses. So to spare him the stress and trouble, I lied with an excited smile and later took out a loan that I am very much unsure how to pay off now.

Thus, securing a job in Asphodel City was first on my list.

"Okay, then," Idrina began, hanging the cloth to dry over the curved faucet. "There's all sorts of jobs available around here. Personally, I'd try my hand at a corporate office somewhere. They pay decently and it doesn't require you to be on your feet constantly."

I smiled, warmed to the idea. "Yeah, that sounds good."

"You should have seen the last job my old roommate had," Idrina recounted. "It was a very good high-paying job at some magazine firm that deals with the city's creme de la creme. She got a lot of perks that way. Too bad I couldn't stand her."

I leaned against the marble counter. "Oh?"

"Yes. Literally, she was the worst. Irresponsible, inconsiderate, and never communicated over important things," Idrina was on a roll now. "She even trashed our apartment after throwing a party *she didn't tell me about*. Said it was to build connections or whatever. The final straw was when she missed her rent—*twice*. I had to cover her ass and sell my furniture to make up for her part. *And* I was a junior resident struggling to pay for my bills and student loans already."

My eyes widened. "Did she ever pay you back?"

Idrina scoffed. "No. I ended up kicking her out. Come to find out, she got fired from her job a week later. Just goes to show you, be a decent responsible person or you get the boot. *So* glad you're nothing like her."

Idrina smiled and patted my arm gently before walking away. For a moment, I stood there frozen, anxiety creeping up my belly. I glanced at Idrina as she made her way to the stainless steel fridge, back facing me. I swallowed before looking away.

Message received. Be financially responsible or my ass was in hot water.

After retrieving two cold water bottles, Idrina handed me one. I thanked her.

"So what about school?" Idrina continued, suddenly very curious about me. "Have you decided on a major yet? The medical field is always a secure route, you know. Oh! You can try nursing."

"Erm—"

"Or better yet, criminal justice. Ryan is an attorney at Sean & Shawn's," she said, looking proud. "It's a high-end law firm in downtown Asphodel. You're into that kind of stuff, right?"

And off she went. I didn't have the heart to tell her I had no interest in medicine. Maybe law, I liked the thought of justice, but the thought of going to law school and dealing with court proceedings was enough to put me off. I could only handle that stuff on TV.

I liked gardening, but I didn't fancy mixing my soothing hobby with academic stress. I thought about finding a part-time job as a florist somewhere, but there's a reason I consider it a hobby only. Aside from seeing dead people, I had this weird quirk that required me to handle plants with intense concentration and calm for small periods of time.

"Hey, um, I'm going to check on Sir Harry real quick," I said, backing away. Idrina had moved to the couch in the living room, scrolling through her phone.

"Tell your naughty boy he better not be up to anything," she said playfully.

I wish. I locked him in my room earlier so he wouldn't wander Idrina's apartment before she got comfortable with him. After causing a run in her knit top when they first met, I didn't dare encourage any more encounters between him and Idrina's expensive wardrobe.

My eyes swept over the balcony doors one last time. To my relief, Burngemear was gone. It was clear and bright outside, the cityscape view absolutely stunning despite the less than stellar weather predicted to appear tonight and the rest of the week.

I smiled wide before turning away.

Upon opening my bedroom door, I noticed Sir Harry wasn't anywhere in sight.

"Sir Harry? Where are you?" I called, taking a few steps forward.

The spare room Idrina gave me was fairly large. It was originally a beach themed guest room, but after it was confirmed I was staying with her, Idrina emptied the space save for the bed and dresser. She wanted to give me a chance to feel more at home and decorate the place to my taste. The only catch was that heavy gothic/voodoo-ism aesthetics were not welcomed. Idrina was a non-practicing Christian with a healthy fear of the occult so her request was a fair thing to ask. Not that I was into that stuff. Just because I was familiar with the supernatural didn't mean I wanted to be constantly reminded of it.

In fact, to further safeguard my new home from any unwanted visitors, the first thing I did when I moved in was take out my Spirit Repellent and assemble it.

It currently sat on the dresser. Beams of sunlight filtered through the curtain, draping itself across the repellent's wood surface. The charm had been a gift from *Abuela* SaRosa, my father's mother, for my *quinceañera*. Intricately carved and varnished in clear gloss, the Spirit Repellent was a circular disk the size of my hand and about two inches thick with five holes housing five colorful pegs. The letter that came with it hadn't explained what it was, only that she hoped it would help me relax at home. It took me a few weeks to realize the charm kept spirits away, but only if all the pegs were in their respective holes.

I dubbed it Spirit Repellent ever since. Thanks to it, I've been able to relax without worry and keep my childhood home ghost-free.

Nervous Sir Harry might have messed with it, I checked to make sure the Spirit Repellent was untouched, all holes securely covered. Out of everything in my arsenal, which was really just two charms, the Spirit Repellent was the most valuable.

Relieved to find nothing was amiss, I was about to continue my search for Sir Harry when Idrina shrieked. Running back to the living room, I spotted Sir Harry, a hairless sphynx of mottled gray and black, perched on the counter in front of my startled cousin.

"Sir Harry!" I hissed. Like usual, he paid me no mind. "Sorry Idrina! He must have escaped when I left the door open."

"No, it's fine," she said, hand on her chest. "I was not expecting him to be there when I turned around."

"I'll put him back in my room. He probably wanted company," I said, walking to grab him. He scampered away to the other side of the kitchen. I scowled, not pleased by his behavior. Normally I would be fine with him roaming around, but this was Idrina's expensive home, of which I was to pay for an equally expensive portion soon. So now was not the time for him to antagonize my cousin, cause any damage or make a fool of me. The latter tends to regularly occur with great embarrassment.

Idrina observed the two of us as she walked into the living room again.

"Well, it's fine if he wanders, just as long as he doesn't—"

Offended by the ceramic coasters next to his majesty, Sir Harry lifted a paw and knocked them off the counter. I shrieked and dashed forward to grab them only to slip backwards on a small puddle of urine. The sudden pain in my skull and rump was rivaled by the humiliation of glass breaking against the tiled floor.

Silence.

My olive skin-toned didn't show it, but my face was cherry red.

"Phani!"

I quickly sat up and assessed the damage. To my relief only one ceramic coaster broke, the rest were cushioned by the gold holder. I glared at Sir Harry. He peered down at me, meowing.

"Idrina, I'm so sorry!" I began, placing the coasters back on the counter. I took off the shoe that touched Sir Harry's watery offering before grabbing Sir Harry himself.

"Phani, are you okay? You're not bleeding are you? Here let me see."

"No, no, I'm fine. I'm really sorry about Sir Harry and the coasters. I think he's just confused about his new environment," I babbled, face still burning. I backed away from her outstretched hand. "I'm gonna put him back in my room. I'll clean up the mess!"

I ran to my room before she could say another word. That's another thing I owed Idrina. Could this morning get any more overwhelming?

"My roses!" Idrina squawked from the living room.

Oh no.

After locking Sir Harry in my room, I dashed to the living room in time to see Idrina fussing over her once-beautiful roses. The lush ruby petals I had admired earlier were a dull, shriveled husk with dark weak stems drooping like wet noodles.

I blanched.

"Ryan literally gave me these yesterday," she said, her touch gentle. "He knows the red ones are my favorite. I can't believe they died so quickly! I could have sworn they were vibrant this morning."

Idrina grabbed the vase and walked towards the kitchen. I bowed my head.

The reason I never risk the idea of being a full-time florist or hang around plants all day is because every time I get the slightest bit upset, depressed or dismayed, the plant life around me begins to wilt and die in solidarity—I assume the quirk has some relation to my seeing dead people, though the specifics of how and why escape me. The phenomenon is uncontrollable, inconvenient, and the reason I can't garden unless I'm completely calm and content.

Eyeing the roses in the tall trash bin, I sighed.

One crisis at a time.

Staying in my lane, I made sure to clean Sir Harry's mess first. After discarding the ruined roses, Idrina announced she was going to lay down before getting ready.

"Ryan will be here in a few hours. He's taking us out. Make sure to dress nicely."

I nodded in response. As soon as Idrina closed the door to her bedroom, I quietly grabbed my longboard stored inside the closet by the front door before swiping my keys from the catch-all bowl on the counter. Making sure my wallet and phone were on me, I snuck out of Idrina's apartment before locating the nearest store selling roses.

It was the least I could do.

II.

PERCIPIENT SEES PARANORMAL

WHEN MY FATHER AGREED—BY the sheer miracle of God—to let me move to Asphodel City without him, he gave me two conditions: that I call him every week so he knew how I was doing and that I see a psychiatrist and continue my psychotherapy.

While I had no problem with the first bit, the second condition may be a problem.

I had yet to make an appointment with the new psychiatrist my old one recommended. I had hoped my father wouldn't insist too much on the whole ordeal. At least for the first few weeks. I did not like having my head examined for something I now knew couldn't be fixed. Other than seeing dead people, I was just like everyone else.

Kind of.

I was careful not to hit anyone as I weaved through the crowd on my way to the convenience store. After searching the internet, I discovered the nearest place selling roses wasn't too far—a mere three blocks—which made this little in-and-out mission perfect. It was tricky trying not to gawk at everything like an outsider. I was successful for the most part, passing by a few jaded locals before the lunch rush.

Turning onto a congested street, I noticed familiar blue-gray smoke swirling over a dead body laying on the road. The torso and hips were severed. Rotten pale guts lined with spidery red threads spilled like slippery sausages onto the concrete in a congealed pool of blood. No one was pointing out the gruesome sight. Cars drove over it like nothing. If the blue-gray smoke hadn't been a dead giveaway, everyone's disregard for the carnage would have been a clear indication that I was staring at another ghost. I looked away.

I was about two blocks from my destination when I gasped.

There, sitting in a decorative pot on a window sill, was a cluster of out-of-season Asphodels, Asphodel City's namesake. Having researched the local flora like a true botanist nerd, I learned the city was named after the garden plant when it was first introduced to the area a few centuries back.

I was a little skeptical at first because asphodels weren't known to survive the New England climate. They thrived in places with well-drained soil and lots of natural lighting. And yet, as if eager to prove everyone wrong, the asphodels bloomed like clock-work every spring. They were like venerated weeds in that way, seen just about everywhere from small cracks on the sidewalk to large stalks growing on balconies. During the springtime, the city was a known popular tourist destination resembling a picturesque postcard with its many quaint brick buildings, glass skyscrapers, and sunny blue skies. I know this because the city's website doesn't shy away from posting dozens of gorgeous photos yearly.

Sadly, it was currently fall. The tenth of October to be exact.

Overcast weather was a normal everyday sight, the streets wet and glassy with a familiar chill in the air threatening to take hold. The asphodels were less noticeable now, smaller, wilted. Just like the ones on the window. I admired whoever was keeping the darlings alive. Tending to it will only get tough once winter comes around.

I took a quick photo of the asphodels with my phone when I noticed my reflection in the window pane. My face was riddled with tiny moles, a few clusters placed in various spots near my eyes and mouth. I had more around my body. It used to bother me when I was younger, but over the years, I forced myself to think positively of my appearance. If nothing else, it certainly helped me achieve a strong self-esteem.

I checked to make sure my stud earrings made of wood were still in place. They were the size of a dime and sported unique Mayan symbols carved onto it. I treasured my earrings greatly. They were a gift from *Abuela* SaRosa when I first met her at seven years old while visiting Guatemala.

After catching me talking to a spirit—who I assumed had been a real person—she gifted me the earrings several days later. She never spoke of the incident or looked at me oddly like a few of my aunts and uncles had done over the years. *Abuela* had simply kissed my cheek, patted my head, and told me to do my best. Her non-judgmental response and trust in my sanity made such a lasting impression. I've tried to do just that ever since.

I smiled at my reflection, doe green eyes sparkling as the magic of the new city filled me with excitement. I sent the picture of the asphodel to my father before continuing on my way.

When I finally arrived at the convenience store, it didn't take me long to find the flower stand near the cash register. I was disappointed but not surprised by their limited selection. Only five bouquets of tulips, roses, and carnations were available. Judging by the smell of the water and the dull color on the petals, the flowers were not being maintained properly.

I wasn't bummed by the revelation, however. Even though I was able to suck the life out of plants if I got too upset, I noticed perked right back up if I got really excited. The reverse wasn't always easy to do because whatever this phenomenon was, I wasn't able to control it.

Still, at twenty years old, I was confident I could give the dull roses I grabbed a boost of vitality. I wasn't confident enough to wander the city for an actual flower shop right now anyways. Maybe another day. For now, cheating would have to do.

Walking towards the back of the store, I stood in an empty aisle and made sure no one was around, security cameras included. With the bouquet in hand, I held them gently and stared with determination. Recalling my initial excitement of moving to Asphodel City and the bubbling feelings of eagerness to begin my adventure was just enough for the red in the petals to deepen and the stems to firm up. Soon, the roses weren't sad, neglected beauties any longer. Happy with their lushness, I quickly got in line for the register.

Ahead of me, two elderly ladies spoke together in hushed tones, pointing their spindly fingers to the newspaper next to them.

"—about time someone like that died—"

"Brenda, I couldn't agree more! Less crime in the city now. You know, I heard—"

When they moved forward, I glanced at the headline on the *Hermes Herald*. It was big and bold, impossible to miss.

CRIME BOSS FOUND DEAD AT ORPHEUS THEATER

No wonder the ladies were pleased.

It was a bit fascinating to know mobsters were still a thing. But then, where there was crime, there was always someone managing it from the shadows. And Asphodel City, like any other city, was rife with crime and corruption.

My father once mentioned, in an attempt to dissuade me from going, that Asphodel had been ranked as one of the top ten cities with the highest crime rate in the country. When I researched the information, I discovered that the article my father had cited had been written ten years ago. At least he had the nerve to look sheepish when I confronted him over his outdated information. Regardless though, my father had a small point.

Despite improvements, Asphodel City still had its problems. Idrina confirmed as much when I asked, letting me know the city wasn't for the weak. I wasn't surprised murder and drama of all kinds flooded the streets daily. It explained the unusually high number of paranormal wandering around, far more than what Miami had.

I'd cry and throw fits as a child whenever I spotted large groups of spirits upon visiting downtown. I hadn't known how to handle them without freaking people out and it didn't help that a lot of spirits were equally clueless around people who could see them. Some begged me to do this and that for them while others simply wanted to scare the melanin out of me.

While I was no longer easily frightened by mean spirited ghosts, what never failed to give me nightmares was Tenebris.

But that's a story for another time.

After paying for the roses and stepping outside, I got on my longboard. I was so focused on my own thoughts and the roses in my arm that I didn't see the woman standing a few feet in front of me. I nearly crashed into her. Thankfully, my many years of longboarding kicked in and saved us both from last minute injury and humiliation.

"Oh! Sorry!" I apologized, stepping off.

The woman turned to me in surprise, brown eyes framed by thick sooty lashes widening as her red lips parted. If there was one dazzling feature about the mysterious woman I could easily point out, it would be the golden brown waves tied into a high ponytail. The ends of her hair touched her lower back. It wasn't the strangest thing about her though. She was wearing thick heels, skin-tight black pants, a velvet cropped top, and above-the-elbow opera gloves. An overall misplaced ensemble but not the strangest. I've seen people dress odder then she, especially during ComicCon.

"You," the woman began, "you can see me?"

"...yeah?"

She stood to the side when I almost crashed into her so I didn't see her neck, especially with all that hair. When she turned her body, I regretted stopping for her. At first glance, she looked to be wearing a dark, ruby chandelier necklace. But upon closer inspection, a bloody bullet hole with chunks of flesh hanging revealed just who this woman was.

"Oh good God!" I said, looking away. "Sorry! I'll just leave."

"No! You can see me! I need your help!"

"Nope." I hopped on my longboard and skated past her. To my dismay, the woman followed after me, keeping up with my pace.

"Dammit, girl! Listen to me!" She snapped, her beautiful face wrinkling in anger.

"My request inbox is closed," I said.

Ignoring her wouldn't do me any good if she was determined to follow me home. That was the problem with spirits. Once they sensed I wasn't a blind sheep, they converged on me like mosquitos to a rare slab of meat. Thank God for my *Abuela* SaRosa and her Spirit Repellant. She had also given me the Be-Gone Beads but those and the pipe were stashed back in my purse at Idrina's apartment. I had been confident this quick adventure of mine wouldn't have warranted such weaponry.

I should have known.

"This is urgent!" The woman insisted, icy hand reaching out to grab my forearm in a hard jerk.

My earrings burned hot, almost searing my skin. I swerved.

"What the heck?!" I shouted, tugging back my arm in alarm.

Did she just touch me? Me? Had a ghost really just *touched* me? That's never happened before! It was already worrisome that the woman wasn't dull and pale or transparent-looking. Her vibrant coloring and complete similarity to a living being was what made me stop myself from crashing into her in the first place, but that in itself warranted the questions of why and how she was able to touch me when all others phased right through. I *really* regretted leaving my Be-Gone Beads at home.

Home! I just needed to get to Idrina's apartment and I was saved. I was only two blocks away but they felt endless with my unwanted shadow.

"Stop or I'll make you fall," she threatened.

I glared at her as my longboard slowed to a stop.

"It's rude to accost people."

She snorted, sharp nails encased in silk gloves brushing aside some waves from her face. Her neck no longer looked like a crime scene. Instead, a gold polished choker with three red stones embedded in the middle hid the gore.

"I'm dead," she said. "It doesn't matter."

I used the roses as a shield.

"Leave me alone!" I shouted, frustrated this was happening in the middle of a crowded street. People were already beginning to look at me funny as I stood my ground.

"Not until you hear me out," she said calmly.

I grabbed my longboard and jogged away.

"*Oi! Cabrona!*" She called in Spanish, reappearing right in front of me again.

Normally, I have the Be-Gone Beads to help me out when it came to annoying spirits, but sometimes, if I concentrated hard enough, I could banish spirits to the Aether Realm. The Aether Realm is what I call limbo. It's not quite Tenebris, which is literally Hell, in my humble opinion, but it certainly wasn't the Physical Realm. I *assume* it exists after reading about it and asking kinder spirits when I was younger. None of them wanted to get stuck there, but some did if they weren't careful. No one has ever escaped it though.

"Stay back or you'll regret it," I threatened.

The woman laughed, the sound high-pitched and filled with so much derision. "Or what, little girl? You gonna cry because a big bad ghost is being mean to you?"

That stung. I closed my eyes and concentrated hard. I imagined her getting sucked away by some unseen gravitational force until she was—

Wait.

There was silence and an intense prickling cold that made the fine hairs on my arms and legs stand on end. It hurt to breathe. When I opened my eyes, my suspicions were confirmed.

Gone were the people, anything living, the sunlight, the purple gray and red of the city streets. The sounds, the smells, the foul taste of traffic, and savory aroma from the New York style pizza joint I'd passed earlier. I swallowed, my grip tightening around the roses and longboard.

The rude spirit was gone. Instead, I saw the same small streets and large brick buildings, only they were abandoned and decayed. Piles of rubble littered empty storefronts and cement walls cracked dangerously. Fog was everywhere, the sky above me forever overcast. Shadows whispered and transparent silhouettes followed silently.

I paled.

I was in Tenebris.

The last place I ever wanted to be in.

III.

TENEBRIS

Sunday. March 15, 1999. That was the day I met the devil *in hell*.

Or what I thought was hell, anyways.

Tenebris wasn't lit in flames like I'd been led to believe. It was, however, a desolate realm with a cold, barren landscape that seeped into my pores and reached me even in my dreams.

The first step on the frozen asphalt was heavy. I glanced around, hoping I wasn't being followed. I knew I was the only human around for miles, but that didn't mean I was *alone*. Even now I could feel distant stares boring into my back. I shivered, clutching the roses tighter. The cold permeated my skateboard's metal truck, biting my fingers the longer I gripped it. I needed to get out of here.

Whenever I accidentally end up in Tenebris, I stay very still in the hopes that the next blink that brought me here would also send me back. It would take a few minutes. Each passing second threatened to knock me unconscious however. Not because the air in Tenebris was deadly but because the fear of the unknown inspired terror. Especially with Burngemear around.

I placed my skateboard down and sat on it while I waited for my return to the land of the living. I kept my gaze solely on the roses, refusing to glance at any shadow specters and whatever else lurked behind the thick fog.

I was five when I first found myself in Tenebris. I hadn't known the name for it then, but it eventually came to me, as if Tenebris itself had spoken to my subconscious. Back then, after the passing of my mother Wilma, dad became an enthusiastic church goer. Sometimes attending service three times a week. When I went with him, I was always placed with the younger kids and for the most part, it was a fun time.

Until one Sunday service in March, when everything changed.

Held in my dad's arms, dressed in a cute white dress and shiny black shoes, I watched as the service progressed, bored out of my mind as I attempted to amuse myself with my stuffed bear. Something about the temple that day made me feel uneasy and fidgety. Being near my dad, inhaling his soap and cologne and touching my stuffed bear's fuzzy fur made me feel better. Safe. That was until the temple darkened and turned gray, the cool temperature in the room dropping like dead weight, and all sounds of the pastor speaking ceased.

Everyone had disappeared.

Empty, decayed chairs, peeling walls and crumbling stone, even part of the roof was missing. It revealed an overcast sky as fog coated the dusty ground. Everything smelled like wet dirt and cement dust.

I remembered clutching my dad's shirt tightly and asking him what was going on. Only, when I turned to look at him, he wasn't there. The alien skull of some demon creature with massive horns greeted me instead. A single silver dot gleamed from one eye socket. Housed in a black hood, Burngemear loomed over the empty space, his robe licking the ground in black puffs of smoke.

He had said something to me, but I can't remember what it was. Not that it was important. I screamed and wailed and fussed in his cloaked arms, throwing the first biggest tantrum in my little life. I had dropped my teddy bear in the process. When I finally calmed down and opened my eyes, Burngemear was gone and in his place was my dad looking terrified and worried for me.

It was a relief to know I wasn't in Tenebris anymore. I was finally home.

Sadly, the teddy bear *Großmama* Stephanie sent me as a gift wasn't. He was left behind, never to be found, never to know the warm embrace of a child ever again.

I shivered, this time more aggressively. I glanced at my phone and was dismayed to find that I'd been sitting in silence for about ten minutes. That's odd. It's time I was back in the Physical Realm. I blinked several times, willing my return with each fervent meeting of the lashes. Instead, my eyelids grew tired.

Just as I stood up to pace for a mini brainstorming session, I saw them.

Tall blobs of murky substance slowly emerging from the wall of fog. There were five and each one had a slender, growing smile as they drew closer.

I blinked.

Nope. Nope. Nope.

I hopped on my skateboard and took off like a bat out of hell, desperately adding speed and distance behind me. The roadway was deserted, thankfully. It didn't obstruct my get away in the slightest. When I looked back, I was startled to see the amorphous blobs following me, their smiles now wide grins as they loudly guffawed. I added more speed.

Oh my god, oh my god, oh my god! I don't have my Be-Gone beads! Why didn't I take my Be-Gone beads and the blow pipe? Why did I go out and buy roses anyways? Why couldn't I just control my emotions in the first place! Please, please, *please,* let me return home!

Another cackle from behind. I made a sharp right turn and zoomed headfirst into another wall of fog. I didn't stop, but I probably should have slowed down a little because my wheels got caught in something and I ended up flying through the air.

I shrieked in terror.

My fall from grace was even more embarrassing and dangerous than when I had slipped on Sir Harry's urine earlier. My elbows were scraped and my back felt like one giant bruise when I finally rolled to a stop. Miraculously, the roses survived. They were still lush and velvety smooth, not a petal out of place. Better them than me, I guess. I struggled to my feet and saw that my embroidered bag was open. A few of my things were scattered on the sidewalk. Sighing, I winced when I pulled the muscles of my back too hard.

Thankfully, I didn't hear the demon blobs anymore so I was able to gather my wallet, phone, keys, lip balm, and pencils before returning them to my bag. I also picked up the bouquet and double checked the roses. Once I was sure they weren't damaged in any way, I searched for my longboard. I limped a little as I looked through the dense fog, eyes squinting as the air thickened, puffs of white escaping past my lips after every exhale. The warmth from the adrenaline finally faded from my limbs.

Why wasn't I back home already? It's been almost twenty minutes, I'm sure. I've never lingered for more than five before. I hissed when my elbow began to throb more insistently.

Ugh, this blows.

Chilling laughter echoed ominously through the fog, coming from no particular direction but feeling close all the same. I froze, terror settling back in at the disembodied sound.

I abandoned the search for my longboard and ran in the opposite direction. I blinked once, twice, thrice in a desperate attempt to transport myself home. On the fifth try, I crashed into a couple. My roses went flying again and my unfortunate victims stumbled onto the sidewalk with me.

"What the hell?!" shrieked the girl as she turned to her side. The guy groaned.

"O-Oh my god, I'm so sorry!" I blurted. "I didn't see you!"

"Yeah, same here," mumbled the guy as he struggled up. I got off them and apologized profusely, adrenaline still high as I belatedly realized I wasn't in Tenebris anymore. I smiled widely. The couple looked at me oddly before they left.

"I'm back!" I cheered to no one.

I received more stares from people near-by, but I didn't care. Mood in the clouds, I picked up the roses, still beautifully intact, and began limping home. Which to my delight, wasn't far at all. In fact, I was in front of Idrina's apartment building. The doorman waved and I smiled even brighter.

Once upstairs in the apartment, I bandaged myself up in secret. Idrina was still in the bathroom which gave me a chance to replace her new roses in the empty vase the old roses had occupied. After adding a little bit of sugar to the water with a mental note of acquiring some plant food in the future, I began cutting up the stems and arranging the roses artfully.

It was peaceful for a time. At least until I remembered that my longboard lay forgotten in Tenebris. Just like my old teddy bear.

"Dammit."

⚜

LATER THAT DAY - 3:04 AM

SOMETHING CLATTERED TO THE FLOOR. It was a hollow sound, reverberating through the room like an ominous chime from a grandfather clock. I sat up quickly with an unladylike groan.

Struggling to keep my eyes open, I rubbed my face in frustration before staring into the darkness.

What was that?

Crawling out of bed with reluctance, I fiddled with the lamp on my nightstand and cringed when the bright light nearly blinded me. A faint meow from a certain mischievous feline told me he was out and about and most likely the cause of the noise that woke me.

By the time I shuffled over to him, Sir Harry was on my dresser, reclined like a tiny, satisfied sultan. The Spirit Repellant was overturned on the floor, bright colored wooden pieces scattered everywhere.

I blanched.

Oh no, this can't be good!

I glared at Sir Harry. It was far too early—or late—to deal with the consequences of his actions. I quickly gathered all the pegs, even going so far as to crouch and stick my arm beneath the dresser, cursing under my breath for this tiring inconvenience at...at...

"What *time* is it?" I muttered to myself in frustration.

"Three in the morning, I think," answered a feminine voice from behind me.

It wasn't Idrina.

I shrieked, yanking my arm out from under the dresser and scraping it in the process. I paid the stinging and throbbing little mind as I stood and whirled around.

The ghost woman from earlier in the afternoon was leaning against a stack of unopened cardboard boxes. I placed a hand over my heart and waited for it to calm down, hating how easily startled I was despite having been exposed to this for years.

She was dressed in the same get-up from earlier, lips red and ponytail high on her head. This time, however, there was no gaping hole in her throat. Instead, a thick gold choker hid her wound, matching her gold hoop earrings. It was a beautiful piece of jewelry with a smooth, gleaming surface. Embedded in the gold were three oval shaped garnets. From where I stood they almost resembled burning coals. Would it be cool to the touch or would it burn with piercing heat?

"I used to own this necklace," the woman said, as if reading my thoughts. Her Spanish accent was faded but noticeable despite her perfect English. This surprised me as I was now mildly curious about her heritage.

"I figured you wouldn't want to see what killed me since it freaked you out the first time," she continued.

Well, she was half right. Mostly, I don't like interacting with spirits in general. Even the most innocent were known to attract darker beings.

I got up and peeked outside my door, hoping Idrina hadn't woken up from my outburst. Once I was sure she was still in her room, I closed the door and stared at my uninvited guest.

"Did—"

"I need your help."

I sighed.

"Listen," I began. "I don't really do the whole 'ghost request' thing, okay? Why don't you go find a spirit medium instead? I'm sure there's someone in this city who can help."

The woman narrowed her eyes.

"I'm not interested in moving on and you're the only one who can actually see me."

I smiled. "Hold that thought."

I rushed over to the Spirit Repellent and assembled the loose pieces back in place. Once it was placed on the dresser, I exhaled in relief and looked over my shoulder. She was still there.

Dammit.

Why hadn't my charm ejected her out? It was called a Spirit *Repellent* for a reason. Any spirits or entities present inside whatever home I'm in always get forcibly sucked out before they can even blink. This ghost woman should've already joined her kin outside my window.

The Spirit Repellent had never failed before, even when I took it with me outside. It doesn't cover a huge amount of square footage, but it covers enough for me to feel normal. Idrina's apartment gets full coverage, thankfully, allowing her place to be a haven for me, and there were few places I could count as safe nowadays.

Seeing my openly dissatisfied expression, the woman smiled, her eyes cold.

"Don't look so *triste*, *chiquita*. I taunted your hairless rat into knocking the charm over; otherwise, I wouldn't have gotten in."

"Who are you?"

"Catalina Patron," she said, stepping further into the room. Her heels made no sound. "And I need your help as soon as possible."

I stared at her wearily, awed by the solidity of her presence. Catalina looked eerily real. Her body wasn't transparent or pale like most spirits. She didn't emit a gray-blue spiraling smoke nor did her form flicker once. If a haughty Sir Harry hadn't walked *through* her legs, I would have been fooled into thinking she was real. There was no doubt Catalina was powerful. Most spirits would fizzle out after having taken a corporeal form for only a few minutes—it takes a lot of energy to maintain. But this woman looked fresh as recently baked bread and I didn't like it one bit.

To expedite her departure, I sat down on my bed with my hands over my knees. I smiled politely at her.

"Okay then, what can I do for you?"

"I need you to find out who killed me."

I blinked, my smile melting. "What?"

When most spirits approach me, they ask for messages to be delivered to their loved ones. If it seemed harmless, I'd do it, especially if it wasn't unreasonable—they end up leaving me alone once I finish.

The most ridiculous request I ever received was to bury half an onion and a bottle of salt beside the deceased's grave as soon as the clock struck midnight on the fifteenth of May. And I did it, believe it or not. It was weird, but I did it, mostly because the pestering ghost would not stop singing Ukrainian folk songs for three days straight until I agreed. And he was horribly off key every time.

But this request of Catalina's? Murder investigation? That was new.

"Listen," I began. "I'm not sure I can help you there. I'm no detective and I'd rather not get killed for the trouble. Besides, aren't the police investigating your case?"

Catalina scoffed. "They have no idea who the killer is. They haven't made any arrests yet."

I scratched my scalp, short hair messy and sticking every which way. At least this bizarre turn of events was happening in my room where no one could see me.

Catalina's face contorted in anger. "I don't know how that little shit got through my security, but he did and *dared challenge me.* In the middle of act one too! Couldn't have waited till after act two or when my boss came and left."

I sighed. This was starting to sound more and more like the sort of trouble any sensible person would avoid. Catalina sensed my reluctance and approached me, her expression morphing into one of surprising gentleness since at no point in her body language did I get soft maternal vibes.

"Please help me," she said. "If we don't stop this murderer, others will die. In fact, he'll probably go after my darling. And I don't want him getting hurt because of me."

I hesitated. Sensing my weakness, she went in for the kill.

"And it would help me...*move on.*"

Damn it. That doesn't help *me* though!

Catalina tapped my knee. Or attempted to. Her ghostly fingers felt like ice when they disappeared through my skin. *Now* it decides to do that, huh? I sighed again. Catalina appeared sympathetic to my internal struggle and smiled at me with indulgence, as if I were the one that needed help.

"I can see you need some time to think it over. I'll give you twenty-four hours."

By the tone of her voice, it sounded like she expected me to say yes. I was suddenly afraid of her reaction if I denied her. Majority of ghosts don't take it well when I say no, some discovering poltergeist abilities in their rage. And if Catalina was powerful enough to look real, I can only imagine the temper tantrum she might create.

With one last pointed stare, Catalina phased through the wall on my left. I got up and pushed the curtain of my window aside, peering into the dark alley below. I couldn't see her anymore.

"How considerate of you," I said aloud, knowing Catalina wouldn't respond back. I turned and gave Sir Harry a half-hearted glare. "Thanks a lot."

The feline continued to stare at me from his perch on the cat tree. He meowed, rolling over to hide his face. I had been dismissed.

Rolling my eyes, I pulled the curtain closed before crawling back into bed. I was going to need some shut eye. I had a long day ahead of me.

IV.

JOB HAUNTING

THE SQUARE CLOCK on the bare wall ticked, ticked, and ticked. Each passing second was a maddening kernel of anxiety piling within me. It was only a matter of time before they all popped.

I glanced at the receptionist who'd been sitting erect since I arrived. She wore a permanent, lipstick smudged scowl, cat-eyed glasses, and the dullest shade of brown on a cardigan I had ever seen. She inspired little conversation from anyone with each glare she bestowed. I had hoped she would have called someone into the manager's office by now. Preferably me. I was the next one up and it's been over an hour since I first entered the waiting room. Two other applicants had arrived and were currently waiting after me. To make matters worse, it was nearly six in the evening.

Looking away from the receptionist, I kept my hands clasped over my lap, resisting the urge to sigh or look anything but patient, lest she sense my weakness and report it. I didn't want to give anyone a reason not to hire me.

To keep myself from walking out of the office, I grabbed the nearest crinkled newspaper—the waiting room consisted of exactly two fashion magazines and a handful of old newspapers. Not a very inspiring start.

At least the headline of the *Hermes Herald* was dramatic: SHELTER BOMBED IN MOB WAR!

According to the paper, there were two factions—Erebus and Thanatos—that had been at war with each other and caused quite a bit of damage around South Coast. Figures the low-income areas were the places getting hit the hardest.

I frowned and glanced at the grainy image of a burned, run-down structure in a sea of charred remains and smoke. My heart ached for the victims caught in the crossfire. Nine dead and ten injured. Among the deceased was a young woman of twenty-three, Katie Dawson, a student at Asphodel University who had volunteered at the shelter every weekend for over four years. The name was unfamiliar, but something about her sweet smile on the grainy image caused the hairs on my arms to stand on end. The newspaper was dated August. She had died two months ago.

Exhaling, I noticed my breath become foggy. Stiffening, I looked up and saw a shapeless cloudy outline of a ghost. I refrained from sighing. This was the last thing I needed.

"Este...fani...Caramel...Boomer?"

I stood up quickly and walked over to the receptionist as she got up from her creaky seat. I didn't bother correcting her about the pronunciation of my name.

My shoulders sagged in relief when the ghost shape didn't follow.

I was led down a narrow, gray hallway until we reached a partially opened wooden door with a plastic plaque reading Manager on it. The receptionist knocked once and indicated that I was present. She gestured for me to sit in the chair opposite a wide desk and left. I sat across a tweedy looking man with a comical combover inside a strangely austere office. Even the chair I sat on was a nondescript gray color, plastic and unyielding. The urge to stand at attention and end my sentences with "sir" when the manager began asking me questions was strong.

How the business thrived without an ounce of warmth was beyond me. If I hadn't been flat out rejected by my previous interviewers, I would have left Fine Ink Co. ages ago. In fact, I would have skipped the location entirely if it hadn't been for Idrina and my own desperation. But as my cousin pointed out, they were paying well, and it was only thirty minutes away by bus.

It was worth a shot.

"So tell me about yourself," the manager, whose nameplate identified him as Paul Walder, said, watery eyes fixed on me.

I opened my mouth, about to reiterate the same spiel I told my last four interview appointments, when a cold pair of brown eyes stared down at me with all the judgment of a Supreme Court Justice. The words died on my tongue.

Catalina stood behind Mr. Walder, one opera gloved hand on her hip, hair flowing down her back like a veil.

"Are you *still* interviewing? Why bother? This place is lame," she muttered, sharp gaze piercing the oblivious man before me.

I refrained from glaring at her in response. This was the third interview she has crashed and it still caught me off guard. At least she hadn't blurted out something embarrassing about Mr. Walder. I knew far too much about the last hiring team's illegal cock-fighting rings.

"This guy didn't even have an applicant in here, did you know?" Catalina continued as Mr. Walder began introducing himself. It was hard to focus on him, especially since Catalina moved to my side. Great.

"—and I'm the regional director of—"

"—he was on the phone with his ex-girlfriend the entire time! And do you know what he was doing?"

"—promises to be a fruitful branch so I'm glad to see people applying—"

"—so pathetic! I'm getting figurative goosebumps just thinking about it! Seriously, Phani, he's a wimp! And I've met plenty at my—"

"—offers great benefits! Including dental! We even participate in—"

"—but the crux of it all is that he was just *begging* her to come back because he finally took a *seminar* on BDSM and pony play!"

"Ah! Shut up!" I snapped, horrified by what she was telling me and the cacophony of sound echoing in my ears.

Mr. Walder looked taken aback. His bushy brows furrowed.

"Excuse me?"

I nearly gasped at my faux pas.

Catalina cackled, drifting to the window.

"Is what some people think when I get inspired by my work and become a diligent employee," I lied in a rush, smile brittle. "I just get so passionate that I talk about my work and all the ways that efficiency can be used in the workplace. They eventually go, 'ah, please stop Phani, we get it!'."

Mr. Walder blinked. "...okay."

"Not the worst lie I've heard," Catalina informed me.

"Well then, let's get started," Mr. Walder continued, glancing down at his paper, "so why do you want to work for Fine Ink Co.?"

"Their name is Fine Ink? And it's not even a tattoo parlor?" Catalina laughed, lifting a hand to cover her lips.

"I understand this place is a small company," I began, ignoring Catalina, "but I believe Fine Ink still has the resources that will allow me to build a professional portfolio. It's a reliable and steady company that has stood the tests of time and still operates with increased profits every year."

Mr. Walder seemed impressed. "I see you've done your research."

Yes, mainly because Idrina helped me research the companies I was applying for. Thank God for my smart and helpful cousin!

"They make increased profits? Impossible," Catalina scoffed, eyeing the papers stacked on the desk. "They sell ink. They're a middle-man. Why buy from these guys when companies can get it from the source? There's a front here, I can smell it."

I almost told Catalina she was being paranoid when Mr. Walder continued.

"Your resume doesn't have any work experience listed," he mentioned, tapping the paper. I kept my smile in place. "Would this be your first job?"

"That's correct," I said. "I've been focusing on my college classes. I recently finished getting my associates degree."

"That's wonderful. What are you majoring in?"

My mind blanked. I still hadn't decided on what. In fact, getting my AA was the only concrete plan I had in regards to my education. Everything else was up in the air. Thankfully my father's patience was endless when it came to my college journey. Some might even say supportive with the different amount of career articles he would print out to interest me. So far he hasn't had much luck.

"Uh, communications!" I blurted.

Truth was I was still undecided, but communications wasn't a bad start. Even if I just made it up on the spot.

"How boring," Catalina replied.

"How wonderful," said Mr. Walder.

Suddenly his phone rang. He eyed it in shock. Catalina smirked.

"It's his ex, the one who thought he was boring and frigid in bed. Do you think she bought what he was selling her?"

I pursed my lips and gave her a "Shut Up" look. Mr. Walder started sweating as his hand hovered over the flip phone. He glanced at me, almost unsure if he should answer. I was going to tell him to take it, but the phone stopped ringing. His expression melted into pure devastation. This delighted Catalina. She laughed at his expense.

"*God*, he's so pathetic!"

"Leave him alone!" I snapped, glaring at her.

"Miss Carmel-Bomber?" Mr. Walder eyed me. Catalina floated to his side and blew on his neck. He shivered, beady eyes squinting in confusion.

"Baumer," I corrected, "and it's nothing. Just thought I saw a fly on your side."

He looked around himself but found nothing. When the nonexistent fly remained elusive, Mr. Walder glanced at his phone longingly before facing forward to continue the interview.

"Alright, Miss—"

His phone rang again. Mr. Walder stilled, sweating once more. Catalina glanced at the tiny screen and snickered.

"He has her under Mistress Kelly with a heart next to it. I'm honestly embarrassed for this guy." She turned away. "I can't watch this pathetic show. Call me when it's over."

With that, she phased through the wall on my right and left. I sagged in relief.

The phone still rang, however, and for whatever reason, Mr. Walder continued to squirm.

"You should answer it," I finally said. "If Kelly is calling you back, then she's probably not over the break up. Maybe she's even impressed with the seminar you took."

"She didn't sound impressed—" Mr. Walder stopped talking. He whipped his head in my direction and stared at me as if I'd grown two heads. The phone stopped ringing.

"What?" I blinked.

Then it hit me. My eyes widened in horror.

I raced out of the bland walls of Fine Ink Co. with a weak excuse and a red face. I knew without a doubt I wasn't getting that job.

Once I was safely a few blocks away from my disastrous interview, I began to feel the ache in my feet. After wearing kitten-heeled wedges for most of the day, I didn't blame my soles for complaining. I would have worn flats if I had any, but the kitten wedges were the only pair of professional shoes I owned. Not that it would have mattered—Idrina insisted on heels, saying they were the only way to go.

A heavy weight settled on my chest when I thought of her. Going home empty-handed was depressing. Especially after Idrina's morning pep talk did, in fact, cheer me up. I had felt as if I could take on the world. Instead, the world chewed me up and spat me back out.

I sighed.

What was wrong with me? Why couldn't I ace any of my interviews? Catalina aside, I should have had the restraint or charm to interest one of the hiring managers. I liked to think I was a sensible individual that took direction well. I was malleable. A rookie employee that could be professionally taken advantage of. What was not to like? Nobody knew I was a diagnosed schizophrenic and it's not like talking to one's self was anything to be alarmed about. At least not with me. Not really.

I glanced at my reflection in the store window and glared.

"Shut up."

The lady behind the window looked at me oddly. I blushed before dashing away.

I needed to stop doing that.

When I made it to the nearest bus stop, I sat down and rubbed at the sore spot on my foot. The heel wasn't even a full two inches. I had to do better for womankind next time.

A sleek Rolls Royce in black drove to a gentle stop in front of me, waiting behind several cars for the red light to change. Tinted windows hid the passenger from view. My reflection greeted me, instead.

I wasn't a huge car nut, not like my maternal cousins in Palm Beach, but occasionally I found myself dreaming about a cute Volkswagen in forest green. Of course, I'd have to get a license first. There was a lot I hadn't done after being diagnosed with schizophrenia. My father's overprotectiveness also didn't help.

When the traffic light turned green, the Rolls Royce sped away and revealed, to my surprise, Catalina standing across the street. She stared after the car as if entranced, an almost tender look on her face. Suddenly I felt awful. Here I was bemoaning the fact that driving would be a huge hurdle for me when Catalina would never drive again. Had she owned a Rolls Royce as well? Or would it forever remain a dream car for her?

Suddenly, Catalina turned her head and spotted me. I smiled awkwardly in response. She appeared startled that I had been watching her. She straightened, a cold mask replacing the softness from her face. She turned away from me, disappearing into nothingness.

Well, so much for that. Today was *so* disappointing.

The bus finally pulled up to the stop in front of me, hissing loudly before kneeling. The doors opened. I got up and climbed aboard, inserting my cash card before taking a seat towards the middle.

I was glad Idrina was working late today. That meant I wouldn't have to see her and endure questions about my employment status, or lack thereof. She was being generous with me, covering the cost of groceries for two, the extra power I was using, the discounted rate for the rent I'd pay in the future, and I hadn't even factored in her gracious concession for Sir Harry—and he was quite a handful sometimes, fur or no fur. If I was going to make it out on my own—and I had every intention of doing so—I had to pull my own weight somehow.

The bus rolled to a stop. More folks got on, an elderly homeless man among them. The people in his immediate vicinity moved away, ignoring him while others stared in suspicion. He shuffled over to the railing near me and stood, all other seats taken now that the bus was close to bursting. I got up and tapped his shoulder, startling him. I pointed to my seat and stepped back, gesturing for him to sit. He blinked in confusion before smiling, his grubby beard lifting a few centimeters as he nodded in thanks. I smiled in return, grabbing hold of the hand strap above me.

When the bus finally arrived at the next stop and emptied half its occupants, the old man left with them. I didn't sit when seats became available though. I found myself restless, desperate to get home and lick my failed job-hunting wounds.

In fact, I should indulge in a pity smoothie.

As I debated what flavor to get, the bus drove over a pothole and someone bumped into me from behind. Startled, I turned and saw a guy around his mid-twenties look apologetic.

"Oh! Sorry!" he said, one hand gripping the hand strap above him and the other holding tight to a plastic grocery bag. He was dressed casually in a gray hoodie and jeans.

"It's okay," I replied. "Bumpy ride."

"I usually have better balance," he joked. I smiled.

We were silent after that. I stole quick glances at him when he wasn't looking. He was rather cute, this stranger. Messy chin length brown hair, faint freckles, button nose, and really tall. Or at least taller than me. Not to mention he smelled pleasantly of detergent, eucalyptus, and something else that was both smoky and nutty.

Because I was so engrossed in the stranger next to me, I failed to keep a tight grip on the hand strap above me just as the bus made a tight right turn. I yelped, crashing into the guy. Quick as lightning, he used his arm as a bar to prevent me from falling on the floor. My hands grabbed a fistful of his hoodie.

"Whoa! Are you okay?" he asked, eyes wide.

I hadn't noticed before but his eyes were a pretty blue-green color. And the warm chest beneath my hands was definitely solid. In fact, I'd wager his hoodie was a thin one because the muscle definition felt generously proportionate to his slender build. I blinked, realizing I had spaced out and was semi-groping him. He smiled, either unaware or didn't mind the lingering hands. The temperature of my face became a burning inferno.

"Here, why don't you sit," he offered, pointing to the empty seat in front of him.

"Sorry about that," I said at last, unsure what else to say once I was settled before him.

"That's alright. We're near South Coast. The bus ride is a hazard at this point," he reassured me. I smiled again, feeling a little braver.

"Thanks for rescuing me, Mister...?"

"Call me Charlie," he replied. "Mister sounds like I'm old."

"My name is Estefani, but Phani is fine," I introduced, shaking hands. His grip was steady and warm. Suddenly *I* was feeling very warm underneath my collar.

"By the way," Charlie began, looking at the floor, his gaze serious. "I saw you give up your seat for that homeless man earlier. That was really kind of you."

I blinked, surprised. "Oh! Well, I mean, it was nothing."

"Not a lot of people in the city are considerate enough to give up their seats for a stranger," he explained, his stare returning to me. "Seriously, it's very dog eat dog out there."

"I'm sure there's nice people around. It's probably just hard to find them."

We smiled at each other. Suddenly, his cheeks turned red.

"Hey, if you don't mind me saying, your haircut looks very cute."

Wait, was he...?

"Are you flirting with me?" I blurted, instantly horrified I hadn't kept that question inside my mind.

Charlie appeared sheepish. "Was it that obvious?"

"I'm sorry!" I apologized, cheeks definitely hot enough to melt ice.

Charlie laughed, eyes alight with pleasant levity. "Don't apologize. I guess it's unusual for a guy to compliment a girl's hairstyle."

I touched the sleek, short strands of my dark hair self-consciously.

"No, it's okay. I just don't hear compliments about *my* hair very often."

I found that keeping my hair short was easier to manage. Not to mention, it was sort of like keeping an homage to my mother. I didn't remember much of her since she passed away when I was two, but every photo I saw of her, even the ones before she met my father, had her modeling a cute blond pixie cut a la Lady Diana Spencer.

"I think you look cute in whatever hairstyle you take an interest in," Charlie replied with dazzling confidence. His infectious good mood had me giggling. He grinned.

A familiar coolness chased away the stuffy warmth of the bus. My smile melted as soon as I noticed a spirit materializing behind Charlie. Despite its transparent misty form, it began to loudly wail, drowning out everyone on the bus. I clutched my bag firmly as fear—familiar to me as my own name—kicked in.

I tried listening to what Charlie was saying but the spirit's wailing made it impossible. I gave him a brittle smile and nodded when I thought his expression called for it. I even tossed in a "hmm" and "oh!" for good measure. I wasn't sure if I was successful but Charlie didn't seem to notice. He did, however, suddenly stop talking mid-sentence, frowning and touching his temple as though it pained him. He wobbled when the bus ran over a pothole.

"You okay?" I asked, reaching out to grab his arm.

"Uh, yeah. Just feeling...drained. Sorry," he mumbled.

I gave the spirit a surreptitious glare. It figured a parasitic entity with a somber mood would affect a nice guy like Charlie. I hadn't noticed it when I was looking at him before, but the purple smudge underneath his eyes, the withered and extra pale quality to his freckled skin were minor symptoms of being haunted long-term by the parasitic spirit.

With one hand guiding Charlie to sit in my seat, the other quickly dug into my embroidered purse, retrieving a Be-Gone bead. It was pea sized and made of wood colored in yellow faded paint. It didn't look like much at first glance, but the charm always prevented weak spirits from approaching me. Just one touch and they dissipated into nothing. Which was perfect since it took a lot of energy and time for them to reform back into their corporeal bodies. I'm not sure why and how it works the way it does, but I'm just glad it does period. If only Catalina had been a weak spirit, then I wouldn't have had to worry about her deadline.

"Here," I said, offering him the precious bead.

Charlie arched a brow in confusion, but accepted the strange gift with grace.

"It's a positive vibe charm," I explained, fudging the truth. "If you keep it with you always, it'll make you feel better."

He smiled, staring at the bead with a far-off look.

"That's really thoughtful, Phani. You're really kind. Thank you."

Oh, don't thank me yet.

The spirit was still sticking to him like glue, sobs morphing into screams of despair. I winced, digging into my purse again for my small blow pipe and another spare bead. Charlie eyed the wooden pipe in surprise as I loaded it up. It was a beautiful smooth pipe with Mayan symbols carved into it, a gift from *Abuela* SaRosa for my tenth birthday. She had it commissioned by a local shaman who special-ized in wood carvings. So many questions surrounded the gift, but I had been too timid at the time to ask any further.

I brought the pipe to my lips and blew.

The hit was a bullseye as the red bead flew through the spirit. It gasped before dematerializing into an even weaker fog. Three blinks and it was gone, returning the stuffy warmth it had stolen. Everyone on the bus gave me strange looks. I hastily stowed my blowpipe away, cheeks red as I gathered the rolling bead and turned around to face Charlie.

"What was that?" he asked, head cocked, lips quirked, eyes curious.

"Uh, it's a...spiritual tool! My grandmother from Guatemala gave it to me. It's supposed to ward off bad energy. I figured, why not?"

Charlie smiled warmly. "That's sweet. If I carried anything from my grandmother, I'd probably break it by accident."

I nearly placed a hand over my heart. Charlie didn't think I was a weirdo. Bless his heart.

"In fact," he continued, "I do feel a little better."

I'll say. His skin didn't have that waxy quality to it anymore. His cheeks were flushed and the bags underneath his eyes didn't look bruised anymore. What a difference getting rid of a parasitic spirit made.

"Here, you sit," Charlie began, attempting to stand. I quickly stopped him.

"No, no! You sit! I'm nearly at my stop."

"Same here, actually."

He laughed, lifting a hand to rub the back of his neck. The hem of his sleeve pulled back enough for me to notice a tattoo on the tender part of his wrist. The design was abstract, but delicate and lovely in its simplicity of thin lines and curious shapes.

"That's a pretty tattoo, by the way," I complimented.

"Oh this? Thank you," Charlie said with a beaming smile. "Out of all the designs I have, this one's my favorite."

"Where's it from? Do you know what it means? Ah, that's if you don't mind me asking!"

"I don't mind. I don't know what it means, but my friend does. He designed it after some goddess statue he found in a garden. It's supposed to represent purity or something. I used to be the only one with a design like this, but then my annoying roommate copied me." Charlie rolled his eyes. "Whatever, I guess."

"Did it hurt? I hear wrist tattoos are painful."

"A little, but I've felt worse." Suddenly, his gaze became serious. I fidgeted, unsure how to take the full force of his unwavering attention but secretly pleased that I warranted it.

"Hey," Charlie began, "do you mind if I give you my number?"

I nearly squealed. No, I did not mind at all! No one had ever given me their phone number before, nor asked for mine. After I saved his number on my phone, courage allowed me to offer the same. We exchanged numbers with excited smiles.

"Text me whenever," he said. "If I'm busy, I'll respond when I have time."

"Of course. I'm not doing much at the moment, but same with me."

As if to complete the fairytale, the bus slowed to a stop, hissing just as the doors opened.

"This is my stop. Thanks for the bead, Phani. I'll see you later?"

"Yeah," I said, waving at him as he stepped off the bus. He waved back. The bus closed its doors and continued forward. My gaze followed him through the streaky window until he was out of sight. I shakily exhaled, surprised by the last ten minutes. The phone in my hand burned, thrilled to know that I now had a cute guy's number saved inside.

Now if only landing a job was as painless.

V.

FAUST BREEZE AND WONDERLAND LEAVES

When the bus arrived at my street, I hopped off. It was around late afternoon and Idrina's apartment was a couple of blocks away. I took the opportunity to celebrate my potential romance with something ice cold and fruity. I entered the nearest Club Smooth, a popular smoothie and boba tea shop, and reveled in the AC working full blast. It may be fall, but *hot damn* did the city feel like a sweltering summer day.

I got in line and glanced at the menu, absently reaching for my coin purse. The flat screen in the corner was on the local news channel where an anchorwoman reported on the latest Asphodel had to offer. I paid it little mind until the group in front of me kept freaking out.

"He's just so hot! I can't believe a man like that exists!"

"Do you think he swings my way?"

"I think he's dating some actress. Typical."

I turned to look at the TV and found that the camera had shifted to reveal a handsome man around his early thirties with thick brown hair. His charming smile was directed at the audience, light refracting off his gray eyes like precious gemstones. He spoke with gentle confidence towards the anchorwoman, giving her his undivided attention.

"—worked on it. It's why I genuinely think this will benefit many of the citizens in Asphodel City," he concluded, not a single styled strand of hair out of place.

The man in front of me sighed. "I'm so glad I'm into men."

I giggled softly in agreement.

"Thank you so much for coming in today and talking about the newly built Charon Bridge, Mayor Warringson. I had—"

I coughed, blinking several times in shock. *That* guy on TV was Asphodel City's *mayor?* Well damn! The upcoming local elections just got a whole lot more interesting.

As I searched for my wallet, I struggled to recall how much I had left in my bank account. This would have to be the last smoothie I got until I landed a job. My financial situation was beginning to enter the reds and if I didn't find employment soon, I'd be in some serious hot water.

The TV in the corner continued to barrel out the city's news at an obnoxious volume.

"—they still haven't caught the killer, but it's suspected that this was a result of a turf war between two rival mafia factions, Thanatos and Erebus," another anchorwoman reported. She stood on the steps in front of an impressive opera building closed off by yellow police tape. "Reports have mentioned nothing stolen from crime boss La Patrona, also known as Mad Dog Patrona. The police are cautious about keeping—"

I turned my attention away. That's the third time I've heard the mafia being mentioned. I wonder what the odds are of bumping into one of them with how active they were in the city. Hopefully not too often.

"—and even more interesting, we've confirmed with the police the real identity of La Patrona who's lived and terrorized South Coast for almost a decade. Not much is known other then she was originally from Southern California—"

The minute the news station showed the photo of a woman with her hair piled into a high ponytail, gold choker gleaming, red painted smirk practically feral, my blood ran cold.

"—and her real name is Catalina Beatrice Patron—"

My coin purse fell.

After hastily excusing myself from the line, I left Club Smooth. It was balmy when I stepped outside. The sky was a bright orange hue, my skin almost glowing from the afternoon sunlight. With how mundane the day appeared, my embarrassing interviews and Charlie aside, I had hoped to rest and recover in peace. Apparently, that was not to be.

"Catalina?" I whispered, hoping she'd hear me from wherever she was so I wouldn't have to raise my voice and catch unnecessary attention. After a few minutes of nothing, I tried again.

"I need to talk to you," I added, a bit louder.

"Yes?"

I jumped, my heart racing at the sudden scare. She needed to stop doing that! I turned and saw Catalina standing close by with her arms crossed, expression expectant. I eyed the crowd and motioned for her to follow me.

I took us to Hesiod Park. It was a modest-sized city park with a decent playground, large walkways, and small elm trees; a mere stone's throw from Idrina's apartment. Because of the setting sun washing everything in hues of orange, the park looked as if it were drowning in flames. It certainly felt hot enough for it.

I stayed away from the children on the playground and the afternoon joggers on the walkway. Instead I settled on a random patch of grass far enough away from anyone within hearing range. Once I was sure no one would hear me, I took out my phone and held it to my ears before looking at Catalina. She remained on her feet. Waiting.

"So," I began, "you're the crime boss La Patrona?"

Catalina preened, looking mightily pleased by the revelation. It was obvious she took great pride in the title.

"Catalina Beatrice Patron, Erebus's Watchdog, La Patrona. How do you do?"

I rubbed my forehead. "I can't believe my luck."

"I can't believe mine, either. To think I'd stumble on someone who can see and talk to me without complications!" She placed a hand on her hip. "Of course I was rather insulted you hadn't heard of me. If anything, my face should have given me away. I get photographed so often. I thought to myself, could I be lucky enough to sucker this girl into helping me?"

I arched a brow, but the woman remained unapologetic.

"You do realize helping you will be dangerous, right? Because I'd have to interact with people who can very well make me swim with the fishes."

"You're not going to interact with my people," Catalina reassured. "You're a civilian and no one in their right mind would believe my own ghost would make *you* find my killer. Which, of course, makes our investigation *perfect*. No one knows you have ties with me. No one knows who you are. This will allow us to find the bastard without difficulty."

I frowned, not sure whether I should feel flattered or insulted. Why did this have to happen the minute I settled in the city? Couldn't she have approached me after I got a job? That way I'd have less to stress over.

"Listen, Catalina. As much as I want to help you move on, I—"

Catalina interrupted me, placing a single gloved finger against my lips. It was like kissing an ice cube.

"If you help me find the killer," she said, "I will tell you the location of my savings. It's all in cash and tucked away in case of emergencies. It's about a little over 100,000 dollars and no one, except me, knows where it is. Just be sure to deposit the lump sum in small increments so no one questions you."

My eyes bulged.

100,00 dollars?!

Just like that? That would set me up for years!

If I had a hundred thousand dollars, Idrina wouldn't have to subtly intimidate me for rent, bills would get paid, I could get my own place, and I wouldn't even have to rent it! I could continue to pay for my studies when I figured out what I wanted to do and most importantly, I could help my father pay off his debts. After all, raising a homeschooled daughter diagnosed with a schizotypal personality disorder wasn't cheap. Especially if the one parent doted on the daughter and wanted her to function successfully in society. With the hundred thousand, I could make my father cease worrying about my mental health hindering my future success.

A cool breeze picked up and scattered fallen leaves around us like confetti. I shivered, but not from the cold. Catalina arched a perfect brow after a few minutes of silence.

"Well?" She prompted. "Do we have a—"

"Deal."

❧

ACCORDING to popular mystery novels and crime thrillers, the first step in tracking down a murderer was to start at the scene of the crime. So, the very next day, after fibbing to Idrina about going out job hunting again, Catalina and I set out for Orpheus Theater.

The theater was on the northeast side of town called Wonder-wood. It was a community where the wealthy and artsy folk mingled amongst graffiti brick walls and decorative boho-themed trash cans. Orpheus Theater was large and painted in white with glossy glass walls. It almost resembled a jewelry case in the daytime.

However, it was the garden to the left that caught my attention.

Called Proserpina's Garden, the six acres of grass and shrubbery were stunning in its unique architectural design. The hedges were neatly trimmed, colored white or blue in between the various shades of nature's green. The flora wasn't native to the environment, but it added fun pops of color here and there. Wooden signs hung on compact A-shaped pine trees, written in fun fonts and skewed slightly to amuse. The footpaths themselves looked magical, unevenly placed flat stone almost hidden in the trim grass. Everywhere I turned, whimsy and marvel greeted my eyes.

It was Wonderland recreated

I took an eager step forward, intent on exploring the garden when Catalina cleared her throat.

"Oh no you don't!" She scolded, jerking a thumb in the theater's direction. "We're here for *that*. Now close your mouth and let's go."

Embarrassed to have forgotten our true objective, I turned away from the garden path. The action was heart-breaking.

"I didn't know Orpheus Theatre had a garden! It's gorgeous! And well-maintained," I said to her, making sure my headphone wires were showing so people wouldn't think I was weird for talking to myself out loud. I had prepared myself for sneaking around so I wore one of Idrina's party wigs— it was a simple red one with long loose waves. Black jeans, sneakers, and a maroon sweater completed the ensemble.

As I walked up the wide steps, I noticed that the potted evergreen shrubs were spaced evenly apart, framing the path to the front of the theater. They were uniquely colored in jewel tones and smelled sweet and piney. I smiled wide when the silver one shimmered under the sunlight.

"Oh that's gorgeous! I wish I could join their landscaping team."

"Why don't you?" Catalina floated beside me, not giving the plants a sliver of her attention. She was focused on the front doors of the theater. We were getting close. A group of three walked down the stairs past us.

"I have a complicated relationship with plants," I said, distracted by the fact that one of the lovely shrubs had a gaping hole in it. It marred the uniform perfection the rest presented. I was about to wander over when Catalina placed a cold hand on my arm.

"Focus, woman! You're worse than a kid at a carnival."

"Sorry," I mumbled, glancing at the poor shrub one last time before continuing up the stairs.

Our first obstacle of the day came in the form of a cop stationed in front of the glass doors. Dressed in the iconic uniform blues, the officer deterring anyone from entering was a tall figure in his mid-thirties with short blond hair. He cut a handsome figure despite the vicious scar stretching over the side of his neck and the intimidating bored scowl he wore that never eased even as I approached.

Hello anxiety, my old friend.

Sticking to the plan, I plastered a wide smile on my face and greeted the officer.

"Hello, sir!"

"The theater is closed, currently under investigation," he replied, voice monotone. He gave me a quick glance before looking away, uninterested.

"Well, isn't he yummy looking," Catalina purred, eyeing the man with a pleased expression.

"I know that," I explained, taking out my folded resume with a flourish. For safety reasons, I created a fake one with my name purposely misspelled. "I'm here for my interview. It was supposed to be yesterday but because of what happened, management rescheduled it for today."

Cornflower blue eyes focused on me from head to toe. The intensity had me sweating bullets.

"Who did you communicate with?"

"It was..." I began slowly, waiting for Catalina to chip in.

"Nate Rashark. He's a manager, always very accommodating to me and my men," Catalina supplied, looking thoughtful. "And he's not a spineless worm like the other guy."

"Nate Rashark, Officer..." I continued, ignoring the rest of her words as I glanced at the man's name patch. "Scrow."

"—too bad he's married. Two kids. Couldn't stop gushing about them. It's kind of sweet now that I think about it, but at the time it was *too* sappy—"

Officer Scrow eyed me suspiciously before glancing at his watch. I kept my smile plastered despite Catalina's continued chatter in my left ear. I swear it was going to drive me up the wall if I had to carry two simultaneous conversations, one of which only I could hear.

"It's currently mid-afternoon," Officer Scrow informed me. "He'll probably be in his office. Can I see your ID?"

Now here's the hurdle.

"Actually, I don't have my license yet and I just moved upstate last week. Would my student ID card work?"

"You don't have a state ID from your old state?"

This guy was tough. Still, my smile remained.

"No, I lost it a week before the move. I figured I would get a new one here."

Officer Scrow's suspicion remained, but he allowed me to show him my student ID which incidentally also had my name badly misspelled. Stefany Caramel Boomer. Officer Scrow's brows furrowed but he didn't say anything about my weird fake name. He did, however, look closely at my picture. It was something I had hoped he wouldn't pay too much attention to. The photo was from two years ago and my hair was longer then. Shoulder length and stick straight. Would he see that my current hair was obviously a fake? Would he call me out on it?

"He's taking forever! You're not even the most suspicious thing around here either!" Catalina complained, tapping her feet impatiently. I didn't bother to correct her that I was definitely the most suspicious thing here today.

"Is something wrong, officer?" I prompted.

Officer Scrow blinked, as if startled. He quickly returned my student ID.

"No, nothing. You just reminded me of someone."

"Ah, probably an old flame," Catalina nodded sagely. "If it was a relative he would have had softer eyes. Right now he's as closed up as a bank truck inside an iceberg."

I was curious enough to almost ask her to elaborate but remembered myself just in time.

"Alright," Officer Scrow said with finality. "You can't come through the front doors, but you can walk to the last set of doors on the far right. Employees who aren't coming through the back enter there. Another set of officers should be there to check your ID again, so have it out and ready."

I nodded and waved good-bye before following where Officer Scrow had pointed to. I didn't exhale until I felt the weight of his stare lift from my back when I had walked far enough that the curve of the glass and wall blocked him from view.

"Geez, that was stressful," I said, wiping my forehead, "and I'm not even inside yet."

Catalina glared at her hidden nails. "I'll say. He's lucky he's a stud. Perceptive cops like him irritate me."

While not irritating to me, they were definitely troublesome. I did not want to come across him again during my investigation.

Soon enough, Catalina and I arrived at the last set of glass doors guarded by another pair of officers. They were a contrast to Officer Scrow, all smiles and laughter as they chatted amongst themselves. One of them was even holding a cup of coffee.

"—funny seeing him knocked down a few pegs—"

"—serves him right—"

"Excuse me, officers?" I called out. They stopped talking and glanced at me curiously. I smiled. "The other officer out front told me to come this way to enter for my job interview with Mr. Rashark."

"That the Indian guy?" one of them asked, Boston accent heavy.

Catalina nodded to me. I nodded back at them. They inspected my student ID in five seconds and waved me inside with little fanfare. As soon as my sneakers stepped onto the plush red carpet inside the large foyer, I grinned. Catalina and I exchanged glances before nodding.

Show-time.

VI.

THEATER CONSPIRATOR

"Where to now?" I asked Catalina as we traversed inside the foyer.

The theater lobby was open and large. White marble walls with gleaming gold metalwork, red plush carpet with gold patterns, and to my awe, a large, but elegant statue of a lyre stood proud like a trophy in the middle of the lobby. Even the air smelled like freesias, white tea and ginger with hints of something sweet, but still light. I inhaled deeply.

Catching sight of my face, a smug smile appeared on Catalina's.

"Yup. Orpheus will do that to a girl. Now follow me. My box is on the third balcony, so fourth floor," she said, walking up the wide carpeted stairs, shifting her weight on each foot as if she weren't dead. I was surprised she didn't just float up like a normal spirit. How great was her energy to keep sustaining such a realistic form? It had to be grossly draining her.

Because we wanted to avoid anymore unwanted interactions, I bypassed the elevator in favor of hiking up the stairs, which I later realized I should've just taken anyway. By the time we made it to the fourth floor, I was leaning against one of the polished gold handrails, huffing and puffing like an exhausted asthmatic. Catalina tsked, unimpressed by my lack of stamina.

"You need to exercise more," she admonished, hair floating around her. "How else will you keep up with me? I can recommend a couple of exercise routines."

I grimaced. That sounded like a horrible idea.

"Were you active when you were alive?" I asked her, mainly so she could stop that horrible line of thinking.

"*Claro que si!* How else would I be able to take down six men single-handedly? Which I did by the way." She continued to brag as we passed numerous doors. "Ever since Darling gave me the opportunity for a better life when I was sixteen, I've trained my body, mastering all kinds of martial arts and fighting techniques. I've never once slacked off."

I arched a brow. Just the thought of doing a single push up made my bones ache. I couldn't imagine going through all that; it seemed excessive. Was it a prerequisite for the mob boss title or was that purely a Catalina thing?

"Who's Darling?" I asked her instead.

Catalina's expression softened, her eyes staring into the distance. "He's the most wonderful person I know. Brave, reliable, clever. Stubborn and manipulative too, but still wonderful."

"So...your boyfriend?"

Catalina laughed, the sound ringing clear across the hall.

"Once, but I could tell he didn't feel the same. He only agreed to it because it made me happy. Once we had my first kiss, I realized I didn't like him in *that* way after all. He can be so sweet sometimes, when he's not being an idiot." She stopped suddenly. "Anyways, no. Darling is, or was, my best friend since I was thirteen. I wish I could tell him I'm doing alright."

I stared at her for a moment before looking down at my sneakers.

"You know, I can deliver a message to him when this is all over," I offered, the words torn from my tongue despite my better judgment.

I made it my policy not to engage in delivering messages from spirits unless I absolutely could not get rid of them. Never mind that I didn't like interacting with the supernatural world on a regular basis, but letting anyone from the living know I could see ghosts and then some? My psychotherapist may as well ship me to the nearest psych ward, no questions asked.

Still, I was beginning to soften up to Catalina's forced presence and her existence no longer bordered the AVOID column. My offering this small reprieve of worries seemed like the kind thing to do.

Catalina's brows rose. "Oh?"

I fidgeted with my wig. "Yeah. I don't make it a habit. I can get inundated and overwhelmed fast. It's like the spirits just *know*—"

"You give off a pulse," Catalina interrupted, eyes trained on me. "It's a specific energy, like a lighthouse. It's how I was able to find you after seeing you for the first time. In a sea of nothing special, something about you made it easy to find you. Other spirits probably wouldn't have been able to track you, but for me, once I saw you, it was over."

That sounded...terribly scary in hindsight. I wonder why that is. Regardless, I was glad Catalina was as bad as it got for me. If I had to deal with any of the dark beings in Tenebris, I would have probably lost my mind.

Seeing my attention wander, Catalina patted my head. Not that it did any good as it phased through my hair. I shivered.

"Now, now," she said. "Don't let it worry you. You've handled yourself fine with me. You can handle any lesser being that crosses your path."

I smiled. "That's nice of you to say."

It was a surprise seeing a different side to Catalina, one that made her approachable. She still came across as intimidating, arrogant, and confident, but knowing she wasn't completely self-centered was comforting.

Catalina shifted her weight and moved a few strands of hair from her face. "I'm just calling it like I see it. Also, I really don't need you breaking down on me. We have a mission to accomplish and time is valuable right now. So focus, got it?"

Ah. Never mind.

"If you still feel like helping me communicate with Darling after everything, I'll take you up on your offer," she added.

I raised a brow. "Really?"

"Of course. I'm not about to turn up my nose at an offer like that. I know how to capitalize."

I nearly laughed. At least she was being honest and still better company than anything from Tenebris. I shook my head and gestured to the hall covered in vintage gold wallpaper and white crown molding.

"Shall we continue on then?"

Catalina crossed her arms and smirked. She cocked her head to the side, indicating the door next to us covered in yellow police tape. I blinked, startled to realize I hadn't noticed it at all.

"No need," she said. "We're here."

For this misadventure, I came prepared.

I searched up important gear would-be detectives should have on hand and found a decent list of things to carry. Gloves were one such item as they prevented any fingerprints from being left behind. It would also prevent me from touching anything weird. I had all my items stored in my Phani pack tucked underneath my oversized sweater. I swung the pack around to face me and extracted the purple nitrile gloves that I got from Idrina's makeshift medical cabinet.

Once they were on, I carefully opened the doors, hoping there wasn't anyone on the other side. The room I entered was colored in shades of red and gold. Ornate style furniture was strategically placed so it wouldn't block the comings and goings of the theater patrons. A lush velvet curtain hid Catalina's balcony.

I glanced at the tiny air vent in the ceiling before walking to the scarlet curtains.

"There's only one entrance," I pointed out, pushing the surprisingly heavy material aside just a little bit. "The killer would have had to come through the main door."

The box mirrored the elegance of the private room; lush red carpet, gold crown moldings, more Victorian vintage wallpaper. It also sported a pair of velvet chairs facing an empty stage. Catalina floated to my side and stared at the balcony with an impassive expression, her eyes darting around with caution.

"What do you think you can find?" she asked.

"Honestly? I don't know," I admitted, sitting in one of the chairs. I relaxed, finding it easy to imagine myself high up enjoying a stage show. "What show were you seeing that night?"

"Blood Brothers," she replied, moving to stand before the balcony wall. She leaned over. "I came here to meet someone."

"Who?"

"My employer."

"Your boss? What mob faction were you in again?"

Catalina made a disapproving noise. "Not important."

I raised a brow. "What do you mean? I think it's extremely important. I can't evaluate a painting if there's no paint on it."

"It's dangerous for civilians."

I rolled my eyes and took out my phone.

"What are you doing?" Catalina snapped.

"Looking it up. I found your real identity on TV," I said. "I'm sure some news site will have written a more extensive article. A mob boss gunned down in a ritzy place like this is big news after all."

Catalina's eyes narrowed in fury.

"Fine! But don't complain if your world suddenly becomes more violent and dark."

Cheek in palm, elbow on the armrest, I used my other hand to point at my eyes.

"Catalina. I can see ghosts, remember? As well as other dark creatures that may or may not be demonic in nature. Anything violent in the physical realm just kind of pales in comparison."

She rolled her eyes in response. "Fine, but listen well. I am—er, *was*, one of four crime bosses that worked in the city's underworld. We all reported to our main boss, Erebus. I controlled the South Coast territory and had other assigned tasks that made me useful to him."

I blinked, sitting up. "Why were you meeting up with Erebus that night?"

"I had some information I wanted to share with him."

"What was the info?"

"Not important," she gritted her teeth. Her tone told me she would not be elaborating. I sighed, lightly scratching my forehead.

"Alright, then how did you die?"

"Shot in the back of my neck," Catalina replied in a snarl, eyes darkening as she clenched her fists. "The nerve!"

I got up from the chair and took a closer look at the carpet, feeling it for any kernels of evidence. Instead, the area was devoid of blood. Had forensics wiped the place clean already? Besides the chair I sat on, the antechamber and balcony appeared clean as a whistle. It didn't look like a scuffle had even taken place.

I scratched my head.

Catalina mentioned that she had died three days ago. Had the proprietors been allowed to rearrange everything back to the way it was?

"I don't see anything useful here," I said, closing the curtains. "Let's go over the facts."

After a small huff, the former mobster floated to the center of the room. I sat down on a maroon couch and nodded my head.

"The night I was murdered," she began. "I was sitting in the balcony chair, waiting for Erebus. Intermission was only twenty minutes away so I knew Erebus would arrive soon. My men, two of them, were guarding the entrance to my box. Considering what kind of reputation I had, I never thought someone would be so bold as to challenge me behind my back." She spat the words out as if it were bitter poison. "So imagine my surprise and outrage when I hear the pop of a bullet and a stinging sensation at the back of my scalp—"

"Stinging? Didn't the bullet kill you...?" I trailed off, confused by her confession. I shook my head. "Wait, never mind. Continue. I'll ask when you're done."

Catalina inclined her head before continuing.

"I was shocked at first. Who would dare shoot me in my own box while I was in attendance with my bodyguards? It took a few seconds for me to react, but by then the killer was already out the door when he realized he hadn't killed me. *The coward*." Catalina's hands closed into tight fists. "When I followed after him, I found my bodyguards dead outside my door. I took their weapons and ran after the culprit."

From there, Catalina revealed that the chase had led her to the employee's area, but she paused.

"What's wrong?" I asked, leaning forward in my seat.

"I...I followed him, guns ready," she continued with hesitation. "I found him and there was fighting..."

I got up and approached her. "Are you alright?"

Catalina bit a plump scarlet lip and squinted hard at the carpet before sucking her teeth and shaking her head. She turned to me.

"I don't remember."

I blinked rapidly. "Oh."

I scratched the wig covering the itchy spot on my scalp. The revelation was an inconvenient one, but not surprising. Some spirits don't remember their final moments, especially if it was gruesome. They do, however, tend to remember their emotions during that time, heightened and almost tangible depending on the circumstances.

"Okay, well, drive me through the emotions you felt leading up to your final moments then."

Catalina turned her head, eyes faraway. "I was furious. Furious, impatient, confident, triumphant...suspicious and then...shocked. Just shocked."

I nodded, unsure how to decipher all that. At least we have some clue. Knowing the type of person Catalina is, it's not hard to imagine she was feeling triumphant when she had the upper hand with two or three guns. Then suspicious when...when...

"Why were you suspicious?" I asked.

Catalina shrugged. "I don't know. Something about the guy was off, like he seemed familiar maybe, but again, I don't know. I can't really remember."

Hmm. I decided to circle back to my list of questions from earlier.

"What about when you mentioned you were shot in the head and all you felt was a stinging sensation? And if he shot you, why weren't you dead sooner?"

Catalina smirked. She turned and floated in front of me until she was nearly in my face.

"Within the underworld of Asphodel City, I go by many names. La Patrona, my formal title, Mad Dog Patrona, a personal favorite, and most notably, Bulletproof Betty. Betty is short for my middle name, Beatrice. Do you know why I have that name in particular?"

"Because you're...bulletproof?" Even saying it sounds silly, but Catalina only smiled.

"Exactly. I am literally bulletproof," she said, stroking her choker. It gleamed brightly despite the laws of physics. "Or, was. I could be shot with any gun in the world and not a single bullet would penetrate my skin. I was like Superman. This convenient talent had me feared in the Underworld and so very useful to all the right people."

I blinked rapidly. "H-How is that even possible?"

Catalina's gaze became thoughtful.

"My choker was a gift given to me during my *quinceañera*. My *abuela* from Mexico came to visit and placed a spell on the choker when I showed it to her. It's an open secret in my family that she dabbles in the occult, even calls herself *La Bruja*. The witch. She said wearing it would make me bulletproof, but that I should be careful because it had one weakness. And if I was unlucky enough to get shot there, I was dead. I didn't think much of her words or the spell for years. It wasn't until one fateful night when I wore it during a party gone wrong that I realized it was all true."

I shivered, her story weaving a cold web over my skin. As far-fetched as Catalina's explanation sounded, I knew I couldn't dismiss her words. Not when I knew that impossible things existed in this world, like a girl able to speak to ghosts and kill flowers without touching them. Having a witchy grandmother cast a bulletproof spell over a necklace sounded so normal in comparison.

I nodded. "Okay."

"Anymore questions?"

Nope, still processing the first one. I shook my head in response before Catalina nodded.

Eyeing the room one last time, I gestured for Catalina to follow me out. Once out in the hall, I closed the door behind me as quietly as I could and fixed the police tape. As I did so, I realized her body-guards would have stood right where I was, guarding her box from any intruders. A suspicious guy like the killer would have been stopped easily, right?

"There's not much to glean from your box. What about your guards? Was there anything weird about their deaths? How were they killed?"

Catalina's brows furrowed. "Their weapons were still in their holsters."

Now I furrowed my own brows. "What? Are you sure?"

"Yes. I remember seeing Benny and Farlo slumped over. Their guns weren't drawn." Catalina's teeth clenched shut. "They weren't even given honorable deaths!"

I fiddled with the strands of my wig. "Holstered weapons imply your men felt at ease with the killer, or at least knew the killer enough to think they wouldn't need their guns in that instant. Maybe it was one of the theater staff?"

Catalina shook her head. "Everyone knows not to disturb my box, under *any* circumstances. Management has always been good about this unspoken rule for years and I periodically have one of my men check for any new hires. I come here often so I don't like surprises."

"How often?"

"Every two months or so."

I suppose that ruled the staff out. I started walking.

"You mentioned the killer felt off. Maybe it's someone you know?"

Catalina frowned, serious eyes trained on the carpet as she followed me further down the hall. I let her think as I headed to the employee area.

I read several news articles that mentioned finding Catalina's body in a storage room in the employee area downstairs. From her opera box to a storage room. The killing wasn't just a random lucky hit or a crime of passion. It was premeditated. Or at least that was the feeling I got. Sure, Catalina gave chase, but she had been angry and goaded into retaliating. And knowing Catalina as superficially as I do, all it would take was some blow to her pride. One audacity. Honestly, if it was someone who knew her, then it would be pretty easy to lure her away and finish her off. Which begged several additional questions:

1. How did the killer know to shoot the only place she could be killed from?
2. Did the killer personally know Catalina or was he really just a lucky random hit man?
3. Was she killed for personal reasons or business ones?
4. Why risk killing her in such a public place surrounded by her security?

"Hey, how many guards did you have with you the night you died?" I asked.

Catalina glanced up. "Four, I never really need more than five."

"Where were the other two stationed?"

"I left them in the lobby downstairs. They're supposed to report to me if there's anything suspicious. I didn't receive anything or hear Benny and Farlo make any kind of fuss, which is why I was caught off guard." She hesitated a moment before continuing. "I didn't recognize the killer but if it is someone I know, then this makes our investigation even more difficult."

I was already through the employee door and eyeing the several flights of stairs. We were apparently on the fourth floor. Before taking another step, I stopped and turned to look at Catalina.

"What do you mean?"

"Phani, everyone I know is from Asphodel City's underbelly. They're dangerous people. If cops have a difficult time simply talking to them, a civilian like you wouldn't stand a chance."

I swallowed. I returned my gaze to the hand gripping the railing. White paint chipped away to reveal silver metal. I shook my head and continued downstairs, determined to leave behind the weight of Catalina's words.

"It's fine," I said. "I wasn't planning on talking to your colleagues.

It's not like I can go around telling people the reason I'm asking these scrutinizing questions is because your ghost is over my shoulder demanding the truth. However true it is."

I laughed lightly.

I could feel Catalina's stare burning my back, but instead of voicing any objections like a normal human being should have, she simply floated ahead of me and led the way down.

I should have insisted she explain herself further, should have thought about where this investigation I agreed to do on her behalf was really leading me, but like the coward I knew myself to be, I let it go and thought of the reward money and all the financial problems it would solve. I thought of the cute little two bedroom, two bath apartment I could rent on my own without having to burden Idrina and how much more confident and self-assured I would come across to my dad if I could just trek it out on my own. I focused on those things instead of the scary truth that hid beneath the surface of the situation I was in.

At this point I figured, in for a penny, in for a pound.

VII.

INTERMISSION

"So, can you think of anyone who wants you dead?"

This time it was Catalina's turn to laugh, only she sounded derisive and high-pitched. I suddenly felt like an ignoramus.

"Oh sweetie," she said, eyes full of mirth. "*Everyone* wanted me dead. I was the most notorious crime boss of them all! La Patrona! Ready to hunt anyone down and destroy them!"

She couldn't have been prouder.

I frowned.

"But no one's made a move towards you before and succeeded. A blow to the neck this time around seems too easy." By the end of my speculation, I found the metal door of the underground floor and opened it up, revealing teal painted walls full of colorful papers and gray speckled linoleum floors. I inhaled faded paint, dust and old perfumes. "Looks like we're here."

Catalina eyed the closed wooden doors with suspicion. "I do remember this hallway. I was on a warpath."

"If you were watching Blood Brothers before intermission then–"

My phone vibrated in my pocket with an incoming text message. I cursed myself for neglecting to turn it off. A lot of internet sleuths warned me about cell phone towers tracking my location with any incoming calls or text messages. When I saw that it was only a message from Charlie, a bright smile appeared on my face.

Hey Phani, what are you up to?

Charlie ended up texting me yesterday night in between bouts of research. It irritated Catalina as she believed he would only distract me and be her downfall in our quest for the killer. Even now, Catalina sent me an annoyed glare as soon as she caught the goofy grin growing on my face. I turned away.

Just woke up, feeding Sir Harry

It was a blatant lie, but I couldn't let him know I was in the area. The less that led this entire ordeal to me the better.

You woke up? It's nearly 12 lol

I checked the time on my phone and cursed when I saw he was right.

I was up late researching a project

"Phani! *Ya basta!* Enough! Concentrate, would you? We're in the middle of something here," Catalina complained as she towered over me. She glanced down at my screen with disdain before turning away impatiently.

"Sorry," I mumbled.

I gotta go and work on some chores. Txt you later

Wait! Could I interest you in a date later today?

Heat broke over flushed cheeks as my heart began to pound thunderously.

Charlie was asking me out? *Today? Me?* I fumbled with a response. I was so glad we weren't having this discussion face to face because I would have stuttered and looked like a fool.

Sure, what do you have in mind?

"Phani!" Catalina called. I looked up and followed after her, still flustered by the turn of events. Another vibration alerted me to Charlie's response. I peeked a glance.

I thought we could grab some food at the Foodtruck Square. I get off at work in a few hours and if you didn't mind, I'd like some company for an early dinner. I'll pay of course! Gentleman's honor!

"That's so sweet!" I whispered aloud, smiling widely.

"Phani!" Catalina called impatiently.

"Sorry, sorry! Charlie asked me out on a date!" I told her, my smile firmly in place as I followed her.

Catalina wrinkled her nose before rolling her eyes. I quickly sent an affirmative to Charlie before turning off my phone. Excitement buzzed in my veins as I looked around. Just thinking about the potential of where our little date might lead to, whether friendship or something more, changed my cautious mood into a confident one. Catalina couldn't remember where it was that she ended up, but I figured a door blocked with police tape was bound to be it.

As time passed, I became conscious of the fact that there wasn't anyone around. The teal underground level soon morphed into utilitarian white walls. I eyed the signs next to the doors, hoping I'd find an exit or some sign that let me know the police had been there. Desperate for some clue, I peeked inside a dressing room I assumed was empty.

It wasn't.

There was a woman inside. Late thirties, curly hair a frizzy mess, glassy eyes tinged red as if she had been bawling her eyes out. The words MIRIAM THORTAN IS A STAR was written on the dressing room mirror in red lipstick. After writing the phrase several more times in angry forceful strokes, the woman I assumed was Miriam hurled the ruined tube at her reflection before turning around.

I almost closed the door, ready to make a run for it when I noticed a silk scarf tied to an exposed pipe in the ceiling. Realization dawned on me too late. Miriam climbed on a nearby chair, placed the thin noose around her neck and stepped forward.

I slammed the door shut.

My mind blanked, my heart hammering violently in my chest. Dread choked me as I struggled to breathe evenly. Against my better judgment, I looked inside again.

Miriam was still there, swaying gently as if blown by a draft, her face blue, lips white. Her neck was bruised purple and her clouded eyes sunk into her skull. She looked as if she had been dead for at least twelve, maybe fourteen hours. When I blinked, she was gone, as were the words on the mirror. Miriam stood back where I found her. She wrote the same message on the mirror over and over again before chucking the lipstick tube and turning.

I closed the door again. This time for good.

I crouched on shaky legs and placed my head between my knees. So much for my shiny happy mood. I took a few deep breaths in an effort to repress the dry heaves as my stomach churned.

Of course this place would have an atmospheric haunting. The theater world was bound to have its fanatic members clawing for the limelight until it was all that remained, that energy, that fire, that hunger for more that not even death could extinguish. Still. I did not appreciate coming across Miriam's death like that. It did, however, make me vaguely wonder if Catalina would have a similar atmospheric haunting despite her current spirit slowly approaching me.

"What is it, Phani? Did you find something?" she asked, placing her gloved hands on her wide hips.

I shook my head. After calming down, I looked up. I was relieved to see there was no one around. I wiped my eyes with the palm of my hand before standing and giving the door a final glance. Catalina arched a brow, but said nothing. I didn't volunteer what had upset me so much.

We continued on.

The tunnel I had wandered in housed ten different dressing rooms, a couple of empty conference rooms, an office which I quickly bypassed after hearing clacking computer keys from behind the closed door, a costume design and wardrobe studio, and a dance hall with mirror walls and wooden floors.

Once I passed that door and turned a corner, I spotted a pair of metal double doors at the end of the hall. It was covered in yellow police tape.

"Found it!" I whispered, skipping forward. Catalina followed.

"This feels familiar," she said.

I smiled. "Then we're on the right track."

Cautiously pulling the police tape aside and opening the door, I briefly wondered if I would see anything unsavory, supernatural wise, considering it was a murder scene. I hoped not. Peeping inside the dark storage room filled with miscellaneous props and large set pieces, the sound of a door not too far from me opened and closed. Heavy footsteps became audible as they neared. Catalina and I both eyed each other in panic.

Fuck!

I ducked inside and hid behind a hollow dresser, hoping whoever was nearby hadn't seen me yet as I waited for the moment of discovery to pass, body tensing. Seconds ticked by from a clock some-where inside. The darkness inside the room somehow made the sound of the clock and my shaky breath louder than it really was. After a few minutes of nothing, I moved from behind the dresser to stare in apprehension at the outline of the door. Light from the hallway escaped through the seams. I worried that as soon as I let myself relax someone would burst in and catch me.

"They're gone," Catalina whispered from somewhere.

I took out my phone and turned on the flashlight. Catalina's body appeared solid under the diffused light. She was standing by the door, keeping watch for any unexpected intruders. I moved the phone and illuminated the rest of the chaotically organized room. My father would have called it messy before his OCD kicked in. I walked over to a section of the cavernous storage unit that was taped off from the rest.

Catalina joined me with furrowed brows. Plump lips thinned as she gazed at a fallen metal shelf and the large brown stain on the cement floor not too far from it.

"So this is where you... you know, passed," I said, scratching my neck.

Catalina crossed her arms. "Just say it. I was murdered here. The concept of murder, even my own, isn't a stranger to me. I've had to murder people before, usually people who deserved it or got too close to Underworld business."

"O-Oh."

I kept forgetting Catalina was a crime boss of almost six years. Of course the thought of people dying doesn't really phase her anymore. If anything, I'd wager she was more furious about the inconvenience and mystery surrounding it then her actual death.

"Alright then, so you were murdered here," I turned to her. "Does anything come to mind? Ring any alarm bells? I know you mentioned emotions, but what about any images? Shapes? Impressions?"

"Impressions...?" Catalina stared at the dark spot on the floor and tilted her head. "I do remember...I remember...a tacky tattoo."

I blinked. "...okay, yeah, we can work with that. How tacky?"

Catalina paced. "It's simple. Boring. Anticlimactic. No artistry at all."

I shook my head. "Okay, simple tattoo. Do you remember what it looks like?"

"Yes, an oval. With a line in the center. Black."

I blinked again. "...so a pill?"

Catalina shrugged. I groaned.

This investigation was a mess. It didn't help that the detective was an amateur and the murder victim didn't remember her final moments. I opened the notes app on my phone and started writing all the clues I had so far on the killer himself. From what Catalina was able to recall, her assailant was male, very fit, had passable knowledge of firearms, and sported an ankle tattoo that looked like a pill. More specifically, I summarized he was mid-twenties to early forties, weighing between 150 to 190 pounds.

I frowned. The killer's description was much too generic for my liking, pill tattoo aside. I needed something else.

I looked at the crime scene again and noted small bits of glass scattered everywhere. Using my flashlight, I spotted lots of headlights piled to one side not too far from the twisted metal shelf. I counted the shelves on the wall and saw an empty spot where the sixth shelf was supposed to have been. It must have fallen during the commotion. The broken glass would have been cleared away ages ago if this room was frequently used.

"Do you remember anything about this fallen shelf?" I asked, turning to look at Catalina.

Catalina glanced at the pile of broken headlights and the shelf. She was silent a moment, neat brows furrowed. "You know...I do remember the shelf. It was going to fall. There were so many of those lights on it and they looked heavy . It was close to me so I ran–"

Catalina blinked sharply. "Wait! Wait, I remember! I remember what happened!"

My face lit up like a Christmas tree. "What? You do? What do you remember exactly?

"The killer! He pulled a rope and the shelf came crashing down. I tried to run before it could but he shot me then, when my back was turned. He shot me exactly where no one had before."

Her gloved hands balled into tight fists. I almost lifted a hand and patted her back, but remembered last minute it would do no good. Instead, I chose to focus on her words.

"The killer pulled a rope, you said? Like a trap?"

"Or a distraction. It wasn't meant to kill me, I don't think," Catalina surmised, suddenly pacing. "Something like a falling shelf would be easy to hear and dodge. At least for me."

"He shot you when your back was turned. Sounds like that was all the opportunity he needed."

That was another thing I could add to the killer's profile: workable knowledge of Orpheus Theater.

Catalina was convinced the killer entered from the back area where only employees were allowed. While he could have just walked in from the front using a ticket, judging from how he lured her downstairs after failing to kill her the first time and the trap he set up to distract Catalina, the killer was familiar with the storage warehouse and had spent some time down here without interruption to set up the trap.

"Hmmm," I hummed, feeling on the verge of something. Of what? I wasn't sure, but I sensed I was looking in the right direction and asking the right questions. I took a few pictures of the crime scene before deciding to call it quits.

"Okay, we can leave. Catalina?"

Catalina floated several feet in the air, neck craning as she searched and spun around for something in particular.

"What's wrong?" I asked, walking closer.

"I'm looking for my choker."

"You mean the wide gold one with the three stones?"

"Yes. After I was shot, it went flying somewhere in here. I want it back. I don't want it falling into the wrong hands. Darling gave it to me as a gift and my grandmother blessed it. It's sentimental."

I wouldn't call putting a bulletproof spell on a choker blessing it, but to each their own. Instead, I nodded and helped Catalina search for her choker. I didn't think we'd have much luck finding it and I was right, it was too dark in the warehouse and I didn't want to risk someone finding us by turning on the lights. My phone light could only illuminate so much so try as we might, we couldn't find it. Twenty minutes passed before I gave up.

"I don't think it's here," I said, wiping the sweat from my forehead before pulling my wig back into a ponytail. "Maybe the police found it and bagged it as evidence."

Catalina frowned, clearly not pleased with the likely scenario. "...I *suppose.* They won't know what it is exactly so I guess it's okay. For now."

Sighing in relief, I escaped the dark cavern of props and set designs. I righted the police tape carefully from outside before turning and leaving the hall.

"Now what?" Catalina complained. "Did you get an idea who it might be?"

"Not at all," I laughed. "But I made a list so we can go over that at home. Maybe I can buy a whiteboard on the way–"

"Hey you! What are you doing here?"

I jumped.

Busted.

VIII.

OVERMUCH COMPANY KILLS

BEHIND ME, a frail, old man hunched over a medical cane shuffled his way towards me. He was bald and dressed in gray overalls splattered with paint. The bony hand on his cane shook with each step.

"No one's supposed to be here," the old man continued, dark beady eyes squinting as he smacked his lips. "Cops and Mr. Rashark told me so several times."

"I'm sorry. I was looking for the bathroom after my interview and got lost," I lied, hiding my gloved hands behind my back. I quickly tugged them off and stuffed them in my back pocket.

"What? What was that?" he yelled, turning his head slightly, hearing aid exposed. He fiddled with it until his face relaxed. I repeated my response when he prompted me to speak.

"Restrooms are on the other end," he began, "and an interview, you say? Didn't think Mr. Rashark had any today. Theatre's closed until next week."

"Well, I just finished," I added hastily, just in case the old man decided to follow up. "I'm Stefany. Who are you?"

"Eustace Shern. I'm the glorified custodian supervisor," he said. He didn't sound overly impressed with his title. "Supervising what exactly, I don't know considering Mr. Marler, one of the managers, keeps chasing away all my hires! Now I'm the only one here!" He sighed, as if the topic was one he talked about often. "Follow me, I have a pot of tea in my break room. I'm the only one who uses the place, so I can offer a cup before I show you the exit."

I turned to Catalina and saw that, much to my indignation, she was gone. My jaw dropped. Did she really just leave me to the metaphorical wolves? Miffed, I gritted my teeth and kept my head down as I followed Mr. Shern.

Much to my horror, the old man decided to continue chatting as we walked, pace slower than normal because of his cane. I tried to tune him out when he wasn't talking about his latest watercolor masterpiece, but it was hard. Mr. Shern had a strong southern accent, and he spoke with such vigor that the words flowed easily from his mouth like a waterfall.

I didn't realize it was common for random people to be so chatty with strangers. I always kept to myself and never initiated conversations with anyone I didn't already know. Sometimes, whenever a stranger approached me and started talking my ear off, they turned out to be ghosts. Now that I think about it...

I surreptitiously poked Mr. Shern's arm. Solid. He didn't notice. Mr. Shern had moved onto the subject of his failed acting career. I nodded my head and sprinkled in a few murmurs of sympathy.

I wonder if I could ask him for his take the night of Catalina's murder. Surely he remembered something useful.

"Excuse me, sir?" I interrupted casually. "Do you know where the employees enter from down here?"

Mr. Shern looked at me. "Enter? They have their own entrance at the back of the tunnel near the loading bay. They're not allowed to use the front. Mr. Marler is *real* strict about it, the old coot."

"Is it always locked?" I asked. "My friend who works here told me she got locked out once."

Mr. Shern scratched his head in confusion as we turned a corner. The halls looked dingier the more we walked through the tunnel. It fascinated me to know that the backstage area was really just a large underground tunnel crowded with wooden pallets wrapped in plastic and rolling carts. Flyers and signs along with framed playbills from past performances hung on the walls like beloved trophies.

"Strange," he said. "The doors shouldn't have been locked. We have a security guard, Bob, likes to smoke, owes me twenty bucks, he does. Well, Bob guards the doors for the actors, so he lets them in. Odd that he locked it. Doors are locked now on account of the murder."

Perfect segue. And if Bob had been guarding the back the night of Catalina's murder, it would have been all too easy for the killer to distract him and slip inside.

"Did you see anything the night it happened? Heard anything maybe?" I asked, hoping I wasn't coming across as intrusive.

"I didn't see anything," Mr. Shern answered. "I was minding my own business, cleaning like mad since my workload suddenly doubled. I wouldn't have even been there that night if Mr. Marler would hire some extra help already and stop chasing away the ones I do hire!" He sounded very bitter about this. "I didn't see anything, but I did hear strange noises in the warehouse. When I checked and saw no one, I figured it was one of the visiting actors hooking up. Oh, how wrong I was!"

He shook his head before stopping and turning to whisper. "Whatever happened down there, they certainly made a mess of things! I even found a damaged prop piece by the door. I knew I had to fix it before Mr. Marler complained I can't do my job. Has it out for me, he does."

He didn't elaborate further on what he found.

We finally made it to Mr. Shern's break room. It was far removed from the main areas where the stage, dance hall, and dressing rooms were. It was a small miserable space with white linoleum flooring yellowing from age and dead bugs trapped in the overhead lights. The room smelled of burnt toast and mildew, the tiny kitchenette overcrowded with used paper towels and dirty dishes. A partially closed window across from us—the one thing cheerful about this place—showed the theater's deserted loading bay.

I glanced up at the overcast sky, hoping it wouldn't rain by the time I left. I hadn't thought to bring an umbrella with me.

"Thirsty?" the old man asked, grabbing a banged-up tea kettle.

"No, thank you," I said, pausing a moment. "So, you didn't see anyone suspicious that day?"

"Conniptions in May? Course not! I'm as healthy as an ox, I am! Survived the war in Nam, don't ya know? No one more fit around here than me!" He paused, his body half in the pantry closet. "Well, except for my last hire. He was a stud—oh bother!"

Mr. Shern carried a round tin in his gnarled hands—one that looked like it used to have whole wheat saltine crackers in it. He was quite put out when he showed me the empty container.

"I'm all outta tea," he said. "I'll have to fetch some in the back. Keep all my good stuff there. Who knows when some sticky fingers, like Meghan from ticketing, will try to swipe from me?"

He waved my help away, assuring me he was perfectly capable of fetching a box of tea himself. When Mr. Shern disappeared through what appeared to be the boiler room door, I sighed before blowing a strand of shiny hair from my face. This wasn't what I had in mind when I followed him. At least I wasn't in trouble.

"Look, look!" Mr. Shern cried as he returned a moment later.

He held up a small blue canvas the size of a hardback book. It appeared wet and shiny but, upon touching it, the paint turned out to be dry. I recognized the smell of oil paints with faint traces of varnish from my few art classes in college. It wasn't a heavy smell that clung to the walls but all the same, I resisted the urge to wrinkle my nose.

"It looks nice," I said, unsure what I was seeing.

"Isn't it? Finished it this morning, brought it to show Nate. One of my crew before he quit had a nifty tattoo and I got inspired by it. Reminds me of the statue in Proserpina's Garden."

I smiled, remembering my own excitement about the garden. "That's great Mr. Shern. But um, what about your tea?"

He looked startled.

"Oh yes! I'll leave this here. Take a looksy if you want."

He shuffled to the door again. I glanced at the painting and scratched my scalp. Lots of abstract swirls and angles with faint traces of green and black. Not sure what tattoo design this was but good on Mr. Shern for trying his hand at art. Despite how fun art class was, my projects hadn't been the most beautiful to look at.

"Having fun?"

I jumped when I heard Catalina's sharp voice. She stood in the corner, arms crossed.

"Jeez. Don't scare me like that," I said, placing a hand over my chest. "How long have you been standing there?"

"Long enough."

"Where did you go?"

Catalina walked to the window. "I thought I sensed...something."

"Something?"

"Something dark. Ominous."

My eyes widened. "You mean, supernatural ominous?" As in Burngemear?

Catalina stretched her hand before clenching it. She turned away from the window.

"Yes."

I shivered. I needed to leave.

"Well, next time warn a girl, will you? I don't appreciate you leaving me in trouble."

Catalina laughed. "With Eustace? He's harmless. Practically lives here and management lets him get away with it since his cousin owns the place. I was actually in talks to buy Orpheus before I died."

Wow. I eyed Catalina with suspicion.

"What?"

"I didn't realize it but...you're a theater nerd," I pointed out, unable to hide my smile.

If Catalina could blush, her face would have been red. Having hit the nail on the head, she blustered, speechless for once. I giggled softly, enthralled by the idea that crime boss Catalina Patron enjoyed thespian culture. It humanized her, made it less awkward to work with her.

"Enough talk!" Catalina raged, sneering at the shabby break room. "What's the plan now that we're in this place?"

The boiler room door remained closed, but I could still hear faint shuffling from inside. I eyed the rest of the break room before shaking my head.

"Nothing here, although…"

"What? Out with it."

"Well, did anyone know about your weakness?"

"No. Only Darling knew. Not even my grandmother knew where it was. I found it myself when I was accidentally nicked there years ago."

If Catalina's darling was the only one who knew, then that narrowed down my suspect list considerably. From what Catalina described and the way the murder scene was set up, it sounded as though her death was premeditated. The first kill shot was a hopeful one, but the second, a planned contingency.

"Hey listen," I began. "Do you think maybe your darling—"

The tea kettle on the portable stove top across from me exploded without warning. Hot pressurized water burst in the air like an angry geyser. I shrieked and scrambled away, heart pounding at the near scare. The ruined tea kettle was definitely Catalina's doing. How powerful a spirit was she to exhibit poltergeist abilities? And why was she so powerful already? Something like that for any human spirit was rare.

I lifted my wide gaze to stare at her. The tea kettle bursting did little to assuage Catalina's fury and disgust. All of which was aimed at me.

"Don't you ever dare accuse Darling! I won't hear it!"

"I was just asking! I didn't say it was him that killed you," I shot back, irritated by her unreasonableness. Before she could say more, there was a shout from the boiler room followed by a clang of metal hitting the floor. The noise had me racing to Mr. Shern, Catalina hot on my tail.

"Hey, are you okay?" I called out.

The boiler room had dimly lit, exposed brick walls and was

stuffed full of cleaning supplies. There were stacked chairs on one end of the room and closed pantry food on the other. I was positive this place alone had to have about a dozen OSHA health violations. For example, it was a random can of paint rolling on its side that caused Eustace to trip in front of a pantry shelf housing unopened boxes of tea, coffee, sugar, plates, and plastic cutlery. I ran over and helped him up with great care, making sure to kick the paint can away from him.

"You alright, Mr. Shern?"

"Yea, yea," he replied, clutching an unopened box of tea to his chest. "Happens every now and then. My hip is still strong, though, don't you worry. I'll go pour us some tea."

I smiled, glad to know his injury wasn't severe. When he left, I belatedly remembered that the kettle he had set on the portable stove top was ruined. I hoped he had a spare lying around somewhere.

"Aside from accusing my darling, have you figured out anything else?" Catalina demanded suddenly, halting my progress towards the door.

"Hey, I'm trying. It's not like I've done this before. And if you must know, I asked Mr. Shern if he knew anything about the night you were murdered."

She snorted. "Doubtful. The man forgets where he is half the time..." Catalina trailed off, her unhappy expression melting into shock. She stood frozen for a moment. I waved a hand in front of her face.

"Catalina? You alright?"

"Phani," she whispered.

My brows rose. I had never heard Catalina use my first name before, especially my nickname. I frowned, sensing something was the matter with her strange behavior.

"What? What is it?"

She pointed at something behind me. I turned but saw only closed boxes and a shelf full of broken knick-knacks. Just as I turned away, I noticed it. The dim light from the single lightbulb above illuminated the gold hidden underneath a gray rag. When I pulled the cloth away, I saw three oval garnets embedded in a solid gold choker, the surface gleaming like a forbidden treasure.

I couldn't believe it. Catalina's choker in the proverbial flesh. It sat on Mr. Shern's shelf, a silent witness to the murder of its previous owner. Catalina's story suddenly felt tangible.

"This must be what Mr. Shern found when he entered the warehouse," I said, grabbing the gleaming bit of gold. The choker appeared to be in pristine condition, if you didn't mind the dent in the back. The clasp was undone. "He told me he fixed it up so Mr. Marler wouldn't get on his case."

Catalina's fists tightened, her nails digging into her gloved palms.

"Take it, Phani," she said. "Before it falls into the wrong hands. I'd hate to see someone else bulletproof."

The choker didn't look particularly powerful, but I've often learned looks can be deceiving.

"What do you want me to do with it?" I asked, tucking the choker into my bag.

"I don't know. I'll figure it out when–"

Glass shattered. It came from the break room. I winced. I hoped Mr. Shern hadn't fallen again. I'd hate to see him cut up by broken glass. I walked into the other room, ready to lend Mr. Shern my assistance when I stopped short.

Mr. Shern wasn't here. Where'd he go?

I noticed the kitchenette window was partially opened. Had Mr. Shern been struggling with it before knocking a mug over or something? Thinking I'd do him a favor, I was about to open it further when I spotted a man clad in black running through the empty back lot as if the devil were on his heels. The sight was so odd that it took me a second to realize that something was wrong. Very wrong. My instincts screamed that I was watching Catalina's killer escape.

"Catalina!" I cried.

She was after him before I could blink. The killer turned a sharp corner before I lost sight of him. I couldn't believe it. The killer actually came back. But why? I soon found the answer when I turned around.

Mr. Shern lay broken and lifeless on the floor next to the table, hidden from my initial view. The ceramic mugs of tea he had been fixing were cracked and shattered beside him, steaming liquid blending into the leaking pool of blood around his head. Bits of pink brain matter was splattered along the floor. The smell of iron began to permeate the airless room.

I gagged before covering my mouth and backing away.

Oh God. Why hadn't I heard any gunshots? Did the killer use a silencer? Was it the same gun he used on Catalina? I should call the police! I should—

I stopped thinking when I noticed the room darken, bright colors dulling ominously. Speckled white-washed walls faded to dark gray as the fluorescent lights above flickered a few times before shutting off. The room became nippy at an unnatural pace, causing the tiny hairs on my arms to rise. Black fog began to appear, filling the room like noxious gas.

I knew what this signified.

Grayish blue wispy smoke began to rise from Mr. Shern's body. I inhaled sharply, taking a cautious step back. Not that it would do me any good.

It happened slowly.

A pale, semi-transparent image of Mr. Shern rose from his cooling body. He appeared to be in a daze, blinking a few times before taking a gander at his surroundings. He didn't notice the pressing darkness around him nor appeared bothered by the hole in his forehead. The blood smeared across it shined like rubies. It was a neat bullet hole otherwise, if one didn't mind skull shards peeking through.

"Did I fall again?" Mr. Shern murmured to himself. He smiled in apology when he spotted me. "I'm sorry. This old body of mine is really getting on."

I stared with wide eyes. The room grew cooler with each passing second until the goosebumps on my skin hardened. I had never seen a spirit remove itself from their physical body before. It was both a fascinating and spine-chilling sight; one that'll likely haunt me in my sleep.

Mr. Shern saw his body sprawled on the floor and frowned, touching the back of his pale head. When he turned, his back facing me, I realized that a portion of his skull was missing. His head now resembled a cracked bowl filled with lumpy beet soup and raw bits of steak. I swallowed my bile, not wanting to appear rude lest he be offended.

"Well, I'll be!" he said. "No wonder I don't hurt anymore."

"He came in here," I blurted, mouth working faster than my brain. "La Patrona's killer. He shot you. Did you see his face?"

"Oh! I can hear better!" The old man exclaimed with a toothy grin, staring at his outstretched arms in wonder. He did a little jig. "Maybe this dead business isn't so bad. I wonder if I'll see heaven. I hope so."

I'm glad one of us thought about his death with some positivity.

"Mr. Shern? Do you know who shot you? Did you see his face?"

"I didn't see his whole face. He wore a mask covering his mouth and nose, but when I saw him at the window, his silhouette kind of reminded me of John."

"John?"

"My former hire. Nice kid, real quiet."

"Former hire? You mean the one Mr. Marler chased away?"

Mr. Shern stomped his foot. "Yes! That old bastard! When he found out I hired the boy under the table, he chased him straight out. I felt so bad. He was a decent worker too. Very meticulous, knew his way around the place after I showed him the ropes."

Suddenly the dots started connecting. Could Mr. Shern's former employee...

"What did this new hire look like? What was his name?" I could feel it. I was getting close.

"John Forty. He was tall, a bit too skinny for my liking. He should eat more. Always smelled like he might have been smoking something." Speaking of, the smoke around his slain physical body was beginning to dissipate, his ghostly form melting away as the oppressing darkness began to swallow him whole. Why was that exactly? Was he ready to go? Was he too weak to keep a consistent solid form like Catalina? Questions for another time.

"What was his race? Any memorable markings? Tattoos maybe?"

"Caucasian for sure. Don't know much else about him. Never spoke about himself much. Just showed up in my office one day, heard I was hiring. He did have a tattoo."

My eyes lit up. "On his ankle?"

"Arm."

I deflated. So maybe it wasn't John Forty, not that a tattoo on the arm eliminated him from my suspect list. He could have more than one tattoo.

"His design inspired my latest painting," Mr. Shern continued. "You should keep it."

I smiled sadly. "Thank you. I'm sorry you had to go this way."

Mr. Shern waved my apology away. "Don't worry about me. I feel so light! No pain! And I've lived eighty years! Would've been nice if I left for my great reward until after I had my tea, though."

I gasped suddenly and took a fearful step back when *he* appeared behind Mr. Shern. Like a figure of doom, Burngemear remained impassive, face forever masked by a creepy demon skull. He didn't acknowledge me, something I was glad for. Even though I see him almost three times a month lately, he's never said a word to me since the first time I met him fifteen years ago.

Mr. Shern seemed oblivious to Burgnemear's hulking presence behind him. "Oh, and Stefany? Catch this killer fella, will you? I hate when criminals get away. I apologize for the lack of tea. Help yourself."

And then he was gone. His spirit form disintegrated into bits of glowing light until they joined together, forming a small gold butterfly. It emitted a faint sound of tinkling bells as it flew.

I never understood why souls took on the form of butterflies, but I was glad their harmless shape gave me some comfort. The soul flew trustingly into the black clouds that surrounded Burngemear. It disappeared and Mr. Shern was no more.

IX.

NOOKS AND CRANIES

TO MY SURPRISE, neither the dark clouds nor Burngemear dispersed after Mr. Shern left.

Burngemear looked up instead. Silver dots glowed inside the hollow darkness of his eyes. Or at least where his eyes ought to have been. As usual, he didn't say anything. Instead, he raised a soot stained hand, fingertips dark and pointy. The black from his hands faded around his forearm and thick red, glowing lines outlined his veins.

The gesture he made wasn't a hello, I knew, but the meaning was lost on me. He repeated the gesture. Pointing towards the window and then himself. Three times he did that. My anxiety rose steadily the longer I didn't understand. I decided to nod, just to see if that'll make him go away.

Burngemer did something odd this time. He bowed. An inclination of his head, a little bending of his waist. Subtle, but telling. Suddenly, and much to my relief, the dark swirling smoke at his feet grew and grew until it swallowed him too.

Burngemear was gone and so were all the clinging traces of Tenebris.

I inhaled and exhaled slowly. Once. Twice. Five times. Finally, I was able to move again. I grabbed the small canvas Mr. Shern gave me and stuffed it into my bag, sharp corners sticking out awkwardly. After that I booked it. With each step I took away from the break room, my relief grew. Hot tears pooled in my eyes, but I blinked them back, forcing myself to keep any sadness at bay.

When I found the exit doors to the loading bay, I burst through them. A security guard was seated just outside the doors to my left. He was asleep, snoring away. His name tag read Bob.

No wonder the killer got away twice.

Outside in the crisp fresh weather of Wonderwood, I found the nearest pay phone and dialed the police, fumbling with the keypad when my fingers wouldn't stop shaking.

"911. What's your emergency?"

"Someone's been shot by La Patrona's killer at Orpheus Theatre," I told them, speaking a few octaves lower, knowing it probably wouldn't fool them. "Send help quick!"

Just as I hung up, an explosion sounded from behind me. I gasped and turned in time to see black smoke smothering the entrance of Orpheus Theatre a few blocks away. People around me began to freak, some running away from the explosion and others running towards it.

Confusion gripped me. I briefly wondered if the unexpected explosion was Catalina's killer's doing.

I readjusted my grip on my bag and rushed down the street away from Orpheus theater, passing confused Wonderwood tourists, a Rolls Royce with tinted windows, street performers holding guitars and violins, and artists painting a mural on the side of a cupcake store. I saw a waiting cab the next block over and hailed it down. Once inside, I gave the cabbie Hesiod Park's address instead of Idrina's, just in case anyone followed me home.

AQUAMARINE, cobalt, cerulean, lapis, and navy. Various shades of blue formed striking thick whorls of different sizes.

Though his painting was small and simple, the message contained within was a complete mystery. I wasn't sure what design Mr. Shern saw on John Forty to inspire him. The whole thing reminded me of the swirling mists and fog that coated the icy atmosphere of Tenebris. I rubbed my eyes when they began to sting after staring at the painting for too long.

This morning's horrific events left me drained, nothing having gone the way I hoped. Too much adrenaline pumped through my system and seeing someone's spirit physically leave their body was kind of having a traumatic effect on me. One I would suffer with later. After returning home from Orpheus Theater, the first thing I did was take a hot shower. I may not have witnessed Mr. Shern get shot but seeing the aftermath was just as bad. I wanted to wash away any and all taint, any minuscule reminder of the last hour.

While seeing spirits was a daily occurrence, I never actually saw a dead body until I was eight years old. I hadn't been allowed to see my mother during her funeral when I was two. So imagine my surprise when my father and I were summoned by *Großmutter* Stefanie to attend my mother's aunt's funeral in Germany.

Tante Hilde's husband managed to scrounge up enough money to have a splendid service and procession. She was to be buried, a tradition the Baumer family firmly believed in—most of them being Roman Catholics, in the yard of her family home, a large house centered amongst acres of grassland.

The service happened on a cold, overcast morning. Dressed in black, everyone was silent and solemn as the coffin bearers came through. One of them slipped on a muddy patch of grass, losing their hold on the coffin. The scene that followed would have been comical if not for the embalmed body of *Tante* Hilde slipping out and landing in front of me. My screams had been hysterical. Partly because of the dead body sprawled at my feet and partly because *Tante* Hilde's spirit appeared before me. In angry German, she yelled at the fallen coffin bearers, claiming they made a spectacle of her funeral and that she could never have anything go her way, even in death.

I was startled from my reminiscing when I felt something touch my bare foot. Sir Harry jumped on my bed with exaggerated grace, looking determined to have his nap on my pillows today. I didn't stop him, even after he left greasy spots on my comforter.

Turning my head, I was surprised to see Catalina floating outside my window. She was impatiently waiting for me to notice so I could let her in, much like Sir Harry would do. I chuckled at the comparison.

I got up and uncorked the middle peg from my spirit repellent charm. The minute she was in, I corked the charm back up before some other spirit invited themself in. It still bothered me that Catalina was able to withstand getting forcefully sucked out of the apartment, not that I would ever tell her that. The loophole around her does beg the question of whether there were other more powerful spirits out there able to do the same. I hoped not.

"He got away," Catalina admitted, expression frustrated. "I lost sight of him once he ducked into Chinatown."

"It's alright," I said, heading towards the kitchen. Orange juice sounded like a heavenly liquid right now and I could sure use a distraction.

"It's not alright! That bastard came back and for whatever reason offed Eustace! There's gotta be a connection there!" she exclaimed. She followed me all throughout the pristine kitchen as I retrieved the OJ and a clear glass—Idrina didn't believe in plastic cups. "The longer that man is out there, the more Darling is in danger. I have to stop that son of a bitch!"

"So you're confirming Mr. Shern's killer is definitely your killer?"

Catalina nodded. "Yes. As I was chasing him, it felt right. He's definitely the same man who killed me."

That is interesting then. Why would Catalina's killer come back and kill Mr. Shern? A bullet through the head implies the kill was purposeful. He definitely wanted Mr. Shern dead and no one else. He didn't even bother to break into the building. Opening the window had been enough.

"When you left, Mr. Shern's spirit rose from his body," I told her. "I asked him a little more about the night you were killed and if he saw anyone. Apparently, he had hired a guy under the table recently before Mr. Marler found out and cut him loose."

"What?!" Catalina snapped, eyes wide and furious. *"Eustace hired someone under the table?!* Not that that's what I'm enraged about. My parents were illegal immigrants so I support undocumented people, but any new hires should have been reported to me! Why didn't Marler report this?!"

Oh she was seething. If flames and smoke could burst from her body, they would have. Instead, the toaster next to me began to tremble. When I brought her attention to it, she huffed angrily and started pacing the kitchen in an effort to calm down.

"Your parents were undocumented?" I asked.

I was surprised by this. Catalina exuded so much confidence and entitlement, not to mention insensitivity and selfishness that learning about this aspect of her backstory confused me. One would think she would exhibit consistent signs of compassion or some form of kindness growing up with disadvantaged parents.

"Yeah? So what?" Catalina snarled defensively, turning to face me.

"Nothing," I said, holding up my hand in appeasement. "My aunt and uncle were undocumented too. When my cousin Idrina turned 21, she asked for them. It took a few years but they were finally able to get their green cards."

Catalina relaxed. "The doctor cousin? I bet they were thrilled. My parents have no idea I'm a crime boss. I just tell them I work as a corporate manager and send them money every month."

I winced before sipping my orange juice. If they didn't know before, they were bound to know now. Her face and name was splattered all over the internet, across various news outlets. It was impossible not to know who she was unless one lived in a different country. I kept my thoughts to myself however.

"So what did you find this afternoon?" Catalina asked, changing the subject.

I straightened away from the counter and told her to follow me. Once inside the bedroom, I placed my glass on the dresser and took out an old notebook that had plenty of empty pages left. After securing a mechanical pencil, I placed the notebook on the carpet and knelt down.

"If I can summarize this insanity," I said, organizing my thoughts on paper, "there were two attempts on your life. One in your box seat which failed. This caused you to be lured downstairs to the set design warehouse where the killer was able to spring the trap that distracted you enough to kill you."

Catalina nodded in confirmation.

"Now we move to speculation territory. How did the killer get inside? How did he know where to go downstairs? And most importantly, how did he know where to shoot to get past your bulletproof armor?"

"Valid questions."

"I suspect he came through the employee area in the back and set up the trap if it wasn't already set up before. This brings us to the list of suspects."

I flipped to a new page.

"First on the list: John Forty."

"The illegal hire?" Catalina asked, bent at the waist as she stood watching me write over my shoulder.

"Yes. Mr. Shern's spirit told me that he briefly saw the killer and for some reason, it reminded him of Forty. Forty was his former employee before Mr. Marler found out. He claims that the guy is nice, tall and quiet, but also really good at getting around. It might be a stretch to accuse him, but he's a pretty good lead."

Catalina straightened and rubbed her chin. "How long do you think he was around before he left? And when did he leave?"

I paused before grimacing. "Damn, I don't know. I didn't think to ask that."

"If I had access to my men, I could find out employment details and anything Eustace might have recorded," she muttered.

It's suspicious that the only person to know anything about John Forty was a deceased Mr. Shern. Unable to tell anyone...even the police....

Underneath his name, I scribbled the details of my theory. If John Forty was the killer, then he came back and killed Mr. Shern to prevent him from speaking to the police. I could be wrong but it would be a neat way to tie up a loose end. It's a shame I couldn't confirm whether Mr. Shern had mentioned John to the police already. If what he told me the first time I asked was the same thing he told the police, then they definitely didn't know. But they would soon, once the police discovered Mr. Shern's body and started investigating his death. Mr. Marler was bound to mention it.

"It should also be noted that John had a tattoo. Mr. Shern said it was on his arm though." I looked up at Catalina. She frowned, arms crossed. "He painted it, sort of.

"He painted the tattoo?"

"Yeah," I said, getting up and grabbing my glass of juice, taking generous sips of the citrusy liquid. "I'll analyze it later and see if I can recreate it. Then I can take it around different tattoo parlors."

Catalina arched a brow, nodding in approval. "You're very thorough about this. I'm impressed."

I ducked my head. "I'm just fascinated with mysteries. It's unfortunate that a lot of mysteries tend to coincide with murder. Really puts off a career as a police detective."

Catalina made a face. "You as a detective? Please don't. I can't stand cops. There's far too many bad ones for the good ones to balance out, especially in Asphodel City. You would have been miserable. A private eye would be a better fit."

I rolled my eyes. "You're exaggerating."

"I'm really not." Catalina crouched and read my work. "Oh? What's this? You wrote a general description of the killer?"

"Just what I think he might look like based on what everyone told me. It's still inconclusive."

"Male, Caucasian, very fit, passable knowledge of firearms. I'd say expert level. Ankle tattoo, looks like a neat pill maybe." She nodded her head. "And you think he's in his early twenties to early forties?"

"I know that could be anyone, but I'm just covering all the bases. He could also weigh between 150 to 190 pounds and has some familiarity with the backstage area, specifically the warehouse. That trap he set up looked like it needed time and rearranging. That's why John Forty is suspect number one. I could—wait! Don't blow on the page!"

Too late. Catalina blew on the page to turn it and found her darling also written down as suspect number two. She was not happy about that.

"*What the hell?!* Didn't I say Darling was off limits?!" Catalina straightened while I retrieved my notebook. The trinkets on my dresser and lamp on my nightstand began to tremble forcefully. I sighed.

"I have to cover all my bases. Your guy is the only one who knows where your weak spot is located. Unless your grandmother started talking and the gossip reached across North America, he's logically the next we should look at. I'm not saying he's the killer but maybe he accidentally said something to the wrong person. Maybe he got drunk and blabbed."

"Darling isn't careless," Catalina argued. "He's methodical and precise, always thinking ten steps ahead and he's super discreet. He's also my best friend and he would *never* betray me like that. *Not ever.*"

I sighed before placing my notebook on my dresser. I returned to the kitchen in lieu of answering her, placing my empty glass in the sink and washing it before placing it on the drying rack.

Catalina didn't follow me. I was glad for it since I wasn't sure what to tell her that might make her see reason. It's not like I'm accusing her friend of betrayal, but the information got out somehow. I mean, how else was the killer aware that the only way to kill Catalina was precisely where he shot? It might have been a lucky shot, but given all the evidence and everything I was told, Catalina's murder was premeditated and something told me that maybe her darling had a clue.

An incoming text from my room had me racing over. It was Charlie, checking to make sure if we were still on later today. I smiled widely. Thank goodness he reminded me because I completely forgot about our date! Catalina was currently eyeing the painting I had placed on the dresser, trying to decipher it as if it held all the clues to our case. Hopefully she found something that made my job easier and cooled down her temper.

"Hey, I'm going to get ready for my date with Charlie," I said.

Catalina waved me away. Shrugging, I opened my closet and tried finding the cutest outfit I possibly owned. Sure it was simply dinner at a food truck square, but I wanted to make a good impression on Charlie and considering this was my first date, I did not want to be the one to screw this up.

Just as I picked out a black floral patterned dress, my phone rang. This time it was Idrina. I brought the phone to my ear while I searched for the perfect pair of shoes.

"Hey Idrina, how can I help you?"

"Phani! When you get a chance can you do me a favor?"

"Yeah, what's up?"

"I left my wallet at home when I rushed to an emergency surgery," she explained.

I nodded, remembering Idrina running around like a headless chicken after she got the call some four hours ago. I had just finished preparing for my mission to Orpheus Theater when Idrina instructed me to eat yesterday's leftovers since her preparation for tonight's dinner was ruined. Her announcement had saddened me. I had been looking forward to her cooking. On the flip side, I was glad she wasn't here. It made talking to Catalina easier.

"I'm staying until," Idrina paused, probably checking her watch, "eleven, so can you pretty please bring my wallet over? I'm starving and there's no way I'm going to let *Travis* treat me so I can 'pay him back in favors'. The man doesn't even respect that I have a boyfriend!"

"Hear ya loud and clear. I'll be over soon. See you later."

"Going out then?" Catalina remarked, moving to hover over my comforter by a few inches. She crossed her legs at the ankle and continued to examine the canvas.

"Have you found anything?" I asked, pulling my dress over my head and tugging it into place before grabbing my brush and fixing my hair. I shooed Sir Harry when he tried pawing at my shoes.

"Not yet, but the painting does remind me of the Plum Island

Sound. I drowned a subordinate there once for betraying my orders," Catalina admitted.

I looked at her in alarm. I needed to stop forgetting that I was helping a full grown, unrepentant mobster and that her sins were just as great as the killer's. If aiding her wasn't so beneficial, I would have run for the hills.

After making sure my dress and hair were neat, I added deodorant and a spritz of a citrusy perfume my father got me for Christmas last year on my pulse points. I even brushed my teeth just in case, though I cringed when the lingering taste of orange juice and spearmint clashed. Once I was done, I left the bathroom and grabbed my embroidered bag.

"Hey, I'm gonna deliver Idrina's wallet to her and meet Charlie after. You wanna tag along for the first part?"

Catalina laughed. "As if. I'm not your hairless rat."

"He's a cat."

"Same—*cómo se dice?* How do you say it?—nuance. Besides, it's a pain having to enter your apartment with the stupid spirit repellent on all the time."

I rolled my eyes. "Alright, but play nice."

I grabbed Idrina's Kate Spade wallet and stuffed it inside my small bag before walking over to the hallway closet. My spare longboard, Cosmos, was stashed safely inside. It wasn't as pretty as Pansy, my main board, but it still rode smoothly. Eventually, when I've gathered enough courage and end up in Tenebris again, I'll retrieve Pansy. For now, Cosmos the Reliable will have to do. I locked up the apartment behind me before heading towards the elevator.

It had been daylight when I left Orpheus Theater earlier, so I expected some warmth to linger in the air. The chilly breeze that washed over me told a different story, however. Judging by the orange hues in the sky, twilight would arrive by the time I met up with Idrina.

Plugging my earphones in, I looked up my favorite playlist before hopping on Cosmos and setting out for Asphodel General. I was careful to maneuver my way through the streets while playfully dancing on my board. It was a neat skill I was really proud of, even if it didn't really serve me any purpose.

As I skated down the sidewalk, my eyes swept past a pink second-hand bookstore. I blinked before stopping my board, turning my head to look back. Curiosity got the better of me and before I knew it, I stood in front of the two-story structure.

Like a square peg in a round hole, Chariclo Books looked out of place between the two gleaming office buildings on either side. It had a quaint Victorian construction, the storefront painted rose pink and the display window themed Halloween with hanging grinning pumpkins. Put together, the different mishmash elements made the book store come across as kind of endearing.

The bell hooked on the door chimed when I stepped inside. Oranges, amber, and hints of mocha coffee stirred in the air. I inhaled the addicting scent in big gulps as a warm feeling seeped into my limbs.

Chariclo Books was decked with dark wooden bookcases from ceiling to floor. They were lined with books separated by genre and categories. Near the front, several tables stacked with local books sporting dynamic covers greeted patrons as interesting trinkets from TV shows and movies lay spread out on any hard surface. I smiled when I spotted a Batman figure in a glass case. Dark academia music at a low volume played from a hidden speaker somewhere in the store. I looked around and greedily took in the atmosphere. What made this place even better was that not a single spirit floated around. My shoulders relaxed.

"Hey ho, welcome to Chariclo Books," called a soft husky voice from behind.

I turned and saw a black woman dressed in a form fitting orange plaid pinafore dress greet me with a wide plump smile. Though her shimmery make-up was flawlessly applied with honey blonde tresses flowing prettily to her bust in mermaid waves, there was something aside from her pretty appearance that had me staring longer than normal. I couldn't figure it out for the life of me though so I shook my head and smiled at her in greeting instead.

The woman must have sensed my confusion as she neared, however.

"What's the matter, kid? Never seen a drag queen before?"

I blinked in shock. "You're a drag queen? But you don't look it."

The woman stopped walking before laughing, blonde hair thrown back. "Thank you! I was going for an everyday glam look. I call this Autumn Librarian. It's part of my Subtle with Style collection."

I eyed her modest 3-inch loafer heels and navy blue tights. It all looked well put together with an additional flair that wasn't out of place. If my personal style didn't already veer hard into Guatemalan mountain village girl with lots of embroidery and light, flowy fabrics, I'd be tempted to mimic her style.

"I think you look exactly the right amount of extra," I said.

The woman grinned. "My sister said differently, but you know what? I like you. Is this your first time meeting a drag queen?"

I nodded.

"Well then, I'm honored to have popped your drag cherry. Trust me though, you haven't seen *anything* yet," she snickered. "The name's Tirisha Jordan, Know-It-All extraordinaire. Now tell me, little chip, what can I do for you today?"

X.

WONDERS NEVER CEASE

Tirisha held out her hand as though waiting for it to be kissed. I took it, staring at the back of her hand in confusion before doing just that. She gasped before throwing her head back again, disturbing the near-by patrons in the store with her boisterous laughter. I quickly let go.

"What?" I asked, blushing.

"I can't believe you went ahead and did that! Oh, you're too precious! What's your name?"

"Phani," I mumbled, embarrassed.

Tirisha smiled. "Well it's nice to meet you, Phani. What can I do for you?"

"Um." My mind blanked so I said the first thing that came to mind. "Are you the owner of the store?"

Tirisha laughed again, using her glittering long nails to push her hair away from her face.

"Goodness no. I just help around whenever my sister Abbie begs for a favor. She's the owner of Chariclo Books. Won't be back until tomorrow though."

"Oh."

Tirisha caught the disappointed tone in my voice. "What's wrong?"

"I was just wondering if I could apply for a job here."

I might as well ask while I was at it. It hadn't been my intention when I came in, but the pleasant book-worm atmosphere encouraged me to try. Seeing Tirisha's pitying face, however, quickly dunked my hopes in the cold, gritty waters of reality.

"Sorry, kid. My sister already hired her people for the season and has her stand-by list full. You'll have to try again next year in August. Staffing here gets really competitive, although I don't see why," she said, wrinkling her nose at a replica of the Star Wars Millennium Falcon in a glass case by the front counter.

It was clear Tirisha enjoyed a livelier and less nerdy scene.

"Oh, okay," I said. "Then I suppose you don't know if this place has any paranormal books?"

Tirisha's eyes alighted with interest. "Paranormal? Now why would a cinnamon roll such as yourself be interested in that? You're not secretly into the occult, are you?"

I blanched, cringing at the thought. "No. I-I was just curious."

She examined me for a moment before humming to herself.

"Okay, I think I have just the books for you. It'll be on the second floor though. Hey! Laila!" Tirisha called, turning to look at the register counter where an Indian girl with long dark hair looked up from her novel. "Man the first floor, will ya? I'm going to show this customer something."

She responded with a thumbs-up before going back to her book. Tirisha took the lead and led me over to an antique spiral staircase near the back of the store.

"Whoa," I said in excitement.

"I know. Abbie loves all things old. Which is all fine and dandy, but please don't bring in the dust, am I right?"

To my delight, the second-floor smelled of vanilla and old parchment. The shelves were just as crammed here as they were on the first floor, except the books and tomes present were more research material and less popular fiction. Two large bay windows overlooked the busy Asphodel streets, inviting anyone to wander over and sit in one of the plush chairs provided. The entire place was cozy and aesthetically pleasing. I loved it.

"This is nice," I said, looking around with a smile.

"It's certainly quieter. Not a lot of people linger, which makes me have to periodically check this floor to discourage any hanky-panky activities," she complained, her thick heels muffled by the dark green carpet.

"Do you catch people doing that often?"

"All the damn time." There was a mirror next to us. Tirisha stopped in front of it to fix her hair and wipe away any stray smudges from her lips. "No drama today though and thank the Universe. I have to change into my full glam look in an hour and I have no interest in dealing with horny teenagers right now."

I giggled. "If you don't mind me asking, isn't it too early to be in full glam drag?"

"Too early? Nonsense! Drag is a lifestyle. It's never too early! But if you must know, I do have an audition I have to be at in three hours," Tirisha admitted, pride evident in her tone.

"Audition to what?"

"To perform at an exclusive club for exclusive people this Thursday. When I get it, I'll officially be a part of the top tier queens in Asphodel City. And that's no small feat let me tell you."

I smiled. "Sounds fun. Good luck."

Tirisha winked. "Thanks. I have a strong *feeling* I'll make the cut."

At the very back next to the historical research materials was a single shelf dedicated to the serious paranormal pursuits of truth. I touched the titles from authors I'd never even heard of in utter fascination. New books meant new information. And with that, a better understanding of my abilities.

"So, what exactly are you looking for?" Tirisha asked.

"Um, well, I was hoping I'd find something about the afterlife," I admitted, refusing to meet her eyes. A lot of people looked at me funny when I mentioned anything of the sort.

I pulled out a thick book titled *Paranormal Theories for the Interested Mind*. This looked promising.

"Afterlife?"

"Yeah, like, what afterlife is there? Why do spirits linger? What can be done to help them move on to a better place? Etc. Topics of that nature."

Tirisha snorted. "Sounds like a mixture of religion."

I shrugged. "Maybe."

"I can sort of understand why a spirit would want to linger around here," she said, laughing a bit. "If they're too naughty, Hell would be far too cold a place to wander around in for all eternity. Not to mention it's empty and boring. No fun to be had anywhere if you ask me."

My hand stilled over a page. I lifted my gaze in time to see Tirisha examine her lacquered nails. Shock filled me.

"What makes you say that?" I asked, standing. She glanced at me as if the answer were obvious.

"God has a funny sense of humor on how people should suffer. Although a frozen Hell sounds strange, it's no less cruel." She turned and walked away from the paranormal section, stopping by the stairs before glancing at me. "At least that's what I think. Now, shouldn't you be going somewhere, my little chocolate chip?"

I blinked, Idrina's face coming to mind. Damn! I jammed the book back in its original place before scooping my longboard up and following after the mysterious drag queen.

"That's a very interesting theory you have there," I tell her as we travel downstairs. "And um, thanks for showing me the books. I'll have to come back later when I'm not busy."

Tirisha glanced at me and smiled. "Hey, do you mind if I touch your hair?"

After shaking my head, she reached a hand out to fix my bangs—they had gotten tangled during my ride.

"No problem, kid. You know, with your moles, you look like an adorable chocolate chip cookie." I grimaced, embarrassed by the attention to the many moles littering my face and body. Funny enough, my dad says the same thing. Apparently that's what my mother used to affectionately call me.

"Thanks," I said once Tirisha was done adjusting my hair to her satisfaction.

"You know, you should carry a small pouch full of beauty essentials for any emergencies. It'll take the edge off when you go on your date."

I blinked, surprised by her words. "H-How did you know that?"

Tirishia winked in reply before another customer approached her with a question. Before I could patiently wait for her, my phone dinged with a new text message. Two messages actually. One from Charlie asking if I wanted company going to the food truck square or if I wanted to meet him there instead. I smiled widely, warmth striking my heart. How thoughtful!

The other text was from Idrina.

Where are you? Did you get lost?

And I had to go.

I bid Tirisha a quick goodbye, promising to come back soon before running towards the front door. Before I could even touch it, someone stepped in front of me at the last moment, their back facing me. I squeaked when I crashed into broad shoulders and a slim waist clad in a black blazer and slacks. To my relief, my weight combined with that of my longboard wasn't enough to run the stranger over.

"Sorry," I mumbled, stepping back and rubbing my nose.

The man in front of me turned and I froze.

Before me stood the most handsome man I'd ever seen. Six feet tall, lithe figure with a well built chest, dark hair, thick brows, gray eyes like storm clouds, an aquiline nose and an angular jaw that I'm positive Idrina would describe as cutting glass. He was dressed in dark slacks, black loafers, and a wrinkle free lavender dress shirt. He even smelled of sandalwood and cloves with a hint of peppermint. Then the man smiled at me. I was stunned.

I must have spaced out for a solid minute because the next thing I know, Tirisha was giggling behind me like a schoolgirl and the handsome man in front of me was waving a hand over my wide eyed, shocked face. Heat quickly flooded my cheeks.

"I'm so sorry!" I blurted out, embarrassed. I stepped back.

The man appeared surprised, but his smile remained in place. "It's no problem. I should be the one apologizing. Are you alright?"

His voice was deep and soothing to the ears. I could have swooned at the sound. How was this man real? Before I could embarrass myself further, my phone began to ring *Material Girl* by Madonna, reminding me that Idrina was getting impatient. Shit!

"I have to go! Sorry about that!" I tell the man, rushing past him and opening the door. Cosmos landed harshly on the pavement before I pushed off and raced down the street, swerving around crowds, parked Rolls Royces, and a group of senior cyclists. It would only get more crowded as I continued.

ASPHODEL GENERAL—A good twenty minutes from Idrina's apartment by car located in Downtown Asphodel—was an old red brick construction. It was under constant renovations ever since it was labeled a historical landmark.

By comparison, the newer buildings attached were modern with sleek lines and glass hallways. While it wasn't much to look at—not like Orpheus Theater—the place did give off a sense of professionalism and healing. It was probably why Asphodel General was the most popular hospital in the city. That and the new high-tech equipment recently donated made one feel less like they were on death's door.

I walked inside the spotless lobby and approached the salt-and-pepper-haired receptionist.

"Yes?" she asked.

"I'm looking for Dr. Rivera's office?"

I may act like coming to a hospital was no big deal, but really, I avoided these places like B-rated horror films. They were always festering with malformed phantoms, weeping spirits, and shifting shadows. They also tended to carry a taint of melancholy so thick it left a metallic taste on the tongue.

I did my best to ignore the half-formed apparitions flickering in and out of existence around me. Most appeared less grotesque, merely looking sick and dazed. The ones coated in blood generally came from the ER. The spirits that creeped me out the most, however, were the ones that died with gaping wounds from surgery, their insides on blatant display. One such spirit floated past me, their heart exposed, bloody skin pinned back by metal needles.

After receiving my ID sticker and pinning it to my chest, I walked over to the hall on my left, following the directions the receptionist gave me. It didn't take long to find Idrina's office. As soon as I knocked and entered, she flung herself at me, eyes bright as relief rolled off her in waves.

"Oh, thank God! Travis has been knocking on my door all afternoon. I swore to myself if I saw his face one more time I would slap him silly with my clipboard. Like, I'm *so* done with him I swear."

"There, there. I think this will assuage your deadly urges," I laughed, handing her wallet over.

Idrina's lips stretched into a wide smile.

A sudden knock on her door revealed two women dressed in scrubs. One pale with red hair and the other with brown skin and dark curly hair.

"Oh! Who's this?" the redhead asked.

"This is my little cousin, Phani," Idrina introduced. "Phani, this is Rosie and Hailey, my after work drinking buddies. I assume you girls came in here to pester me about Travis."

Hailey grinned. "Guilty!

"So this is your baby cousin? She looks so cute!" Cooed Rosie. She tapped my cheek gently without permission. "I knew she was coming to live with you, but I had no idea she would be this adorable!"

My ears began to burn as Hailey shook my hand.

"Are you in high school? My brother's a senior at Asphodel City High. What year are you in? Sophomore? Homecoming is right around the corner. You should get yourself a date before all the good guys get taken."

"Or all the good girls," Rosie added, rolling her eyes. "Don't be so archaic."

"Ladies," Idrina interrupted with a raised brow. "She's in college."

"Oh! Oh no, I'm so sorry!" Hailey gasped. "That was so embarrassing of me! What year in college are you? What are you studying?"

"Have you found anyone cute at Asphodel U? A patient of mine swears up and down that all the business major seniors this year are hot," Rosie whispered, bumping her elbow against my arm.

There was a few seconds of silence and I realized, to my horror, they wanted me to reply.

I dreaded the moment when people asked me what I was doing with my life. I generally replied with honesty, but whenever I did, I was either given a pitying look or a judgmental stare. Then the anxiety would build up. Before long, I would find myself hyperventilating; proving to my psychologist once more that I wasn't ready to leave the gentle folds of their influence. And like a sucker, my father would take their word as law.

It would have been easier to let Rosie and Hailey misunderstand.

"Um, I just finished my Associates degree," I told them, trying to appear put together, as if my life wasn't currently a bewildering mess. "I'm taking a year off before I start on my bachelor's degree. I'm not entirely sure what I want to do yet."

They nodded in sympathy.

"You poor thing," Rosie sighed. "I didn't have a clue what I wanted to do either. I switched from zoology to biology until I finally settled on nursing. Wasn't easy, let me tell you, but it certainly pays the bills in this pricey town."

"What about a boyfriend? Or girlfriend?"

"Hailey," Idrina interrupted again. "Phani doesn't have time for stuff like that. She still hasn't found a job."

And oh, how that one-liner opened up another ten-minute one-sided conversation about all the places I could try looking at, and how I shouldn't worry about the economy here in Asphodel because there was always someone hiring. As if.

Still, I smiled politely, suffering in silence.

Sensing her mistake, Idrina didn't add anything after that. She allowed us to remain in her office until she finished signing and stamping some papers.

When it was finally time to leave, Idrina asked Rosie and Hailey to meet her at the cafeteria. Unwanted hugs and loud kisses ensued before they left us in peace.

I whipped my head around to stare at my cousin, eyes wide. "Idrina, *what* was that?"

Idrina chuckled. "I know, I know. I was overwhelmed when I met them as well, but they keep the seriousness of my job from getting me down. Now, enough about them. How was the job search today?"

Ugh. I never win. I was hoping she wouldn't bring that up.

As we walked away from her office, I confessed to her there hadn't been much luck today, but that I felt I'd find something soon. I knew this wouldn't lessen Idrina's persistence, but hopefully it would buy me some time.

"You know Phani, if you can't find anything by the end of the week, I could try pulling some strings for a job here," Idrina whispered. I avoided colliding with a twirling spirit flashing their derriere in a hospital gown. I hastily looked at my feet.

Idrina continued. "I heard there was a position open in housekeeping. It's nothing glamorous, but it should do until something better comes along."

I wasn't sure what was more embarrassing, having Idrina get me a job because I sucked at landing one myself or working housekeeping at a hospital. Not that working any custodial job was something to be ashamed of. I just knew they were strict on cleanliness, more so than a regular hotel. How would I succeed in such a demanding environment when I could barely keep my own room in order? Would my qualifications be enough? Did I even want the job with so many spirits around? It was almost as bad as working in a cemetery. And if I did land the job, it would only be a matter of time before I was let go for poor performance. I could just imagine it now. Although, if the days continued to be anything like today, trying my hand at house-keeping at a hospital for however long I lasted was going to be a godsend.

"I'll think about it," I said.

Idrina patted my back in sympathy. At least I hoped it was sympathy. I couldn't show my face if it were pity.

"Or I could ask Ryan if there's something at his firm," she said. "I know he's always going on about needing someone to get the office coffee and how the files were never organized right because his boss keeps firing all the temps and—"

Okay, I needed to nip this in the bud.

"Idrina, that's really sweet and all, but don't worry about me. I'm on the verge of something, so I should be fine by the end of the week," I said with a confident smile, feeling anything but.

I sincerely hoped that was the case. I mean, who knows? Maybe Catalina recognized the symbol in the painting and we could wrap up the mission so I could finally get paid. Wouldn't that be beautiful?

"I better get going," I said.

"Alright. Remember, I'm always a phone call away. Take care and I'll see you home later tonight. Oh, and it's late, so take this twenty and grab a cab, got it?"

Idrina hugged me before running off towards the cafeteria. I looked at the crisp twenty in my hand.

Andrew Jackson mocked me, frowning at my freebie-accepting shameless behavior. But what could I do? I would have refused Idrina's offer if I had anything left in my bank account for a cab. And with rush hour still happening, she wasn't wrong about longboarding this late in the day being a risk. It was a long way home and troubling my cousin recklessly was foolish. Besides, getting hurt cost money and I was a jobless bum. If I didn't find something soon in my job hunting or in the chase for Catalina's killer, I was going to end up a homeless bum too.

And then how would I support Sir Harry?

Going back home wasn't an option anymore. My father sold our childhood home shortly before visiting *Großmutter* Stefanie in Germany, and there was no way I was going to intrude on my aunt and uncle here in Asphodel either. The whole family would know about my situation in a matter of hours. The gossip would then somehow travel overseas to Guatemala and Germany and, before I knew it, I would be the object of pity in my family. Always referred to as the one who "didn't make it." I could just see everyone sighing over how darling Wilma would turn in her grave if she knew she'd given birth to not just a mentally ill child, but an unsuccessful one with no future, at that.

And I had to be worth something more. I refused to let my mental-health and ghost problems bring me down.

IT WAS dusk by the time I walked outside, the sun low, streaking the sky with violet and pink hues. I inhaled the fresh air before checking my phone for the time. Six twelve. The food truck square Charlie was meeting me at was about a ten minute walk from the hospital. I should probably text him that I was on my way. He already sent me a text when I arrived at the hospital earlier that he was close and would meet me there in accordance to my wishes.

As I walked and texted my response to him, I spotted the taxi cab area. Just as I stuck my arm out, a Rolls Royce pulled up in front of me. The door opened automatically, the interior a warm cocoon of leather. I blinked in surprise. From where I stood, I could see the silhouette of a man inside.

My brow furrowed in confusion. This wasn't a taxi, I don't think, and it certainly wasn't for me. Before I could turn away, someone from behind shoved me inside, causing my forehead to knock against the door frame. I was out like a light. The door was promptly shut before the car pulled away.

XI.

DINNER WITH THE DEVIL

WHEN I CAME TO, the first thing I became aware of was the instrumental music playing. It was smooth and fluid, sending chills down my spine when the vibrations of the notes in the air touched my skin. Next was the delectable aroma of grilled meats and exotic spices. If I inhaled deeply enough, I could smell an expensive perfume mingled within.

I opened my eyes and blinked several times, my eyelids heavy. I squinted when gold bokeh orbs obscured my blurry vision. A faint throbbing on my forehead made me groan and close my eyes. I rubbed at the spot, surprised to find a small bump there. After a few seconds, when my sight began to sharpen, I realized I wasn't in Idrina's apartment. In fact, I wasn't in Asphodel General or any place familiar to me.

Glancing at my surroundings, I realized that I was seated at an empty square table in what appeared to be a stylish spacious restaurant with warm ambient lighting and waiters dressed to the nines. Red and orange hues complimented the creme colored walls and foliage scattered around, bringing to mind a Mediterranean tropical night.

If I wasn't so confused and terrified, I would've been very impressed by the establishment.

I tried standing, but found, to my alarm, that I couldn't. My legs were stuck to something. When I moved the white table cloth aside, I found my ankles tied to the legs of the chair with rope.

That was not a good sign. My heart began to pound a mile a minute.

As I searched the place for help, I noticed the restaurant was empty of patrons. Only waiters and waitresses went around cleaning tables, folding napkins, chatting amongst themselves as the faint clanging of pots and pans from the kitchen sounded. No one approached me. Not even the staff to ask what the hell I was doing here because clearly, I did not enter this place with consent. Instead, everyone minded their own business.

"Hello? Guys? Help?" I called out. The staff merely glanced up before looking back down. Miffed, I tried grabbing their attention again, but they ignored me. Even when I screamed and banged on the table.

"Am I being punked or what?" I called out loud. The staff chose to leave instead of answering. "Cowards!"

I was alone. There wasn't any silverware on the table. Just a leather bound menu with dishes written out in Italian. I placed it back on the table and looked at my ankles again. I tried shimming my foot back and forth, hoping to loosen the bonds. I pushed my chair back and tried pulling at the ropes. They were tight, but I kept wiggling my feet. Whoever had tied the knot was an expert because it was not giving no matter what. I wasn't going to get out of this by normal means apparently.

That's when it came to me. I pushed my chair back on its hind legs, lifting the front two. I made sure to keep one hand on the table so I didn't fall and hurt myself. With my other free hand, I pushed the ropes down the leg of the chair until presto! One leg free! I did the same for the other leg until I was finally able to stand up. Rope anklets aside, this was a successful escape.

I wasn't sure if the staff was in on my kidnapping, but I had a feeling if they saw me up and about, they'd alert whoever was responsible for bringing me here. Avoiding the back kitchen area, I ran to the front doors. The restaurant space was large with three different sections tucked away from each other. My section had been at the back. I was relieved to see no one up here when I made it to the front where a wrought iron podium stood. I was about to push open the doors when baritone voices on the other side made me hesitate. Panicking, I spotted the bathrooms. They didn't have doors but the walls were enough to hide anyone inside.

The bathroom was shiny, clean and made of sleek beige tiles. It smelled of cedarwood and sea salt and was a lot larger then I thought. Instead of cheap paper towels, folded cotton terry cloths sat neatly stacked on a carved platform next to the marble sinks. Sadly though, there wasn't a window I could sneak out of.

"This is different," said a silky voice from behind me.

I gasped and turned. My shock doubled when I realized that I was looking at the handsome man I had crashed into earlier. He was staring at me with wide eyes, sitting down on a velvet bench tucked into the corner near the bathroom entrance. Apparently I had missed him when I dashed inside. He had two smart phones in each hand and a notepad flipped open on his thigh.

"W-What are you doing here?!" I whispered, eyeing the entrance of the bathroom with worry.

The man continued to blink in surprise. "I had to check on something. They wouldn't leave me alone. I'm sorry."

"Do you work here?"

The man sat up straighter. "No."

He turned one phone off and the other he silenced before tucking them into separate blazer pockets. He grabbed his notepad and flipped it closed before standing.

"Damn," I muttered, looking away. "You wouldn't know how to get out of this place, do you?"

The man came near before ducking his head slightly. "Aside from the front door? And why are you whispering?"

"That's not important!" I whispered again, beginning to pace. "I think there's someone at the front door. We need to get out of here without being seen."

"We?"

"Fine. *I* need to get out of here without being seen."

"Why? It's dinnertime."

I gestured to the ropes still tied to my ankles. "I've been kidnapped!"

The man glanced at the ropes for a moment before laughing heartily. I gawked.

"So that's what happened. I should have known." He turned away and stopped when he reached the bathroom entrance. "Come outside. You're in the men's bathroom."

I sputtered. "As if that's important! And I told you I'm trying to get out of here without being seen!"

"There's cameras in the restaurant so that's a little impossible," he explained, smiling apologetically. "But don't worry. No one's going to touch you. I've ordered them to ignore you."

It took a minute for that to process.

"*What?!*"

❧

SO THERE I WAS, sitting across the most handsome man I'd ever seen. The very same one who orchestrated my kidnapping. Today was definitely not shaping up like how I thought it would.

The only reason I'm even sitting across from him now instead of bolting for any exit was because the handsome man had pointed out that his men—one of which opened the front door to wave at us—were stationed outside all the exit points. Mainly for security reasons, he assured me, but they would stop me if I tried leaving early.

Despite my angry petulant glower, the man looked at me with a soft smile on his lips, gray eyes crinkling. Even in the evening light, surrounded by the bizarreness of my situation, he looked impeccable. Not a crease or wrinkle in sight. But I knew better. Not because I knew him, but because something about that smile of his, the one meant to relax, disarm and charm with its endearing amicability? The one that looked sinfully beautiful? That smile was fake. Which meant I was in major trouble.

I stayed silent as the handsome stranger perused the restaurant's menu with leisure, as if my being here against my will was of no consequence. After a few minutes of tense silence, at least from my end, gray eyes flickered away from the menu to meet my ogling gaze.

"Miss *Estephanie,* am I right?"

I eyed him with suspicion. His Spanish pronunciation was on point, though a bit of gringo lingered. Seriously, who was this guy? Why bother tying me to a chair at a fancy, but empty restaurant with my mouth and hands unrestrained? If this was the beginning of me being sold into the human trafficking ring, then this guy was going about it oddly.

"What do you want?" I asked. Then I remembered. "And where's my longboard?"

And oh my god, I had stood Charlie up. I hoped he didn't think I ditched him. Did I even send out my last text? Before I could spiral, the stranger chuckled softly. I looked up.

"Of all things to inquire about, your first thought is your skateboard?"

"I have to make sure my getaway ride is intact," I quipped, hands clutching the fabric of my dress. How I sounded steady and calm instead of shrill and hysterical I'll never know.

"Then allow me to get to the point," he said, leaning forward and fastening his fingers together. I was all eyes and ears. He had quite a demanding presence, as if anything else that wasn't him was irrelevant when placed at the center of attention. And those eyes. They were steady and heavy, the intensity never letting up. Even if my ankles had remained tied, his gaze alone would have pinned me to my chair.

"Call me Aedes. I represent the interests and petty affairs of my employer," Aedes began with a polite expression. "I have 'kidnapped' you for your own safety. I can't be seen meeting with you in public unless it's under...questionable circumstances."

I nodded, not truly understanding.

A waiter with a trimmed mustache appeared at our table with a pad and pen in hand. Before I could say anything—like HELP—Aedes spoke, smoothly ordering in fluent Italian without missing a beat, probably having done this a thousand times before. And he didn't just order for himself, but for me as well, mentioning he hoped I wouldn't mind pasta in English. I could only stare at his audacity, words unable to form on my tongue. Aedes smiled and the waiter soon left.

"I assume you're not allergic to anything on the menu?" he asked.

"Bold of you to assume I want to eat anything from someone who's kidnapped me," I challenged. Two seconds later, my stomach growled shamelessly. I flushed, mortified.

Aedes looked down and brought his hand up to cover his face, his shoulders shaking. If I thought that was the picture of remorse, I was sorely mistaken. I gritted my teeth angrily. He was laughing at me!

"Listen," I said, eyes narrowing. "I don't know what you want but I think you've got the wrong person here."

"Actually, I don't. Estephanie Cora Carmel-Baumer Xiu. Five foot four, twenty-years-old, born February 21, recently graduated with your AA from Miami Dade College, major undecided, currently unemployed and living with your cousin Idrina Glenda Rivera Carmel Xiu, a cardiac surgeon at Asphodel General, as of ten days ago. That sound about right?"

I leaned back, my eyes so wide I was sure they would pop out. My expression must have been comical to Aedes because he began chuckling again, shaking his head.

"*What the hell?* Y-You *researched* me? What do you want from me?!"

"Now, now, no need to be alarmed." Aedes said. "My employer and I aren't going to do anything with this information nor shall we harm you. Yet. You see, we are merely curious about you, Miss Estephanie. You were seen entering and leaving Orpheus Theater earlier this afternoon. Shortly after, an explosion went off in front of the theater entrance. It didn't damage the front doors, but left a mess on the steps."

Huh, so that's what happened.

"Do they know who caused it?" I asked.

Aedes's lip quirked. "No, but cameras in the area saw that it originated from a potted shrub a few feet from the entrance."

It dawned on me that the marred shrub I saw earlier today, the one that looked as though someone had punched a hole in it had actually been housing a bomb this whole time. If I had gotten closer to it, if I had inspected it like I wanted, would I have found the bomb? I would have alerted the police for sure. Maybe with the increase in police in the area, the killer would have delayed Mr. Shern's execution. It would have ruined my own investigation as well, but what was an afternoon ruined when a human life could have been spared? Though if Catalina's killer was determined, Mr. Shern's death would have been inevitable. If not at the theater then in his own home.

I sighed. I was thinking in circles. I stared at Aedes as he waited for me to say something. I briefly wondered how he knew about what the police had found. Was he a part of the mob? The Erebus faction maybe? Did they have crooked cops reporting to him? While the thought was alarming, it wouldn't be terribly surprising.

"I hope no one got hurt," I said at last.

"Not at all. It appeared the bomb was more of a distraction than anything deadly. Though an hour later, the police stormed the theater after receiving a tip that the janitor, Eustace Shern, was murdered."

Despite the levity of his tone, his gaze was piercing. I blanched.

"It wasn't me, I swear! Catalina's killer was the one who shot him!"

Aedes stiffened. "Oh?"

I could have kicked myself. This was not the time to blurt out the truth. The minute he knows what I know, Aedes will either dispose of me for knowing too much or have me installed in a psychiatric ward somewhere. I had to be careful.

"My cousin mentioned she'd lost her favorite pair of earrings there last week," I said, smiling. "Her birthday was today and since I didn't have any money to buy her anything, I thought I'd see if maybe someone like the janitor might have seen them."

To my surprise, the more I talked, the more the lie sounded plausible. Maybe I had some potential in acting after all. Aedes's face was unreadable as I spoke, but he wasn't saying anything to contradict me. I looked down at the table cloth.

"I entered and got lost before Mr. Shern found me," I continued. "He told me he hadn't seen the earrings but felt bad for my situation, so he offered me some tea. As I was leaving, I heard a gunshot and saw the killer escape."

Now that I thought about it, my thorough perusal of Aedes did check some of my killer's description boxes. Tall, Caucasian, fit body, mid twenties to early thirties max, etc. But if Aedes was the killer, wouldn't it make sense to just kill me like poor Mr. Shern instead of doing whatever it was we were doing? What I wouldn't give to have Catalina beside me right now.

"Interesting," murmured Aedes at last. "Never mind that you didn't stay behind to report to the police in person, why did you figure Eustace's killer to be Catalina's?"

Oh damn. I shouldn't have said her name. Was her real name used frequently in these dark circles? I doubted it.

"I mean, Mr. Shern was talking about it before he died. I figured the killer must have come back, thinking to silence a witness," I added hastily.

Aedes smiled gently. "I think you've stumbled onto something messy here. You are aware that the crime boss La Patrona was killed a few days ago, no? The police have their own conclusion and suspects. My employer, well, he's trying to get to the bottom of this mystery as well."

I was afraid again.

"My condolences. I'm assuming she worked for your employer."

That smile remained. "Of course."

Our drinks arrived. Aedes chose a fancy cabernet for himself that the sommelier had insisted would pair exquisitely with our dishes. I, on the other hand, was given a glass of ice-cold water. I frowned, upset the waiter hadn't called the police nor warned anyone of my situation. Aedes smirked into his wine, inhaling and swirling the bloody liquid around the crystal-clear glass.

"How come you get something good?" I asked, annoyed to have so little control over the situation and my unwanted dinner.

"Despite the questionable method of your arrival, I don't condone underage drinking," he quipped, waving the sommelier away.

"How thoughtful of you," I muttered sarcastically. I suppose it was better this way. I couldn't lose myself even a little bit right now.

My polish-free nail clinked against the cool surface of my drink, condensation dripping down the glass. I took advantage of the pause to gather my thoughts. I had to have all my mental faculties in working order if I was going to make it through this bizarre situation. In contrast, Aedes appeared relaxed, taking tiny sips of his wine as he leaned back in his seat.

"After this dinner, will I go home?" I asked.

Another chuckle. "Of course. I had to question you to see how much you knew about the shooting and how involved you were in it. Now I see you're merely an innocent bystander caught in the crossfire. My apologies for this most unusual invitation to dinner."

Unusual indeed.

It wasn't long before our waiter returned with a picturesque appetizer of red glazed fruits sprinkled over a small hill of what looked like salad and something else. Set between us, the white china plate dwarfed the dish. Aedes pushed it toward me with a kind smile.

"Please enjoy the food. *Il Melograno* is one of my favorite restaurants here in Asphodel City," Aedes praised. "And I'm personally paying for dinner."

I blinked. He's paying? Well I should hope so! I didn't ask for my food truck dinner with Charlie to be replaced with a five-star interrogation.

"Are you sure it's not poisoned?"

Aedes looked offended. "That'd be a waste of food. I don't condone such methods of disposal."

Well, nice to see where his priorities lay.

Would I get murdered after this though? I hoped not. Didn't seem like Aedes's style, but then what did I know? I wasn't even screaming for help. At least Aedes didn't think I had anything to do with Catalina's death. Did the police? Suddenly I was grateful I had worn gloves for the majority of my investigation. Even though I had taken them off when I met Mr. Shern, I hadn't touched anything in the break room. They wouldn't find my fingerprints anywhere.

My stomach growled again. I blushed, refusing to meet Aedes's gaze. Instead I eyed the fancy salad. It did look rather inviting, and if the man was offering to cover the check...

I picked up a fork I hoped was for salads and speared one of the ruby glazed fruits from the dish. Even from a distance it smelled divine. It certainly topped anything I had planned to make tonight. As I took a bite, the tart flavor of the berry exploded on my tongue. I swallowed, pleased with how fantastic the food tasted. I vaguely wondered if the fruit would stain my lips and teeth. I sipped my water.

"What's the red berry? I don't think I've tried it before."

Aedes gave me an odd look, as if he couldn't believe it.

"It's a pomegranate seed. I ordered a pomegranate and pear green salad as an appetizer."

"How fancy," I said. "Do me a favor in the future though? Don't ever take me to dinner."

Aedes raised his glass in my direction, a gleam in his stormy eyes.

"Here's to you being an exceptional dinner partner," he toasted.

I grimaced. As if I had a choice. I raised my own glass in response.

"And here's to having had better nights with better company."

Aedes chuckled behind his glass.

XII.

WORD TO THE WISE

Despite the low hum of anxiety pooled in my belly, dinner was delicious. The company though? Not as terrifying as it could have been.

Having Aedes for company wasn't terribly awkward or tense and to my surprise, he was nothing but pleasant and charming. Sometimes even funny. I had no doubt in my mind that had I met him under different circumstances, I would have swooned over his sweet smile and inviting eyes. It didn't help that his congenial personality and handsomeness sweetened the pot.

But as it was, the rope still tied around my ankles kept me firmly anchored to reality. So instead of having a great time smiling and laughing like I had been hoping to do on my date with Charlie, I simply nodded and delivered an occasional quip. At one point I remembered that I owned a bag with a phone in it.

"Where's my stuff?" I asked, looking around.

"With your skateboard." He signaled to a waiter nearby.

I got nervous when he returned with a knife. I was prepared to claw his face off and run, but instead the waiter asked to see my ankles to remove the rope. I hesitated at first, but one look at the "I just want to clock out already" expression on his face had me relenting. The waiter bent down and cut my ties with little difficulty. I exhaled in relief when he left.

"I can't believe I forgot about those," said Aedes, looking horrified. I gave him a dirty look, not believing him for a moment. "How barbaric of me. My apologies, Miss Estephanie, especially when you went through the trouble to dress so cutely for our date."

I scowled and stood up, glad this dinner was finally over. "I had an *actual* date planned tonight with someone who has way more integrity than you and doesn't need to kidnap me for my attention."

It was wonderful to see my spine return in full force. It was a little hard to act defiant when I was at a stranger's mercy and his henchmen surrounded the area like statues. Aedes didn't take offense to my response however. Instead, he smirked.

"And yet, I was the victor tonight," he said, standing up and taking out two hundred dollar bills from his wallet as a tip. My jaw dropped.

"What? The serving industry is not an easy job. I like tipping well," he explained, leaving the bills on the table. "And considering he had to cut you free, it doesn't hurt to compensate him for the trouble."

My mouth remained open. There were so many contradictions about this man. If Aedes hadn't kidnapped me tonight, his generosity would have had me falling for him like an easy sucker.

He offered his hand. "Shall we proceed outside then?"

I frowned, crossing my arms in protest. Aedes acquiesced.

Once outside the restaurant, Aedes gestured to a man in a black suit—he must have been one of the men waiting outside. The man took out a phone and I surveyed my surroundings, wondering where in Asphodel City I had been taken to.

To my surprise, *Il Melograno* was located next to the infamous Tinsley's—a sleek modern jewelry store with black spindly letters for its logo. I recognized it from all the times Idrina pointed it out in her favorite bridal magazines. She had ambitious hopes that Ryan would pick up her future engagement ring there and propose.

Across from *Il Melograno* sat a large hotel made of red and white bricks, domed spires, and bright lights outlining its heavy Vienna architectural influence. I spotted a Porsche and Mercedes-Benz enter uphill on the curved valet entrance. I briefly wondered what the inside looked like.

"What are you looking at?" Aedes asked, interrupting my observation.

Deciding to test his knowledge of the city, I pointed to the hotel.

Dark brows nearly touched his hair line. "The Grand Gatsby Hotel? Sorry, I don't normally sleep with a girl on the first date so I'm going to have to decline."

I sputtered. "No! I just wanted to ask what that place was! I don't want to sleep with you!"

Aedes snickered. "Then we're in agreement."

I rolled my eyes. "Where are we exactly?"

"Vanit Town," he said. "It's far west of Wonderwood. Vanit Town is the part of the city one tends to see in classic Hollywood films. Think Rodeo Drive and Upper East Side meets New Orleans's Garden District."

Well this certainly wasn't somewhere I would have wandered into on my own. And to think little 'ol me got kidnapped to dine here of all places. If Idrina knew, she'd freak out in more ways than one.

A familiar Rolls Royce pulled up in front of Aedes and I. Even under lamplights and nighttime illuminations, the paint job and windows remained glossy. It occurred to me then that I had seen this car before. Several times in fact. Today when I left Orpheus Theater and again when I left Chariclo Books. And again when it pulled up in front of Asphodel General to spirit me away. I nearly gasped. Aedes really had been stalking me all day. His bumping into me at Chariclo was no accident either. With maybe less than seven hours, Aedes was able to track down who I was. All so he and his mysterious employer Erebus would be assured I wasn't really involved with Catalina and her killer.

I was too frazzled to think clearly before, but it appears I've caught the attention of Erebus, the crime syndicate Catalina once worked for. I knew then Aedes wasn't Catalina's killer, but he was still someone dangerous. This was further confirmed when he opened the back door. His blazer opened just enough for me to catch a glimpse of a gun tucked into a shoulder holster. I swallowed nervously.

"What? Not going to push me in again?"

He smiled. "Not tonight. Are you going to run away again?"

I eyed the spot on his blazer where I knew his gun to be. "Can I walk home instead?"

"Sure," he said, getting in the car anyway. Another man dressed in a black suit with purple accents approached the door but didn't close it. "Just know from where you're standing it'll take you 4 hours to walk to your cousin's apartment. And I don't know about you, but even I wouldn't walk around Asphodel City alone at night."

I clenched my fists and stared angrily at the asphalt beneath my shoes. I wouldn't be walking alone at night if I hadn't been kidnapped in the first place. Couldn't he have just called me? It would have saved us a lot of time and unnecessary stress.

"I promise to drop you off at your cousin's with no detour and free of any manhandling," Aedes offered, leaning back against the seat with a relaxed expression, arms crossed.

I hated how care-free he looked, as if doing all this was just another regular Monday. Which, if he worked for Erebus, it probably was. I huffed. Walking for 4 hours in Asphodel City at night with little clue as to where exactly Idrina's apartment was without my cell phone did seem like a really bad idea. I took a gamble and climbed into Aedes's vehicle. If worse comes to worse, I could always try blinking myself to Tenebris. At least from there I could wait a bit and transport myself back to the physical realm before trekking to Idrina's on foot.

The door closed firmly behind me. To my surprise, Aedes handed me my longboard Cosmos and my embroidered bag. I eagerly took both and inspected them to make sure nothing was missing or added. My phone still had plenty of charge and about a dozen texts from Charlie. I winced. It's probably better if I don't open them right now. I'll grovel for forgiveness when I get home.

There was a dark window separating the back from the front,

hiding whoever it was that pulled us away from the sidewalk. The restaurant soon disappeared from view.

"Now that we're officially alone," Aedes began, "let's talk."

I turned away from the window. "You mean we weren't before?"

Aedes tsked, shaking his head. "We were merely getting to know each other, Miss Estephanie. What I'm about to say now can only be said within a secured, private environment."

"Then what was the point of kidnapping me and taking me to the restaurant?"

"I was hungry," Aedes explained, as if that answered everything. "I had reservations at *Il Melograno* weeks ago. It would have been disrespectful to make the owners close the restaurant to patrons only to have me cancel last minute."

Oh, so that was disrespectful but bringing me along tied up wasn't?

"Did they say anything when you dragged me in?"

"You weren't dragged in. I carried you. You don't weigh a lot." Aedes frowned. "You should eat more."

I blinked, astounded by his audacity yet again. I had no words.

Sitting inside a dark car alone with him was certainly private and secure at least. The pit of my stomach felt heavy again, adrenaline kicking in as panic began setting in like an infectious disease. Was I going to be killed then? Were my organs going to turn up in some freezer on the black market? Was I going to be sold into the slavery ring after all? Or worse! Was I going to be sold to some occult?

Oh God, and I just ate dinner with the devil, I thought wildly. *What if there were drugs in the meal? Damn my hunger!*

I swallowed, my body tensing. "What is it you want to speak to me about then?"

"I know you're trying to find the identity of La Patrona's killer."

Aedes's face betrayed nothing. He spoke as though the statement were fact. And it was. But how could he have known that? The pounding in my heart became rapid as I waited for him to continue.

"I don't know why you're doing this," said Aedes, "but my employer isn't angry with your investigation."

Then that's one worry off my chest.

"So, he cares then? About what's going on?"

"Of course. La Patrona was one of his most prized crime bosses. He was supposed to meet up with her the night she perished. It's in his best interest to find out who had the audacity and luck to murder her and why before any necessary retaliation."

My brows rose. Then it's confirmed that Erebus had plans to meet Catalina the night of her murder. Was it business talk or personal? Normally a setting like that would be personal, but seeing how Catalina liked mixing business with pleasure, I couldn't be certain. Catalina still refused to tell me what it was she wanted to speak to Erebus about. Was the topic the reason the murderer was desperate enough to kill her before the meeting?

Ah, theories. My head began to ache.

"That's a relief then," I said carefully. "I didn't figure this Erebus person was into theater shows."

Aedes's lips quirked. "For him it was purely business."

Another confirmation. Now if only I knew what about. The topic might be nothing related to her killer, but what if it was? I had to know! I was invested in this mystery and not just for the money, though that certainly helped incentivize me. I doubt I could trick Aedes into telling me the specifics, especially if it was related to crime syndicate operations. Ugh, how messy.

Why couldn't I have had the ability to read minds instead of speaking to dead people?

"—do you understand?"

I blinked. Aedes was staring at me, waiting.

Oh sweet God, I hadn't been listening!

"C-Could you repeat that?" I asked hesitantly.

Aedes moved before I could blink. He took my chin in his leather-clad fingers until we were face to face. From this close up, I couldn't make out the gray in his eyes. The darkness in the car was too pressing even as we sped through the city. I sensed his body heat, though. And from the small puffs of breath he exhaled, wine and peppermint permeated the air between us. It was a strangely intoxicating scent, but I longed to back away from it, from him.

"Miss Estephanie, listen closely," he said in a smooth and seductive voice. "I don't know why you're investigating La Patrona's killer, but I'm going to assume you're just an innocent and curious civilian who was simply at the wrong place at the wrong time. As a result, I'm warning you to cease your investigation."

Wait, what?

"I—"

"Shush, now. Don't speak. This is just a 'friendly' warning. I've warmed up to you, so I want you to stay out of trouble," he confessed, flashing an innocent, charming smile. "Do you understand?"

I nodded carefully. He let me go, satisfied by my response. I rubbed my chin, still feeling the ghostly impression of his fingers.

Aedes wasn't kidding around. He meant business.

We didn't say anything else after that, the ride home almost feeling like purgatory. This was the worst after-dinner experience ever. I sat as far from Aedes as I could without it being obvious. I was acutely aware of his presence and wondered if he felt the awkwardness building inside the car. I kind of hoped he did. This entire night was his fault, after all. But knowing my luck, I was probably the only one able to see the elephant in the room.

Before long, I felt the car slow to a stop.

"We're here," Aedes said, facing forward. "Your company this evening has been lovely."

"I'm sure," I said, eyeing the door.

I was so ready to run away, but at that moment, Aedes turned in his seat and placed one arm on the backrest behind my head. He was crowding me; ready to deliver another warning, no doubt. He lifted the hand resting on my lap and held it loosely in his, just in case I wanted to pull away. As if I had a choice.

"Truly Miss Estephanie," Aedes reassured. "This was an interesting evening. Of course, I must ask if you've obtained any information from your investigation so far."

Nothing I could share without putting my life in danger.

"Not really," I answered, hoping he'd buy it.

Aedes didn't seem convinced, but he didn't argue further. As subtle as a ninja, he slipped a small business card in my palm. I tried to pull away, but his grip on my hand tightened.

"If you have any information or see something, call this number. It will get you in touch with me and I will handle whatever problem you're facing, alright? The police won't know what to do with the information you have should you turn to them. Now, don't give me that look. It's better this way. Any questions?"

"Is your name really Aedes?"

Aedes laughed. "Of course not, but I've been told the name makes me sound mysterious. Anything else?"

I shouldn't but...

"Does Erebus know what Catalina wanted to speak to him about the night she died?"

His easy smile morphed into a smirk. He lowered his head and pressed his lips against the back of my hand, causing goosebumps to rise on my skin. His lips were smooth and pliable, warm to the touch. He released my hand just as the car door next to me opened.

"Stay out of underworld business, Miss Estephanie."

Stepping out of the car, I noted with relief that Aedes had dropped me off in front of Idrina's apartment building. And then it hit me. Aedes knew exactly where I lived. This begged another crucial question, what else did Aedes know about me?

Fear made my heart pound. I adjusted the grip on my longboard.

"Don't forget what I said," he said from behind. "And do stay safe. Wouldn't want anyone else getting any ideas."

I turned and saw how relaxed and confident Aedes came across, completely in his element. I scowled.

"You know," I began, "next time you kidnap me, try calling me Phani. I'll probably like you better."

I slammed the door in his face.

The car drove off without much fanfare, disappearing into the dark belly of Asphodel's nightlife. I stood on the sidewalk and allowed my racing heart to slow. That was the strangest and most surprising thing that had ever happened to me and *I* was the one who could see ghosts. I hoped today's excitement didn't continue or else I'd be mentally exhausted before the week was over.

As it happened, I nearly screamed my lungs out when I turned and saw Catalina standing behind me.

"Geez, don't do that," I gasped, clutching my chest. "Today has been too much for me already."

"I recognize that car," she said. "It's one of Erebus's. Who did you talk to? Why'd you show up late in one of Erebus's cars?"

Once inside the empty apartment and away from prying ears, I told Catalina about being kidnapped and meeting someone who was interested in finding her killer. I also told her about the warning I received. She scowled in response.

"Sounds like Erebus is on the hunt." Catalina began pacing my room. "This complicates our investigation. Damn it!"

To add to her frustration, Catalina hadn't been able to figure out what the tattoo on John Forty might have looked like despite staring at the painting for hours. As a result, she was really fixated on Aedes's impudence.

"How dare a low-tier bastard threaten me!" She snarled.

"He actually threatened *me*," I corrected.

Catalina slowed to a halt. She frowned before turning around to face me.

"You're right," she said, a gleam entering her eyes. "In fact, from what you've told me, you acted remarkably."

Now *I* frowned. "Did I? Seemed like I was one wrong move away from being killed."

Catalina looked offended. "Hey, we're not barbarians. We don't just kill civilians indiscriminately. We do scare them a bit, which is what Aedes did to you. Besides, if they really wanted to harm you, I wouldn't be seeing you right now breathing or in one piece."

"That's not very reassuring, Catalina."

"Oh toughen up. You made it out fine."

Anger bubbled up in me. "How can you be so insensitive? It's one thing to investigate your death, but I got kidnapped! I'm not just over that! I was really scared!"

"So he treated you to dinner, so what," Catalina said, rolling her eyes. "When I first got kidnapped, I was nearly raped."

I jerked at that. "Then why aren't you more upset? It could have been me!"

"Because I killed them. Because I joined Erebus's ranks to reform the underworld so to speak. There are a lot of dirty, dark sins in this world. Some so horrible it tears at your humanity," Catalina warned, gaze darkening, "so I discarded my softness and seized power anyway I could so the people I cared about would never get hurt."

She lifted her chin and approached me.

"You may not have asked to be involved in the underworld, but neither did I at first. Now, you can either listen to Aedes and crawl back to the surface with your tail tucked between your legs or you can swim deeper with me and figure what the fuck is going on before it affects your shiny world and its innocent people for good."

I was speechless. I didn't know what to say. What could I say? I wanted to burst into tears because it seemed like no one but me cared about what happened. But if I did Catalina was sure to snap. It was times like these that I missed my father. He would always comfort me when I was feeling overwhelmed or drowning in despair. He wouldn't understand my problem, but he'd at least comfort me the best way he knew how.

I turned and wiped my eyes just in case.

"Are you crying?" Catalina asked. She sounded disgusted. "Oh *ugh*, you're one of those soft baby types."

I looked back and glared.

"I'm sorry I'm not a heartless bitch."

Catalina laughed. My glare intensified.

"Listen, I'm not saying your experience is less than mine. I'm not trying to invalidate it or say that it should have happened. In an ideal world, you wouldn't have been kidnapped or threatened. None of this would have happened and I would be alive minding my own business, shopping and trying to snag a husband." It was odd to imagine

Catalina doing anything so mundane. Catalina continued. "But the fact of the matter is that it *did* happen and now you get to decide what you are going to do about it."

I looked at my bare knees. They were shaking. I shook my head.

"I think...I'd rather be dealing with spirits and ghosts," I said at last, "then this."

Catalina smirked, crossing her arms. "Not as glamorous as the movies make it out to be, huh? Of course, I could say the same. I'd rather deal with underworld affairs than weird supernatural shit. Kind of glad I'm not in your shoes."

I blinked as I realized something. At no point while in Aedes's presence did I see any paranormal phenomenon. Which was ironic considering he worked for a crime syndicate. He'd have to have at least a couple of angry spirits following him around since I had no doubt in my mind that he was responsible for ending quite a few lives.

I sighed before laying face down on my bed. Sir Harry chose that precise moment to climb on my back. He circled a few times before settling down. I didn't have the heart to disturb him.

"Well?" Catalina prompted.

"I'm still traumatized," I said, "I don't want to feel helpless again. Or caught off guard."

"Hmm, you'll keep facing surprises in my line of work, no matter how much control you try enforcing. However, I *can* teach you how not to feel helpless," Catalina offered.

I lifted my head. "Really?"

"You're a plucky girl. You deal with the supernatural on the daily and you handled yourself really well with Aedes. Some guidance under my tutelage will serve you well, I think."

"Are you sure? Because contrary to what you may think, I really like being alive and I'd rather not swim with the fishes because I was too stubborn to listen to the warnings of the mafia about staying involved. Besides, with the resources they have, I'm sure your boss Erebus will find the killer before we do."

"No! *Yo dije que no!* Erebus cannot get involved."

I raised a single brow. "What? Too dangerous for a mob boss?"

Catalina laughed before sitting on my chair. It both amazed and creeped me out when she performed normal acts like that. It gave the illusion that she wasn't dead.

"Listen little Phani, Erebus is much more than just a petty 'mob boss.' In this town, he is what mob bosses fear the most. Despite his fearsome reputation, he has plenty of enemies from every corner that will do anything in their power to destroy him. That's why I must resolve any loose ends even from beyond the grave. This is my duty as his watchdog."

Her loyalty was both admirable and extreme. Could I be that loyal to whatever cause I followed even after death? I imagine it wouldn't matter much anymore by then.

I closed my hands into fists. Sir Harry purred from his perch on my back.

"Was your word about the reward money true, Catalina?" I asked.

Catalina was affronted by the mere suggestion.

"Of course! I wouldn't lie. My word is law."

Well, I *have* made it this far, I might as well keep going.

"Then I'm still in. But we *have* to be careful about moving forward and you *have* to teach me everything you know about not feeling powerless. I don't ever want to feel like that again."

Catalina was on her feet. In a blink, she stood in front of the dresser where her gold choker sat untouched. Through the mirror's reflection, I saw a gleam enter her dark gaze. Were ghosts supposed to have reflections?

Hands on her hips, she turned with a smirk in place.

"I have an idea."

XIII.

STILL WATERS

CHARLIE WAS GUTTED to have been stood up on our date. I knew this not because he told me, but because he was less bubbly and talkative as we spoke over the phone. He tried to sound as though the whole ordeal hadn't bothered him, but I knew it had to hurt.

"No, trust me, Phani, I understand," he reassured, his voice sounding far through the speaker phone. "I'm not blaming you."

"But we made plans and I can only imagine what a horrible feeling it was to be left there without even an explanation," I said, pacing the length of Idrina's balcony.

Her roses inside the mini 4-tier greenhouse I bought were coming along nicely despite the cooling climate. Even my oriental lilies were thriving, though that was mainly because of my touch. While they were easy to grow flowers, they were mostly summer bloomers. Their progress now was an uphill battle. Maybe when I get the chance and funds, I'll buy Idrina some poinsettias to mark the winter holidays. She'd appreciate that.

"You had a family emergency and lost your phone in the chaos. It happens. At least you found it again," said Charlie. He completely bought the story I fed him, or at least, didn't ask too many questions. I couldn't be more grateful.

"Let me make it up to you," I said, touching the plastic cover of the greenhouse. "You're working right now, right?"

"...yeah..."

I checked the time on my phone. "Let me bring you lunch! There's this Honduran restaurant near Idrina's place. I can pick it up and bring it over."

"What?" Charlie sounded surprised. "You don't have to do that. I'm fine."

"No, no! I insist!" I opened the sliding glass door and entered the living room. I was about to keep going when I spotted Sir Harry on Idrina's pristine white couch. I scooped him up before he could protest.

"It'll also give me a good excuse to find some place hiring along the way. Your workplace isn't in need of some extra personnel, right?" I joked, placing the phone on my shoulder just as I grabbed the doorknob and entered my room. I placed Sir Harry on the bed before grabbing my embroidered bag from my dresser and closing the door behind me. Sir Harry meowed indignantly.

"What? N-No, not really, but Phani wait you don't have to do that! I understand, really!"

I was already grabbing my longboard and locking the apartment behind me.

"It's my treat! Plus," I paused, blushing, "I kind of want to see you in person. I was really looking forward to our date, you know."

Charlie was speechless, or at least I assumed he was. He didn't say anything for a minute. When he did, his soft-spoken tone only made him more adorable in my eyes.

"Alright, you can drop off lunch but I insist on treating you to a proper dinner."

The elevator dinged. Metal doors slid open and I stepped inside.

"It's another date then. I'm in the elevator by the way so text me your location and I'll swing by. I'll text you when I'm near."

"Okay," he said. "Um, I'll see you soon then."

There was a hopeful note in his voice that warmed my heart. I smiled before giving one last goodbye and ending the call. My chest felt light and I sighed, happy as a clam that I hadn't messed up my chances with Charlie.

I hoped he liked the food. Despite being half Guatemalan, my father made sure to get take out from nearly every Central American restaurant just so I was better familiar with my cultural cousins. I briefly thought about getting Charlie something American just so he was more familiar with the food, but since I had already promised him Honduran and he hadn't protested, I figured this would be a nice little cultural cuisine exchange.

The restaurant *Catrachos Eats* was only five minutes away by foot. Charlie's workplace was about thirty minutes by bus. I looked to see what bus route I could take when I noticed Chariclo Book was on the way. Excitement coursed through my veins.

I was dying to see Tirisha again. Her comment about hell being a frozen wasteland rather than a burning pit left me insatiable for answers on her opinion. While it's not a new concept, my gut told me she knew more about Tenebris then she let on. At least I hoped so. I resolved to stop by for a quick visit before seeing Charlie.

Catalina had left two days ago after her idea announcement, claiming she needed to scout a few places and people before executing our next course of action. I didn't mind the respite as it allowed me to breathe and destress from my unexpected meeting with Aedes. Even just thinking about him, his beautiful face and deceptively charming smile had me shivering. Whether it was the good kind or bad, I couldn't tell, but I definitely did not want to see him any time soon, that's for sure.

After ordering some *baleadas* and sodas in Spanish from a kind older lady behind the counter and paying, I made quick work of skating to Chariclo Books. Traffic was mercifully minimal today.

Inside the store, I searched for Tirisha all over the first and second floor, but she wasn't anywhere in sight. When I approached the counter on my way back to the front, a young black woman with dark box braids and an anime T-shirt greeted me with a radiant smile. The ID clipped to her collar read Abigail Bryan. I knew then this was Tirisha's sister. She looked nearly identical to her, except

Abbie was smaller and less sparkly, though no less dramatic apparently.

"Well aren't you the cutest little ducky I've ever seen!" she gushed behind vintage-esque pink and white nails. "Phani, right?"

I blinked in surprise. "Yeah, how'd you know?"

"You look like an adorable chocolate chip cookie," she said. She took something from behind the counter and handed it to me. It was a chocolate chip cookie wrapped in plastic and a designer sticker. Chariclo Sweets, it read. It was still warm.

"Wow," I laughed.

"Don't mind the randomness. It's a Bryan thing. Tirisha told me you wanted to see if I was hiring. Sadly, I'm good for staff right now, but if you leave me your information and resume, I can always give you a call once I have a spot open."

I perked up. Waste not, want not.

"Do you know when Tirisha will be back?" I asked, handing over a folded resume I always kept on hand just in case. Abbie didn't seem to mind its less than presentable state.

"I know she got the gig she auditioned for so she's practicing her act, even as we speak," Abbie revealed with a wink.

"Really? That's great! Where is she performing?"

"The Candle Lounge in South Coast! I'd go, but I'm helping host a book signing tomorrow that clashes with her performance. Normally her shows are at eight in the evening, but this one's at six!"

Huh. Well, good for Tirisha. Abbie was kind enough to share Tirisha's social media account with me in case I needed to speak with her sooner. After a cheerful good-bye and another promise to return, I resumed my journey to Charlie's.

The GPS brought me to the border of downtown Asphodel. Two streets away and I suspected I'd be in South Coast. From what Idrina told me, the south eastern portion of the city didn't have the most stellar reputation. In fact, a lot of low socio-economic families tended to live down there because housing was so cheap. Or at least, used to be cheap. Rumor has it a lot of developmental corporations were interested in buying property and gentrifying it, pricing out many locals from their homes. It didn't sit right in my spirit, this greed and heartlessness. I hoped something was done soon so the locals of Asphodel wouldn't suffer.

After texting Charlie I was about five minutes away, he immediately called me.

"Phani? Where are you?" He asked, sounding winded.

I stopped my board and looked to my left. "I'm next to Lisandra's Laundromat. By 187th avenue."

"I know where that is! Stay there. I'll come meet you." He hung up.

That was unexpected. I glanced at the window to my left and fixed my appearance using the grimy reflection. I smiled. This was it! I stood to the side and waited, butterflies in my stomach. I noticed a few spirits milling about before dispersing into fog.

One in particular looked strange, draped in black shimmering robes and sporting a lost sleepy expression. He had delicate features with long, flowing hair so platinum blond it resembled fresh snow. Despite his pale coloring, he didn't appear transparent like the other spirits. When he caught me staring at him, he stopped moving.

"Oh!" he said, sounding surprised. "Oh what a coincidence! Fancy meeting you here!"

His voice was ethereal and soft. Eyes blue and icy like a submerged iceberg. As he approached me, his waist-length hair floated around him.

"Hello!" He said again, once he was standing in front of me.

He was so tall, almost six foot five. I craned my neck just to look at him. He didn't give me any hostile vibes or overwhelm me with his energy. He seemed almost harmless, the expression on his face ever kind. I covered an upcoming yawn.

"You've grown so big!" The mysterious spirit remarked. "Do you remember me?"

I paused, unsure whether I should acknowledge him. I made it a policy not to interact with spirits. I just wasn't cut out for the medium thing. The reason I'm even speaking to Catalina was because she offered me money. It's a selfish reason, when I should be using my gift to help others, but I just don't want to do it. I don't want to be in charge of someone else's happiness like that. Their emotions, their memories, their energy, their *soul*. It was overwhelming. By ten years old I was able to stop crying and trembling when a spirit approached me. By thirteen, I was able to snap back when they got rude or intrusive. By fifteen, I was able to defend myself from unsavory intentions. Little by little, I was able to carve out a life despite Burngemear stalking me and Tenebris kidnapping me.

I looked away.

The spirit frowned, studying me for a moment. He seemed to understand that I wasn't going to say anything to him the longer I avoided his gaze.

"Ah, forgive me for disturbing you. I just thought it'd be nice to speak to you now that you're older. Maybe another time," he said, inclining his head. He sounded apologetic and sincere. A scent like chamomile wafted from his floating hair as he turned away.

I lifted my head and stared at his retreating back. What did he mean by "now that you're older"? I've never seen him before. I certainly would have remembered a spirit like him. Curiosity and a little bit of guilt had me breaking my policy.

"Hey," I called suddenly, startling a passing woman carrying paper grocery bags. She gave me an odd look before continuing. The spirit turned, eyes wide in surprise.

"Yes?"

I stifled another yawn. "How do you know me? I've never met you."

The spirit smiled. I belatedly realized that he was actually quite beautiful. Not in the seductive, human handsomeness that Aedes had, but something other and breathtaking.

"Of course you've met me. Many times in fact," he said, "but for this cycle, we met when you were little, so you probably don't remember me. And I don't blame you. The human mind is fragile and fallible."

I blinked. "...what?"

Before he could elaborate, I heard Charlie shout my name. I

turned and saw him jogging up the street, waving a hand. I automatically waived mine in return.

"It looks like you're busy," the spirit continued, eyeing Charlie curiously. "I don't want to disturb you. We'll meet again another time."

He dispersed into a shimmering fog which caused my breath to come out cold. Charlie arrived then, exhaling rapidly as he caught his breath.

"Sorry for the wait!" he said, standing straight. He was dressed in a white T-shirt and dark washed jeans.

"No trouble," I mumbled, eyeing the spot the spirit had occupied. I never even got his name, but he definitely had my interest now. My gut told me he knew more about me then he let on. I shook my head for now and concentrated on Charlie. I presented him with the plastic bag carrying lunch.

"Here you go! On the house!" I said, smiling.

Charlie chuckled, placing one hand behind my back and leading me to a small park near-by. He offered to carry my skateboard and together we sat on an empty bench circling a bronze statue. The park wasn't large like Hesiod, but it had enough greenery that one could pretend they were getting their daily dose of nature.

"Thanks for bringing lunch over. You didn't have to," Charlie began.

"Don't worry, I really wanted to," I said, unwrapping the bag and handing him a flat rectangle wrapped in tinfoil and a soda. "So this is a *baleada*. It's like a taco, but not really. It's a soft flour tortilla with refried beans, this salty soft dairy spread, cheese, and I even added a strip of steak so you can have some protein."

Charlie unwrapped the tinfoil and raised a brow. "This smells fantastic. I think the most foreign thing I've eaten is American Chinese food."

"I think the most American meal I ate was a hot dog," I said, unwrapping my own *baleada*. "My dad cooks strictly Hispanic food."

"Do I eat it like a regular taco?" he asked. After an affirmative, he bit down and ate a portion. His eyes lit up. Once he was able to talk, he looked at me and smiled. "This is delicious as fuck, Phani!"

I giggled. The warm feeling in my chest grew and we remained this way for the next twenty minutes. Charlie, a fan of his new meal, suddenly became more animated. The subdued vibe I got from him earlier seemed to have dissipated. He was asking me questions about my home life, my hobbies and what I was doing in Asphodel.

"I just thought it was time I moved out and figured things out on my own," I said, the soda can cool against my palm. "I was feeling very stuck and claustrophobic being home all the time and after getting my AA, I realized I didn't know what career I wanted to pursue."

Charlie nodded, sipping from his can. "I get that. After high school, I didn't bother with college. It was too expensive and I didn't have a clue what I wanted to pursue."

My eyes widened. "Really? No college at all?"

"Nah," he shrugged. "I barely graduated high school, though not for lack of trying. My home life had just been...difficult." I nodded. He continued. "I was mostly focused on raising my little sister and keeping my part-time job."

"Oh! You have a sister?" I asked, smiling. I always wanted a sibling, but for obvious reasons, it just wasn't meant to be. "What's she like?"

Charlie hesitated. "She...was kind-hearted and selfless. Almost to a fault."

I nearly gasped at my blunder. "Oh, I'm sorry. I didn't meant to–"

"No, no, you didn't know and I don't normally talk about her anymore," he admitted, his voice quiet. "She...died almost three months ago. Got caught in a gang war."

"Gang war? Like, the mafia...?"

His eyes darkened. The empty soda can in his hand crumpled from the pressure. "Yeah. Erebus."

The good mood left me.

"Oh. I'm so sorry," I said.

Even though I hadn't been here when the chaos happened, the

fact that I was working with Catalina, former crime boss of Erebus, and had talked to Aedes, who was working for Erebus right now, and thought him handsome felt like a betrayal to Charlie. And he deserved better than that. He had his own charm and boyish good looks. Eyes a bright blue-green, lips small, but red, jaw-line prominent, and an upturned nose. He was nothing to sneeze at. Even the faded linear scar on his left cheek bone added to his appeal.

In an effort to change the subject, I pointed at my own left cheekbone.

"How did you get that scar?" I asked.

Charlie touched his face gently. "Oh this? One of my bosses from a previous job gave it to me. Didn't like that I stood up for myself when their order was stupid."

I gasped. "That's terrible! How dare they! Did you go to HR? Did you report them?"

Charlie smiled at me. "I couldn't, but it doesn't matter. I left that place behind and don't regret it. What about you? How was your home life?"

I frowned. It was apparent he wanted our conversation to sail on lighter waters. The topic of his rough upbringing and previous toxic workplace was obviously a sore topic, or at least one he wasn't ready to divulge on our unofficial first date. I crumpled up the tinfoil my *baleada* came in and stuffed it into the plastic bag next to me. I held out my hand for his trash. He was surprised at first but handed it over without protest.

"My home life was...safe," I said. It was the best way to describe it without saying too much myself. "My dad tried his best to raise me after my mother passed away."

Understanding flooded Charlie's blue-green gaze. He ran a hand through his shaggy hair.

"Oh. I'm sorry."

I smiled. "It's fine now. I didn't really know her. I was only two years old when she left."

"...h-how?" he asked, hesitation clear in his voice. "But only if you want to say it. You don't have to."

"It's fine, Charlie. She was in a car crash. It was too late when the ambulance arrived. My dad took it really hard for years. Still does sometimes, when I'm not looking."

"Really? Has he moved on or tried to date anyone else?"

I shook my head. "He's moved on the best that he can, but I know he constantly thinks about her. I haven't ever seen him bring anyone home. Never really talks like there's anyone else in his life. It was like she was his one and only."

"That's...kind of romantic," Charlie murmured, leaning back against the bench.

"I know," I said. "My family tends to mention that. But honestly, that kind of romance scares me."

"Eh?" Charlie turned his head to look at me. "What do you mean?"

"Well, just think about it," I said, turning to him. Our knees touched. "You have this important person in your life that you love with all your soul and then they're gone. The love and memories that you once had becomes painful and suddenly you can't function. You can't eat, you can't sleep, you can't even enjoy simply living because it feels almost hollow. And you know you need to find some way to move on, but it only becomes harder and harder the longer it sinks in that they're gone. They were your everything and you were their everything. The reciprocation is suddenly gone and everything just feels meaningless. Love like that, that's all consuming and passionate and fixed, it's terrifying."

Charlie blinked, exhaling slowly but shakily. "...oh. I...I never thought of it that way."

It was an observation I had noticed in my father over the years. My first memories of him were of a quiet and soft spoken man who mostly stayed indoors when he wasn't working. Subdued, introverted, overprotective. I wasn't sure if he was like that before my mother died, but his behavior shaped me into the awkward homebody I am today.

I know my father did his best to raise me as a single parent. He made sure I was fed, clean, clothed, and socialized with my cousins from my mother's side. He bought me toys and taught me to speak both in Spanish and English—not that his skill of the anglo language was any thorough—despite being homeschooled. I would have thought him completely normal if it wasn't for the little things. Something was off when I would speak to him sometimes; his face never registered having heard me at all. As if he were lost somewhere else. Or when tears suddenly leaked from his eyes when he was driving or cooking. The house remained exactly as is, nothing changed, dust settled around her knick knacks and picture frames of my parents sat untouched. Wilma's loss was always noticeable, almost as if my father were afraid to touch anything of hers.

As I grew older, I decided I never wanted to be so dependent on someone that I became an entirely different person. Not that my father being who he is now was bad, but his recovery into a functioning adult with aspirations and attachments outside of his deceased wife had been a grueling process. If he had been like his old self, I wonder if my childhood would have turned out different. Would I have turned out different? An interesting thought for another day.

Charlie placed a gentle warm hand on my head. I turned, curious. He leaned so close to my face I could see the flecks of brilliant blue in his cool green eyes. My face grew hot. He wore a very sincere expression, one of comfort and reassurance.

"I think," he began, "that if you're with the right person, all of your concerns might not seem so scary."

I blinked. "O-Oh?"

"I can understand not wanting to be so vulnerable," he admitted, eyes downcast, "loving someone shouldn't ever feel like a burden. But sometimes, that's just life. What can we do but hold the memories and try to find a way to make things right?"

I said nothing, taking his words in. He had a point, but must we always resign ourselves to such a heavy outcome? I look at Idrina and Ryan sometimes, the few times he's over, and wonder how far they'd be willing to go for each other. Were their feelings sincere enough if they decided to call it quits? Was it worth it if they faced downhill problems? I suppose it does depend on the person you've chosen and whether that person can mesh with who you are yourself.

Charlie laid his cheek on my head, the pressure steady and gentle. He was warm and smelled of earth, like potatoes or poppy seeds. It wasn't unpleasant and with the birds chirping in the park and the distant sounds of traffic, the moment was soothing. I sighed happily.

Maybe exploring my feelings with Charlie wouldn't be so bad. He was cute, patient, and thoughtful. As first relationships go—kind of, we were still getting to know each other—I had to be doing well for myself. With my free hand, I interlaced my fingers with the hand Charlie left on his lap, the one sporting his elegant tattoo. He jerked a little, surprised, but when I didn't pull away, he leaned into me again.

His palm was rough, fingers deeply calloused, but warm. My finger traced the pattern of his tattoo. Charlie shivered.

The next twenty minutes remained like that. Us leaning into each other and chatting about small stuff; my love of fruit smoothies, his fanaticism over the Beach Boys, Sir Harry, his annoying roommate who dabbles in illegal things, my dream of owning my own apartment, his going to culinary school, etc. Eventually, we were interrupted by several insistent dings coming from Charlie's phone. He straightened up and checked what the fuss was about.

"How long have we been here?" I asked, looking at the blue sky and gray clouds.

"About an hour," he murmured, replying to the messages.

I jumped up in shock, getting to my feet. "Oh no!"

He looked up, confused. "What's wrong?"

"You're late! I don't want you to get in trouble," I explained, throwing our lunch into the nearest waste can across from us. When I returned, Charlie still looked confused.

"What?" he said.

"You're break! I don't know how long it was supposed to be."

Understanding dawned on him.

"Oh! Oh, no you're fine. I had an hour lunch," he explained, hastily getting up. "But you're right. I should head back."

"I'll walk you," I said, grabbing his hand. To my surprise, he jerked away.

"No! No! You don't have to. I can go by myself," he insisted. His phone dinged again, several more times in fact.

"Is that your work?" I asked.

Charlie sighed as if exhausted. "Yes, they can't seem to function even with the most basic instructions."

"You said you worked in catering?"

"Yeah, *Delizi Dilettos*. It's Italian," he said, tucking his phone into his back pocket. "It's not a big business, but there's a promising job we have next Thursday so my team and I are prepping up."

I smiled. "That's good. Then I should let you go. Text me when you can."

Charlie looked up and met my gaze with a smile. "Yes, I will. Thank you, Phani. You really didn't have to meet me today."

I blushed. "I wanted to."

With a lingering glance from him, Charlie jogged away, his pace set and determined as he looked both ways before crossing the street. I sighed and walked back over to the bench, picking up my longboard and setting it down.

It might have been my imagination, but it almost felt like Charlie was going to kiss me. The idea didn't repulse me, if anything it added butterflies to my stomach. I was probably getting ahead of myself though. I only just met Charlie three days ago, hardly enough time to warrant falling helplessly in love. At least for me anyways. I've had crushes on guys in class when I attended college, but I never did anything about it. Even working on projects, the guys in Miami hardly seemed interested in pursuing me.

While I did believe what I told Charlie about being scared to fall in love to the degree my father did, I wasn't opposed to some romance or being swept off my feet. I firmly believed I had what it took not fall over the edge like everyone else. Not because I thought myself superior or special, but because no significant other would ever understand the complexities and emotional turmoil I experience from being spirited away to Tenebris and seeing dead people on the daily.

That's not even taking into consideration Burngemear stalking me. The crazy supernatural part of my life was just enough to keep me from truly opening my heart.

Some might think it unhealthy, but for me, it was perfect.

It took me forty minutes to eventually arrive a few blocks away from Idrina's apartment. Cutting through Hesiod Park, I didn't make it far before Catalina popped up in front of me without warning. I shrieked and swerved, falling off my board and rolling onto the trimmed grassy area beside me.

I groaned, feeling like one giant bruise as my elbows throbbed.

"Finally, you're here," Catalina remarked, hovering over me. She didn't look the least bit remorseful. No surprise there.

"No laying down on the job now! I gotta prepare you for the next phase of our investigation," she continued. "That means no staying up late tonight and texting lover boy."

"And why's that?" I mumbled, sitting up and feeling my head.

Catalina grinned, causing shivers to run down my arm.

"Because, *little girl*, we're going shopping tomorrow."

XIV.

BATTLE PREP

THE NEXT DAY rolled around and with it anxiety gathered at the pit of my core the more Catalina clued me in on her big idea.

According to her, the next phase of our investigation would be taking place at the Candle Lounge in South Coast. I wasn't sure why the name sounded familiar, but I later realized it was because Tirisha would be performing there. The thought of seeing her gladdened my heart, which made the undercover portion of today's mission less nerve-wracking.

"We need to get you a suitable dress," Catalina declared. "This portion of our investigation requires you to look like you belong in the Underworld. We're talking about the Candle Lounge, after all! This is not some low-class bar anyone wearing cheap polyester can saunter in. And first impressions are *everything* in the Underworld."

That I could understand, but did first impressions have to be bought from an expensive boutique in Vanit Town, of all places?

Located in none other than Vanit Town near the border of Wonderwood, Astora's Room, the store we were currently in, was certainly not for those who earned less than forty thousand a year after tax. Astora's Room was a sleek and modern boutique with glossy wooden floors, teak displays, and glass shelves. The ceiling and walls were crème colored, giving the space an open concept not normally seen because of the enclosed windowless design. Even the air smelled fancy, with traces of—according to Catalina—Guerlain meteorite foundation powder and Chanel No. 5 perfume. I wasn't sure what all that was, but I liked that the scent was light and floral with hints of bergamot and rose.

Elitist vibes aside, I liked the store. It carried a lot for a boutique and was surprisingly big. As soon as we entered, Catalina directed me to the back where the occasion dresses were hung. Half way through browsing and arguing with Catalina that I was *not* wearing anything explicit—her style was more on the daring apparently—a sales lady came over.

"Excuse me, ma'am? Are you okay?" she asked, giving me a look that clearly said she didn't think so.

I faced her in confusion. "Yes? Why do you ask?"

"It's just, you're *talking* to yourself," she said, nose wrinkling.

It took herculean strength to keep my facial expression neutral and not twisted in horror.

"Oh! Sorry, I, uh, have a tiny bluetooth earbud," I responded hastily, backing away. "Don't mind me!"

I've refrained from responding to Catalina aloud since.

"Take this dress and put it on," she ordered, pointing to a forest green number with long glittery fringe.

The confidence in her demeanor was intimidating and hard to deny. Like a resigned subordinate, I swallowed my words and grabbed the dress before entering the nearest unoccupied dressing room. I've learned that my peace of mind generally remains intact if I don't question the older woman. That and the rich residents of Vanit Town browsing nearby would definitely have side-eyed me for talking to myself again.

Had Catalina always been this self-assured? I wondered what she had been like as a child. I know I had come across as a timid little push over. My metaphorical spine didn't exist in those days, but I've since grown a stable one.

For the most part, anyways.

I stopped paying attention to whatever Catalina was going on about outside the stall. One good thing about not having to respond to her was that I didn't have to listen. I was surprised to discover in my partnership with her that Catalina was a talker. It was as though she enjoyed the sound of her voice because she just couldn't get enough of it. And I didn't entirely blame her. Spanish voices were pleasant on the ears but her accent didn't even slow her down in the slightest!

Had she been a voiceless stone in her past life? A silent tree? Something that made talking a wondrous hobby for her now? Catalina could talk for hours sometimes and show no signs of boredom. While bits of conversation with her were interesting (wolfsbanes were her favorite "flowers" despite being poisonous plants) if a bit overwhelming (her sex life was never something I needed to know), Catalina was a woman with no filter, no shame, and other then Underworld business, no secrets.

I glanced at myself in the mirror and frowned, self-conscious of the way my partially-clothed body looked. It was rectangular in shape, resembling a washboard despite my chest fighting to reach B cup status. Curves were all the rage in my family, a dominant gene that skipped over me vindictively.

If you were tall and curvy, you were considered a bombshell in both the Carmel and Baumer families. Idrina was a shining example with her pear-shape figure and shiny straight hair. Every family reunion consisted of lovely compliments of what an accomplished young woman my cousin turned out to be—even I was among them. In contrast, when people spoke of me, they weren't exactly impressed. Looks of sympathy and words of encouragement everyone knew would never come to fruition were tossed my way.

I sighed. Oh well.

I adjusted the dress until it sat right. It was mostly a slip cinched at the waist and covered in long fringes that swayed with movement. The fit was exact and comfortable when moving my legs. Cleavage showed and the back plunged a bit, but otherwise, I think this one was it.

"Are you done yet?" Catalina called.

With my casual clothes folded under one arm, I got out and showed her the dress. I made sure to stand in front of the full-length mirror so the woman standing two racks down wouldn't get suspicious of me. The sales lady who caught me speaking to Catalina earlier lurked near-by, probably thinking I was a crazy loon seeking to cause mischief. I tried my best to ignore her.

Catalina stared at the dress with a critical eye. She turned me this way and that until she nodded in grudging approval.

"It will do. It's too bad we can't shop at my favorite store though."

"Why not?" I whispered, turning my back.

"Because I'm dead, duh."

I glanced at her with one arched brow, lips pulled to the side. "*I* can't go in there because *you're* dead?"

"Damn right! You wanna torture me with all the beautiful things I can't buy or wear? Anyways, this place isn't too bad. If you're desperate, that is."

Desperate? The price tag on the dress alone nearly sent me into cardiac arrest! This place was not for the desperate *at all*.

I followed behind Catalina as she went about picking shoes and accessories for the dress. The more she added, the more my anxiety skyrocketed. The only thing running through my mind was the question of payment. How on earth was I supposed to pay for all this? I had no money to hand over and Catalina didn't have any cash on her either.

"Hey," I whispered, looking out for anyone near me. "Are you sure we're going about this the right way?"

"Of course! The thick fringes on the dress will make your *chiches*," she said, cupping the air in front of her generous chest, "look bigger."

I looked at her in confusion before I realized she thought I was talking about the dress.

"Or at least disguise their modest handful," Catalina continued. "It won't help us if you can't look great during an interrogation. Undercover work is no excuse to look a hot mess."

I wasn't sure what to make of her response, but I didn't bother clarifying or contradicting her comment about my chest. She wasn't wrong.

After what seemed like forever and a half later, Catalina had me put on the whole ensemble. I declined putting on the earrings she recommended. I couldn't bear taking mine off for sentimental reasons. She huffed in response but didn't comment.

We ended up grabbing some black tights—the kind that made my legs appear longer—and an elegant pair of black leather gloves to go with the black ankle boots I wore. Catalina's choker was already in place and hidden away by a silk jade scarf. Add together the shoulder-length honey blonde wig from Idrina's closet—she had a total of three; for what exactly I hadn't a clue—and I looked ready to step into a James Bond movie as the cute, but mysterious femme fatale. While the entire trip felt superfluous, I smiled when I saw the final result in the mirror.

"I love it," I admitted, adjusting the green scarf around my throat.

Catalina laughed. "Good. If you feel confident and amazing, everyone else will think you're a big deal, including Garcy Maroone, owner of The Candle Lounge. She's a fountain of Underworld gossip and a go-to for people who need a hit-man. I met Garcy years ago when I first moved to Asphodel City. She can get wily sometimes, so I tend to keep an eye on her."

I grimaced. Catalina's casual confession was an ugly reminder that where I was headed, mobsters weren't fantastical figures. They were scary real and something I was only recently exposed to thanks to my partnership with Catalina. If it wasn't for the reward money, my sensible world would have never crossed hers.

"Did you find everything you were looking for, ma'am?"

The sales lady that had stalked me all over the store appeared from behind a display of folded cashmere sweaters.

"Um, yeah. I'm ready," I said, feeling just a little bit small and foolish in my dress now that an outsider was present. I looked to Catalina for guidance. She rolled her eyes in response.

"Take out the note I told you to write and hand it to her."

I fetched the index card I had folded and stuffed into the pockets of my shorts earlier. The sales lady named Casey, according to her name tag, pinched the note I gave her between long trimmed nails. Contempt marred her pretty features as if she were preparing to battle against an intrusive homeless person. The second she read the words on the index card, however, her entire demeanor performed a one eighty-degree transformation.

The way Casey *fawned* over me with such fervor made the smothering dressing room I'd been in earlier seem mild in comparison. She asked me a series of questions non-stop: Did I need anything else? Was I happy with my shopping so far? Did I want to sit and have her bring me any more dresses and shoes? Did I want some sparkling water with watercress sandwiches to nibble on? Was the atmosphere of the store to my satisfaction?

She even went so far as to redirect a snooty customer, one who clearly belonged in Vanit Town, to another sales lady. It was wild!

"Ask her if they have any venetian masks," Catalina added. "The wig is good, but I want your identity kept firmly hidden. It'll make our mission flow smoother if no one remembers your face."

I relayed the message to Casey, who scurried to the back like a woman possessed before promptly returning with a velvet tray showcasing venetian masks of different styles, shapes, and make. As she explained the materials of each piece, I wasted no time picking out the one Catalina pointed to. It was a green half mask made of stiff lace formed into vines and flowers, a perfect match for the dress. After adding a pea coat, everything was finally rung up. Not once was I instructed to hand over cash or show any cards. When the receipt was handed over, I noticed the prices for the items were missing. That was normal on this side of the world, apparently.

Once it was over, I couldn't get out of there quick enough. Seeing Casey go from *Ugh!* to *Oh!* was disturbing. All I had written on the index card was: *On the House of Van Darlington tab. Orders from Erebus.* That was followed by a serial code number underneath.

"Hey Catalina, is your darling the same person I wrote on the card? Did we just buy all this stuff on his tab?" I asked worriedly.

Finally freed from the shopping excursion, I stepped onto the sidewalk outside with relish. It was afternoon time in Asphodel, the city smelling of faint gasoline and autumn. Despite the sun's beaming presence, a familiar chill began to seep into my skin.

Winter was nearly upon us.

"We did, but it's all chump change," she said, not the slightest bit worried. "Darling never checks his account until it's tax season so don't worry your pretty little head."

That wasn't reassuring, especially since Catalina had written that the charge was on Erebus's orders. I hoped Catalina hadn't endangered me again. There was enough on my plate without having to worry about Aedes kidnapping me for using his boss's name to charge some poor sucker's bank account.

Hailing a cab, I half-listened to Catalina's bragging as she recounted in great detail all the different outfits she owned thanks to her darling's unsuspecting generosity. She listed several that would have been perfect for the mission.

"Tear-away skirts are ideal if I need a flowy look. Since I'm a form-fitting kind of gal, if the dresses don't fit my body like a glove, it's a no," Catalina explained inside the taxi cab. She gestured to the tight pants and snug top she wore when she died.

Forget clothes. I was far more impressed by her ability to stay within the moving vehicle instead of phasing through. How was she doing that? Just how powerful was this woman? What made her so special that she could keep up with me like any normal person?

"Darling understands this. Whenever he gets me clothes, it's never loose. Unlike *some* women," she continued, oblivious to my awe. "He knows me so well. I don't even have to tell him what to get me. He just knows."

Her tone became sad, a rare moment of vulnerability. Despite my best efforts not to care about her situation, I found myself concerned. To my relief, the taxi driver paid me no mind. He appeared distracted by his Russian conversation over the speaker phone.

"My offer still stands you know," I reminded her. "I don't make it a habit, but I wouldn't mind finding your darling and letting him know you're doing alright."

"Oh God no, not right now! He would know I'm getting into trouble and scold my gravesite. When all this is finished, you can just write him a note and deliver it."

That sounded painless and a far better option. The less interaction with people who knew I was able to communicate with ghosts, the happier I was. Also, speaking of gravesites...

"Do you know when your funeral was supposed to be held, by any chance?"

"I do actually. My funeral is today. I'm not sure what time, but with most of Erebus in attendance, today will be the perfect day for you to briefly slip into the Underworld for a few hours. This Aedes guy will never have to know." She paused, brows furrowing. "Who even *is* that guy?"

"What? You don't know?"

She shook her head. "I've never heard of his name before and I know near everyone in Erebus. I only know for certain that he's legit because of Rory and Chensing guarding him. I recognized them from the front windshield."

"Good to know I wasn't kidnapped by a complete stranger then," I remarked dryly, crossing my arms. I pushed the mystery of Aedes aside when I remembered another thing I wanted to ask Catalina.

"Hey, how did you know joining the mafia was what you wanted to do with your life?"

Catalina laughed. "I didn't. I appreciate that Darling took me out of poverty when we became friends, but honestly, if I hadn't met him and lived life normally, I might have hustled my way into modeling or becoming a TV personality, maybe even a motorbike racer." She paused before smirking. "Or even a housewife! Maybe all four! But instead, I chose him. There's just something about Darling that inspires my loyalty. I wanted to be involved in his life more than I wanted to do anything else. No matter the cost."

I frowned. "That's...intense." Not to mention a little unhealthy.

Catalina smiled. "Isn't it? He's lucky. I'm a very selfish person and I hate thinking about others if they don't interest me. But Darling and I have been through a lot and we've grown so much. Well, mostly me.

To be honest, he's pretty much stayed the same since the day I met him: fearless, clever, and annoyingly confident."

She's one to talk.

"What's his name?"

Catalina winked before turning her body away. "*Not spilling!* You'll end up falling in love with him and he'd make mincemeat out of you."

I sputtered. "Excuse me?! That's quite the assumption!"

She shrugged. "It's true. It's happened so many times. I've had many female friends fall victim to broken hearts. Darling is not for the faint of heart. Stick to your lover boy. He seems harmless, if a bit weird."

I didn't have the words to respond to that. The entire conversation about Catalina's best friend was so bizarre. I could never possibly mold my entire life around a guy. In addition to being doted upon, my super overprotective father had drilled into me that I shouldn't let peer pressure dictate my actions and thoughts. While I was still a push-over sometimes, I wasn't about to let anyone steer my life unless I wanted them to. Of course, if only I knew *where* I wanted to steer my life in the first place.

I rubbed my forehead, taking notice that the streets outside the cab were starting to look more shabby and less chic.

"—it's just as well," Catalina said. "I hate being upstaged, but Darling is lucky I love him. Otherwise, he'd be on my shit list right next to Bian."

Oh my god, was she still talking?

I chuckled, going along with whatever Catalina had said.

"Who's Bian?" I asked.

Catalina curled her lip.

"The Vile Serpent. A *perra* from hell, figuratively speaking. I'd sooner throw myself off a cliff then shake her hand. She's part of the Upper Circle, another Second-Tier crime boss. In private, I like to call her Bitchy B, BB for short." She frowned, brown eyes downcast. "Not that it matters anymore."

Her silence was telling. Catalina had lived for her former life. She had derived pleasure from shooting up rival gang members and bringing down order with an iron fist. Would Catalina have chosen a career as a law enforcer if things had been different for her? Maybe. Maybe not. Knowing her, loyalty to blind authority would chafe unless she was personally invested.

I shook my head. What a way to live.

Ten minutes later and our destination was finally insight.

The Candle Lounge, from what Catalina had been telling me all day, was an old nightclub turned jazz lounge situated in South Coast, a dangerous neighborhood home to the projects on the other side of the Odium River. The front entrance looked as though it had been abandoned for years with windows boarded up and its red-brick foundation cracked here and there. Even the paint outside was chipped and peeling away. The only thing modern about it was a neon candlestick holder sign that had been placed over the blocked entrance. Dim light flickered weakly as it struggled for a pulse. There was no other indication that declared this battered building to be the infamous Candle Lounge.

If it hadn't been for Catalina's confident expression and the faint noise of jazz music seeping through the cracks of the broken windows, I would have thought the taxi driver had tricked us. I clutched my pea coat and pulled it close when I got out of the cab. I glanced at the rundown neighborhood around us with trepidation.

We definitely weren't in Vanit Town anymore.

As my eyes swept over the colorless area, I heard a sharp gasp from Catalina. I glanced at her and panicked when I saw the source of her distress.

Burngemear was here, blocking The Candle Lounge's abandoned street entrance. I backed away, my stomach hollowing with dread. His presence never meant good news to anyone, least of all me.

"What the fuck is that?" Catalina demanded, following me in haste. Even she was taken aback.

"That's Burngemear," I told her, the words feeling odd in my mouth. It was then that I realized I had never said his name aloud before. "You've seen him, right? He lives in Tenebris."

"Tene-what?"

I stared at Catalina's furrowed brows, the wrinkle of skin between them, the twist of her pouty lips as confusion rolled off her in waves. Why was she acting like I was speaking gibberish? Surely, she's had to have seen Burngemear before, or even Tenebris? She's a ghost! Of course she would have ended up on the other side.

"Catalina, where do you disappear to when you're not in the physical world?"

She shrugged, keeping a wary eye on Burngemear.

"When I close my eyes, I find myself in this thick, dark void with other pitiful spirits floating around. Unable to move, forced to be carried away by an invisible current. I know they're crying, screaming, but I hear no sound. Just piercing silence."

Huh. That's...different.

"How do you get back here then? To the physical realm?"

"I just move. It's easy for me but impossible for the others. If I want to leave, I just picture where I want to be and poof! There I was. I've been using your cousin's apartment building as a safe point."

That's fascinating. How was Catalina able to do that? Why her, specifically? I knew there were odd quirks she had, like her solid colorful appearance, her endless energy to maintain said solid colorful appearance, and her emotional poltergeist abilities. But was all that enough for her to break out of that purgatory-like void? So many questions floated through my head, but sadly, not enough answers presented themselves. I briefly wondered if Tirisha might have a clue, assuming she knew more than she let on. It was worth investigating on our off time.

Before I could respond, I spotted two women leaving the right-side entrance of The Candle Lounge. They walked away briskly, focus zeroed in on their phones as they spoke softly to one another. High heels clacked with finality as they ate the distance to the sidewalk. It took me a moment to realize that I recognized one of the women.

"Tirisha?"

Tirisha looked up at the sound of her name. Her dark lashes fluttered apart upon seeing me, here of all places. She quickly approached me, never missing a steady step. Everything about her tonight screamed big, blonde, and bodacious. She looked stunning, like a glamorous Hollywood starlet.

"Phani?" she said. "What are you doing here? Goodness you look gorgeous! Like a Bond girl!"

I grinned.

"Stick to the story," Catalina reminded me.

"I have a date here tonight," I said. "Who's your friend?"

"Miss Quim a la Mode. She's my companion tonight. Quim, this is Phani, a cute girl I met a few days ago," Tirisha introduced.

While Tirisha Jordan's style of drag involved glitter, big blonde curls, and a modern movie star flair, Miss Quim a la Mode was made to be displayed in an expensive art gallery in Wonderwood. She was super tall, with five-inch platform heels that only added to her dynamic colorful look. Her make-up was bold, but it was even more striking when she grinned.

"Is this the one whose drag cherry you popped?"

Tirisha laughed. "Almost. She still hasn't been to a show."

Miss Quim tsked, snapping her claw-like fingers. "And she won't see today's either. Bad timing, girl, but there's always next time at the Gays Inn. Now I gotta fetch the car, but you stay put, Ti. I'll be quick. Nice meeting you, Phani!"

With a final wave, Miss Quim sashayed away.

"So...not today, huh? I thought you were performing here," I asked the blonde, a bit saddened by the news. The mission just went from exciting to burdensome real quick.

Tirisha smiled wryly.

"I was, but I've recently been made privy to a bit of shocking news. I was forced to cancel tonight's show as a result. Trust me, little chip, no one's more upset about this than I," she sighed. "And just when I was getting my big break."

"What's the news?"

Tirisha shook her head, sleek curls bouncing. She was really spiffed up with flawless make-up and delicious perfume. Her sequined fitted gown shimmered like a disco ball and her white fur coat looked exceptionally expensive. Even her heels, five inches at the very least, were glittering. What a shame she couldn't show it off in full.

"I can't say," Tirisha said. "But Phani, once you find your date, *get the fuck out of there*. In less than forty minutes, I wouldn't recommend being seen at The Candle Lounge."

I opened my mouth to protest, but her serious gaze made me chicken out. Her words sounded foreboding. And Burngemear's presence wasn't helping matters. I nodded instead.

"*Qué le pasa a esta loca*? Seriously, what's wrong with her? Why would she say that?" Catalina muttered, crossing her arms.

"Tirisha," I began, ignoring Catalina's muttering, "if you don't mind me asking, remember when you said hell was a cold place? I, uh, well, you might be right."

Tirisha paused, her jewel polished nails hovering over her smartphone. She turned her head, attention fixed on me entirely.

"Oh? What makes you think that, little chip?" My neck began to feel unseasonably warm.

"Well, it's possible," I said, briefly eyeing Burngemear. He remained where he was, simply hovering, face turned away, biding his time until tragedy struck. I shivered. "I also think this frozen hell has a very creepy harbinger of death."

"Burngemear."

It was a shock to hear those words fall from someone else's lips. Was I hallucinating? I pinched my cheek, causing Tirisha to laugh in response. She patted my head sympathetically.

"What are you doing to yourself?" Catalina asked.

"Sorry, I thought I heard wrong," I said.

Tirisha smirked. "You heard right. Those paranormal books you wanted the other day, were you hoping to find more information about the frozen hell called Tenebris, by any chance?"

Christmas sure came early today!

"Yes! Yes, that's right!" Then I found myself divulging more than I would have normally been comfortable with in my excitement. "You know about Tenebris then? And Burngemear? How? What do you know?"

"My, my, slow down!" Tirisha chuckled. She fished into her sparkly clutch, handing me a business card with her name, phone number, and email on it. "Here's my information. You'll have to come see me next time. I dare not linger here, and you shouldn't either."

I nodded eagerly, taking the card as if it were the holy grail.

"Yeah, totally! I—" I stopped when I remembered something. "Ah, Tirisha? You wouldn't, you know, happen to know anything about an in-between place spirits go to after they die that isn't Tenebris, do you?"

Tirisha looked thoughtful as she placed a sharp nail to her lips.

"You might be talking about the Aether Realm. Weak spirits with no purpose and little energy tend to get sucked there. It's been said that once there, you're stuck forever. At least until someone gets you out."

"Someone?"

"Burngemear."

She winked just as Miss Quim pulled up, classical music blaring full blast from the car speakers. Tirisha gave me a quick hug, her perfume wafting all around me.

"Gotta run, my spotted cookie. Ta!"

"Later Phans!" called Miss Quim.

And then they were gone.

By how brisk their departure was you would have thought they were being chased by a mob of telephone marketers. Still, I was glad to have stumbled upon Tirisha. It's not every day I met someone in the know about Tenebris and Burngemear. Even the extent of my knowledge was based solely on what I've experienced. I hadn't found any source materials anywhere mentioning Burngemear or Tenebris specifically, just vague theories about hell and the devil. After a while, reading too much of it became dark and depressing.

"What the hell was all that? Who was she?" Catalina demanded.

"Her name's Tirisha," I explained. "I met her at an indie bookstore on my way to Asphodel General a few days ago. She was friendly and helped me find some paranormal books. She mentioned that to her, hell was a barren world made of ice. I was hoping to speak with her about that, but I never thought she'd actually confirm my wildest nightmares!"

Catalina was not amused by my gushing. "Okay, but answer me this: what the hell is Tenebris and Burngemear exactly?"

"Well, I think Burngemear is a grim reaper. He came to me when I was very little. I don't remember what he said to me at the time, but I knew the place we were in was called Tenebris. Hell, in other words. At least I think it is. It's an empty, cold realm where the air dries your skin and everywhere you look, the demons and the dead peek around cracked corners."

Catalina cringed. "Fuck. I hate creepy shit like that. I try not to think about what'll happen to me after all this is over. But...you make it sound like you've seen this place first-hand."

"I have. I don't know why I get transported there, but I do. Even when I don't want to. I hate it." My fists tightened until I felt my nails digging through the leather fabric. "But it's not like I can control whatever it is I'm doing. Or not doing."

I didn't mention that sometimes, I felt trapped. Like I was never going to return home. Never feel the sun warm my skin or touch the smooth, green leaves of my potted plants. The thought made me feel strangely claustrophobic.

We were silent as we walked toward the real entrance of the Candle Lounge, each of us lost in our own thoughts. Burngemear, I noticed, had moved to the roof of the building, growing larger and larger until he was the size of a blimp. That did not bode well at all.

When I finally stood in front of a green, rusted metal door, I paused. Sensing my dismal mood, Catalina placed a cool hand on my shoulder.

"Listen, Phani," Catalina began, brown gaze serious, "you're stronger than you think, so *never* underestimate yourself. That kind of thinking kills you faster than any knife wound. I believe you'll survive whatever situation you find yourself in, since it's you."

It took me a moment to shape my lips into a shy smile, warmth pooling in my chest. No one had ever said that to me before, and with such confidence. For once, I didn't feel like a crazy person. Someone was in my corner, convinced that I was able to handle myself just fine. I hadn't felt like that in a long time. Not many people thought I could navigate my issues with my sanity mostly intact. I've been treated with kid gloves or outright dismissed for most of my life so listening to Catalina's words was refreshing. She might not be aware of the impact her words had on me, but the pep talk meant a lot.

"Thanks," I said, ducking my head in embarrassment.

Catalina's toothy grin was boyish.

"Don't worry about it. Now enough emotional talk," she said brusquely, ruining the moment. "Our mission starts now."

XV.

SLEUTHING IS SUBTLETY

"Knock seven times, wait five seconds, then do it again," Catalina ordered.

Strange, but understandable considering the metal door didn't have any door knobs or handles in sight. After knocking, the entrance creaked open a fraction, halted by five security chains. A dwarf-sized man with a wicked dark beard appeared through the narrow opening. A cigar was tucked in between his chapped lips. The name Tino was tattooed in urban gangster font above his right brow. With slicked back hair, pressed slacks, and a gold chain round his neck, Tino looked the part of a shady bouncer of an equally shady establishment.

"Tino's here!" Catalina cried with a smile. "I was wondering where he disappeared to for the last couple of weeks. I thought Garcy had fired him."

Tino greeted me with a menacing stare as he puffed on his cigar and sized my inconsequential worth. Clearly, this was a man who could take care of a gang of hooligans by himself without much trouble.

"Who're you?" He spat.

"Like we practiced, Phani," Catalina reminded.

"Can't a girl get a decent drink around here?" I sighed dramatically, rolling my eyes. "Or are you gonna make me wait for my date out in this dirty alley?"

My words seemed to have the desired effect. Tino huffed in irritation before closing the door and unhooking the safety chains. This time he left the door wide open.

Entering, I noticed we were in a large antechamber made of dark polished wood. There was an archway up ahead, colorful shiny strands of beads blocking the view of the lounge area. Two large men sat by a table, poker cards and drinks in hand. They were obviously waiting for Tino to rejoin them. They didn't glance at me.

"You look too young for a drink," Tino remarked snidely as I walked past him.

My face remained neutral even as I blushed. I was thankful my dark olive skin made it difficult to show any cherry-colored cheeks. How could I forget I was underage? My twenty-first birthday was in February. I had less than half a year to go.

"I'm glad," I heard myself say. "If people didn't card me I'd throw a major bitch fest."

Oh god, what bull. Was Tino even buying this? How could anyone believe me? I looked like a chubby faced child playing dress up with her big sister's party clothes. To my surprise, despite Tino eyeing me like a rotten fish, he let my lie slip uncommented. He shook his head before walking away, flicking the ash from his cigar.

"Sign the guest book before you step inside," he muttered.

I smiled at my good fortune. I approached an old leather-bound ledger on a podium next to the archway. Catalina had explained earlier that it would be a good idea if I used a fake name. After much deliberation, I chose my current alias: Cora Greene. I even came up with a backstory for my arrogant, but ditzy character. When I mentioned it to Catalina, she had curled her lip in response before advising me to keep it to myself until someone asked. I suppose she had a point.

After signing the book, I parted the beaded curtain.

The Candle Lounge was a place I never thought I'd find myself in.

Granted, I never pictured myself dining at *Il Melograno* in Vanit Town either, but it's amazing the places I've been finding myself in a week after Catalina enlisted my help in finding her killer.

The smell of tobacco mingled with alcohol and savory spices. Coupled with smooth jazz music playing from the speakers, the entire atmosphere was easing my nerves. Musty shelves lined with old tomes, lit scarlet candles of cinnamon centered on wooden tables, carved paneled walls, and a ceiling filled with exposed rafters gave the entire establishment a colonial speakeasy vibe.

I wouldn't have minded coming here more often if the residual energy of spirits passed didn't linger like hardened paint—that, and if this place was anywhere other than South Coast. Traces of sorrow, fury, frustration, desperation, and resignation caused me to blink rapidly, my eyes watering with mixed emotions. It wasn't over-whelming to make me feel ill, but it was enough for me to feel uncomfortable and just a little depressed. I was glad there weren't any spirits with a solid form walking around.

"Garcy should be around here somewhere," Catalina remarked, hands on her hips. Despite inhaling the strong smell of whisky and Cuban cigars, I knew she couldn't really take it in. Her eyes didn't water at the smoky quality tingeing the air in a manner so thick it coated my tongue.

My heels audibly tapped against the hardwood floor. By the time I approached the polished counter of the bar, a burly bartender with slick hair faced me.

"What'll it be?"

"I'll just have water," I said. Then I remembered who I was supposed to be. "For now. I'm waiting for my date."

He raised a brow before silently turning away. I exhaled, taking a seat. Catalina plopped down on the bar stool next to me.

"Tell me again why you couldn't just sneak your way in and over-hear the gossip yourself?" I asked, fingers tapping the counter.

"Silly Phani. One doesn't gossip about the Underworld openly. If Garcy flaps her mouth to the wrong people, her head rolls."

I winced. "So how do I get her to talk to me?"

Plump red lips curled into a smirk. "Leave that to me."

Not like I had much of a choice. I was risking a lot by being here. I had to know I was in good hands, that there was a plan already in place, as well as contingencies for when the original and the backup plan failed. That's how worried I was.

After receiving my water, I retreated to an empty table near the back where a soy candle burned. It was an odd smell that mingled strangely with the tobacco and alcohol but wasn't entirely foul. I sipped my water and kept to myself as Catalina fluttered around before briefly disappearing through a wall.

I ignored the hazy spirits drifting in and out of existence near me, cooling the stuffy air inside. I shivered, missing my pea coat currently hanging in the antechamber. It didn't surprise me that a large concentration of spirits was anchored here. This place didn't exactly scream safety.

"So what does Garcy look like?" I whispered when Catalina returned.

"Short, stout woman. Blonde hair. Always wears red, as if she looked good in the color," Catalina snorted. "A bit of a social climber but knows her place in the Underworld, so she's harmless. Loves talking about everyone, though. Can't get her to shut up sometimes."

I nodded, swirling the ice in my glass.

"But that's not what I wanted to say," she continued. "I checked her office and it was empty. This is your chance to go in and see if there is any correspondence from the killer. Garcy wouldn't know it was from him, but we do. I'll cover for you."

Never mind that I was supposed to sneak into her office as if it were the simplest task in the world, but how was I supposed to know what an incriminating correspondence from Catalina's killer looked like? As it happened though, sneaking into her office was the least of my worries. In fact, it turned out to be downright anti-climactic.

Nearly all the employees were gathered in the conference room three doors down from where Garcy's office was. According to Catalina, the woman was screaming bloody murder at someone over the phone, furious that Tirisha had bailed on them last minute. This probably gave me five minutes tops to investigate.

Her office was a large room with dark green walls surrounded by sleepy Marilyn Monroe paintings and wooden bookcases skimming the ceiling. Picture frames of cats and a ten-year old girl with large round glasses dotted her desk. It would have been a quaint office if it hadn't been for the cluttered mess of bills, letters, binders, notebooks and empty wine glasses scattered around. The place was a pigsty and smelled like one too. I wrinkled my nose, appalled at the thought of me wading through the disorder.

Where do I even begin?

I ruffled through anything that looked like a correspondence. I even went so far as to use her laptop since she had it open to her email. Nothing suspicious. Though I did discover the woman to be a nasty piece of work with a vindictive streak.

She received an accusatory email from her ex-husband, claiming she had meddled and gotten him fired from his last job so she could have a better custody case for their daughter. She responded mockingly at first until he fired back with news that he'd found a better paying job with decent hours, thanking her highly for her interference. Garcy ended up calling the man every name in the sailor's handbook. After that drama, the only other thing of interest was the locked safe and I had no key or time to waste on it.

Hopefully there was only money and jewels stashed inside.

"*Niña!* Hurry up!" Catalina hissed from outside. "Sixty seconds!"

I panicked. In my haste to leave I ended up tripping on my heel. My hand caught the rim of the wastebasket near Garcy's desk and overturned it. I winced at the sudden impact of the floor, my chin and knees throbbing like crazy as the high arch of my shoes killed my feet. I'll never understand how women can stand to wear these things for so long.

To my chagrin, crumpled, torn pieces of papers spilled from the bulging wastebasket along with old pens and pencils, some snapped in half, a moldy brown banana peel, cigarette stubs, empty coffee cups, stiff French fries, and to my horror, a recently used condom.

"EW!" I squeaked, jumping far from the smelly debris.

"Forty seconds!"

I hastily scrapped the mess back inside the waste basket with a random manila folder—minus the condom, I kicked that aside—when a crumpled ball of paper caught my attention. It was stained with red splotches. Wine, I assumed. Hoped, really. I tossed the folder and picked the note up, flattening the torn paper enough to see smudged handwriting.

I WARNED

YOU WHAT WOULD

HAPPEN IF YOU TATTLED!

NOW YOUR A LOOSE END

"It's 'you're'," I corrected, pleased by my discovery. Bingo!

"Phani! Someone—"

I bolted from the room, completely forgetting about the overturned waste basket as I stuffed the note inside my bra. Running down the hall, Catalina's stranger danger warning came too late the minute I rounded the corner and collided into a warm body. Steady hands gripped my shoulders in an effort to prevent my fall. Looking up, a gasp rushed past my lips when I saw who was before me.

Blue-green eyes widened in equal shock.

"What are you doing here?" Charlie and I asked simultaneously.

"I'm here waiting for my date," I blurted.

"I'm here because—wait, date? What?"

Charlie seemed genuinely upset by this admission. I cringed, unable to believe the turn of events. Before I could correct myself or give him a better answer, a door hinge squeaked behind us.

In my panic, I dragged Charlie away from the back rooms. No one followed us. Once in the safety of the main lounge, I let him go. We sat at a small table in a dark corner away from the other patrons. A red cinnamon candle illuminated the small space.

"What was that?" Charlie asked, no longer disappointed but curious and amused. "And why are you wearing a wig? And a mask? What were you even doing back there?"

There was an upbeat quality to him today. He was a lot more animated than yesterday, less subdued. Was he carrying the Be-Gone bead I gave him the first time we met? I periodically reminded him to always carry it around. I hadn't noticed the shrieking spirit yesterday when I was with him so I hope he had indulged me.

Today he was dressed sharply in a black sleeveless blazer, a plum colored shirt, and dark slacks. His hair was still shaggy and wet as though it'd been recently washed. It looked good on him. Charlie looked good. I was suddenly self-conscious of my dress.

"I-I was looking for the restrooms. I got lost but I didn't want to bump into any employees and have them yell at me for thinking I was trespassing," I lied, bypassing the wig and mask part. "What about you?"

"My roommate woke me up at like, three in the morning, and wanted me to deliver a package later today to someone named Ms. Maroone," he said, gesturing to his backpack. "Normally I ignore him, but he gave me the bus fair and swore he'd pay me. Since I could use the extra money, I thought, why not?"

"Do you know what's inside?" I asked.

Charlie leaned forward, voice lowered. "That's the thing, it's just a punch of poppy flowers!"

"What? Seriously? Is he trying to woo her?" I laughed.

"I don't know but he's going about it oddly. Not to mention he's got strange taste in women. But it's free money so I'm not complaining too much," he said, shrugging. "Now the real question is, why are *you* here at the Candle Lounge? This place isn't somewhere I'd ever peg you visiting. And what's with the wig?"

Damn. "The wig is Idrina's. Thought I'd try something new."

"You mentioned a date?" he reminded me, brow arched.

I laughed nervously. Here comes the lying. I couldn't tell Charlie the obvious truth of why I was here but I also didn't want my cover story to ruin anything between us.

"To be honest, I'm not really on a date. I lied because the men here started hitting on me and it was the easiest way to let them know I'm not interested."

Charlie leaned back against his seat, shoulders lax. "Oh, that makes sense, but why are you here in the first place?"

Here's a truth I can toss. "I have a friend who's performing tonight so I came to see her. She said I should dress up since it's a fancy venue."

Charlie smiled. "Well, you look incredible, but this place isn't what I'd call fancy. Sure it looks that way, but it's just a seedy bar draped in aged finery frequented by thugs with money. If we were on our date, I would have taken you to Jack and Mina's by the Board-walk. It's a great eatery with a circus theme."

That did sound like fun. I returned his smile.

"Then we should make that our next date night."

Charlie grinned, excitement in his eyes. "Okay, how about right now?"

"Right now? Isn't it already late?"

He chuckled. "What do you mean? It's only five thirty."

Five thirty? Geez, I could have sworn it was later than that. To leave right now on a real date with Charlie would be a dream and something I would have agreed to in a heartbeat. But I was in the middle of an investigation and I had a strong feeling Catalina wouldn't let me leave once I told her I found a promising lead.

Speaking of, Catalina suddenly appeared behind Charlie, eyeing him curiously before giving me a thumbs-up. I exhaled in relief. Looks like no one noticed the break -in.

"Tell lover boy to beat it," she said. "We need to discuss what you found in Garcy's office."

Disappointment washed over me. I didn't want to reject Charlie's date offer, especially when I blew him off the last time through no fault of my own. But duty called

"I can't right now," I said, eyes downcast.

Charlie's face fell. "What? Why?"

"I–I'm seeing my friend perform tonight. I promised I'd be here. Why don't you join me instead? We can visit Jack and Mina's tomorrow," I offered.

Charlie frowned. "I'm not available tomorrow. Also we *really* shouldn't stay here. This place is dangerous."

"Well, I can't leave right now, I told you my friend is performing," I insisted, watching Catalina grow impatient behind Charlie's back.

"Who's your friend?" he asked.

How does one explain Tirisha Jordan exactly? Lucky for me, there was a flier on the table next to us. I got up and grabbed it, handing it to Charlie before pointing to the tall dark-skinned blonde smiling, one shiny shoulder exposed like the quintessential Hollywood starlet she was.

"Her. Tirisha Jordan. She was really excited when she got the gig and I've been looking forward to seeing her onstage."

Charlie wrinkled his nose. "Your friend's a he/she?"

Catalina gasped. I froze.

"What?" I said, blinking quickly.

"No offense, but it's weird when a man parades around as a woman. What's the appeal?"

I was speechless. A heaviness settled in my stomach.

"I remember going into the Gays Inn once and it was literally the most uncomfortable experience I've ever had," Charlie continued, flipping the flyer over. "Most of them didn't even look believable. It was like watching an ugly clown show. "

Catalina cackled behind him. "What an asshole! Have you ever seen anyone ruin their chances with a girl so quickly?"

I stood up abruptly. "I–I have to go."

Charlie also stood up as well, placing a hand over mine. "Wait! Come with me, don't stay here."

I jerked my hand away. "No! I'm not going with you! How could you say those mean things about my friend?"

"Wait, you're really upset?"

He seemed genuinely surprised. My eyes widened even more, head tilting forward a bit.

Seriously?

"Oh my god, he's an idiot," Catalina commented, rolling her eyes.

"You've just said a slew of offensive and cruel things about people different from you who've never done you any harm," I said, my face and ears suddenly hot. I couldn't even look at him. "I may not know a lot about the world, but even I know what you just said was appalling and unkind. And one of the things I hate most is ridiculing someone because their harmless lifestyle and interests differ from yours."

Whatever Charlie said next was drowned out by a sudden wailing. Next to Charlie's right materialized a cold gray mist that shaped itself into a feminine figure. I instantly knew it was the same spirit from the bus, the one that had been haunting him. She must have gathered quite the energy to reform and follow the man as a parasitic entity. When her face and frame became distinguishable, my eyes widened in horror.

Half her body was burned, her skin black and thin. It was flaky and charred, pale bone exposed in a few areas. She looked absolutely wrecked. Nausea whirled in my stomach. Four blinks later and the spirit's figure blurred, black skin disappearing until she looked the way she did before burning to death. The smell of cooked meat lingered. I resisted the urge to hurl.

Dark hair, creamy pale skin with thin features and a hook nose. She floated like a wilted flower, depressed, eyes droopy. There was a forlorn expression on her face as she stared at Charlie, her sobs thick as she moved around him. Her presence smothered the man, causing his eyes to tighten as he looked down, his lips moving. Was he still speaking? Was he still speaking to *me*?

Seeing the spirit haunting him brought forth another shard of betrayal. I know carrying around a wooden bead from a girl you just met is kind of unusual, but with the revelation of Charlie's transphobia, his disregard of what's important to me felt like a sucker punch to the gut. I couldn't handle being around him anymore.

"I have to go," I said, walking away from the table.

"Wait! Phani, please! At least let me call you a cab! South Coast isn't safe!"

"Go away!" I snapped. "I don't want to speak to you right now!"

"Phani!" Catalina hissed, pointing a finger to my left. "Garcy's here! She's heading towards the bathroom. Go after her now before she's gone! This is the perfect opportunity to corner her!"

I looked over to see if I could recognize the woman. I was partially relieved I wouldn't have to endure Charlie anymore. I felt him tug at my hand and turn me around.

"Charlie—"

"Listen, I can grovel later, but you need to leave here," he insisted, grabbing my other arm to face him, eyes pleading.

"Your transphobic lover boy is ruining our chances!" Catalina snarled, rounding on him. She zeroed in on the sniveling spirit peeking at us from behind him and took a menacing step forward. Her gloved fingers resembled talons as they struck like a cobra, grasping the spirit's arm.

I was surprised Catalina was able to touch her as though she were made of solid flesh. Was this something spirits could do with each other? Another thing to add to Catalina's list of quirks.

"*Vete!* Go! 'Ain't nobody wants you here!"

"I'm sorry!" The weepy spirit sobbed. "It's all my fault!"

The girl spared Charlie a quick glance before the threat of Catalina's anger made her disappear. Charlie blinked several times, aware that the poisonous cloud of heaviness the girl had carried around him was suddenly gone. But honestly, I didn't care anymore.

I took the distraction and shook him off me.

"Phani!"

"I don't want to see you!" I yelled, running away and losing him in the growing crowd. They obviously hadn't heard that Tirisha was no longer performing tonight.

"Wait!" Charlie called, struggling to get through.

I twisted and turned through the throng of regulars until I saw the women's restroom at the very back. I ducked inside, heart pounding a mile a minute. Had Charlie followed?

When I opened the door a tiny bit, there wasn't any sign of him as far as I could see. I exhaled in relief before closing the door and resting my forehead against the tiled wall. I gave myself a minute to calm down. To breathe in and out, and just empty my mind of anything Charlie related, including my feelings for him. Now was not the time to cry about it. I could do that when I got home.

A few minutes later, once I was sure I could concentrate on my mission, I turned around and surveyed my surroundings.

The Candle Lounge restrooms were small but neat with beige tiles, red wine stalls, and fluffy folded towels stacked on a shelf near the sink. Cinnamon and jasmine mingled pleasantly in the air. I nodded my approval.

There was a small closed window across the room, located near the ceiling. Outside, the sky continued to darken.

There was a disgruntled-looking woman standing in front of one of the sinks. It took me a few seconds to realize how scarily accurate Catalina's description was.

Garcy Maroone, proprietress of The Candle Lounge, was indeed a stout woman with short, voluminous blonde hair styled in the 50's Victory roll. A scowl graced her scarlet lips, which only served to pronounce her jowls and match the glittering earrings she wore. At least she knew how to color coordinate.

I swallowed, suddenly nervous about asking this woman anything. She may look harmless, but I had a strong feeling she could easily gut me without chipping a nail.

Catalina phased through the door right then.

"Love boy is gone. Dropped off his stupid package before he ran out of here like a coward—there she is! Say something! Interrogate her!" Catalina hissed in my ear.

My mouth remained shut.

Garcy muttered curses as she dabbed at a wet stain on her skirt. She must have spilled her drink. At least, I hope that was the case. For some reason, seeing her struggle with something so ordinary made me feel a little braver.

"Do you need any help?" I asked.

Her blue gaze flickered in my direction before dismissing me.

"Go away." Her voice was a chain-smoker personified.

"Remember what I said," Catalina reminded me.

I had a feeling I was going to get shot for this. I turned and grabbed hold of the door handle. The click of the lock was audible. It was swiftly followed by another distinct click.

This one from a gun.

"What the fuck do you think you're doing, kid?"

XVI.

PARTY POSSESSIONS

I RAISED my hands and slowly turned around.

Garcy held a small hand-gun in her chubby grip. Its silver round muzzle pointed at me without hesitation. Where had she kept that thing? Her outfit was so skin tight!

"I just want to talk," I said. "Honest. I'm not armed."

"Like hell! Why shouldn't I blow your brains out right here, right now?" She had a strong southern accent made of fresh home-made apple pies and ice-cold lemonade.

I glanced at Catalina, awaiting her signal. Once she gave me the go ahead I took a deep breath before exhaling all the uncertainty away. Time for Cora Greene, undercover interrogator extraordinaire who's been stood up by her transphobic date—God that still hurts— to come out and play.

"I come on behalf of La Patrona," I began. "She has unresolved business and wants the usual from you."

Garcy's face was stoic at first. When she saw I wasn't laughing, she gawked. Incredulity shined from between her spider lashes.

"Do you think I'm stupid? Patrona's dead!"

"Maybe. But you know she never leaves loose ends, Ms.

Maroone." I leaned against the door, feeling surprisingly relaxed despite the threat of her gun. Catalina looked on in approval.

"So? Who are you?"

"Call me Cora. I'm here because La Patrona wants to know the gossip on the state of the Underworld."

"Fuck this shit!"

She pulled the trigger. I couldn't even blink.

The gunshot sounded obscenely loud in the small room. The bullet should have killed me, or at least, injured me in some way. Instead, it simply fell at my feet with a clink, the tip dented. I touched my chest, expecting to find a bloody hole. My skin felt dry and smooth. Clean and intact.

Holy shit, that really just happened!

Garcy's gaze widened in horror. Catalina doubled over laughing.

"She can't believe it! Oh, they never do at first."

I tugged at the scarf around my neck and flashed Garcy Catalina's infamous gold choker. The smaller woman gasped, her gun dropping with a loud clatter as she backed away in haste.

"The choker! That's Catalina's!"

"Answer the question. What's brewing in the underworld?"

"T-There's not much happening. It's the same as usual."

Catalina scoffed. "Not with my death. Tell this bitch to spill the good shit. Mention Erebus. She fears him."

"Catalina was working on something important before she died. In fact, she was going to meet Erebus prior to her death," I said. Garcy's breathing quickened. "He's investigating her ill timed demise, you know. He's very angry."

"I don't know anything about Catalina getting killed!" Garcy cried. "I swear I don't!"

My brow arched. I was getting the sense she knew a lot more than she let on. Garcy shifted from foot to foot, uncomfortable with the change in power dynamics.

"Listen, there's a lot that's been going on. I've been hearing strange rumors," she finally said.

"Rumors?"

"Of an uprising."

"Uprising?" Catalina echoed. "Against Erebus? That's insane!"

"That's suicide," I said.

"I never said it was a smart move," Garcy admitted, wiping her sweaty palms against her scarlet dress. "It's just the vibe my feelers have been picking up. Erebus already knows about it."

"There's got to be something more suspicious," I murmured, placing a curved finger against my chin.

Garcy arched her own brow. "This is a suspicious town, hun. You're gonna have to be a little more specific than that."

I frowned. If the Candle Lounge was truly a wolf in sheep's clothing, a go-to for anyone who needed to hire a hitman, then it's more than likely the killer would have passed through here at least once. But if he had passed through, what would he have gotten from here? Was it just the drinks at the bar?

"Information," Catalina declared suddenly, pacing. "I'm almost positive the killer came here to get information. But asking about me, my weakness, whatever, it would be too obvious and Erebus keeps tabs on people asking around after the organization. Garcy's supposed to report on anyone inquiring, even if it's meaningless gossip."

I nodded. Then if the killer was trying to seek information that wasn't on Catalina specifically, what was he here inquiring about?

I thought back to the killer, to him offing Catalina. The whole ordeal came off as hastily executed in my mind, what with the killer going back to kill Mr. Shern. If Mr. Shern was a loose end the killer needed gone, then he had been actively scoping Orpheus Theater because he knew Catalina would show up. So the showdown had to be there. The first attempt failed, probably knew it would and thus lured her to the trap in the warehouse. It was a very determined attempt especially when Catalina wasn't an easy opponent. She was meeting Erebus that night to speak to him about something she had discovered. Catalina still wouldn't say what it was she found but she had mentioned that Erebus would have most likely ordered her to Fetch and Eradicate.

When I had asked her what Fetch and Eradicate meant, Catalina ominously implied that she acted as both a blood hound and executioner.

Could the killer have known what Erebus was going to order her to do? Did he kill her to stop her from officially hunting down whatever needed hunting down? That wouldn't stop Erebus from making someone *else* investigate and hunt down whatever needed hunting down though. At most, the killer just bought himself time. But for what?

I thought back to the note I'd found in Garcy's wastebasket and the angry words slashed onto the paper with scary and desperate force. I wonder if I was going about this from the wrong —wait.

Desperation!

That's what this reeked of. I always thought the killer going after Catalina to prevent her from getting her assignment was a bold and desperate move. Maybe I could work off that.

I crossed my arms and relaxed my shoulders.

"Tell me, Ms. Maroone, has anyone come to you asking for any gossip, but reeking of desperation? As if whatever you had to say was their last resort?"

Garcy blinked. "Desperation? That'd be a stupid way to get anything from me. I hate the desperate. They're so embarrassing." But she paused, as if recalling a far-off memory. "Well, there was this guy a few months ago, actually. I near had to kick him out of here. I couldn't stand looking at him, so pitiful. But it didn't have anything to do with Erebus or La Patrona. All he wanted—no, *demanded*—was to know any and all information I had on Thanatos. Claimed to be working on Erebus's behalf. Showed the credentials and everything, so I told him."

Erebus's men had credentials? Shaking that inconsequential thought aside, I decided to roll with Garcy's confession, which sadly wasn't much. I had been hoping for someone asking around after Erebus or Catalina, not their mortal enemy Thanatos.

"What did you tell him?"

"Well, there were obviously a few Thanatos stragglers around at the time. The last man I knew lived downtown, dated an old server of mine I ended up firing. That was a year ago, though. I thought they had all gone extinct, but a month ago, I came across my old server's *roommate.* She told me the two were living well somewhere. I thought the whole thing odd considering Erebus's 'Kill Thanatos Supporters' order was still in full effect. I admitted all this to the guy when he asked."

"Who was the guy? What did he look like?"

Garcy shrugged. "I don't know, it's been a while. Didn't give me a name. He was tall maybe, clean looking, short hair, white."

I blinked. That could be literally any white male.

"Okay, well, do you remember how old he was?"

"I don't know. Maybe twenties, early thirties? He had facial hair."

Well, at least it was something more substantial than tall and clean-looking. Not that this guy was the killer. In fact, associating him to Catalina's murder was a stretch without some link or proof to tie him to the scene of the crime. But that note I found...

Something told me the killer was the one who'd written it. Maybe the guy who had inquired after Thanatos was involved in this mess somehow. Or maybe I was just seeking a connection where there was none.

I tapped my chin in frustration. I was running out of ideas and Garcy was becoming dangerously bored. It wouldn't be long before she ceased humoring me. I took one more shot in the dark.

"Have you seen Erebus recently?"

"Just the other day. He wanted to know if anyone had put out a flier for a hitman in the last three years. I gave him the list."

Interesting. I pulled out the crumpled note I had taken from her wastebasket and held it up. Garcy paled, her jowls bouncing as she swallowed.

"W-Where did you—"

"Do you know what this is about?"

"Were *you* the one who made a mess in my office?"

"When did you receive this?" I repeated.

"You little bitch!" Garcy bent and picked up her gun. "Today, okay? But it's nothing special. I get death threats all the time. In fact, that one's tame in comparison to—"

Crossing her arms, Catalina ignored Garcy's rambling and paced again.

"Before dying, I was investigating a few rumors I had picked up as well. It wasn't the uprising, but the supposed turncoat hiding within Erebus's Upper Circle," she said.

"Turncoat?" I looked at her, taken aback. Was that what Catalina had been about to report to Erebus before her murder? That would have been useful to know ages ago!

"It's underworld business," she said, shrugging. "It's still ongoing, last I knew."

"That's still important for me to have known from the beginning. What if that has a connection to your killer?"

"I didn't think it did before, but maybe it does now."

"Please don't keep things from me anymore if you want this investigation to continue," I warned her, crossing my arms tightly. Catalina raised a brow in response.

"Oh my, what a spine!"

"I'm just saying. It's courtesy and if you keep being all 'mums the word' then what am I even doing here? Finding your killer is already difficult. Please don't make it harder. "

Catalina rolled her eyes. "Fine. I won't keep things from you anymore. Happy?"

"God, you're so insufferable sometimes," I snapped, "I'm just trying to help."

Catalina whirled on me. "You're doing this for the money, not because you want to help."

"Well, yeah! I'm not doing this for my health! I want to do this right so we can find the killer, it's the least I can do for sticking my neck out for you. I could have just kept searching for a job like a normal person!"

"You mean, *failing* at getting a job like a normal person? How many applications have you put in already? Thirty? Have you heard back from any of them?" she smirked, tossing her hair from her shoulder.

My cheeks burned. "God, you're such a *bitch*!"

Catalina laughed. "What was your first clue? Is today your first time meeting me?"

"*I'm sorry,* but *who the fuck* are you talking to?" Garcy snapped, bringing my attention back to her. I noticed the gun was back in her pudgy grip.

Blame it on recklessness, frustration, anger at Catalina or the lingering adrenaline from surviving the bullet earlier, but whatever was the cause, it made me do the craziest thing. With a straight face, I pointed at Catalina.

"I'm arguing with La Patrona's ghost. *Do you mind?*"

Garcy blinked several times, causing Catalina to snicker. I tried holding off my own amusement, but it was no use. The giggle came out. Insulted, Garcy's face turned an ugly shade of purple.

"You may have Catalina's necklace, but you're just a dumb, crazy bitch," she spat. "This stupid interrogation is over! Now get the fuck out of my lounge this instant before I have Tino *stab* you instead!"

She stormed past me, unlocking the door before slamming it closed. I exhaled a shaky breath before touching the cold gold around my throat. At least Garcy hadn't tried shooting at me again. That's one experience I could live my life without.

"Did you get what you wanted?" I asked Catalina.

"We got a bunch of puzzle pieces, but no way to fit them together just yet."

I sighed, walking to where I dropped the scarf and wrapping it around my neck, hiding Catalina's choker once more. My hand hovered over the fabric.

"Listen," I began. "I'm sorry I got short with you. I'm just...filled with a lot of disappointment and betrayal right now."

Catalina eyed me, one brow arched. She gave it a minute before grudgingly nodding her head.

"You're also right, you know," she said. "I should have laid every-thing out on the table from the beginning. I should have known better than to believe we could solve this mystery with only the need to know facts."

For real. A turncoat added to the mystery could have given me another angle to work on.

"Why are you still adhering to the rules in Erebus when you don't even work there anymore?"

Catalina hesitated, which was a first for me to see.

"I just...I made Erebus my entire life," she began, "and I don't regret it. I should because we have done some shifty things, but I don't. I loved my life there and even though I'm dead, I still feel fiercely loyal. Maybe it's stupid and I'm a sucker for dedicating every-thing to a crime syndicate that can replace me, but I know who I am and I'll never regret serving anyone I feel deserves my loyalty."

I blinked, awed by the intensity and sincerity in her caramel gaze. To have such conviction, such devotion to a purpose bigger than yourself, even if it was flawed; while worrisome in one aspect, it was reassuring in another. I want to have that kind of confidence in my choices going forward.

"Anyways, let's bounce before Garcy turns Tino on us," Catalina suggested, gesturing to the door. "We can figure out the pieces when we get to your place."

Just as I opened the bathroom door, a group of men poured through the beaded curtain by the front, entering the lounge and effectively blocking the exit. They wore dark sunglasses and shabby black suits with teal accents. They kept looking around as if in search for someone.

The patrons of the lounge looked uneasy. The whispers behind their hands and drinks grew louder the longer the men remained where they were, immovable as boulders. One brave soul tried going around them. He got punched in the face for his trouble, crashing to the floor like a bag of marbles.

"Who are those guys?" I whispered.

Catalina phased through the door, impatient at my hold up. One look at the men and she froze. She staggered back as if slapped, gasping.

"*No, no, no, no puede ser*. It can't be!" She whispered, patting her hips for a gun only to realize she didn't have one anymore. Not that it would do her any good.

"What? What's wrong?" I asked.

"Get inside! Lock the bathroom!" She ordered just as Garcy emerged from a doorway behind the bar.

She scowled at Tino and the bartender, probably annoyed with them for having fetched her. The second her beady eyes spotted the strange men, however, she let loose a pig-like squeal. Garcy reached for her tiny gun, but the men were faster.

One of them brandished a hidden semi-automatic and shot Garcy Maroone, ten-year proprietress of Asphodel City's Candle Lounge, right in the face.

The mirror behind the bar shattered when the bullet drilled through her skull, coating the prepping station in a spotted layer of red. Garcy jerked back from the recoil, sending glasses and bottles of alcohol crashing when her body fell.

Someone screamed.

I slammed the door shut just as the chaos began. Screams, glass breaking, overthrown furniture, and a heavy rumble of footsteps pounded against the wooden floor. More shots were fired in rapid succession. It was clear those men didn't want anyone making it out alive.

Jazz music continued to play undisturbed in the background.

Hyperventilating and sweating like a can of sardines trapped in a sauna, I locked the restroom door before turning around. I searched frantically for a place to hide.

"Catalina, who are those men?" I demanded, inspecting the stalls. "Why are they killing everyone outside?"

This was the last thing I thought would happen. I should have just left the minute I was done with Garcy because this was insanity! Oh God, what if Charlie was out there bleeding to death? Sure he turned out to be disappointing, but I didn't want him dead!

Catalina bit her nail, her gaze flickering between the door and me. Even she had no clue how to help me out of this predicament.

"They're Thanatos's men," she explained. "He's the only one with enough balls to attack an establishment protected under Erebus's name. No, don't go for the stalls!"

Shit! The towel hamper looked big enough to hide me though. I ran for it. Before I even took three steps, the bathroom lock was shot. I cringed at the sound. Ten seconds later and the intruders kicked the door open with little difficulty. Three men came swarming in, guns blazing. I froze before slowly raising my hands, conscious of Catalina's presence behind me.

"Don't scream. They'll kill you faster," she said, her ghostly hand hovering over my shoulder. "You have my choker on so that'll protect you from the bullets. At the first opportunity, make a run for it, okay?"

Easier said than done. I hated feeling so helpless. While I was starting to understand I couldn't be shot dead, that didn't mean they couldn't cause pain using other means. It would be all too easy for them to harm me since I wasn't a hand-to-hand fighting expert. However, if they shot me and I went down acting dead, I could make it out of this alive.

"Hey, this one looks young," one of the men whispered to the others. "She's got blonde hair, dark skin, and moles on her face."

I grimaced.

"Boss said to take a girl fitting that description alive," someone replied.

What? Me? Why? Warning bells started ringing in my head.

Just as I took a fearful step back, the men lunged at me. Startled, my hand jerked and grabbed Catalina's arm. I don't know why I bothered since she couldn't do anything to help me out.

But...that's when the weirdest, most extraordinary thing happened.

As soon as my fingers touched her ghostly skin, Catalina was gone, sucked into me with a vacuum-like force. The wood earring studs I wore grew hot, almost burning the skin of my ear lobes. To my surprise, panic and blinding terror didn't seize me like I expected.

Instead I felt...aloof, detached from reality. As if I were in a trance. As if nothing could touch me. Which was ironic seeing as the three men tackled me soon after. They grabbed my arms and bent them behind my back before shoving my head down and aiming their guns at me.

I wanted to cry. I wanted to burst into tears and plead for my life because while it wasn't anything special, it was still mine and I didn't want to die.

But instead of sobbing and blubbering like an unattractive mess, I could feel myself looking up with dry eyes. Hysteria was absent, so was panic, fear. I was unbothered by the frenzy happening outside my consciousness. It was almost like I was drugged.

Time seemed suspended as aloofness morphed into shock. Tinnitus sounded in my ears between my ragged puffs of breath and the loud beating of my heart. My vision went in and out of focus. Fingers twitched before clenching and unclenching.

Shock gave way to confusion now as my captors suddenly came into sharp focus. I could see the oily pores on their shiny faces, the linty rough texture of their dark suits, the sticking smell of cigarettes and alcohol as their muffled voices finally registered. The sensation was jarring.

Why was everything so... heightened?

I blinked a few times, the sound of my thudding heart slowing until it flat-lined. When the high-pitched noise faded away into noth-ingness, I knew something was different. I was different.

My lips curved into a sudden smirk. Thrill coursed through my veins like an engine revving from zero to sixty.

I was ready. But for what?

"Hey! We found the girl!"

They dragged me into the lounge where the others stood. Some-where along the way, my wig got lost in the shuffle.

Death hung heavy in the air. Bodies littered the floor in puddles of varying amounts of blood. The scent of iron and salt was suffocat-ing, causing a nausea so strong I nearly hurled.

"The Mexican one?" one of them asked.

Ignorant swine! I thought angrily, the sudden urge to cause them so much pain flaring like a wildfire. I blinked, spooked by the abrupt craving for violence. Where had that come from?

The man with peach fuzz on his chin smiled. "If we tell the boss she got caught in the crossfire, do you think we could sell her behind his back?"

"Wouldn't he want to see her body for himself?"

"We could say she ran away. I know a guy who could fetch us a good price—"

"Have you any idea what you imbeciles have done?" I interrupted, my voice husky. Angry. "Why are you doing this? Why did you kill Garcy? This is Erebus territory! When he finds out what you did, he'll hunt you down and sever your heads."

That's when it hit me. I wasn't really saying that. I would never say that and in a tone filled with so much rage. I knew of one person who would though.

"Shut up before I break your face, bitch."

A throaty laugh emerged in response. If I wasn't so shocked that Catalina had possessed my body, I would have been impressed that I was capable of producing such a provocative sound.

The man holding me down twisted my arm further until the pain became unbearable. He whispered directly into my ear.

"What's so funny?"

Oh god, that hurt! Catalina, do something already!

"*Caballeros*. Gentlemen," I heard myself croon. "Your sense of humor is atrocious."

And then it happened.

Catalina slammed my head against my captor's nose in a sickening crunch. He howled in pain and dropped me like a hot potato to nurse the damaged cartilage. My head throbbed, but that didn't deter Catalina. My fingers, quick as a flash, jabbed the eye socket of the next guy. A squirting sound reached my ears as warm blood soaked the leather of my gloves. Catalina withdrew my fingers, causing the man's ruined eyeball to pop out.

If I could, I would have fainted straight away.

The men reacted. They fired five shots. One in my cheek, two in the chest, one in my stomach, and the other missing me by a mile. Despite feeling like stabs, they never penetrated skin. Catalina laughed, finding their antics adorable as the bullets ricocheted.

"You boys *must* do better to thrill me," she said behind stained fingers. She tugged away the scarf hiding her choker. It winked in the light.

Catalina lunged forward and delivered a high kick right across the jaw of my closest assailant. The others stared dumbfounded at the impossible miracle—I was half-horrified and half-awed myself. She grabbed the next man before whirling around and throwing him over my shoulder. He landed on the guy whose nose she'd broken, both of them crashing down like stone pillars. The move caused a burning ache in my arms to flare up. Catalina cursed at the pain.

"If I had my old body, this would have been cake," Catalina hissed. "Time for plan B."

The next man received a kick in the crotch with the toe of my boot. He stumbled. Catalina grabbed the top of his head and jaw before twisting it.

Crack. He fell.

I screamed. It was soundless, heard only in my mind. Bile rose, but it didn't slow Catalina down.

"Calm down, Phani," Catalina ordered. "One distraction from you and it could cost us everything."

Easier said than done considering she just used my hands to KILL A MAN.

Someone came from behind and grabbed me around the waist. They lifted me up, trapping my arms. Catalina laughed.

She stabbed the man's kneecap with my heel. His grip loosened slightly. She grabbed his pinky and pulled it back all the way, stabbing the other kneecap for good measure. He let go.

Catalina twirled in the loose grip of his arms before grabbing his head and smashing it down on my knee. She ignored the bullets ricocheting off my back and swiped the gun from our attacker's holster. A smirk formed. Catalina whirled around and pulled the trigger six times.

I could say with confidence that *this* was the very last thing I expected to happen today. I had never been possessed before. Nor had the intruding spirit saved my skin in a fight against rival mobsters. I know I should be grateful towards Catalina for taking the wheel here, but my senses were too overwhelmed. And I still couldn't get over the fact that *I have been possessed by a ghost!*

Nearly psyching myself out, I blinked and realized the fight was over. The Thanatos men were down, bearing neat bullet holes in their throats. This time I was able to gag audibly. I moved my limbs however I wanted and exhaled heavily when I realized I was now in possession of my body. But where was Catalina? She wasn't beside me or anywhere visible.

I'm still inside you, but you were freaking out so much you took over, she said from somewhere in my head. If I wasn't still freaking out, I would have laughed that at long last I was finally hearing voices in my head like my psychotherapist was convinced I did in secret.

I took gulping breaths as tears pricked my eyes. By the miracle of God and whatever supernatural force made it possible for Catalina to possess me, we made it.

We were safe. I was safe.

The Candle Lounge resembled a macabre butterfly garden with its kaleidoscope of glowing butterflies emerging from bullet riddled bodies like old cocoons. They flew about in a jumbled frenzy, emitting faint jingling noises and high-pitched sighs. One such butterfly soul phased through my chest, warming it considerably for a brief moment before the feeling faded away.

Before I had a chance to gather my mental faculties and examine what the fuck happened exactly, there was a brutal pounding on the bolted front door.

There's more!

Every bang came close to knocking the door off its hinges. I estimated I had about thirty seconds before whoever it was got through and I'd be forced to fight them again.

And I did not want to fight them again. My psyche wouldn't be able to take it a second time.

We have to get out of here. Your body's too weak to do much else, Catalina said as I dashed inside the restroom. The door closed behind us just as the sound of a soda can exploding came from the front door.

I spotted the small window near the ceiling and wasted no time hopping onto the sink. I opened the window with ease once the lock was unlatched. I hesitated when I realized I would have to jump up and squeeze through. I was not physically talented for all that.

Catalina, I'm going to need you for this.

On it, she said, wasting no time in possessing my limbs. Ignoring the ache in my arms, Catalina jumped and grabbed hold of the smooth ledge, slipping through the small opening with ease like an experienced gymnast. For once, I was glad my body was small enough to fit.

The bathroom door slammed open just as my leg went through the window. Catalina swung the rest of my body down with no injury into the empty alley below us. We were outside The Candle Lounge now, on the opposite side of the building's entrance.

As we ran towards the open street away from the Lounge, we found more men dressed in black huddled by the mouth of the alley on the opposite end. They were heavily preoccupied by the commotion inside. We ducked behind an empty car.

Black smoke surrounded The Candle Lounge as though it were burning. It sucked out all the warmth from the wind. I shivered, spotting Burngemear still looming over the building, glowing souls floating around him like restless fireflies.

Through the smoky haze, the Lounge sign glowed. The flame light had gone out, making it seem as though the candle had been extinguished.

I was so focused on this inconsequential detail that I didn't hear the footsteps behind me until it was too late.

"Move and I shoot."

Catalina and I froze, not because of the threat issued, but because of the voice that uttered it. We both recognized that voice.

His voice. Aedes's voice.

Then another strange thing happened—which considering all that transpired in the last fifteen minutes was saying something.

I had no clue how she did it, but Catalina separated herself from me. My body felt weightless for a single moment. Light as a feather, as if submerged in zero gravity. Then, I fell and crashed into the front seat of reality, completely in control of myself once again.

"Darling!" Catalina cried.

Her voice had never sounded so jubilant before. That singular word conveyed her beliefs, feelings, and convictions.

I whirled around, fear seizing me as Catalina rushed to Aedes's side. Four men dressed in black suits with purple accents on their blazers surrounded me, guns drawn.

Gray eyes narrowed balefully when he stepped forward. The hand holding his gun dropped just as he stopped an arm's length away.

"Phani, this is Darling!" Catalina announced with a bright grin. "I didn't think he'd get here before Tundra! We're saved!"

My tongue felt dry against the roof of my mouth. I swallowed the lump in my throat. I had not forgotten Aedes's warning about interfering in underworld business. Nor did he, by the looks of it. The temperature outside matched his mood.

Aedes tutted before eyeing The Candle Lounge, his men securing the perimeter against any remaining threats. There were black cars parked haphazardly everywhere, blocking the street. The familiar Rolls Royce that had stalked me days before was among them. How had I not noticed it before?

"Oh, Miss Phani," he sighed, shaking his head.

I didn't see the blow that came to my temple and knocked me out.

XVII.

TWO IS COMPANY, THREE IS A HAUNT

My vision was a blurry mess when I finally regained consciousness.

My temple throbbed and my neck ached the moment I reoriented myself. Brine, mildew, and rusted iron overwhelmed my nose when I took a deep breath. After blinking several times, my vision cleared. That's when I noticed the cavernous gray metal walls and cement floor beneath my heels. From afar, I could hear screeching seagulls and waves crashing against the shore. That explained the salty tinge to the air.

Where was I?

When I tried moving my arms, I discovered they were tied to the handles of a metal chair. I frowned.

I was tied to a chair. Kidnapped. Again.

I sighed.

An empty chair sat across from me, fueling my unease. One quick glance around told me I was alone. Catalina was nowhere in sight.

"Oh boy," I mumbled, pulling at the thick ropes trapping my wrists. They weren't being careless this time around apparently. As I struggled, a series of footfalls echoed from behind. I froze. The sound became louder as it neared. What made the suspense worse was that I knew who it was.

"Good, you're awake."

Aedes walked into view.

He was dressed in pressed slacks and an oversized leather coat. Making himself comfy in the chair across from me, I noticed that his charming personality with its ready smiles was gone. Instead, a poker face that could make a grown man sweat bullets took its place.

Catalina suddenly manifested next to Aedes, face apprehensive as she eyed her precious Darling. When her gaze found mine, she smiled weakly. I wasn't reassured in the least. I knew then this confrontation was going to be an uncomfortable one, at least for me.

"Miss Phani," Aedes began. "Didn't think I'd see you so soon. Tell me, what brought you to The Candle Lounge today? You're much too young and *innocent*—" The word hung from his tongue like a sarcastic phrase. "— to be hanging around a suspicious place like that."

I swallowed. "I wanted to hear some jazz music?"

Aedes raised an inquisitive brow as if seeming to say "try again".

"Just tell him the truth," Catalina warned. "He's not stupid. He knows the cover story is a lie."

"I was looking for Garcy," I corrected.

"Garcy? What business did you have with her?"

"I-I just had to ask her a few questions. On behalf of a...friend."

"Well I hope you had a chance to ask her your questions," he said, "because she's dead now."

I avoided his intense gaze like a coward.

"But you already knew that didn't you, Miss Phani?" He rearranged himself on the chair, leaning on one side with his legs crossed. "We were tipped about a possible shooting by an anonymous source. Unfortunately, we were unable to prevent it in time."

"The absolute nerve!" Catalina snapped. "And in Erebus territory too!"

Aedes glanced at his watch. "I was expecting to find the perpetrators, you see. But to my surprise, I found you there instead. One of the remaining few alive and the only one with fingers coated in the blood of her victims."

I looked at my hands and found the gloves still on. They were stiff with dry blood staining the fingertips. Memories of what happened flashed through my mind. I suppressed the urge to hurl and shake uncontrollably as I recalled the violence my hands caused. My skin crawled. I wanted to scream.

Ghosts were one thing, but gore was another. I may have been desensitized to the former, but the latter came to an extent. Fresh gore I caused myself was enough to certainly push me to the edge. I understood what Catalina had done was necessary; my life had been in danger and there was no other way—but holy fuck, a word of warning would have been nice. The violence, on top of the possession, had taken its toll on me both mentally and physically.

Catalina stared at me in apology, drifting close to place a ghostly hand over my own. Her touch was glacial. I shivered.

"As I watched the cameras," Aedes continued, "it was clear to me that The Candle Lounge's heroine was you."

"Um, thank—"

I stopped speaking when I saw him pull out a semi-automatic; a dark gleaming creature of cool metal that stared into my soul with a frightening intensity. An unforgiving silencer. Dread crept up my spine when the barrel was aimed at my forehead.

Catalina gasped before whirling around and berating Aedes in harsh Spanish for his callous treatment. But of course, Aedes couldn't hear her. He had eyes only for me and he wasn't smiling.

I tried to swallow but the frozen terror dried my throat.

"But," Aedes added, "I suspect you're hiding something from me. Any sane person with anything to lose wouldn't get involved in the Underworld, especially after I've warned them off. So, here's what I think. Maybe you're just a stubborn civilian who doesn't listen to good advice to save her life. Or you're a spy working for Thanatos."

"Deny it!" Catalina exclaimed. "Don't ever say you're an enemy. He'll shoot you otherwise! Darling has ways of getting information out of spies without interrogating them."

"How charming," I replied faintly before realizing I had spoken aloud. "I—I mean, I'm not a spy! Really!"

"Oh? Then how did you get this?"

From a hidden coat pocket, Aedes pulled out Catalina's gleaming choker. I gasped, suddenly conscious of the fact that my throat was bare. I felt almost naked without its heavy protection.

"That's—"

"La Patrona's," Aedes interrupted, his expression darkening into a glower. "I gave it to her as a gift for her *quinceañera*. Last time I saw it was the morning of the day she was killed. She's never taken it off once in the last thirteen years and it was the only thing missing from her body. How in the fucking hell did you come upon this?"

"The janitor Mr. Shern found it and fixed it up. He thought it was a stage prop. After he got killed, I took it."

And that was when I realized I messed up big time. Aedes stood up, eyes blazing.

"You took it? Did you know it was Catalina's?"

He was so angry that he had unintentionally let slip La Patrona's real name. Unable to watch the train wreck, Catalina covered her eyes and turned away. If she didn't know what to say to him, then I was screwed. No matter what I came up with, truth or lie, it would paint me in a suspicious light and Aedes looked like he was ready to pull the trigger and feed my corpse to a swarm of crocodiles.

I closed my eyes in fear. "Yes, but I swear I'm not a spy!"

Aedes sighed. "You're right."

Catalina and I snapped our eyes open to look at him. One hand scratched the back of his head while the other still held the gun pointed at me, arm steady. The action defied Aedes's accepting expression.

If it was possible for Catalina to become pale, she would have right then and there.

"Phani. Darling has that expression that could kill angels," she whispered, backing away.

What? Oh God. Her fear only heightened mine and it was the last thing I needed.

"You're not a Thanatos spy. I see that now. I conducted my own investigation this past week, looking for Patrona's killer. I've discovered, to my shock and shame, that there had been a turncoat hidden in the upper circle. This was what La Patrona had been about to reveal to Erebus in Orpheus Theater."

Catalina nodded. "Intelligent as always. I knew he'd discover it before the week was out."

Not the time to be singing his praises, I thought hysterically.

"It was her loyalty and my betrayal that killed her." Catalina protested that he had nothing to do with her death, but Aedes continued, oblivious to her presence. "I had the turncoat interrogated this morning before gutting him and cutting his corpse into pieces. After which he was buried in cement. Would you like to know what he said before he died? Turns out he was working with Catalina's killer. He was the one who overheard a private conversation between me and her about her choker's weakness, he was the one who gave away the meeting's existence, and it was he who also told the killer of Catalina's weakness. They knew once Catalina was given the Fetch and Eradicate order, they'd both be dead within twenty-four hours. So you see Phani, you aren't the spy—"

I sighed in relief.

"—you're just her murderer."

What?

"No!" I cried, struggling in my bonds. Aedes brought the muzzle close enough to kiss my cheek. "I swear I didn't kill Catalina! I was just helping her! I don't own a gun! I don't even know how to use one!"

Aedes chuckled softly. "The dead men at the Lounge beg to differ, sweetheart."

Ah, shit. "B-But I'm serious! I know how that looks, but I swear it wasn't me!"

"Prove it then."

His voice was hard and unforgiving, like sharpened nails. He took my chin and our eyes clashed; stormy clouds with flecks of steel ready to drown soft grass. His breath was cool, smelling faintly of vanilla. I was too in awe and frightened to speak, but his grip on my chin tightened when I didn't respond.

"I'm waiting," he said.

"Tell him about me!" Catalina begged, hovering over us. "It's the only thing that can save you!"

Tell Aedes about my ability to see the dead? Why not just ask him to shoot me instead? I've never told a soul about my curse. The only ones who vaguely had a sense of something amiss was my father and *Abuela* SaRosa. Only God knew exactly what was going on with me. Was I supposed to blurt out my deep dark secret to this stranger who was all too ready to off me and make me join Catalina in the afterlife?

"I'm becoming impatient," said Aedes. "You have sixty seconds."

Oh God, what do I tell him? I'm going to die!

My father, Idrina, Sir Harry. I was going to leave them all behind. Unemployed and my major still undecided, my life suddenly seemed boring and terribly unimportant. My "clairvoyance" had to be the stupidest gift in the world, too. It only ever frightened me, made me anti-social, ruined my mental health, made me unsuccessful at forming relationships of any kind, and was probably the reason why I couldn't find a job.

"Tell him the truth! *Dile! Dile la verdad!*"

Catalina's desperate words ringed in my ears. My heart was running a marathon inside my chest, and it didn't help that Aedes's unamused face stared down at me with a baleful expression. The pressure was too much. I snapped.

"If you kill me because you think I'm Catalina's killer, then you're no better than the killer himself!" Shit, that was lame. "If you're so smart, then you would know from your investigation that I'm not the one who murdered her!"

Aedes yawned. "You're not convincing me, kid."

He disengaged the safety.

"Stop being such a bully!" I yelled.

Oh god, I sounded like a hysterical child.

"Phani!" Catalina cried.

Aedes checked his watch. "Time's up. Better luck next—"

"I CAN SEE GHOSTS!" I screamed in his face, tears rolling down my flushed cheeks.

I hate him! I hate him! I hate him! How dare he lower me to this point?

Aedes's expression morphed from shock to skepticism. My blood boiled in response. How *dare* he not believe me after my internal struggle? I let the anger flow through me, latching onto the burning emotion rather than the cold terror threatening to drown me.

"It's true. I can see and speak to the dead," I said, finding that the words just rolled off my tongue with ease.

It seemed too easy. Had I always wanted to tell my story? Discussing Tenebris and Burngemear to Catalina and Tirisha had been one thing, but this was different. This was about me and my ability to see dead people.

"Catalina approached me and offered to pay me if I helped her find her killer before you did."

He blinked. "Why is that? And how much?"

I looked away for a few seconds and forced myself to calm down before I burst into tears. I met Aedes's steel colored gaze.

"She's paying me a hundred thousand dollars because she doesn't want you getting hurt."

The expression on his face was stupefying—and that was saying something because I was determined to hate him right now. His heartless debonair façade melted away, revealing wide eyes and a gaping mouth. When I saw Catalina relax, I knew the tense situation had abated. I continued talking before Aedes could deny my words.

"Catalina wanted me to look at the scene of the crime first, so we went to Orpheus Theater. It was there I met Mr. Shern. He's the one that found Catalina's choker. She told me about the choker's special ability and had me take it so it wouldn't fall into the wrong hands. Shortly after, Catalina's killer had returned and shot Mr. Shern."

Aedes didn't say a word at first. He simply stared at me with wide, confused eyes. After a few moments, he shook his head and retired to his chair, exhaustion etched on his face by the weight of the truth.

"And the events of the Candle Lounge?" He asked. "I saw the video. You were the one that killed those men."

My gaze became far away as I thought about that mystery as well.

"To be honest, I'm not sure how it happened, but Catalina temporarily possessed me. I may be a little active but I don't have moves like that. Not even close. I've never harmed a fly before, let alone have the mental stability to..." I trailed off, meeting Aedes's gaze once more. "Anyways, we were there for Garcy because she's the Underworld gossip girl—"

"Was."

"Erm...was. She was the Underworld gossip girl. Catalina figured the woman was bound to know something she could pick up on. Garcy let slip there were rumors of an uprising against Erebus. After she left, those men came and started shooting up the place. Before they could grab me, I touched Catalina and the next thing I knew, she was handling the problem. We thought you guys were more of the enemy, so we booked it. When you found us, she left my body and flew to you. The rest is history."

I waited for a response.

Aedes remained silent, his eyes distant. The chill of the warehouse prickled my bare shoulders. I looked down and saw that I still had the Lounge dress on. No wonder I felt cold. Aedes leaned forward in his seat. The gun now faced the floor.

"Earlier today," he began, "I got a call from Astora's Room, one of Catalina's back-up stores. They thanked me most ardently for spending over eight thousand dollars with them."

Oh my God.

Was this dress made of diamonds and the cure for cancer?

Eyes bulging, my anger dissipated completely. The poor sucker whose bank account I thought had belonged to Catalina's Darling was actually Aedes's? I mentally screamed in utter embarrassment. Could the floor just open up right now so I can tilt my chair back and disappear forever? I cannot believe the entire outfit I had on was worth over eight grand. And Aedes had been the one footing the bill! And the dress was ruined now, so I couldn't even return it! It was no wonder Catalina hadn't told me a thing! She knew I'd balk and walk out the store the minute I knew who'd be in charge of paying for the extra zeros.

Catalina shook her head. "I should have known they would follow up on that. I betchu it was that Casey girl."

Was that her only concern?

"I'm so sorry about that," I apologized. My ears and neck burned hot. "Catalina made me write something on the card to show the salesgirl. I didn't know what it meant and when I asked, she wouldn't say."

"Is that where you got Darlington from?" He asked, revealing the very note I had given the saleslady. Boy, he *really* followed up on that phone call.

"Yeah. Is that your last name or something?"

He laughed, rubbing his face. "Ghost whisperer, that's a new one. Okay, listen, say I believe you, I still need some proof that what you're saying is true."

I bit my lip, looking to Catalina for some proof I could hand to him. She frowned and fiddled with her hair.

"Why not tell him something personal about himself? Like how he likes designing jewelry in his spare time?" Seeing my hesitant look, Catalina went on, warming up to the idea. "In fact, tell him about the time we skipped class during our college sophomore year. My car broke down and we ended up stranded near a sketchy strip joint. I dared him to go apply for a job. Can you believe they hired him on the spot? The 'employer' wanted to measure his equipment and see if it worked properly so Darling bashed him over the head. We slashed his tires before hightailing it. Oh yes, tell him about that one! I wanna see his face!"

My eyes bugged out. She laughed.

"That's too personal!" I hissed at her, realizing too late that I was sitting in front of the object of our talk as he scrutinized my every move.

"What's too personal?"

I hesitated, attention flickering between the two. "Um..."

Catalina rolled her eyes. "Or you could tell him I had a brief fling with Huey, his second-best friend. Me being the first, of course. We broke it off when I realized a few days in that I didn't feel *that way* for him. Still adore him though. Darling knows all about it."

That seemed safe. Though I'm confused as to why she would so blatantly tell me the friend's name and not her actual best friend's name. That would be proof enough right? As if to explain my confusion, the older woman's lips curled into a smirk.

"Darling's last name is Darlington," she said. "Van Darlington to be precise. I call him Darling because it always bugs him so technically I *did* tell you his name."

Ah. I'll just stick with the friend thing.

"Okay, so Catalina had a brief fling with your friend Huey—"

I yelped when he suddenly launched himself at me. My exclamation was soon cut off when he placed a cool hand over my mouth before glancing around at the large empty warehouse in suspicion. Catalina reacted accordingly and whirled around, brown eyes scrutinizing the area for any eavesdroppers.

"Miss Phani, it may appear as if we're alone, but I have people surrounding this place. Speak softly. I'll still hear you. I'd rather this be between us," Aedes whispered against my ear. The heat from his face made me shiver. I nodded before he let go.

Speak softly? So when I hysterically shouted about seeing ghosts his people were nearby to hear that? The revelation did not please me. I pray his people didn't take anything I said seriously.

I flinched when I saw Aedes take out a small knife. To my relief, he began to cut the tight ropes wrapped around my sore wrists. I glanced at him. He merely smirked in response, his cheekbones becoming more pronounced in the pale light. He looked much too pleased with himself, like Sir Harry when he's eaten all the creme.

The Aedes from *Il Melograno* was back. I knew then I wouldn't be dying today. I tried really hard not to cry in relief like an overly emotional sissy. Now if I could just get him to apologize for emotionally tormenting me, that would be great.

"I believe you," he said, making Catalina beam. "However, never mention that name to anyone ever again."

I nodded quickly, having already risked my neck for a bit of gossip. I hoped this Huey friend was nothing like Aedes.

"So how exactly was Catalina planning to pay you?" Aedes asked once my legs were freed.

"Well, she was going to tell me the location of her secret stash…" I trailed off when I saw Aedes pull out a checkbook and pen from inside his coat. What was he doing?

"I'm giving this to you on the condition you stop your investigation on Catalina's killer," he said. His tone left no room for argument.

Catalina sputtered in anger. "Excuse me? Tell him he better not!"

I was torn. "Uh…"

Aedes surprised me yet again by turning his head to where Catalina stood, looking her straight in the eyes. His accuracy raised the hairs on my arm.

"I've been watching you look to your right for the last fifteen minutes and I can only assume Catalina is hovering around you like a pesky fly."

"Bitch! The only fly here is you!" Catalina quipped. "Kidnapping girls because you can't date them the normal way? How amateurish! I can't believe you're a year older than me! Hmph!"

"What did she say?" he asked me.

And now I've become their translator.

"She said the only fly here is you."

"She used colorful language, I know," he said, chuckling. Then his expression turned somber as he turned away. The jovial air that floated around us dampened.

"Catalina," he began. His voice was calm, almost peaceful. It belied the hands curling into fists. "I'm going to catch your killer and stab him in the face. Then I'm going to shoot him and anchor his corpse to the bottom of the Ignis river. So for once, just once, do as you're told, Catalina. Leave everything to me. And don't ever involve a civilian again."

Her normally expressive face was wiped clean of her usual haughty cheer. Instead, she wore a heavy, crestfallen expression, one that almost had me stepping forward to comfort her. But I stayed where I was, and Catalina didn't say anything after that. She vanished on the spot.

Aedes and I were finally alone. He glanced at me. We stared at each other without saying a word for a couple of minutes. My skin prickled the longer his gaze remained.

"She's gone?" he asked at last.

"For now," I admitted. "She'll turn up when she's cooled off."

"She's so sensitive. I had hoped she would learn to be mindful of others without taking offense," he complained, tucking his gun away and straightening his coat.

Sensitive? That is not a word I would use to describe Catalina at all. Maybe vulnerable sometimes, but it was not something she was willing to show or dwell on for very long. But then, Aedes knew her better than me and for far longer. I wasn't going to argue against him.

"Oh well," Aedes continued. "Shall I take you home, Phani?"

He held out his hand for me. After a few beats of silence, I took it.

XVIII.
DON'T SHOOT THE HARBINGER

"How's Asphodel treating you, Phani?" asked my father in Spanish over the phone. His voice sounded tired, but I imagined dealing with *Großmutter* Stefanie could make one feel that way. I heard she was quite the interesting character.

Above me, an ominous sky of ashen cotton blanketed Asphodel City today. The filtered sunlight struggling through the clouds was weak, hardly giving my brown skin a challenge. I was currently chilling on a bench in Proserpina's Garden, using the serenity to call my father before he freaked out over how I hadn't contacted him.

A week had passed since the events of the Candle Lounge and just like the tension that followed, the weather became icier. It forced me to wear thick pants and plump jackets, a survival tactic I was most peeved about. If I had been living in Miami, I wouldn't have had to worry about the winter climate at all.

"It's been eventful," I said, half-lying. "I've been trying to settle in so there was a lot to focus on. Are you well? How's *Großmutter* Stefanie?"

"Surprisingly pleasant," he responded with awe in his voice. "Everyone's been giving me the side eye, but she hasn't said an insulting or sarcastic remark at all. I was sure she'd comment on the state of my shoes, but she's been the picture-perfect host."

"Huh, I guess the rumors were wrong," I said, remembering talk of how *Großmutter* Stefanie supposedly hated my father for taking her precious only daughter away.

"Right? That's what I said! Despite the language barrier, we've actually chatted quite a bit. About you in fact."

I froze. When I spoke, my voice was surprisingly steady.

"All good things, I hope?"

"Of course! She's keen to meet you, you know. She even invited you to check out her famous Baumer garden. No wonder your mother liked gardening so much. I showed her pictures of you and she started gushing!"

My ears grew hot. Thank God I hadn't been present. I was already embarrassed when my father fussed over me, but for him to share that with other people? I couldn't possibly show my face!

"You should visit Germany," he continued. "It's an interesting environment and I've gotten a lot of inspiration for the novella I'm writing. I keep imagining Wilma walking alongside me and just pointing out all the places and people familiar to her."

I glanced at my shoes, sensing the mood turn somber. Even after eighteen years since my mother's passing, my father was still ardently in love with her. One could see it in the way his eyes lit up when he talked about her, or when his smile curled into a playful smirk when he thought of funny memories.

"Um, anyways," he continued, "have you scheduled an appointment with your new psychiatrist? What's their name? What are they like? I hope they speak Spanish like your old one."

Oh boy. Here goes.

"Hey, dad, I, uh, haven't scheduled an appointment yet."

A pause. "Oh. Well, you should get on that soon. Preferably before the week is over."

And the cringe begins.

"Listen, I was thinking about not continuing the sessions," I said, tracing the floral design pattern on my pants. "Dr. Suyapa mentioned that I was making progress since the last relapse. Which, by the way, was years ago. In fact, I feel really great right now and I've been on top of my game and it'd be super hard to—"

"Phani. The deal was you attend your sessions if I let you move to Asphodel City." His tone left no room for argument. But still, I tried.

"Dad, please. These sessions are expensive, and now that you're self-employed they can't be easy to pay for. Plus, I'm twenty! Not a naïve little twelve-year-old who doesn't know any better. I really feel like I'm in a good place and—"

"Phani. Make an appointment before the week is out. I appreciate your thoughtfulness, but this is for your own good. I'm not ever going to compromise your mental safety and the fact that I'm in Germany, leaving you without any protection or guidance is testing the limits. Don't make it worse."

The strain in his voice was noticeable.

I bit my tongue to keep from lashing out. Why couldn't he just trust me? I've grown up! I'm not the broken nine-year old he used to know anymore!

I clenched my fist. After a few beats of silence, I sighed, the tension leaving my body.

"Okay."

"That's my girl! When you meet the new psychiatrist, give me the details. I have to run now, but don't forget to call! I love you!"

"Love you too. Talk to you next week."

When I hung up, I leaned back and rubbed my eyes, feeling as though I've aged a few years. One day I won't have to worry about psychotherapy sessions anymore. I'll be freed from the mistakes of the past until none of it matters. If only that day could come sooner.

When I stood up and stretched, something crunched underneath my feet. To my alarm, the grass underneath the bench, the bushes near-by, and half the tree that shaded my little spot was brown and shriveled, as though something had sucked all life and vitality out of them. The smell of rot reached my nose. In my frustration and anger, I must have unknowingly zapped the life force from the surrounding plants. Thank God no one was around. I definitely could not have explained this unnatural phenomenon.

I forced myself to think happy thoughts, moving my arms wide to help encourage some leafy growth. The grass returned to its green happy color. The bushes and trees needed a little more encouragement, but it didn't take them long to return to their natural color, minus a few leaves that had fallen when they died.

Once everything was nearly as it should be, I exhaled in relief. As a treat, I decided to check out the maze at the center of the garden. The shrubs were tall and cut neat and evenly. The round pattern of the maze was visible only to the tall buildings surrounding and overlooking the small pasture of land. Giddiness filled me when I entered the maze.

Mazes always brought a smile to my face. Most people hated them because it was easy to get lost, but I'd rather get lost in a labyrinth of plants than set foot in Tenebris. I stared at the minute details embedded in the hedge walls, fascinated by the craftsmanship. Smooth multi-colored pebbles were strategically scattered on the ground, making it easier for those more inclined to get lost to find the center or exit.

As I walked, I fingered the few remaining white narcissus struggling to live in the changing climate.

One was all by its lonesome, wilting and pointing its petals to the earth. To my surprise, in another crevice I found a small bushel of lilacs. From far away, the deep purple had me thinking it was wolfsbane. While Catalina would have been thrilled at the prospect, one wrong touch of the poisonous plant and it was curtains for the unfortunate. When I realized the purple plants were just lilacs, however, my shoulders slumped in relief.

"False alarm, Cata—" I began, turning my head only to see the maze wall behind me. I frowned.

Catalina wasn't around anymore. She disappeared after our second quarrel the same day Aedes brought me home after The Candle Lounge. Idrina had been called away to the ER that same night—certain critical condition patients from a certain shot-up club in South Coast had been transferred to Asphodel General via helicopter. It was lucky she hadn't been around because if she had heard me raising my voice, she would've chalked it up to my schizophrenia and insisted I book an appointment with a psychiatrist *ASAP.*

"What do you mean you're not doing this anymore?! Catalina exclaimed, hair floating wildly around her. "I can't believe you're listening to him!"

"It's for my own good! I let it slide the first time, but I was literally almost kidnapped by a second rival mob gang and then *actually kidnapped by Aedes! Twice!* Who, by the way, ended up being you're Darling this whole time! And you didn't even tell me!"

"He goes by Orcus in Erebus! How was I supposed to know he made up a stupid name to keep you from learning about the real one?! And you wouldn't have been kidnapped if you'd just kept up!"

"*What did you just say?!*" I could practically see red.

"I feel like you didn't even try! You just want to listen to Darling and stay out of Underworld business despite agreeing to help me!"

"Catalina, are you hearing yourself? I placed my life in dangerous situations numerous times for you, and believe me, I don't do that kind of thing for just anyone. In fact, death is something I avoid religiously!"

Catalina rolled her eyes. "*Ai, no seas cobarde!* Don't be a coward! Learn to live. Life isn't meant to be wasted! If you were that afraid to take the lead, then you should've let me take over from the beginning. We could have made progress in our investigation!"

I sputtered. "Hey! I'm trying my best here! Don't dictate how I should live my life! I'm not like you, I'm not outgoing nor do I care to *live* dangerously like that, especially when I have no real power! I told you I never wanted to feel powerless in that way again!"

"And thanks to me, you weren't! You were kicking ass and taking names! Once I possessed you, you were the farthest thing from powerless! So I kept my promise! If we do it again, you won't have to worry about your safety."

"Catalina, are you obtuse?! Your way of going about this entire investigation is selfish and tone death! You need to remember I'm not like—"

"Yes, yes, you're not me. Instead, you're boring and wasting away." Catalina interrupted with a sneer. "Is that why you attract the dead like maggots to a carcass?"

I clenched my fists and snarled at her. "How dare you! I can't help that! And I will not let you possess me again! It's invasive and creepy!"

"Excuse *me?*" Catalina's outrage made the furniture in the bedroom shake. "Then next time I won't save your sorry ass from getting sold and slaughtered! Next time, you're on your own!"

The argument spiraled out of control. Neither one of us had refused to back down and apologize first this time around. After shattering a light bulb, Catalina disappeared with a string of Spanish profanities. I haven't seen her since.

Despite still being upset by her insensitivity, I worried she was gone for good. Sure the circumstances that brought us together hadn't exactly been ideal, but, much to my own surprise, I found myself liking Catalina. Barbed thorns and all. Sure, she was capricious, crass, overconfident, and manipulative, but she was honest— when it wasn't underworld business. I admired her for daring to be herself. For breaking the mold and being unapologetically Catalina. I wasn't sure if she felt the same way, but I considered her a friend, a mentor almost.

When I glanced at the lilacs again, I gasped. They were wilting before my eyes! Violet faded as petals drooped, brown leaves curled in tight furls.

Ugh, not again.

I backed away and tried stifling my dismal mood. If all the plants here ended up dying because of me, I'll snap. Frustration and stress tempting me to scream bloody murder at the heavens.

Once the lilacs were saved, I stuffed my hands, numb from the cold, in my jacket pocket before continuing down the maze's foot path. I yawned. I stopped walking when my fingers touched wrinkled paper.

Oh yeah. Almost forgot about that too.

I pulled out a creased check, dark inky zeros engraved on the parchment with heavy permanence. The evidence of my meager involvement in the Asphodel underworld had never felt so tangible until this moment. It mocked me for passively accepting Aedes's bribe. But how could I not? Unemployment had reared its ugly head. Even if I had stupidly said no, Aedes would have probably added me to his hit list. At least now the man didn't have to worry about me, though I felt dishonest about the whole thing.

After Catalina disappeared, I thought long and hard about the check. In the end, instead of depositing it like any sensible person would, I went out and searched for another job.

And this time, I was successful. Sort of.

Earlier this week, about fifteen minutes away via the subway, I walked into Kyle's Chili Wraps and Salads on a whim and *demanded* a job, as if I were entitled to one. Not only did I not bother flashing anyone my resume or cover letter, I wasn't even professionally dressed! Ten minutes later, I was hired on the spot by the aging manager and instructed to hold the Kyle's Chili Wraps and Salads sign outside the store.

It wasn't a glamorous tale, but it was a sign that I was capable of making it out on my own. Not to mention, I was relieved that I wouldn't have to worry about rent. Though to be honest, I was not looking forward to standing outside in the cold with indifferent Asphodelians who would sooner knock me over than look at the direction my sign was pointing to. At least they paid minimum wage, which was a lot more than Florida's.

I jumped when I heard my phone go off. The tune of Material Girl filled the nippy air as I groped myself, searching for the elusive device before it stopped ringing. I knew who it was even before I looked at the caller ID.

"Idrina? What's wrong?"

"Phani! You'll never believe it! Come home quick!"

"Why? What's wrong?"

She hung up. I looked at the phone for a second. Idrina sounded frantic, as if completely caught off guard. But if whatever she was dealing with was an emergency, why call me?

I sighed in resignation. The maze would just have to wait another day. Before I turned away completely, my eyes caught a glimpse of the maze center through a narrow opening. Intrigued, I took a step closer.

A fountain made of glass and marble shaped in circles and odd lines stood at the center, water dribbling down. It was very abstract in its minimalist design, but despite that, I could make out the feminine outline of a young woman kneeling down. I tilted my head. For some odd reason, the fountain statue looked familiar, though I couldn't place my finger on it.

Shaking my head and yawning once more, I turned and rounded a corner in time to see someone on the opposite end hastily retreat behind a hedge to my left.

Well, isn't that sketchy?

I wasn't sure whether to call out or just silently slink away. Stealth seemed like the better option. I took a different path and left the maze.

When I returned to the outer portion of the garden, I found no one else around. My longboard Cosmos didn't look disturbed. Maybe I had imagined someone back there. Could it have been a ghost?

I jumped again when my phone dinged with an incoming text message. It was from Idrina. Stifling another terrible yawn, I summoned a taxi cab by text, since Cosmos was not going to be a fast enough method of transportation for Idrina it seemed.

I wondered where Catalina was and what she was doing right now. Was she in the Aether Realm? I still couldn't believe she hadn't seen Tenebris yet. It's nearly impossible for me *not* to see Tenebris once every week, and I'm not even dead!

At this point, the abandoned cityscape had been carved into my dreams: ice and thick ropes of vine smothered streets and crumbled buildings, the sky forever dreary, and swirling misty figures and walking shadows haunting every crevice. And don't even get me started on the different frequencies of breathy whispers, hollow winds, and eerie squeaks that followed me even after returning to the physical world—

I stopped walking.

Something, or someone, was following me. Please let it be a ghost and not a serial killer.

I turned around.

It was him. The ethereal spirit that smelled like lavender and chamomile from last week. He smiled at me, icy blue eyes twinkling from between pale lashes.

"Hello again," he greeted, voice soft and melodious. He sounded happy, relieved almost.

"You. Wait, what's your name?"

"You really don't remember me?" he asked, concerned. The closer he got, the more my eyelids felt heavy. "That's fine. I go by many names, but I'm most fond of Hypnos."

"Hypnos?"

"Ringing any bells?" Hypnos asked, voice hopeful.

I shook my head. He sighed.

"No matter. It is nice to see you again. How have you been?"

"Since the last time you saw me? I've felt better," I admitted, ruffling my hair. I yawned.

Hypnos cocked his head. His robes skimmed the walkway as we walked towards the entrance of Proserpina's Garden.

"I'm sorry," he responded, "I know the human realm has always been challenging. Sometimes, I wish it were easier to navigate. It would certainly make it less aggravating for everyone."

Hypnos had to be the strangest and least scary spirit I've seen to date. He didn't seem like the other spirits I've met who were desperately clamoring for my attention or upset that I was able to communicate with them but refused to. For once, I didn't mind speaking to a spirit.

"Why do you call it the human realm? Are you not human?"

"Me? Of course not," said Hypnos, "I'm an immortal deity."

I skipped a step and nearly fell. When I righted myself, I turned to look at him.

"An immortal deity? What? You mean like a god?"

"In other words, yes," he said, smiling gently. "You are one too. Technically."

Okay, now he was talking crazy. It figures that Hypnos had a flaw. Still harmless compared to Catalina.

"I don't think so, buddy," I said, chuckling.

By then we had arrived at the drop off area. My cab should be arriving in the next five minutes, according to the update. I covered an incoming yawn.

"But it's true, Kore. I don't jest."

"Kore? You mean Cora? How do *you* know my middle name?" I asked, arching a brow.

"Is that what you call yourself nowadays?" he asked, hands clasped behind his back.

"Well, my name is *Estephanie*," I said, spotting a cab heading my way, "but I like when people call me Phani."

"Phani," repeated Hypnos, seemingly entranced by this information. "I like it. I technically have another name I used to go by. Joshua."

Joshua? That's a stark departure from Hypnos. Before I could even figure where this odd conversation was going, my sticker covered taxi cab had arrived. After confirming my ride, I looked back to Hypnos. He stood to the side, eyeing the cab with sadness. Icy blue eyes eventually met my own. Pink cupid bow lips curved into a soft smile.

"Until next time, Phani."

Then he was gone.

Somewhere along the way to Idrina's apartment, I dozed off. When we arrived, the cabbie was nice enough to verbally wake me up. I was a little alarmed to have let my guard down in such a way, not because I thought the cabbie was dangerous, but because a girl traveling alone in a city, especially when she had no control over the vehicle she rode on, should always be cautious and aware of her surround-ings in case of unsavory situations.

Thankfully this was not the case. I paid the driver and walked to the elevator inside, resolving to get a better night's sleep.

When I entered Idrina's toasty apartment, Sir Harry greeted me first on the kitchen counter, wearing the adorable pumpkin sweater Idrina had gotten him as a housewarming gift. I chuckled and scratched his little chin. He purred in content.

"Phani? Is that you?" Idrina called. "Finally!"

I followed her voice to the master bedroom.

It was decorated in the same contemporary design prevalent throughout her apartment. Colored in hues of red and creme, it contrasted the green and beige color palette used in my room. Idrina reassured me that I could redecorate the space however I pleased—save any gothic themes. She had a not-so secret fear that I dabbled in *santeria*, devil witchcraft. It stemmed from the rumors that spilled forth from my freaking out about ghosts and the devil when I was younger. It was kind of funny when I thought about it, but Idrina needn't have worried. Why would I want to theme my bedroom around death and the afterlife? I already faced that stuff on the daily!

Inside her walk-in closet, Idrina struggled to zip her dress. Judging by her colorful Spanish curses, she had been at it for a few minutes. Another hot second had her throwing her arms up in exas-peration.

"Idrina?" I said, knocking on her door.

"Phani! Thank goodness you're here!" Idrina exclaimed, turning and rushing towards me. "I got a call from my boss earlier and you'll never believe what he surprised me with! Guess!"

"Um—"

"He said I was invited to the Asphodel City Hall Gala!"

I blinked twice. The what?

"Can you believe it? Me? I was so shocked I simply had to call you home so we could make necessary preparations."

So...there's no life-threatening emergency? I rushed home like a zealous marathon runner and spent twenty bucks on cab fare for this? I felt the small coil of tension melt as exasperation took over. Idrina paid my frustration little mind as she whirled around to check herself in front of a full-body mirror.

"I know it's last minute, but anyone who's anyone in the city will be there," she continued. "I called Ryan immediately after, and it turns out, he was invited today too! Glad I'm not the only one scrambling for clothes last minute. Anyway, my invitation has a plus one and I thought, to celebrate your new job, you could come with me!"

Whoa, wait, what? Me? At a fancy shindig? With my current state of mind and lack of prospects?

"You didn't send out the RSVP, did you?"

"Of course! I had to answer within the hour. Anyways, I have a few possible outfits I could parade in front of the bigwigs. Did you know Mayor Warringson will be there too? How exciting! I hear he's even more handsome in person and quite the dancer! Hmm, I think there might be something in here that could fit you," Idrina mumbled absently as she ransacked her closet.

I frowned, fidgeting and scratching the back of my neck as Idrina changed back into her normal clothes. I wasn't sure how to bring up my refusal to attend. I would have left it at that and let her have her way, but then Idrina started talking about possible makeup combinations and I knew I had to act fast.

"Listen, Idrina," I began. "This is going to be awkward, but I don't think I should go."

Idrina stopped posing in front of the mirror and looked at me. "What?"

"I'm no good at these kinds of functions. I can't dance, and I wouldn't even know what to say to these people. I'd only embarrass you and Ryan."

Instead of looking furious or relieved, Idrina's expression softened like warm butter. She came over and gently took my hand in a grip that smelled of her favorite rose scented lotion. It was bizarre seeing her react this way. She looked almost...maternal. Which was odd because the words Idrina and maternal in the same sentence seemed like an incongruous pairing.

"Sweet, sweet Phani," Idrina began, voice gentle. I wondered if this was the voice she used on her patients. "You don't have to go if you don't want to, but don't ever do it because you feel inadequate. You are not invalidated or unimportant because certain people happen to be well-known, well-off, or even of sound mind. You got that? And I know you think you'll be a mess because you've never been around these types of people, but remember, everyone's gone through what you're feeling at least once. Even me."

What? "Really?"

Idrina blushed. "To be honest, I'm a little nervous about going too."

Who was this person speaking to me in a relatable manner? Where had the confident, no-nonsense, but ever dramatic Idrina gone? Was I being punked?

We sat down on her bed, perfectly made with fluffy pillows propped up against the headboard.

"When I first came to this city and began working at Asphodel General," she began, eyes downcast. "I felt so out of place being the outsider surrounded by professional and talented people with years of experience. I couldn't even find the parking lot my first day and ended up working on the wrong patient that same week!"

"What changed?" Cause she certainly wasn't that way anymore.

Idrina sat up straighter, shoulders back, face upturned as she cracked a secret smile.

"Baby steps. That's all I did and still do. Eventually, all those baby steps will take you exactly where you want to go. No one's an expert from the get-go; we all have strengths and weaknesses. It's up to us whether we decide to let it hold us back."

"And you think that will help me with this crowd?"

Idrina leaned back. "Look at me, Phani. Do I look like I'm going to let these people intimidate me?"

"No."

"Exactly. Even if I feel the opposite, I pretend."

Well, that is one way, I suppose.

When I searched Idrina's brown gaze for sincerity, I was awed to see she meant every word. It was like I was seeing her in a new light. One where she wasn't this intimidating, perfect figure, but instead a compassionate and understanding person. I nodded in response. Idrina patted my hair gently before pausing.

"Hey, by the way, have you seen my blonde wig anywhere?"

I struggled to keep my face from contorting in horror. Instead, I mentally cursed myself. Her wig was The Candle Lounge's property now.

"Blonde wig? No, I haven't seen it," I lied. "Why?"

Idrina pouted, looking at the carpet. "Ryan's a bit of a nerd and he wanted to attend an anime convention coming up dressed up as a couple of characters."

"Oh. You dress up?"

Idrina laughed. "I dress up to go to *bars*. It's fun wearing different wigs, but with Ryan, I have another purpose for them."

"That's interesting," I said, surprised to learn about this side of Ryan. He always came across elegant and gentlemen-like. This nerdiness humanized him.

Idrina gave my hand a squeeze before getting up and grabbing her keys from the dresser.

"If you change your mind, call me. I'm heading over to Tatianna's. She's got better options for me to choose from than my own closet right now."

"Who's Tatianna?" I asked.

Idrina paused, blinking before gasping. "Oh, that's right! You haven't met her yet. Tati's my best friend. I met her when I first moved to Asphodel. She works at the Leda Sanctuary, a charity foundation her family built that helps victims of sexual assault, domestic violence, and homelessness. It's her passion project and she takes it very seriously."

Wow. I wondered if Tatianna's charity was hiring. It sounded like a great place to work while also positively contributing to society.

After shooing me away so Idrina could change again, I retreated to my room in a thoughtful haze. Normally I would have agreed to go to such an exciting event, but after the last few weeks, all I wanted was some peace and quiet. And as encouraging as Idrina's words had been, my new job was nothing to celebrate. No way was I going to tell anyone about my job at Kyle's Chili Wraps and Salads, least of all at a gala where the city's handsome mayor was supposed to be attending.

An incoming text from Tirisha interrupted my musings.

Be very careful today.

I frowned at the message. I was aware that Tirisha had been feeling uneasy lately, but this was just concerning.

After inquiring about my well-being following the events of The Candle Lounge over the phone, Tirisha had invited me to hang out with her while she was marooned at her sister's bookstore all week. Turns out Abbie had left for a writers conference in New York and asked Tirisha to hold down the fort.

When I arrived, I was surprised to see Tirisha out of drag wearing a tight plain shirt, a maxi skirt, and prescription glasses. Her heels were at least two-inches, her make-up minimal, and she was rocking a curly blonde bob, a lovely contrast against her black skin. She flipped through a magazine, looking utterly bored with the calm silence of the store.

I was amazed. She was usually dolled up the few times I'd seen her, so seeing her blend in with the conventional was odd yet extraordinary. It was like finding a diamond in the rough.

"Tirisha?" I called, approaching the counter.

When Tirisha spotted me, she straightened and smiled, her eyes a pretty caramel brown. Even without the heels, she was still tall, easily towering over me.

"Little chip! Glad you could visit me today."

"Of course," I said. "Um, if you don't mind me asking, out of drag, I still call you Tirisha, right?"

She laughed. "Yes, you may. It's both my legal first name and stage name."

I nodded, thankful for the clarification.

"Did you still want to talk about Tenebris and, um, Burngemear?" I asked hesitantly.

Tirisha winked before signaling Laila to take over the front register. She led me to her sister's back office painted in shades of green and yellow. The wooden floors gleamed with polish while the air smelled strongly of oranges and lemons. I sat in a floral settee across from her—it was identical to the one *Tante* Hilde had stowed away in her attic. Once we got comfortable, Tirisha cut straight to the chase.

"How do you know about Tenebris, Phani?"

After Aedes's interrogation, I found it easier to let slip the truth.

"I can speak to the dead."

She hadn't laughed or looked at me like I was a deranged loon. Not once. Tirisha simply nodded, taking in the information like a fact of science before continuing. Her reaction left me wind-blown.

"You believe me?"

"Of course! I have no room to doubt you considering I'm clairvoyant," Tirisha admitted with a smile. "Born with it all my life."

I blinked. "Whoa."

"The past, present, and even future. I can see it all." She continued, lowering her tone for dramatic effect. "Sometimes, I can even see *Other*."

"Other?"

"A world not like our own." She straightened and leaned back in her chair. "It's random though, and the visions can either be vague in detail or really vivid. I can, however, look for a specific vision about someone or something, but whether it will be well-defined is never a guarantee."

My eyes resembled saucers.

"Tirisha, that's mind blowing. Was it something you discovered by accident or trained yourself to accomplish?"

"I've had to hone my intuitive instincts over the years. It helps me decipher most visions with little difficulty."

"So...The Candle Lounge?"

Tirisha grimaced, brown eyes gazing at her clasped hands. "I only saw the floor, but it was smeared with blood. I heard gunfire and screams in the background. Self-preservation and experience told me to get the hell out of dodge, so I canceled my performance. Glad to see you followed my advice."

Well, almost.

I stroked my invisible beard, the questions about her ability just buzzing to the forefront.

"Can you see past events of certain people you've never met?"

Tirisha shook her head. The light from the window glinted off the gold hoops in her ears.

"Nope. I can only see the past, present, or future of people I've seen physically from five feet away max."

Huh, I suppose that axed using her as a resource for Catalina's killer. Why I was still even thinking about the closed investigation, I don't know. When we approached the subject of Tenebris specifically, Tirisha turned out to be a wealth of knowledge.

"I've only seen the place through visions," she admitted, shuddering.

"Do you know how Tenebris came to be?" I asked.

"I couldn't say. It's ancient though. Probably been around since forever. Think of it like this, if Tenebris is hell, then what is heaven?"

I hesitated. A sinking feeling settled in my belly.

"If we go by that comparison, then Burngemear could be—"

"The devil? Who knows. Or he could be a grim reaper, an angel of death, if you will."

Now it was my turn to shudder.

"I always suspected he might be, but I didn't like placing any importance on his presence, hoping he'd just go away for good. He talked to me once, you know."

Tirisha's lashes flew wide open. "What? He spoke?"

I nodded. "When I was five-years-old, my father took me to a church hosting a visiting prophetess. When he went up front, I followed him and insisted on being held. Before she could even anoint oil on my forehead, she disappeared. Everyone disappeared. I was still in the church, but it was abandoned, crumbling. It was cold and gray everywhere. I also realized that I was still being held. By *him*. Burngemear."

Tirisha leaned forward in her seat, hanging on my every word.

"What did he say?"

I glanced at my hands, the nails pink, squared, and clean.

"I don't remember what he said exactly, I just know...that he's frightened me ever since."

Tirisha tapped her chin. "I would ask if you owe him or a demon something over a broken contract maybe, but—now, now, don't look so horrified. I've seen it happen. They come to me begging for help. These people communicate with creatures far beyond their understanding and make deals with them, letting them control and ruin their lives. It's horrific."

"Oh, thank God I haven't seen that!"

"Wouldn't be so sure," said Tirisha, looking almost apologetic. "I have a feeling you'd be a ripe pick for them to go after. If they haven't, then—"

"It's because Burngemear told them to back off," I whispered, realizing what she meant.

"Which brings me to the question of why Burngemear would bother with you? What makes you so special? Sure, you speak to the dead, but so what? There are plenty of other mediums who communicate with the dead. Is it because you can transport yourself to Tenebris? How can you even do that? No, why are you the one who can do that?"

All vital questions I wish I had the answers to.

Idrina's voice sounded distant as I stood immobile on the threshold of my room. Huh. Hadn't realized I'd spaced out. Before I could even step inside and lie down, my phone rang. One look at the caller ID had me scowling.

Charlie.

XIX.
CLUES IN THE RUSE

CHARLIE LEFT me thirty missed calls and forty three text messages since the night of The Candle Lounge. Apparently he heard about what happened from the news and had been beside himself with worry. I texted him that I was okay and alive, but refused to interact with him after that.

He hasn't let up despite my cold shoulder. Everyday since, he's called me twice a day and left a message asking if he could apologize in person or if there was some way he could make it up to me. Aside from seeing the error of his way and apologizing while also making amends, I wasn't sure what else he could do. I've never been in this situation before.

I didn't have any friends back in Miami, or at least any I could hang out with after classes ended. My social life mostly consisted of my cousins living in West Palm which was quite a drive. The neighborhood kids thought I was weird and wanted nothing to do with me ever since I spotted a shadow figure stalking one of them and pointed it out.

Tirisha may not be my best friend or one I've known forever, but I value the friendship we struck. It was highly insulting he would insult her for being different. What did that say if he ever learned the truth about me?

I silenced Charlie's call and sat on my bed. Sir Harry jumped up and settled himself on my lap. Smiling, I scratched his little head, mindful of his big ears and feeling the vibration of his purr. A ding from a text sounded. I didn't even turn to look. Instead, my eyes caught Mr. Shern's painting on my dresser. The blue stood out, vibrant against the green and beige of my room. My brows furrowed when I noticed something amiss with the painting, however.

Standing, I went over and picked it up, inspecting it carefully. Just as I suspected, there were tiny scratches alongside the edge of the canvas. I gave Sir Harry a half-hearted glare which he ignored, choosing to lay on his side and lick himself. Rolling my eyes, I placed the canvas down just as something caught my eye.

Mr. Shern's painting had remained indecipherable to me, but as I turned it around, I could see that the broad-brush strokes of cyan and cerulean formed several semi-circles. I turned it another way and realized the pattern of lines and circles was familiar.

I took out a piece of paper and pencil and began copying the design from each angle of the canvas. Once I was done, I assembled the shapes into the feminine pattern I had seen erected in stone in Proserpina's Garden. This was it. This was the design Mr. Shern had seen on John Forty.

This was also the design Charlie had on his wrist. The one I had traced with my finger last week when I brought him lunch.

I blinked. No, it couldn't be. I glanced at my phone, silent as a gravestone resting comfortably on my bedspread beside Sir Harry.

I searched for my investigation notebook and settled down on the carpet once I found it. I looked back at the evidence and theories I had put together, then at the list of suspects. I added my new findings and realized that Charlie matched John Forty's description, especially the tattoo on his left wrist.

Could John Forty be Charlie? It was a jarring thought and one I couldn't assume because of how out of nowhere it was. I was convinced that John Forty was either the killer or had been helping the killer because the one who shot Mr. Shern was definitely Catalina's killer. Catalina mentioned investigating a turncoat in their ranks and was simply waiting on Erebus's Fetch and Eradicate order to officially take care of the problem. Thanks to Aedes, I knew that the turncoat had been working alongside Catalina's killer.

I frowned, realizing another important fact.

Charlie had an annoying roommate who kept odd hours and dabbled in illegal activities. Could one of those illegal activities involve Erebus and underworld business? He did pay Charlie to deliver a package to Garcy shortly before she was murdered and copied Charlie's tattoo design. I gasped. The clues were all starting to add up and one thing was clear, Charlie was my ticket to the truth.

I grabbed my phone and saw the message he left me: *I'll leave you alone then. I'm sorry.*

I texted him a response and waited, anxious about my new theory. I had to know more about his roommate. Was he the turncoat, or was he the killer?

Charlie responded five minutes later.

Yes, absolutely you can come over! But are you sure?

More sure than I've ever been in my life.

If my father ever discovered that I had gone over to a male stranger's apartment alone and defenseless, I have no doubt he would have had a conniption and given me a three-hour long lecture.

Thankfully, I wasn't a complete airhead or defenseless. Idrina had given me a taser and pepper spray as part of my welcome package my first day in Asphodel City. I was too nervous to carry the taser before, but now I carried it concealed in my pocket. Dressed in jeans, a flowy shirt, and a knit cardigan, I walked to Charlie's apartment.

I needed a closer look at Charlie's roommate. If he was the turncoat, then he should be missing and if he was, then maybe he left behind some clue as to who the real killer was. If he wasn't...well, I just had to pretend I knew nothing and make my escape.

This begs the question of who *would* I turn to with the results of my investigation if I did find something? The police was the obvious choice, but for some reason, Aedes's handsome face popped into my mind. I grimaced, shaking my head.

One thing at a time, Phani.

Charlie's apartment was a shabby complex in South Coast. It was tucked away from the main street behind some shops and accessible only through a narrow alley, as if exiled from the public as punishment for being unlovable. Charlie lived on the third floor and much to my knee's chagrin, there were no elevators available. He was already outside, however, leaning against a wall scrolling through his phone by the time I came near.

When he saw me, Charlie straightened up, putting his phone away.

"Hey, Phani," he greeted, wiping his palms on his thighs. "I'm happy you wanted to see me. I was sure I'd never hear from you again."

I smiled. "Well, you seemed insistent on apologizing and trying to make amends so I decided to hear you out."

Charlie nodded, cracking a small smile. "Yes. We could have done this at a park though, in case you feel uncomfortable."

How considerate. Too bad it was against my plans. I shook my head.

"It's okay. Wanna lead the way?"

As we walked upstairs, I decided this was a prime opportunity to bring up his roommate.

"Is your roommate around? I just remembered you don't live alone and I'd hate to intrude."

"Actually, he's not right now. He's visiting family," said Charlie, leading the way. I avoided a brown stain in front of one of the apartment doors.

"Has he paid you for delivering the poppy flowers?" I teased.

Charlie laughed, shaking his head.

"No, uh, not yet."

Interesting.

Charlie opened his door and gestured for me to step inside. The first thing I noticed was how dim it looked. Orange-yellow walls, popcorn ceiling, brown shaggy carpet, and lots of battered moving boxes. The smell of burnt popcorn and mildew lingered in the air, even with the window from the kitchen opened wide. In short, this place looked terrible.

"Sorry about the mess," he said, moving some boxes out of the way so I could walk to the couch. "I'm usually up and about so I don't have a lot of time to clean."

"Did you just move in?" I asked, noticing one of the boxes was wide open and filled with packing peanuts.

"No. I've technically owned this place for months, but," he shrugged, "South Coast real estate doesn't give me inspiration to decorate or wanna stay here long enough for it."

With how rough South Coast looked the deeper one went in, I could understand where he was coming from. I eyed the kitchenette separated from the living room by a counter. There was a long hallway next to it. That must be where the rooms were.

Charlie finally sat beside me and ran a hand through his shaggy hair. I noticed the intricate tattoo on his wrist. It stood out like a lighthouse now that I knew that design was what John Forty had tattooed on him. Charlie had previously mentioned that a friend designed it for him, that it was only one of its kind. Unless his friend sold it to a tattoo parlor or posted it online, I was getting close.

"Listen, Phani, honestly, I feel terrible about what happened," Charlie began, looking down at his shoes. They were black leather sneakers mostly hidden by his jeans. "I'm sorry I said what I said. I shouldn't have said it and you were right that it wasn't very kind."

I stayed silent, allowing him to say his piece.

"I've grown up in a very narrow-minded environment and the influences around me weren't the most tolerant. I'm not saying this because I'm excusing what I said. I've had time to reflect and I realized that if Katie heard me speak that way, she'd be furious too."

"Your sister?" I asked, remembering our previous conversation about her.

Charlie nodded. "I wasn't kidding when I said she was kind. She was also very open-minded and couldn't understand why I spoke the way I did sometimes. I thought I was better, but I realize I have a lot to still unlearn."

I wasn't sure what to say to him. This topic wasn't one I had any authority to educate on. I was relieved that Charlie knew what he said was unkind and was willing to unlearn his previous mindset about trans people and drag in general, but that didn't mean I was willing to let everything go back to normal quite just yet. Discovering this part of Charlie made me realize that I didn't really know him and that I shouldn't have rushed into anything with him. Because of my awe at having a guy like me and finding Charlie cute, I had been all too ready to say yes if he had asked me to be his girlfriend. I needed to be better about romance and relationships in the future.

"You don't have to say anything if you don't want to," Charlie continued. "I realize I may have put you on the spot."

"I am," I began, fiddling with the hem of my shirt, "glad to see that you're willing to work on yourself. Obviously, actions speak louder than words so I can't really say much until I see you prove it."

Charlie nodded, smiling. "I understand. I—"

His cell phone went off. He looked at it in irritation until he saw the caller ID. He grunted before answering.

"Yes?" After a moment, he looked at me in apology. "Sorry, I gotta take this."

"Can I use your bathroom?" I asked, using the distraction to get started on snooping.

"Sure, last door down the hall," he said, pointing to the dark hallway. "I'm gonna step outside for a moment."

We left simultaneously. I was in the bare hallway when I heard the front door close. With only three doors available to explore, one of which I was sure was the bathroom, I opened the first door I came across.

It was locked. I cursed, jiggling it a few times before giving it up.

The next door I opened was dark and smelled of men's cologne. When I flipped the switch, I grimaced at the lone mattress on the carpet and the piles of clothes scattered around along with a few large, black cases. There was a single dresser that was overflowing and a cardboard box acting as a nightstand. A disassembled handgun lay on top of it, along with a photo frame facing down. A familiar red bead sat next to it.

This was Charlie's room, I realized. But what was he doing with a gun? Did he know how to use it? I walked over to the nightstand and lifted the frame. A younger version of Charlie and a familiar brown haired woman greeted me with a smile. The names Charlie and Katie were inscribed on the bottom. I gasped. The weeping spirit tailing Charlie was this woman in the picture. Katie, his dead sister. To think she must have burned to death in a gang war. That's really no way for a young woman to die.

I frowned, placing the photo frame back how I found it before turning around to leave. My foot kicked one of the black cases open by accident, revealing a fully assembled sniper rifle.

What the hell?

I turned off the lights and rushed back into the living room. I jumped on the couch in time to see Charlie open the front door.

"Hey sorry about that," he said. "It looks like I have to head out soon. Work and all that."

"With Deli-something? The catering company?" I asked, trying hard to calm my heavy breathing. I was dismayed that we would have to cut my visit short. I hadn't even searched his roommate's room yet! I wondered if I could sneak back here when he left, though that still left me the dilemma of the locked room.

Charlie laughed. "*Delizi*, yeah."

"Hey, do you think I could get some water? I'm a little parched," I said, trying to stall.

"Oh! Of course!" Charlie headed to the kitchen to grab a sealed water bottle from the two packs stacked on top of each other. It took no time at all and as he maneuvered his way around some boxes, his foot got caught on a ten pound dumbbell partially hidden by a rag. He went down like a felled tree, a heavy thump sounding as his body hit the floor.

"Shit," he muttered.

"Charlie, are you okay?" I asked, getting up and going over to him, careful of the dumbbells littering the path.

Charlie was sitting down, looking at his foot, rotating it slowly.

"Yeah, I'm fine," he said, "I'm just super annoyed at John for leaving his shit–I mean, stuff everywhere."

I froze. "John?"

"Yeah, the roommate. Most times he's not here but the few times he is, he makes a mess and leaves me to clean it. I'm also really busy so it pisses me off when he can't follow directions."

The discovery of his roommate's name practically gave me a rush. What were the odds? I might be jumping the metaphorical gun assuming his roommate John was John Forty, but it all fits! I decided to test it a bit.

"And to think he also copied your tattoo. Didn't you say it was one of a kind? That a friend of yours made it?"

Charlie sighed, handing me the water bottle before nodding his head. "Yeah. I can't tell you how annoyed I was when I found out."

In offering my hand to help him up, I noticed a dark mark above his ankle. Charlie saw where I was looking at and smiled.

"That's just another tattoo I got. Not a favorite, but it was necessary for work."

I raised a brow. "They require you to get one?"

"Just this one," he said, lifting the hem a bit.

Black, oval-shaped with a line going through it. An alarm bell rang in my head.

"A pill?" I asked, both brows furrowed

Charlie laughed again. "I know, I know, it looks lame. It's supposed to be a theta symbol, you know, the eighth letter of the

Greek alphabet. I was told it also means death, but I still think it's lame."

Oh my god.

"How long ago did you get it?" I was shocked my voice was steady instead of hoarse. My throat felt parched all of a sudden, my hands clammy. I rubbed them against my thighs.

Charlie shrugged. "Like two months ago? I don't know, it's been a while."

I couldn't hold it in anymore. I started hyperventilating, gulping for breaths as the pieces suddenly fit into place. Charlie said something, but I couldn't hear him. I couldn't even feel his hands on my arm and forehead.

Charlie, the guns in his room, the calloused hands, the tattoos, John Forty, the roommate...

I gasped even further, my vision becoming fuzzy. I had to leave.

I struggled to get up, but Charlie held me in confusion.

"Phani....what's...you okay...hello?" His voice kept coming in and out.

"I need to go! I need to go!" I insisted, knocking into another battered box and falling over. Charlie helped me up.

"Do you need to go to the emergency room? What's happening?"

"I just...need to go," I forced out. In and out of focus my vision went. "I have to leave."

"Okay, okay, hold on."

He held my waist as he helped me to the door. Despite the clothes separating our skin, his warmth which I used to find comforting suddenly felt sticky and cloying. I wanted to run from his grip, run far until I never had to see him again. Once outside, we paused by the stairs where I sat down. I was vaguely aware of the distant sounds of traffic and barking dogs.

"Wait here, I'll see if I can get you a cab and escort you home. Are you sure you don't need the ER? I think you're having a panic attack."

"N-No, just home," I said.

I shut my eyes and tried to slow my racing heart. I heard Charlie's footsteps as he raced down the stairs. I was finally alone. My hands rose to cover my face as I tried taking deep breaths. Following that my head began to pound, my palms still clammy as cold sweat broke across my skin.

This was all too much. I couldn't believe it. I just couldn't.

Charlie? Out of all the people in Asphodel City, Charlie was the killer? I was so sure it was the roommate John! It made the most sense, but apparently not because Charlie had been another obvious contender. What were the odds that the first guy I was initially interested in was the one responsible for murdering people? And then one of those murdered people wound up being a mob boss who would hire me in the afterlife to find said murderer! The entire situation was too wild. And to think I had trusted him! I had confided in him! Sympathized even! I felt utterly bamboozled.

I shivered and took in large gulps of air. I fumbled with my embroidered bag and took out my notebook and mechanical pencil. I flipped to the pages containing my notes. Goosebumps rose on my arms, but I ignored it.

So Charlie was the killer. Let's place him back at the scene of the crime.

If he was John Forty, then it made sense Charlie's reason for working under Mr. Shern was to scope out the area and set up his trap in case his first attempt to kill Catalina failed. How would he know to go to Orpheus though? The turncoat—I suspected the turncoat was the roommate, but that's something to inquire about another time. The turncoat was working with Charlie for reasons I didn't know yet. The turncoat told Charlie about Catalina's weakness and that she would be getting the order to Fetch and Eradicate the turncoat soon. If Catalina's track record was to be believed, that means bad news for anyone involved with the turncoat. Would her hunting him down eventually lead to Charlie? Would Catalina have discovered Charlie without the turncoat?

All questions for Catalina to answer. I added an asterisk next to each question.

Was Charlie involved with anything suspicious prior to killing Catalina? If he was rubbing elbows with the turncoat, it stands to reason that yes he was. I didn't have a clue what exactly, but it was probably nothing good.

During the confrontation, Catalina felt something was off with Charlie. Maybe she unknowingly recognized him despite his disguise? If she missed the fact that Aedes had been her Darling, then this probability was certainly a possibility. Catalina then catches a glimpse of Charlie's theta tattoo. Charlie succeeds in killing Catalina and leaves. He must have realized soon after that with the police investigating Catalina's death, along with Erebus, they were bound to question Mr. Shern who would no doubt tell them about John Forty. While nearly everything about John Forty was shrouded in mystery, Mr. Shern knew what his tattoo looked like and painted it. I wasn't sure if Charlie knew Mr. Shern had done that, but regardless, Mr. Shern had become a loose end. He must have returned at the earliest opportunity and killed the old man.

I shuddered violently. The thought of Charlie having been only a wall and a few paces away from me had me feeling ill. I suppose it was a good thing Aedes kidnapped me when he did. I managed to miss out on dating Charlie hours after he had murdered Mr. Shern. Goes to show you really shouldn't pick up strangers just anywhere.

I finished writing the last of my theory, my fingers stiff from the cold. Fog escaped from between dry lips.

I thought back to when I met up with Charlie for lunch. He insisted on meeting me instead of having me walk wherever he worked. He hadn't seemed all that pressed for time despite it being his break. In fact, he got confused when I brought it up. Had he even been working that day? If he had, I suspect it hadn't been for anything legal, that's for sure. I clenched one of my fists.

Then what about the time we met at The Candle Lounge? I flipped to another page. Taped in the center was the suspicious crinkled death threat I had found in Garcy's trashcan. I read the message again. My eyes lingered on the words "loose end".

Charlie had been familiar and knowledgeable about The Candle Lounge when we spoke then. Knowing what I know now, he must have definitely spoken to Garcy before, at least enough for him to write the note. The mention of Erebus and his hatred for him was enough for me to link the two together. With his turncoat dead by then, Charlie must have thought Garcy had mentioned something to Erebus. Instead of poppy flowers, whatever was in the package he planned to deliver must have been bad news.

I wonder how Thanatos factored into the events of that night and why I was ordered to be captured alive, especially since I was a nobody. Was it all just a coincidence or was there something more to it?

Whatever was going on, I knew what I had to do next.

"I have to tell Catalina."

A soft high pitched sigh by my ear startled me enough that I looked up from my notebook and gasped. While I was still sitting on the stairs of Charlie's apartment complex, I was no longer in the physical realm.

Instead, I was in Tenebris.

XX.

DOWN JEOPARDY LANE

For once, Tenebris was a welcome sight. Mainly because I belatedly realized that if I had not been transported away from the physical realm, Charlie would have discovered me scribbling away in my investigation notebook. And if he had, I had a feeling things would have turned ugly.

Tenebris looked the same as always; abandoned and post-apocalyptic. I put away my notebook and pencil before standing up and eyeing the gray sky. I contemplated whether I should stay put or walk to Idrina's apartment. On the one hand, I could probably avoid any unsavory spirits. On the other hand, if I showed up in the physical realm again, I'd have to face Charlie and I was *not* ready to face him at all. Maybe if I just walked a few blocks away I could return in peace.

The apartment complex stairs were half destroyed so I carefully made my way down, avoiding the gaping hole on some and the rocky debris on others. Fog escaped past my lips as I exhaled. Once I was safe and sound on the ground floor, I moved to the narrow alley.

A few orbs of light floated past me. In the distance, I heard soft sighs and dripping water. I crossed my arms and stayed focused. When I made it through, I stood on the sidewalk facing the street. I frowned at the ever familiar wall of fog that hid half the city from view. Hopefully no tall dark blobs make an appearance. I didn't have my longboard with me this time for any quick getaways.

I glanced at the rusted street signs encased in ice, calculating which way to go. With a vaguely familiar direction chosen, I started walking again.

"You can do this, Phani. I believe in you," I mumbled to myself.

When a transparent cloud of mist touched my leg in passing, the skin underneath my pants numbed as though it had been exposed to liquid nitrogen. I cursed silently, but kept moving, trusting I wouldn't bump into anything or anyone through the thick fog.

After what felt like fifteen minutes, I spotted another frozen street sign. I must have crossed several blocks now. When the fog shifted enough to reveal a broken traffic light and the destroyed remains of a convenience store that I had passed on my way to Charlie's earlier, I knew this would be a good stopping point to return to.

I crouched and closed my eyes, praying that when I opened them, I would be in the physical realm again. It usually worked, especially when I was a child. I never saw Tenebris for more than a few minutes. As I got older however, my "visits" became lengthier. And to add to my horror, I could touch things. And those things? They could touch *me*.

I counted to thirty. When I reached twenty-eight, I cheated and peeked between my fingers. Fear doubled when I found myself staring at the cracked walls of the building across from me.

"No, no, no, no, no, no!" I whispered, blinking several times, desperate to wake up from this terrible, lonely place. With each passing second, the dread increased and so did my cries.

That was when a dark, flat figure caught my attention. It was tall and slender; a shadow. It moved leisurely along the wall, two white dots eyeing me from the round blob of its head. I froze, my breath coming out in shallow pants. It stopped moving. A wobbly smile appeared underneath its eyes. Twig-like fingers parodied a wave. It crept closer, hissing, body stretching and shrinking disproportionally.

"Stop," I said. I was surprised my voice sounded steady.

When the shadow figure heard me speak, it frowned in dismay, eyes suddenly glowing red. It peeled away from the brick wall until it loomed over the pothole riddled street.

I screamed and ran blindly into the fog. I didn't even know where I was going. I just knew I had to get away. My lungs burned from inhaling the cold air as I raced through the streets of Asphodel. My heart pounded in my ears as I dodged dark shapes in the fog. One of them growled in passing.

A hidden pothole caught my foot and I fell. Pain flared in my ankle.

"Shit," I muttered, struggling up. I grimaced when my palms touched cold, wet asphalt. Glancing behind me, I was relieved to see no slender man-like figure behind me. I sighed, shoulders sagging. I turned around and shrieked in terror.

Burngemear—a hulking manifestation far more terrifying than whatever it was I had seen earlier—stood a few feet in front of me. Twilight streamed through the clouds. The weak light partially illuminated him, the rest was shrouded in darkness as he approached.

I trembled, taking a step back every time he moved closer.

Why was he coming towards me? Burngemear had never done that before. He had always ignored me for the most part; a constant I lived for when forced to accidentally catch a glimpse of him. My shoulder blades dug into the brick wall behind my back. Dead end.

Estephanie...Cora..., Burngemear rasped.

I gasped, shocked he had spoken. The words came out toneless and penetrating, the volume soft yet loud enough to reach my ears without shouting.

Why was he speaking to me? Now especially? What was different this time? What had changed? I stilled when a blackened hand rose to pull back his hood, revealing a face hidden by the familiar demon skull. Silver blazed from inside dark sunken pools where his eyes ought to be.

Have you come to stay...for good?

"No."

...but you will...

The confidence in his tone had my body shaking with crippling fear. Over my living body was I ever staying here for good! I bolted from my spot and ran to the alleyway next to me. The massive sides of the building did little to deter Burngemear. His shadow loomed over me as I ran.

You will...soon.

I screamed, attempting to drown out his voice. I even used my hands to block my ears.

I burst through the other end and saw through the fog a desolate patch of dirt with rusted benches scattered just across the street. Blackened, dried tree trunks with spider branches greeted me as I entered what must be a park of some sort. I didn't even stop to check if Burngemear was still following me. At one point, I tripped again. I grimaced at the damp earth beneath my palms.

There is little time...

"Go away!" I shouted, shutting my eyes closed.

"Phani!"

I gasped, eyes flying open. I sat up and spun around on the ground at the sound of the familiar voice. Prickly grass touched my muddy hands. Bright sunshine caressed my sweat soaked cheek and ice cold hair. The warmth of the city breeze hit me like a freight truck and there, floating before me, was a confused Catalina.

I laughed in relief and flopped back onto the grass.

I was no longer in Tenebris.

Catalina continued to stare at me as if I were an asylum escapee.

"Phani?"

"Catalina! Oh, thank God!" I cried.

Seeing the bright vivid colors of Catalina's hair and clothes instead of the toned-down dullness of Tenebris nearly had me sobbing in happiness.

"Phani, calm down before you cause a scene," she said, eyeing anyone else that might be too close to us.

I got up and limped to the nearest park bench, groaning when I sat down and leaned back. I stretched my legs and let the heat of the sun soak me.

"What the hell happened to you? You look terrible," Catalina exclaimed, examining my disheveled appearance.

I smiled. "Thanks."

"I'm just saying."

Despite her brash commentary, Catalina crossed her arms and shrunk into herself, gaze looking sideways instead of unapologetically forward. I paid it little mind however. I was just genuinely glad to see her again. A week without her had been far too long. I wasn't sure what this said about my dependency on her friendship and whether it was healthy considering she had to leave at some point, but for now, I was so damn glad she was back! Was she still upset at me from our argument? I hoped not. I only had two reasons for wanting to pause the investigation and it wasn't because Aedes had paid me off.

Reason one was because the flickering flame of my life seemed easily prone to blowing out whenever I involved myself in underworld business. Catalina knew this whole thing was no walk in the park—cut me some slack if I wanted to chicken out for a moment or two. The other reason was because we were technically back to square one.

After the Candle Lounge and Orpheus Theater fiasco, there wasn't much else I thought we could do to figure out who her killer was. That was, until today.

I took a moment to reorient myself. The distant sounds of angry traffic and laughing kids on the playground reminded me it was probably rush hour. I exhaled shakily, determined not to let my misadventure in Tenebris affect me.

"Phani, hello? Are you good? *Te miras pálida*," she said, taking note of my paler than usual dark skin.

"Huh? Oh, sorry! I just..."

"What happened back there?"

"Back there?" I echoed, watching as dead leaves scurried past my feet.

"When you had your face planted on the ground! You looked terrified out of your mind!"

"I-I thought I saw something."

Catalina arched her brow. "Girl, I'm not stupid. One minute I was alone, and then suddenly you pop into existence in front of me screaming bloody murder. Try again."

Shit. She saw.

I've noticed that whenever I end up in Tenebris, my body in the physical realm would either disappear or become transparent. People who've seen me by accident think they've hallucinated or inhaled something strong. But not Catalina.

After the church incident fifteen years ago, my dad sometimes brings up the subject of me disappearing from his arms. He's convinced it had been a sign from God, reminding him that things could have been a lot worse. I could have never been born—I suppose this was where his overprotective streak first flared because it's never wavered since. I was told the church congregation believed the holy spirit had touched them in that short moment. I've never dissuaded them from the theory. It was better that way.

I looked around the unfamiliar park, taking note that I must be south of Downtown. I must have traveled quite a bit to make it this far north from Charlie's apartment. That would explain why my leg muscles ached and my lungs still burned from the heavy breathing. If I wasn't so tired, I would have been a lot more awed by the realization that moving around in Tenebris from one location to another mirrored the same in the physical realm. I thought the one time last week where I lost my main longboard was a fluke.

"I'm sorry," I said, sitting up. "I was in Tenebris."

Catalina's eyes widened. "Again?"

"Yeah. I was having a bit of a panic attack combined with an emotional crisis when it happened."

"Are you alright now?"

I laughed, ruffling my hair. "Yeah, all in a day's work."

Catalina sighed, her fingers toying with her curled tresses.

"Listen, I was lingering here because I was trying to work up the nerve to apologize," she admitted, almost resembling a guilt-ridden Doberman after ruining the family couch.

I blinked several times. Did my ears deceive me? Was Catalina *actually* apologizing? With remorse? Had Hell frozen—oh wait.

"Go on," I said.

"I'm...," she grimaced, straightening her arms as she stared at the ground. "I'm so...so—*sorry* about our fight. In fact, my behavior since I've enlisted your help has been selfish and inconsiderate. And while I'm normally okay with being selfish, you're not the person I should be directing my asshole-ish tendencies on."

Oh my God. I placed my fingers over my mouth, my doe-eyes widened. I stayed silent for a few moments, cautious she'd say something to cancel her apology just when I fell for it. When it seemed like nothing was forthcoming, I opened my mouth.

"That's really kind and self-aware of you," I said, "don't worry about it too much now, Cata. We were just really upset by how things turned out. Are *you* okay now? I was worried about you too."

Catalina's sculpted brows rose, a mixture of conflicted emotions evident on her face. She bit her bottom lip before clutching her forearms tightly. She snapped.

"Don't be so kind to me, Phani! I was a raging asshole! I never realized my death was affecting me in that way, but it makes sense because I was so angry! *Dios mío,* Phani, I'm *dead*. Dead! Deceased! That's not supposed to happen to me! *Me*! Catalina Beatrice Patron! It was *all* under my control. I was on top of the world! I had nearly *everything* I could want and now..."

Her voice cracked. Anguish flooded her eyes as unshed tears glistened. My own eyes began to prickle.

I wondered when Catalina would snap about her death. I thought maybe she'd done so before I met her because she seemed so emotionally unbothered by it before. It was evident now, however, that she had only been delaying the inevitable. Unlike Mr. Shern, Catalina had not come to terms with her death at all. It's probably the main reason why she has yet to move on, her killer aside.

"I can't do anything now," she continued, crouching down until her waves phased through the ground. "No one can see me. It's like I've been forgotten. Like I was never useful, like everything I did in the end didn't even matter, like my existence was pointless."

"That's not true!" I argued, getting down and kneeling in front of her. "You have people who care about you and will remember you forever! I certainly will! Then there's Aedes, and your family. And you can't say you didn't leave a lasting impression, either."

I gestured to the park and what lay beyond. Catalina turned her head, chuckling softly.

"Yeah that's true. I just...I never realized how cold and lonely death was. At least, I never thought I'd experience it. I was so sure..."

"You're only human, Catalina. You were bound to die eventually. It's no fault of yours."

"Yeah...human."

Her eyes took on a faraway look. She lowered her face, suddenly shamefaced.

"I'm–*I'm sorry* I got you involved in something dangerous," she said, standing once more. She began to pace to and fro before whirling around to face me. I stood up as well. "To be honest, I was hoping this would be a simple open and shut case. With my help, I thought we could get this done in under a few days tops. I was wrong and I'm sorry. You almost *died* because of me. *I even possessed you!* I imagine the feeling wasn't pleasant. I know if it had been me, I'd have run straight into the fire in an attempt to exorcize myself."

I frowned. I've tried not to think about the possession since it happened, but I suppose it was time to tell her what I thought about it.

"The possession wasn't a pleasant feeling," I agreed, "but it wasn't the end of the world. Really, I was mostly curious how you did it. I assume it's because you're a strong spirit and I allowed you to take over. I hadn't exactly been protesting given the circumstances. I admit, I won't allow it to happen again. I've never been possessed before. I avoid confrontations and carry charms that protect me from such things."

Catalina looked disappointed.

"But," I added, "if it's *you* and it's an emergency, I wouldn't mind doing it again."

Her eyes grew big. "*Really?*"

I nodded. "Granted you don't do anything weird in my body."

Catalina smiled, holding out her hand for a shake. Even though she couldn't touch me, we still managed to shake hands and nod to each other upon reaching an accord. It was an understanding that suddenly brought us closer than normal strangers forced to work together. I honestly thought I'd never get this far with her. What was probably stranger was that I considered Catalina a close friend. Had she been living, no doubt I would have been warned against her negative influence.

Was it pathetic to feel this way about someone who was dead? Maybe, but I couldn't help it. I've never had friends before. Not to the degree that I considered Catalina who didn't brush me off or look at me like I was some weirdo. If anything, her critical gaze was honest. She saw deeper than most and never judged without being fair. I liked that about her.

Once the air between us settled, Catalina watched as I sat back down before asking me a personal question.

"How long have you been seeing ghosts?"

I hesitated. "Since I was very small."

Her concerned face said a lot as she sat next to me. I admit that seeing her feel genuine sympathy and worry without making me feel awful made me appreciate her more. She stared at the walkway, expression somber.

"I'm sorry for barging into your life when you already had so much to deal with. To make such demands of you, manipulating you with money, it was very crass of me."

Crass, but in character. I didn't really fault Catalina for coming into my life with a very real life or death situation. I smiled, lightly bumping her shoulder even though she didn't move with the motion.

"It's okay, really. I've grown used to it. Sure, ghosts still scare me sometimes, but I'll get over it. I don't have much of a choice."

Catalina gave me a wane smile. She patted my head before

bumping my shoulder in return. Seeing her look carefree reminded me of my very important and devastating discovery.

"Oh, um, by the way, I think I may have gotten us ahead in our investigation," I said.

"Eh? Really? But I thought—"

"Aedes, or Orcus as you know him, may have given me the check but I haven't cashed it in."

"Why not? I would have!"

"It's not right. I promised you I'd help you find your killer. If there's one thing anyone can count on me for, it's that I always keep my promises."

Surprise and relief shined on her face.

"It'll be dangerous," she warned. "I didn't warn you properly the first time. The underworld of Asphodel City is a terrible place filled with terrible people, always waiting for an unsuspecting civilian to wander in. Always waiting for a turned back to stab."

I noticed a dark wisp floating to my right. It whispered softly before fading and disappearing under the shining sun.

"I've noticed. Are you ready then?"

"Ready for what?"

"For the news that's about to blow your mind," I said, unearthing my notebook from my bag.

When I revealed to her the tattoo I had seen on Charlie and all the clues that painted him as her killer, Catalina's face morphed into one of scandalized horror. I was glad she hadn't gone the I Told You So route.

"*Phani*. That must have been *shocking*."

I nodded. "I've reviewed the facts in my head and he's the one that fits the bill. You remember his face, right?"

"Eh, kind of. He's not really memorable to me."

I got my phone and searched for the photo Charlie took of himself before revealing it to her.

"Does his face ring any bells now?"

Catalina scratched her scalp, raising her upper lip in a disgusted snarl. "He looks like a doofus to me. Can't say I—wait, widen the area near his left cheek bone? Yeah there—*dios mío*, it's Dawson!"

"Yes, that's his last name. What—"

"Phani! *Charlon Dawson*. I remember now!" Catalina exclaimed, jumping up and pacing around even more energetically than before.

"I had a rookie in my fifth tier called Dawson. Young lad, forgettable face, promising talent. He disappeared two months before I died. Clawbra, my underhand, tried tracking him down, but no one could find him. His younger sister died a week before he disappeared, during a turf war. He must have wanted revenge. We thought he got himself killed and buried, going after the culprits alone like that.

"He looks so different though. I wouldn't have recognized him if it hadn't been for that scar on his cheekbone. I gave it to him after he *dared* talk back to me after a debriefing, the little shit. He had a goatee and short-cropped hair back then. It's amazing what a little growth and a clean-shaven face will do."

I looked at the photo, unable to picture Charlie with a goatee.

"Why would he want to kill you so badly? He went through an awful lot of effort to make sure you died that night."

"Don't you remember what Darling said when you saw him last? The turncoat knew I was investigating him and that if Erebus gave me the official Fetch and Eradicate order, he and anyone associated with him, i.e. lover boy no more, would be dead. Which means whatever plot was happening, it had to remain hidden, but for whose benefit?"

I thought back to the time I was kidnapped a second time by Aedes, going over what I remembered from the emotionally wringing interrogation. He had accused me of being a Thanatos spy...

Thanatos! What an obvious answer!

When I told Catalina this, her eyes narrowed into slits, burning rage burning bright and furious. The name had been mentioned before but until this moment, I hadn't realized how much the name meant to both Aedes and Catalina.

Thanatos, Catalina revealed, had been the ruling crime syndicate in Asphodel City for many years, long before Erebus began his reign.

When it was clear Erebus would only continue to prosper in both power and numbers, they became rivals for control of the city. The war between them lasted for about a year until Erebus came out victorious. It was ordered that anyone associated with Thanatos had to be eradicated. No questions asked. A few members and followers were known to have survived the slaughter, continuing to cause mischief every now and then—nothing Erebus couldn't quell. In recent years it was emphasized that anyone remotely linked to Thanatos and his ilk would be briefly investigated before they were eliminated.

Most didn't get an investigation though.

"What I want to know," Catalina ground out, "is what his endgame is? What is he after?"

I turned to a fresh page in my notebook and started connecting the dots.

"Thanatos's motives are a mystery for now. If the turncoat was working for Thanatos, then Charlie was also working for him," I paused. "That would explain how Thanatos's men wanted to capture me alive at the Lounge. Charlie must have been working with them and told them not to kill me. I thought it was strange why I was singled out like that. Oh! And the note I found," I showed it to Catalina, "I had a sinking suspicion that Charlie did it, but I didn't understand why. Now I think I do. Garcy said that she once had a guy inquire after Thanatos, claiming to work for Erebus. He was really manic about it too. This was two months ago. Didn't you mention that Charlie disappeared two months ago?"

That's when it clicked into place for her.

"You think when Dawson disappeared to find Thanatos...he *actually* found Thanatos, but instead of killing him, he ended up joining him? But why? Thanatos's men bombed the shelter his sister worked at. He was so consumed with revenge and hatred before he left."

I thought about the burned spirit following him turning out to be his sister Katie. It made sense why she looked the way she did now. Charlie mentioned that she got caught up in a gang war despite warning her not to go near the action that day. I never would have imagined that was how it went down exactly. Poor thing. From the way he described her, it was hard to imagine the once lively and kind girl being the pitiful spirit stalking him after burning to death.

"Charlie is still upset over her death," I said, looking down, "but instead of blaming Thanatos, he's more hostile towards Erebus."

"That little *bitch!*" Catalina spat. "How dare he betray Erebus! And to *think* we even bothered taking him in! *Ugh.* If only I had gotten the official command, him and that turncoat would be dead by my hands right now."

I stood and stretched before stowing my notebook away. Catalina followed as I walked out of the park. I was eager to return home and take a soothing shower before napping for the next several hours.

"Could you elaborate on that?"

"What I was doing prior to my death was only snooping, gathering facts. I don't take any actions to eliminate the problem unless Erebus gives me the green light. The Fetch and Eradicate order, in other words," she said, lifting her nose.

I scratched my head. "Interesting. So would you have found out about Charlie without the turncoat?"

"Hmm," she placed a finger to her lip. "It would have taken me a little longer, but if Garcy had been alive, I would have eventually discovered loser boy."

"How long do you think it would have taken you to discover him?"

"Twenty-four hours."

At my arched brow, Catalina smirked.

"I'm very fast and *very* thorough."

"Then it sounds like you were killed to buy some time."

A hint of snarl formed on her raised lip. "Buy time for *what*?"

Now that's the hundred thousand dollar question. I shrugged in response.

"It's out of our hands at this point," I reminded her. "Should we call Aedes and have him handle the rest? I know you don't want him involved, but at this point he's our best recourse, aside from the police."

Catalina sighed, phasing boldly through a couple openly showing affection. They stopped and shivered, looking around them for the sudden cold blast of air.

"Yeah, go ahead and do that. I can give you his number. Do you know where loser boy will be at today?"

I sat down on the bus stop bench and took out my phone, bringing it to my ear as an excuse to speak to Catalina without getting weird looks from the two old men next to me.

"If he's not at his apartment, then he's probably at work, assuming *Delizi Dilettos* is even a real business," I answered, glancing at Catalina just in time to see her stiffen. "What? What is it?"

"Did you just say *Delizi Dilettos*?"

"Yeah?"

"DD is a popular catering company in Asphodel," she revealed. "A lot of high-profile events hankering for some Italian use them. Hell, *I* even hired them for my birthday last year. Why would Charlie work in such an obvious place? I would have tracked him down within the hour."

High profile events? The light bulb in my head lit up. I searched for the necessary information on my phone. It took me a few minutes but I found it. I held the screen up to Catalina's face.

"Look. The catering company *Delizi Dilettos* has been hired to serve the Asphodel City Hall Gala tonight."

As soon as those words left my lips, Catalina's face paled. Well, it would have had she been alive.

"He wouldn't dare!"

Her outburst caused the overflowing trash bin beside the gentlemen to burst like a geyser, spraying a few days worth of debris to rain over us. I yelped and backed myself underneath the awning in time to avoid smelly food bags, crushed soda cans and broken beer bottles. The men didn't even have a chance to dodge the garbage. They mostly sat in shock, covered in trash rainwater. Children laughed in the distance.

Catalina paid this demonstration of her power no mind, however.

Her hair whipped around her like a wild hurricane, eyes wide in horror.

"Phani! We have to go! *Now*."

"W-what? Why?"

"*Huey*, Phani! He's in trouble! And if there's one rule in Erebus's regime, it's that the Mayor of Asphodel City must *never* be touched."

XXI.

ANOMALIES AFTER DARK

Mayor Hugh Warringson of Asphodel City was known as Huey to a select group of individuals. He was also Aedes's cousin from his late mother's side. The connection was considered confidential. Catalina made me swear not to tell anyone.

The Warringson family was an old friend of the Van Darlington's, both tracing their roots back to the Mayflower. They're so well connected they've even rubbed elbows with the likes of the Vanderbilt's and Rockefeller's. Rumors abound in some circles of their ambitious aims in certain political and underworld pies.

Aedes had to distance himself from high-society so as not to tarnish his friend's image in order to work for Erebus. Whether Mayor Huey or anyone from his circle knew of Aedes's current occupation, I couldn't say. Catalina hadn't elaborated.

I stood to the side, at the very fringes of the gala; the epitome of a wallflower as the movers and shakers of Asphodel City mingled and danced, draped in brand-name finery, sipping liquid gold as they scarfed *Delizi Dilettos's* lip-smacking finger foods. My penniless brethren would have never been allowed to even look at these people, let alone attend such a high-profile event.

I sidestepped a giggling horde of women as they chased a waiter for more flutes of champagne before glancing around. Catalina had gone searching for Charlie earlier, warning me to stay put. She didn't want me risking myself this time, especially when I was no longer in possession of her bulletproof choker. While the thought was sweet, I knew it was only a matter of time before I stepped in.

The music in the ballroom—a separate edifice under minor reconstruction a little ways away from the main city hall building—was a classical rendition of a famous composer tastefully done by a local orchestra. People laughed and danced with such elegance and grace as to make others with little skill feel shame.

Like me, for example.

While I knew how to dance to modern tunes, this type of atmosphere only served to remind me how I didn't fit in, and that my original choice not to attend had been the right call. Sadly, after Catalina surmised that Charlie would be here as a threat to the mayor, I called Idrina to let her know I had changed my mind. She invited me over to her friend Tatianna's so we could all get ready together.

Tatianna, a stunning woman of mixed race and Idrina's best friend, turned out to be quite a bubbly woman. When I mentioned the Leda Sanctuary to her, she had been thrilled to provide me more details about it while scouring her closet for a dress. She ended up snagging one of her younger sister's sparkly dresses. It wasn't anything drop-dead gorgeous or figure-hugging. In fact, the dress was rather cutesy, complete with lace and tulle: a *quinceañera* slash prom dress rolled into one. A single glance at me and anyone could tell I didn't belong with the Dolce & Gabbana, BCBG, Alexander McQueen type crowd dripping in Harry Winston jewels.

"Phani!" Idrina called as she approached. Unlike me, Idrina was a vision in blue; svelte, tall, glowing skin, stick-straight shiny hair, and a figure-hugging dress with a slit up to her knee. It was no wonder Ryan, looking spiffy in a tux himself, followed closely behind, glaring mildly at the men turning to stare at my cousin.

"There you are," she said. "You'll never believe who I just saw!"

"Who—"

"The Mayor!" Ryan exclaimed in excitement, bright eyes accompanied by a huge smile. "My boss is always raving about the good he does around the city."

"How long has he been mayor?" I asked, mainly so it would seem like I was interested. My eyes strayed around the ball for any sign of Catalina.

"A term," answered Ryan. "He was pretty young when he started out. There was a lot of opposition at first, but now that he's had experience, he'll win by a landslide next month. No doubt about it."

"Tatianna's sister was dating one of the secretaries from his office," Idrina added, grabbing a flute of champagne from a passing waiter. "She said the gala was to celebrate the finished construction of the Charon Bridge."

"Wait. You two didn't know what this gala was for?"

Their guilty faces said it all.

"Idrina!" Tatianna called from outside our group. She rushed into the circle like a mad woman. "The Mayor's coming this way!"

"What!" Idrina and Ryan gasped.

"And he's surrounded by your bosses!"

Idrina and Ryan blushed. I looked at them both.

"I thought you guys met him already," I said.

"Well...not *officially*. I kind of bumped into him in the restroom by accident," Ryan confessed. "Idrina was waiting for me outside."

I giggled despite myself.

"They met Huey with this lax security? Unacceptable!" Catalina snapped, lifting her nose in disdain beside me.

I started, my drink of sparkling water almost spilling thanks to Catalina's sudden appearance by my side. She had *definitely* not been there before. Ryan, Idrina and Tatianna continued their chat, oblivious to her chilly presence.

"When you find a minute, meet me in the women's room," Catalina said before phasing through the crowd.

I was about to sneak away myself when Idrina grabbed my arm and dragged me into her circle just as the Mayor of Asphodel City arrived.

The TV interview I had seen with Hugh Warringson a few weeks ago had done him no justice. The man was absolutely *gorgeous*! Tall, brunette, well-built with a square-cut jaw, high cheekbones, and eyes so pleasantly gray that—wait. I didn't think I'd see a resemblance, but I was wrong. Huey's gray irises were eerily similar to Aedes's silver gaze.

When Tatianna noticed my staring, she gave me a knowing smile. I blushed and shifted my attention towards my drink. Wouldn't want anyone to think I was ogling the man. Even though I was. How old was he? He couldn't have been more than his early thirties, maybe late twenties.

Mayor Huey smiled as he listened attentively to Idrina and Ryan's bosses, two older men in crisp black suits, one Hispanic, the other Chinese. When Mayor Huey finally spoke, his voice was soft and pleasing to the ears. I blushed when his eyes landed on me by chance, my ears warming considerably. I looked down.

Mayor Huey hadn't arrived alone to our group with Idrina and Ryan's bosses. There were two other people from his cabinet with him: city councilman, Mr. Rotley, a portly aged man with a thick gray mustache sporting an air of self-importance, and Mr. Lucrum, his freckled assistant. Temporary assistant, Mr. Rotley clarified as he introduced the tall fellow. Mr. Lucrum wore an oversized tweed blazer, clunky polished shoes, thick glasses, and a bow tie. The addition of his dark hair gelled back made him look almost dour. Which is a shame because he couldn't have been more than his late twenties.

Geeky features aside—he made *me* look good in comparison— there was something about Mr. Lucrum that didn't sit right with me. He twitched and fidgeted when anyone gave him the slightest bit of attention. But as soon as he caught me staring at him, he winked. The moment was so bizarre I had to avert my eyes.

"Mr. Lucrum here is filling in for Mrs. Yuu," Mayor Huey told us all, slapping the jumpy young man's back with enthusiasm. Mr. Lucrum winced. "She caught food poisoning, so she sent us her intern. Finest of the bunch, she said."

"Erm, pleasure to meet you," he mumbled in a low, nasal voice.

We all replied with pleasant greetings. Idrina took the opportunity to speak up, though I rather wish she hadn't.

"Everyone, please meet my little cousin Estephanie," Idrina introduced, gently pushing me forward when she turned the spotlight my way. I may have looked shy to everyone but inside, I was freaking out.

"She's taking a year off college and is staying with me in the meantime," Idrina continued. "It's also her first time in the city."

"Oh? And how are you liking our fair Asphodel, Miss Estephanie?" Mayor Huey asked with a smile. All eyes centered on me. I swallowed, fingers fidgeting with the hem of my dress.

"It's a lovely city that's been nothing but hospitable," I said, ignoring my memories of The Candle Lounge and my encounters with Aedes. "I hear it's come a long way from what it used to be."

"Quite right!" Mayor Huey exclaimed, eyes sparkling. "My predecessors worked hard on the reformations. When I took up the mantle, I was determined to keep that same prosperous future going."

Mr. Rotley sniffed. "You should have seen this place before; a work in progress this city was. Why, I remember—"

I ignored Mr. Rotley, turning briefly to glance behind our group instead, wondering if Catalina's patience was wearing thin. Knowing her, she was probably foaming at the mouth. I vaguely heard the music start again. Before I could excuse myself to the restrooms, a well- manicured hand appeared before me.

"May I have this dance, Miss Estephanie?" Mayor Huey asked with a gentle smile. Was he serious? Was Mayor Huey asking *me* to dance? Here? Now? I mean, I'd love to, but I would have thought he'd ask Idrina or Tatianna.

I hesitated for only a moment before nodding. I couldn't very well refuse him, not with Idrina and Tatianna throwing excited glances my way and Ryan taking my drink. Catalina will just have to wait a little longer.

Feeling like a princess or a very elegant lady, Mayor Huey placed my hand under his arm until it rested on his firm bicep. Only then did he escort me to the dance floor. His sleeve felt like silk, the scent of musk, pinewood, and cologne invading my senses. I became super conscious of how close Mayor Huey was after that.

"Um, I'm not really familiar with this," I warned him once we made it to the dance floor. I glanced at the other couples nervously. A few photographers present lifted their cameras in interest when they spotted Asphodel's Golden Boy. I prayed they wouldn't use photos featuring me. Mayor Huey gave me a dazzling smile, ignoring everyone around him.

"That's alright. I can guide you if you follow my lead. I figured I'd christen and celebrate your stay in Asphodel City with a dance from *moi*," he teased.

I giggled softly, following Mayor Huey's moves with care. "That's awfully brazen of you, but thank you."

"You're welcome," he answered, grinning as we sidestepped an incoming couple. "It's nice to see new faces enjoy the city. And with the Charon Bridge finished, Asphodel can be even more accessible to others as well."

Hearing him go on and on about Asphodel City was kind of endearing. His face would just light up like a Christmas tree, excited smile brightening away any gloom. It was fascinating to watch, though it didn't help that he was so handsome I could swoon. No wonder he was a favorite of everyone's; he had a face people could stare at all day and never get tired of. His kindness and polite temperament only further sweetened the pot.

I was thrilled to see that Mayor Huey was in no rush to finish our dance. I even laughed at a corny joke he tried surprising me with after twirling us away from a particularly clumsy couple.

Smiling at him, enraptured by his infectious light and pleasant attitude, I found myself having a great time at the gala. Things continued in this vein for a moment or two until, like all fairy tales, the happy feeling came to an end when I spotted *him*.

Burngemear.

He was here, gliding above the crowd. Waiting. Impatiently waiting. Black smoky robes spread through the ballroom like spilled ink. Reality slapped me. I couldn't believe I nearly forgot why I was here in the first place! Mayor Huey was in trouble and now that I've officially met him, I *definitely* did not want him to get hurt.

I had to stop Charlie.

"Hey, after this," I began, unsure how to phrase my odd request, "um, stay safe, okay? Like, stay near your security people at all times."

Mayor Huey looked surprised. "Of course. They're never far from me, though sometimes I wish they were. Why? Are you worried about tonight's security? Don't be. Mr. Rotley did enough worrying for everyone. He even went so far as to hire extra outside protection in addition to the officers already assigned to the event. And with my security guards, both you and I will be perfectly safe."

If only I could believe that with absolute certainty. If it had just been black smoke, which was what usually appeared when someone died, I wouldn't have worried as much. But a personal appearance from Burngemear meant the night promised to be a tragic one.

"Mayor Warringson!" called a familiar voice.

We both turned our heads in time to see Mr. Lucrum stumble through the dance floor. Out of breath with spectacles askew on his too-large nose, he stood before us bent at the waist with hands on his thighs.

"What is it, Mr. Lucrum?" Mayor Huey asked politely.

"The-The VIP guests of the night have arrived, s-sir," he stuttered, fixing his glasses.

"Already? They're usually fashionably late," Mayor Huey replied, eyes wide with surprise. Still, he smiled warmly. "No matter. I apologize for leaving you here, Miss Estephanie, but I have to personally attend to these guests."

I nodded. "That's fine. Thank you for dancing with me. I'm glad I didn't step on your toes."

Mayor Huey chuckled. "It was my pleasure," he said, lifting my hand and placing a gentle kiss on it. I blushed, embarrassed by the intimate contact, but flattered all the same.

"I'll see you around."

And then he was walking away.

Mr. Lucrum didn't immediately follow. He stood there staring at me with an odd expression, head cocked to one side. I wondered what he was thinking. Did he believe I was a pathetic social climber vying for Mayor Huey's attention?

"Um," I said, turning away, "good night."

"If you reach for that star," said Mr. Lucrum, his voice sounding less nasal all of a sudden, "you'll get burned."

I spun around to look at him, but Mr. Lucrum was gone. Anger flared inside me as my cheeks burned. How rude! How dare he assume I was gunning for Mayor Huey! Because I wasn't! At least not on purpose. Besides, for all I knew Mayor Huey was married or had a girlfriend or partner or something. Was it so wrong to admire him from afar? I didn't think so.

I stalked off the dance floor, instantly peeved.

"Phani!" called Catalina's voice from somewhere.

Realizing that I had been about to leave, I doubled back until I saw Catalina standing in front of the women's restroom door. I gestured for her to come inside so people wouldn't think I was crazy for talking to myself.

The ladies' room was a lovely eggshell white and smelled strongly of jasmine potpourri. While I waited for one lady to finish washing her hands, I pretended to inspect my hair.

The woman ignored me. She did, however, do a double take in the mirror when she spotted Catalina's spectral form looming behind her. She whipped around but saw no one there. When she glanced back at the mirror, Catalina's reflection was gone.

I stared at Catalina, but she shrugged in response.

"It happens sometimes," she said. "I can't control it."

"You okay?" I asked the woman.

She blinked. "Um, yeah."

She left soon after, clearly spooked. Just as well. I checked each stall in case anyone else remained. When I knew for certain the coast was clear, I loosened the muscles in my shoulders before facing Catalina.

"Yes?"

"Finally! Took your sweet time getting here, didn't you?"

I looked down. "Sorry. I—"

She waved my apology away, smirking in response.

"You're fine. Huey was monopolizing you, after all. Drink your fill now girly because that boy is only good for eye candy."

I frowned. "What do you mean?"

"He's off limits," Catalina explained, turning towards the mirror. She grinned when she saw her reflection appear. "Not that it stopped me, but Darling was angry when he found out. No, what I mean is you could try going after him but be aware all his potential girlfriends are thoroughly investigated. The ones who don't make the cut are asked to sign a contract that refrains them from ever contacting him or speaking about him on public broadcasting channels, social media, and online articles. Or else."

Oh my lord! "Why does everyone think I want to date him? And why this bizarre intensity over his love life? Isn't that kind of extreme?"

"His family is grooming him to be the next President of the United States," Catalina explained, fluffing her hair and touching the smear-free lipstick on her lips. "He's got five more years, but that's not stopping the Warringsons. After his next term for mayor is over, it's expected he'll run for Senator."

Holy—

"As you can imagine, they don't want any scandals or gold-diggers attached anywhere near him. And it's imperative he remains protected at all times."

It makes sense now but...

"But what about Aedes? You said they were friends, cousins even. Won't Aedes's connection to Erebus taint Huey once it's exposed?"

Catalina cackled.

"Phani, Phani," she said. "*No te preocupes.* Don't worry about it! Darling is a professional. No one will know anything about him unless he wants them to."

Well, I won't argue against that.

"So, what did you come up with then? You said you wanted to meet me here."

"*Si, si!* I went looking for the catering staff, but I couldn't find Charlie anywhere. I thought maybe he was hiding out somewhere doing something nefarious when I heard some gossip amongst the hired security guards. They were talking about their plans for tonight, you know, when the gala would be 'cut short'."

"Cut short? But it's supposed to last until one or two in the morning. At least, that's what Idrina kept saying."

"That's what I thought, too!"

It was odder still that some hired security guards would be talking about such things. I didn't have much time to dwell on that though since a group of high-society ladies soon burst through the restroom door.

I pretended to look busy in front of the sink. They filled the air with perky laughter and chatter about a much-anticipated celebrity that had finally shown up. Catalina eyed them in distaste.

"Should have locked the door. We'll have to move this meeting elsewhere," she said, drifting towards the exit.

I went to follow her when I paused upon hearing the ladies mention my favorite celebrity of all time: Raisa Hollenburg. A legend and a native Asphodelian, Raisa Hollenburg was a renowned Hispanic actress, singer, and songwriter who married a Danish prince tenth-in-line for the throne just last year. Most importantly, she's the current star in my favorite telenovela, *Cocinando con Vida.* Cooking with Life. I have the whole first season on DVD.

"Phani!" Catalina hissed when she noticed I had stopped following her.

"Raisa Hollenburg!" I whispered, looking at the girls with longing as they whispered amongst themselves. I wanted in on the gossip for once. "She's here at the gala!"

Catalina paused for an intrigued second before shaking her head.

"Damn it! Dead! Ugh, we don't have time for this! Come on!"

The city hall ballroom was large and round with two exit doors on either side. One door led to the city hall garden and the other was connected to a long outdoor corridor. It stretched until it met the main office buildings that ruled the daily goings of the city. Both doors were guarded by a pair of Asphodel's finest. Catalina figured Charlie was lurking around the main city hall building somewhere. It would be the perfect time to strike considering security was at its weakest. Most of the guards were stuffed inside the ballroom.

Leaving the party was an easy task as the few stragglers walking to and from the gala occupied the hallway. The officers on guard checked invitations and ID's before allowing guests inside. They paid little attention to me when I left.

The outdoor corridor was long and curved, cement awning and thick metal pillars the only protection available from the elements. Shrubs and trees dotted the scenery outside as small pathway lights at the edge of the walkway shined against my shoes. After a minute of walking, I noticed I was the only one around.

Just as I wondered where I should start my search for Charlie, I spotted a dark figure walking towards me from outside the corridor. I ducked behind the pillar to my left. When the stranger stepped onto the pathway, the lights illuminated his face just enough for me to recognize his loosely tied shaggy hair.

"Charlie!" I whispered to Catalina. Thankfully, he hadn't seen me.

The spirit of his sister followed behind him like a somber shadow.

"What is—" Catalina stopped when she saw the infamous duo. "Ugh, it's that thing from before."

"That's his sister, Katie," I told her. "I saw her picture on Charlie's nightstand."

"*That's his sister?!* Oh God, that explosion rearranged her face," Catalina exclaimed, lifting a hand to her lips as she no doubt recalled how Katie had appeared to us at The Candle Lounge. "I'm so glad I at least died pretty."

"Catalina," I chided.

Unlike Charlie, Katie spotted us. She yelped upon seeing Catalina before disappearing.

"That little shit," Catalina muttered. "I was beginning to feel crazy, but I *knew* I was right. Dawson really is here. Where's he been hiding though? And what's he been doing?"

Charlie looked around cautiously before straightening his white catering jacket, a smirk gracing his lips. He made his way towards the ballroom. I stared after him, feeling a mixture of disappointment and resignation. He had texted me a few hours earlier wondering where I had disappeared off too. I was relieved he hadn't suspected anything suspicious with the way I had acted before I left his place, though it seemed bittersweet he still cared.

Once the coast was clear, I left my hiding spot and looked in the direction he came from. I checked my phone for the time.

Forty minutes until eleven.

Stepping off the path of the corridor, I navigated my way through shrubs and wilting floral bushes, the flashlight app on my phone illuminating the area.

What I found most surprising and ironic was that the only thing of interest was a hidden outdoor janitor's closet behind the ballroom. It was the only door around. Had Charlie gone in there? I saw the broken silver knob on the door and found it opened with little resistance.

"I could be wrong, but I have a feeling this is it," I said.

"Oh?"

Catalina walked through the wall. I rolled my eyes at her impatience. Inside, the walk-in closet was crowded with brooms, mops, buckets, rags, and shelves full of cleaning chemicals. Nothing looked suspicious. If I hadn't spotted Burngemear in the ballroom, I would have thought Charlie wasn't up to anything after all, despite our suspicions.

"Was he jerking in here? I don't see anything!" Catalina complained, sneering at the boring innocence of the closet. I sidestepped a vacuum cleaner.

Nothing incriminating stood out, though I did spot something small and red on the floor. When I bent to pick it up, I realized it was my wooden Be-Gone bead. At least that cleared up any doubt that

Charlie had been in here. I checked inside drawers and looked behind shelves, but aside from clean rags and dust, I found zilch.

Ugh, this blows, I thought, leaning against a poster of Mayor Huey's re-election slogan from last year. I crossed my arms.

"Now what?" I asked. "How are we supposed to stop Charlie from doing whatever it is he's going to do? Assuming he—"

I shrieked when the poster slipped to the side, causing me to fall against a few mop handles. I groaned, my side throbbing.

"Phani, look! A door!" Catalina exclaimed, pointing towards a dull red door next to me.

I sighed. Of course the poster I had been leaning against would be the one blocking the important clue we were after. I rubbed my sore back and slowly got up, brushing the dust off my dress. I turned the small door knob I somehow missed and saw that the door opened up to a dark staircase. I noticed a switch to my left and flipped it. Dim orange light illuminated the rough steps.

Something told me that if I wanted to know what Charlie had been up to in here, going upstairs was the key.

XXII.

BEWARE IGNIS FATUUS

THE STAIRS WERE endless and steep. It was like traveling up a mountain using forks. Each step I took tired me and pinched my toes—oh, why did I let Idrina talk me into wearing three-inch heels? After what seemed like forever, I almost cried in relief upon seeing an end to the stairway. I leaned against the wall and wiped away the beading sweat from my forehead. Uncomfortable warmth invaded my skin.

I should work out more.

When I turned the knob, the door was unlocked. Once through the threshold, I saw I had made it onto the roof.

"What in the world?"

Catalina phased through the floor, floating high to survey the area. I envied her ability then. My heart was still pounding hard from the exertion I had just put myself through.

The noise from the city's traffic mingled with the music from the ballroom. The odd harmony made our night-time excursion a surreal one. I walked close to the edge and peered over the side. The ground looked far away, almost frighteningly so. I backed away quickly before I did something stupid, like accidentally fall off.

Construction tools and debris littered the rooftop, making every step a calculated one as my phone lit the way. I shivered when a gust of wind blew my dress against my legs. Good thing the tulle under-skirt was keeping me partially warm.

"I heard there were plans to make a rooftop garden," commented Catalina, eyeing the construction equipment.

I smiled. "A rooftop garden sounds like a great idea. When's it supposed to be finished?"

"Beats me."

She approached a large dome ceiling with a metal railing. Different colored glass panes were beautifully lit up as a familiar sound rose from within the ballroom.

It was Raisa Hollenburg.

"She's singing!" I gasped, running towards the dome.

"Hey, hey! If I can't listen to her in peace, you can't either!"

Despite her complaint, Catalina rushed to phase half her body through the glass to look in on the performance.

"Lady Hypocrite!" I cried, out of breath as I climbed over a pile of planks.

In hindsight, I should have probably been more careful. A loose board gave way beneath me. I yelped and sprawled forward, my phone clattering some distance away. Groaning, I coughed and waved away the floating white particles of dust stirred by the fall. Sitting up, I looked to see if the shoes Idrina had bought me were ruined. I'd never hear the end of it if they got scuffed.

"Phani, are you alright?" Catalina came towards me as soon as she heard the noise. "Geez woman, you're so clumsy!"

I was about to say something smart when I saw my phone illumi-nate a lumpy object at the base of the glass dome. A black sheet covered it. I dusted myself off and walked forward.

"Phani?"

"I found something," I said, picking my phone up and revealing the inconspicuous object. Blue light seeped through the cloth. I pulled the sheet away before freezing.

It was square-shaped and made crudely with wires tangled all around. The blue timer screen indicated that thirty minutes remained before detonation.

"Bomb!" I shouted.

Catalina rushed over and gasped in horror.

"What the shit? Shit! Do you know how to disarm a bomb?"

"Are you kidding me?! I was never equipped for this!"

"Neither was I! We have to warn Darling!"

"He's not here!"

"He's always keeping an eye out on Huey!"

"We have to tell the police and get everyone out!"

"Wait!" Catalina screamed. "What if it's remote controlled? If Dawson sees us creating a scene, he'll blow us all up for sure!"

"Can we really take that chance?"

I ran towards the door and raced down the stairs, suddenly gaining a lot more energy.

That's why Burngemear was here! With a bomb like that, with so many people around, death hanging heavy like a burning scent in an airless room would be all too easy! I had to get everyone out of here. Even if Charlie had a remote, I couldn't let these people dance around until they burned in the inferno.

Raisa Hollenburg was here for Pete's sake!

"*Estephanie!*" Catalina appeared in front of me, blocking my path to the ballroom. "*Que vas hacer?* What are you going to do?"

"I'm going to," I panted, catching my breath, "I'm going to cause a scene. One that will make everyone leave this place without knowing there's a bomb in the building!"

My plan was easier said than done. The minute I was back inside the ballroom, my nerves and introverted personality kicked in. It was a recipe for disaster. I was about to cause a scene, one that would bring heaps of attention to me. The realization was terrifying.

But then the bomb came to mind and it was enough to get my legs moving forward.

I reached the platform Raisa Hollenburg was performing on with little difficulty. She was wrapping up her song, an elegant, popular number that lent itself only to her unique vocal cords. Once the final note in the air faded, the applause around the ballroom was thunderous.

Raisa smiled, curtsying.

Face aflame, I proceeded not to think, but *do*.

The moment I hopped on stage, all eyes zeroed in on me. Even Raisa's, which was more than I was hoping for. No one had been expecting me, which bought enough time before security came and tackled me to the ground. I focused on the stained-glass windows behind the crowd and used it as a crutch to keep myself from choking on fear. Wouldn't do to mess up my only attempt at saving everyone.

"Can I have everyone's attention please?"

That didn't sound loud enough.

I looked at Raisa and gestured for her to hand over the microphone. She did just that with a confused look before retreating to one side of the stage. In my mind, I was freaking out over the fact that I was touching the very same microphone Raisa Hollenburg had just used to sing only moments ago! Quelling my inner fan girl until she was under control, I braced myself.

"Everyone! I have an important announcement to make!"

"Phani!" Idrina shouted from somewhere. "What are you doing?"

Murmurs broke out amongst the crowd as they questioned the sudden unanticipated interruption. I flushed, my cheeks burning as blood roared in my ears. I tightened my sweaty grip on the microphone.

"Theres's-There's a—there's a—!" Fuck, I couldn't get the words out. "F-Fire! There's fire!"

Confusion grew as everyone looked around, wondering if this was true as the fire alarms had yet to go off. Shit. I should have pulled that first. I glanced at Catalina and gestured with my eyes for her to look up. She did and saw the sprinklers just as a breathless Idrina got to the front of the stage, her ample chest heaving up and down.

"Phani! Get down!" she hissed, throwing a panicked look around us. "Security is going to throw you out!"

I paused and stared at her. Her eyes. When Idrina turned her head to face me, her dark eyes glittered with genuine worry and fear, but not for herself. Her expression said it all: she thought I had finally lost my marbles. A piece of my heart fractured.

Before I could open my mouth and defend myself, Catalina cursed aloud. Her forehead wrinkled in frustration as her attempts to shatter the safety on the sprinklers weren't working. Apparently, her poltergeist abilities weren't coming to her easily this time around.

"*Ai, esta papada vieja!*" she snapped. "How did I do this last time? It's hard when I'm not furious."

I suspected as much. Catalina had to be emotionally unstable to cause anything to explode. Before I could tell her my theory, I spotted Charlie in the crowd near the catering table. He was staring at me, looking as confused as anyone else was to see me standing here. He turned and spoke into a walkie-talkie. To my alarm, I noted that Charlie stood a little too close to Mayor Huey and his entourage.

Dammit, my plan wasn't working!

"EVERYONE GET THE FUCK OUT NOW!" I shouted just as Catalina's temper flared. One of the sprinklers broke, causing a chain reaction as half the sprinklers in the room went off. Even though it only rained heavily on one side of the room, the sudden commotion was enough to get people reacting. They shrieked and scrambled towards the main exit on my right to avoid the watery deluge. I smiled in satisfaction.

"Phani!" Idrina yelped. Ryan came over and placed an arm around her.

"I'll meet you outside," I said to her, tossing the microphone aside. "I'll explain later!"

Before she could protest, both Idrina and Ryan were promptly swept away by the chaos. About half of the party-goers remained, including Mayor Huey. Both he and the few police officers on duty guided frantic guests out the ballroom. Huey's security detail hung close, anxious looks on their faces. It was clear they wanted him out *now*.

The hired security guards scattered themselves, doing nothing useful. Some stuck close to the police officers like frightened children, others lounged around. The water and chaos didn't seem to bother them.

I sighed and shook my head. So much for their help.

Hopping off the platform, I saw Charlie stare at me with a smile. He didn't look the slightest bit upset that his plan was foiled. My sense of danger tingled, but I ignored him. Escaping the bomb's blast radius was more important right now.

Or at least it was until Charlie pulled out a gun from his coat. Time slowed. There was no hesitation in his blue-green eyes nor in the muscle of his trigger finger. No one saw him aim at the nearest police officer's back. The deafening pop that followed made me freeze. It took forever for the officer's body to hit the floor, but when it did, everything after happened fast.

The once useless security guards snapped to attention. They pulled out their own firearms and fired at the remaining police officers before they could retaliate.

Panicked screams renewed with fervor as people made a dash for the exit. The security guards wasted no time slamming the doors closed. They pointed their guns at everyone, discouraging anyone from coming near.

It dawned on me that the gala had been a set up from the beginning.

"Oh shit," Catalina cursed. "Shit! Shit! He has an army!"

Mayor Huey's security detail surrounded him, their guns aimed at the enemy. A few unlucky guests remained trapped inside, myself included. They kneeled down and cowered, doing little to bring attention to themselves. Even the jittery Mr. Lucrum was present, his face buried behind a clipboard next to the mayor. To my relief, Idrina and Ryan were absent.

"This was not how the night was supposed to end," Charlie announced.

He didn't have to shout to be heard. The acoustics of the empty ballroom carried his voice well. He swaggered toward Mayor Huey.

"I suggest, Mayor Warringson, that you tell your boys to put their guns down or I pull this trigger on a random citizen."

Mayor Huey glared at him.

"I won't be intimidated by you," he said, but gestured for his security detail to put their guns down. They did so with much reluctance.

Charlie's smile became smug. "I don't need you to be, Mr. Mayor. In a few short minutes, you won't exist, and nothing will ever matter again."

Mayor Huey's eyes flickered in my direction, probably wondering if my crazy spectacle from before was to prevent what was going on now. If only he knew it was much bigger than that.

"Phani," said Catalina. "He's stalling."

"Can you try possessing him?" I whispered.

She shook her head. "Believe it or not, I can't possess just anyone. You're the first person I could do that with. I tried with others after I did it with you, but it never worked."

Well that left us in a pickle.

"God, this feels good," Charlie laughed. "I've been waiting to do this for ages."

He stopped a few feet away from Mayor Huey and circled the men protecting him. His curved lips became malicious. How did I ever think of him as cute before? All I could focus on was the cruelty and ruthlessness shining through every step he took.

"And just what have I done to make you act this way against everyone here tonight?" Mayor Huey asked, staying calm and collected.

"It's nothing you did per se, Mayor Warringson. It's more of what a friend of yours did," Charlie answered.

Mr. Lucrum trembled behind his clipboard the moment Charlie neared him. The sight caused him to laugh before mocking Mayor Huey for his pathetic personnel.

"Why did you kill Catalina?" I asked aloud, forcing myself to speak.

I had to get this going before we all blew up.

Charlie whirled around when he heard my voice echo. He looked surprised, as if he'd forgotten I was also trapped inside with him and Mayor Huey. The expression was soon replaced by a poker-face.

"I saw you at Orpheus Theater," I said, "when you killed Mr. Shern. When you came by The Candle Lounge, you weren't there to just deliver poppy flowers to Garcy, you were there to kill her. Then when I ruined your plans, you sent in your men to massacre everyone instead."

Charlie frowned, eyes wavering slightly. "You weren't supposed to be there, Phani. I didn't want you hurt. I told my men to leave—"

"The blond haired, dark skinned, mole girl alive," I interrupted, glaring at him. So he *had* been working with Thanatos! That bastard! "Thanks to that, I ended up figuring out that the guy I was interested in dating was a cold-blooded killer."

Charlie scowled before marching over and grabbing my arm. Catalina gawked but was unable to stop him from manhandling me. The most she could do was phase through him and all that did was give Charlie a chill he easily ignored.

"You don't know anything, Phani. Not all the facts. But I do admit that I didn't know you were such good friends with Bulletproof Betty to go snooping on her behalf. Especially into business that doesn't concern you. I can't believe you've been holding out on me," he accused.

His grip on my arm turned painful, but my bravado held through. "Don't do this, Charlie."

"Are you working for *Erebus* then?" he hissed, anger blazing in his eyes. "*You lying, sneaky bitch.* I can't believe you were trying to get me to fall for you."

"Me? I'm not the one murdering innocent people!"

"You're not hung up on that useless Shern guy from the theater, are you? He was a loose-end who loved flapping his gums. When the cops began asking around after the shooting, I didn't want them catching on to me, especially if one of them reported to Erebus. So I killed him when I had the chance. I couldn't risk any slip-ups."

So he really had been John Forty, I thought. I stared at him in horror, unable to believe I had been so thoroughly fooled. You just can't get taken with anyone off the streets anymore, can you? Charlie tugged me closer, dragging me towards Mayor Huey. I glanced at the large antique clock hanging on the wall in between the stained glass windows.

Twenty-five minutes left.

"I also know about the bomb!" I blurted.

Mayor Huey's face paled. Mr. Lucrum let his clipboard fall.

"You came here to blow everyone up," I said, "*especially* Mayor Warringson. Probably because Erebus told everyone under his rule that the mayor was off-limits."

"Phani, don't provoke him!" Catalina hissed.

Charlie gripped my chin, his thumb pressing against the mole at the corner of my lips. He tugged my face forward until it was a mere two inches from his own. We were so close I could smell the scent of his breath. It was stronger than last time. Earthy, raw, as if he'd been munching on poppy seeds. The smell was almost dizzying. One look at the satisfied expression on his thin face, however, made all thoughts of his breath leave my mind.

"So you know? Seems you aren't as innocent as I thought."

"Why are you doing all this?"

"As if I'd tell you now."

Charlie tightened his grip until I squeaked in pain. Catalina took that as a sign to possess me. She walked into me with ease, like slipping on a fitted jacket. Her presence was a familiar weight against my limbs. They tingled, my fingers twitching despite internally screaming at my body to stay still. Her voice echoed in my mind as she figuratively took over the wheel.

This is safer for you, she said. *If he tries anything, I can put up a proper fight.*

"Please let her go!" Mayor Huey shouted, attempting to break away from the circle of bodyguards that held him in place. "Take me instead! It's what you want, right?"

"No offense, but I'd rather hold onto someone cute. Phani and I have history together, after all. Don't worry though, you'll bite the dust soon enough. We have, oh, say twenty-three minutes left."

Police sirens wailed in the distance, but Charlie didn't seem bothered by them. It was a very worrying observation. Did he intend to get himself blown up too? Did his men? A quick glance at their faces showed a strange feverish gleam in their eyes as though they'd been drugged.

"Alright then, *don't* reveal why you're doing this," said Catalina before I could stop her. My lips transformed into a vicious smirk. "No one wants to hear a sob story from a suicidal orphan anyways."

I knew to expect painful retribution after that. And yet, I found myself surprised when Charlie backhanded me. Maybe some part of me still hoped he could turn this horrible nightmare around. I should have known better.

The Charlie I knew was never real.

My teeth rattled from the force of his blow, cutting the inside of my cheek. It throbbed with stinging pain, my tongue tasting thick copper. He let me drop like dead weight. Unwanted tears pooled in my eyes. I tried blinking them away; showing weakness at this stage was dangerous.

Charlie bent down and cupped my cheek. Despite the surprising gentleness of his touch, it stung like a bitch. He tutted, looking remorseful.

"Phani, Phani, look what you made me do," he said with a shake of his head. "That mouth of yours just now was not cute, and not very you. It hurts me to think of you as my enemy, you know. I thought we had something special, an understanding."

He sighed. "Tell you what, because of my fondness for you, I'll show some mercy and send you off to the afterlife now. That way you won't have to burn to death when the bomb goes off."

I found myself staring at the end of his muzzle when Charlie loomed over me. The look in his eyes made me grow cold. He meant it. Charlie really meant to spare me a fiery death by killing me. Right here, right now. If Catalina hadn't been way ahead of me, I would have sat there frozen like an idiot.

She kicked the gun out of Charlie's hand the same time he pulled the trigger. To my relief, Catalina pulled my head back just as the bullet whizzed past, almost grazing my forehead. I had worried earlier over how things would play out now that Catalina's bulletproof choker was no longer with us, but I shouldn't have bothered. I may be conscious of my near-death experience, but Catalina was not.

The moment Charlie's gun clattered onto the hard shiny floor, pandemonium struck for the second time that night.

The guests that had gotten stuck inside sprang to their feet in one sudden fluid motion. They grabbed hidden handguns from their persons and fired at Charlie's men. A fight ensued, the henchmen giving back as good as they got.

Mayor Huey's security detail brandished their own backup weapons before joining the fray. I didn't even get a chance to blink twice before Mayor Huey grabbed my arm and high-tailed it towards an overturned buffet table with Mr. Lucrum and a few bodyguards in tow.

"Don't let the mayor escape!" Charlie shouted. He was quick to retrieve another small pistol from a strap at his ankle. Shooting his closest opponent in the face, he ducked behind an overturned table.

One of Mayor Huey's bodyguards grabbed a fallen chair. With a mighty heave, he flung it toward the window behind us. It crashed through like a heavy stone. The delicate stained-glass shattered into thousands of tiny shards. Cold wind burst into the ballroom.

"You have to go. Now!" Mr. Lucrum ordered.

He shoved Mayor Huey and I through the makeshift exit before we could say another word. The wind outside was harsh as it nipped our exposed faces. The city hall garden, with its trimmed rose bushes and red maple trees, surrounded us as we ran. I could feel Catalina's presence still inside me, using my weak legs to carry us through the chaotic night.

"Estephanie," Mayor Huey shouted, "where's the bomb?"

"On the roof," I said, panting, "sitting at the base of the dome."

"Gotcha. Get to safety," he said before veering off to one side, heading straight towards the nearest stairs. I gasped. What was he doing?!

"Huey no!" Catalina and I cried. "Come back!"

He didn't listen, and neither did my body's instinct to find safety.

I don't know whether it was Catalina or me who did it, but we both ended up following Mayor Huey. I checked my phone and saw we only had about eighteen minutes left before all of city hall was destroyed. Catalina pumped my legs faster, causing me to huff and puff until we caught up. Mayor Huey was surprised to see me running alongside him. Other than a small frown of disapproval, he didn't say anything.

It took us about four minutes to make it to the roof deck using a different set of stairs. This one allowed me to see the city skyline instead of dank darkness. When we made it, I led Mayor Huey to the bomb sitting at the base of the glass dome. Through the ceiling, the sound of yelling and gunfire became prominent.

"Can you disable the bomb?" I asked.

"No, I haven't a clue how to, but I have to get rid of it somehow," Mayor Huey confessed, extracting the bomb with care. It was small enough that he was able to hold it with little difficulty in one hand. His tense shoulders relaxed when he looked into the distance. "I know, I can toss it into the lake!"

"Are you sure that's a good idea? Aren't bombs fragile? Won't a careless move kill us all?"

Mayor Huey frowned. "Maybe, but we're running out of options here. We won't be able to outrun it and we don't know how to disarm it without blowing ourselves up either. It's our only recourse."

"We might have had a chance if you hadn't run up here," Catalina snapped, placing angry hands on my hips. Mayor Huey turned his head to stare at me with a serious expression.

"I'm not going to let innocent people die so I can survive."

The intensity of his gaze had me shivering. He meant every word. He would rather die trying than do nothing at all. Catalina grit my teeth.

"Fine," she muttered, resigned. "How far can you throw it?"

Mayor Huey graced me with a soft smile. "Pretty far. I wasn't the star pitcher on my college baseball team for nothing."

The lake was next to the gardens across the ballroom. Mayor Huey would have to throw it pretty far to minimize the blast damage.

Police sirens sounded into the night as Asphodel's finest

surrounded the city hall entrance, the ballroom annex located behind the city hall main office building. For the moment, we remained untroubled by the crowds of people and news channels gathering. That didn't stop the helicopters flying overhead though.

Mayor Huey readied his throwing arm.

"Step back," he said. "I'll—"

"I think *not*," interrupted an angry voice from behind us. "I did *not* come this far to fail. You two are going to die here whether you like it or not."

XXIII.

CRISIS APPARITION

CHARLIE STOOD several feet away with his gun pointed at Mayor Huey's torso. Disheveled and wild-looking with windblown hair, he bled from a skin abrasion to the cheek, probably the result of a bullet. Hatred blazed in his eyes.

At the same time, Burngemear phased through the roof. He floated above us like a thundercloud, a rainbow swarm of butterflies following after him. I swallowed.

Catalina moved my body forward until I was shielding Mayor Huey.

"Estephanie," Mayor Huey whispered in surprise. "What are you doing? Get out of the way!"

We didn't move.

Phani, I'm sorry, but without my choker, I can't guarantee you getting out of here alive.

I had a feeling that might be the case. With a gun in enemy hands, my chances of survival were slim. Just when I was anticipating my unfortunate demise, a familiar misty figure materialized behind Charlie's back.

It was Katie. She whimpered behind dainty hands, sorrowful eyes peeking at her brother. Seeing her act pitifully despite persistently clinging to Charlie brought a sudden realization.

I knew what I had to do.

"Charlie," I said, walking forward with care. I lifted my hands. "Don't do this."

"You're not allowed to call me that anymore!" He snapped, moving a few steps forward as well. "You were an Erebitch this whole time! You lied to me and made me crazy about you! But what you didn't know was that anyone associated with that devil doesn't deserve to live."

"Please. You're better than this. Katie wouldn't have wanted this for you," I said.

Charlie's eyes widened. "What?"

"I know what happened to Katie," I said. "Her death prompted this retaliation against Erebus and the Mayor, didn't it?"

"Oh my god. Are you really going to talk me out of this?"

His sarcasm dripped like poison.

"She knows what you're doing," I continued, ignoring his derision.

His smug smile hardened in response.

Katie floated in frantic circles behind him, her face had morphed back to the black charred mess of flaky shiny skin. I could smell cooked meat from where I stood. Acid shot up my esophagus, but I fought the urge to retch.

"She's dead," Charlie snapped with finality. "You better shut up before I stop indulging you."

"Then why go through all this? If you think killing us will bring your sister back, then you're wrong."

"You're right. It won't bring her back, but it'll make me feel damn good. Everyone will get a taste of what I've had to swallow for years in this fucking corrupt and shitty city," said Charlie with a crazed smile.

"There's a better way to do this," Mayor Huey said aloud, voice gentle. "You don't have to go through such dangerous lengths to get your revenge."

Charlie's gaze flickered to Mayor Huey before sneering. "Oh *shut up.* The city's better than it ever was? *Get fucking real.* You haven't done a single damn thing to help anyone in this damn city. You've only gentrified and swept all of the poor and ugly people into one corner, allowing rich assholes to fuck us over. You're a fucking joke, *mayor.*"

Mayor Huey's eyes widened in shock. He was left speechless.

"It can't have been all that bad," I said. "Surely, there were good moments in Asphodel."

Charlie rolled his eyes. "You kids really want to talk, huh? Alright, I don't care. You have less than twelve minutes before the bomb blows up, anyways."

Shit! I had to do this fast!

"Katie," I said aloud, looking at the ghost woman. She stopped moving and glanced at me. Her face was singed, nose missing, exposed eyeballs overflowing with fear as they sunk against the bloody muscles of her socket. I smiled reassuringly, suddenly guilty that I hadn't been kind to her in the past. None of this was her fault, after all.

"Katie. If your brother could hear you right now and you could tell him anything, what would it be?"

Charlie looked at me like I was crazy. As for Mayor Huey, I could feel his puzzled stare, but I bravely faced the girl. Hope filled her. When I blinked, she was suddenly standing in front of me, invading my personal space. I nearly screamed in fright. Dry eyes appraised my sincerity as she circled me. The smell of cooked meat became prominent.

"Really?" she asked, teeth rattling. Her burned tongue stuck to the inside of her mouth, making a wet slapping sound.

I nodded, fighting the urge to cringe.

"Tell him I'm sorry," she whispered, looking down. "I didn't mean to disregard his warning again, but there was a baby that had checked in at the shelter. He reminded me of Timothy. The mother promised me that I could hold him the next time I saw them. I could have waited, but I was so *impatient.* I just wanted to hold him! I wanted to know what Timothy would have felt like in my arms!"

The grief in her voice was thick. I nodded. Much to Mayor Huey's protests, I approached an amused Charlie. I met his gaze and for once, spoke with complete confidence.

"Katie wants you to know she's sorry. She didn't mean to disregard your warning about going to the shelter, but she just needed to go there that day. It was important to her."

Charlie's derisive smile melted. Quick as a cobra, he grabbed the front of my dress and yanked me towards him. He kept the gun pointed at Mayor Huey, preventing him from interfering. Mayor Huey gritted his teeth but stayed put, frantically eyeing the bomb as the seconds ticked by.

"You're honestly becoming kind of annoying, Phani," Charlie declared. "I always thought you were odd, but I found your eccentricity endearing. Now you're just pissing me off."

I clenched my fists. I could feel Catalina rearing to tear into him, but I had to remain in control if I was going to make it out of this alive. I couldn't let Charlie's presence stop me from speaking.

"The reason she went to the shelter," I continued, "was because there was a baby there. He reminded her of Timothy. Katie was promised she could hold him the next time the mom saw her. She couldn't wait until the next day. She needed to know what Timothy would have felt like in her arms."

The tension around Charlie's eyes and jaw grew slack. The transformation was incredible. I didn't know who Timothy was, but it certainly did the trick. Horror entered Charlie's face before he shoved me away.

"Wha-What the fuck? No one knows about Timothy! No one! Not even Erebus! *Who the fuck are you?*"

His trigger finger became uncomfortably twitchy. When my mouth opened, the words flowed naturally.

"I'm the girl who can see dead people. And those dead people, they *speak* to me."

This time Catalina morphed my lips into a smirk.

"*Including* your sister Katie."

Charlie lunged at me like a deranged animal, snarling in mindless anger, momentarily forgetting about the gun. Catalina kicked the weapon from his hand. It arched and clattered some distance away. We looked at each other for a split second before dashing towards it. I fell when Charlie knocked me aside. In retaliation, he scraped his chin when I used my legs to topple him.

Having placed the bomb down when I wasn't looking, Mayor Huey ran towards the abandoned gun. Charlie used his strength to push me aside before going after him. Sensing Charlie from behind, Mayor Huey sped up before taking a dive. His hand grabbed the gun before rolling out of the way just as Charlie pounced. Before he could even sit up and aim, silver light glinted off Charlie's hand as a swift arm grazed Mayor Huey's neck. The man yelped.

I ran towards them and saw that Charlie had cut the side of Mayor Huey's neck with a hidden knife. It wasn't dead center, but it was still substantial enough to look gory when the bleeding started.

"Huey!" Catalina and I shrieked.

Mayor Huey wasn't going to let the gushing slash on the side of his neck stop him. Instead of letting Charlie overpower him, he tossed the gun as he and Charlie tussled, free hand grabbing Charlie's tattooed wrist to prevent him from using the knife. Catalina was torn between staying to make sure Mayor Huey's windpipe wasn't cut open and running after the gun to end the fight.

Just as I moved to run after the gun, Charlie jabbed his elbow into Mayor Huey's face, causing the man to fall back with a grunt. Catalina acted fast. Charlie only had time to roll on top of Mayor Huey and aim his knife at the man's throat before I kneed him in the face.

He let go of Mayor Huey, but not before grabbing my dress and yanking me down. I fell next to Mayor Huey as Charlie rolled away to safety, staggering to his feet. His nose bled and stained his lips and teeth. The injury did little to slow him down. He broke our staring match to make a break for the gun. It was too late to stop him. Swiping it off the ground, Charlie turned and pulled the trigger.

Mayor Huey covered me in time. I heard myself scream as the bullet lodged itself into his right shoulder.

"Oh my god!" I cried.

Mayor Huey didn't make a sound. He brought his left hand to the wound, his fingers coming away red and smelling metallic. At this point he was quickly resembling *Carrie*, half covered in bright red blood.

"Huh. My vision's funny," he said, voice steady. He blinked a few times. My hysteria reached a new high when Asphodel's Golden Boy slumped forward, desperately fighting to stay conscious.

Gravel crunched underneath Charlie's approaching footfalls.

A stray wrench lay near my foot. Without hesitation, I flung it at Charlie's face. He fired another shot just as it clipped his temple. The bullet missed and clinked off a surface behind us.

Now!

I raced at him, Catalina taking control of my limbs.

Despite looking disoriented, Charlie blocked one fist before snatching my arm in a tight grip. Using my full weight, Catalina leaned heavily on one side, counting on Charlie not letting go and using the chance to hook my leg around his knee and yank it forward. Charlie lost his balance and with my free hand, she punched him right in the solar plexus. The air rushed from his lungs. Catalina kicked the gun from his hand. In retaliation, Charlie's grip on my arm slid to my wrist where he tightened it before twisting it hard. My arm bent with the movement, but the bone almost broke. He kneed my stomach after that.

I gasped like a fish as I doubled over.

"So you can see and speak to ghosts then. Fine, whatever," Charlie began, using his other free hand to grip my neck hard enough to leave marks. He lifted my head and smirked, bringing our faces together. "But you've given me a theory. I heard my men at the Lounge were killed. No real loss. I had more. But imagine my shock when I found out through the gossip vine that a dark haired girl in a green dress had been the one to take them out. I couldn't believe it at first. I mean, you? A frail, meek girl? Impossible. And I *still* feel that way because you see, I'm not stupid. I'm starting to see a pattern here. It feels like I've fought you before. These moves, they're good. Almost Bulletproof Betty good."

Catalina screamed and slammed my forehead against his already injured nose in a vicious head-butt. *Crack!* The hairs on the back of my neck rose. Charlie howled in pain, backing away. He didn't let go of me though. His grip on my wrist tightened, his other hand touching his definitely broken nostril. A stream of wetness spilled steadily down my forehead and the slope of my nose until it pooled around my lips. My tongue tasted hot, liquid iron.

Blood. *My* blood.

"Fucking bitch! I knew it! You possessed Phani somehow," Charlie exclaimed with glee, eyes feverish. It was disturbing to see him so unhinged, as if he'd inhaled something recreational. Could the poppies have gotten to his head? "I knew Phani was too good to get embroiled in this mess. If she can speak to the dead, then how far fetched would it be if La Patrona possessed her? It was *you* who killed my men. It was *you* who turned her against me!"

"You're fucking delusional, man!" Catalina spat. "Phani will never forgive you after what you've done!"

He laughed maniacally, sea green eyes glazed with heat. "As if it's anything different from what you used to do. At least I'm only striking in retaliation."

"For a Thanatos foot soldier bombing your sister's shelter?"

"I thought it was Thanatos too," he said, walking me backwards. "That's why I went after him. But when I finally met him, I was surprised to find he was totally different from what Erebus made him out to be. And you know what? He told me a disturbing truth about Erebus. The *real* reason he appeared in this shitty city. It's *his* fault that my sister died. He made me see that I had been blinded and tricked by Erebus this entire time!"

His nails carved crescent moons in my skin, cutting off the circulation and scarring it viciously.

"No! No, it's not!" Catalina snapped. "No one could have known your sister was going to be there that day! Thanatos lied! Erebus had no way of stopping your sister from going to the shelter. *You* told your sister not to go. *You* told her there would be a Thanatos and Erebus gang war on that street. Katie should have *known* better. It was her own damn fault she died!"

We gasped when Charlie let go of my wrist just as Catalina yanked it away. I stumbled backwards, the back of my knees suddenly hitting the edge of the roof—when had we wandered this close to the edge?—and before I could stop the momentum, I fell.

"Phani!" Mayor Huey yelled.

I couldn't even scream I was so terrified.

I was going to die. *I was going to die.*

Thinking fast, Catalina threw my hand out until it caught a protruding ledge. When my body halted its descent, the splitting sensation in my arm caused the muscles to scream. It trembled. My fingers struggled to hold on.

Oh god, when did I get so heavy?

Oh, I can't do this. I can't do this. I can't hold on forever. I'm going to slip and fall to my death.

"Fuck!" Catalina cursed. "Don't let go!"

I panted, feeling the weight of gravity pulling me down. My head became woozy the longer I held on, my grip loosening when something wet trickled down my bruised throat.

Charlie peered over the edge with a smirk.

"This is it. The second time I kill you. Serves you right for interfering, you stupid bitch. And just when things were starting to look up. I guess you can't win everything, huh? At least, I can get rid of you with pleasure!"

Having recovered his gun, my eyes widened when Charlie aimed for my head. My fingernails chipped as they scraped against the dry cinder block. The tears on my lower lids froze from the harsh night breeze. My vision clouded over.

Phani, I'm so sorry!

I closed my eyes.

The sound was deafening.

I shrieked in retaliation, my shoes skimming the wall of the building. When the searing hot pain of the bullet never came, I reluctantly opened my eyes.

"Phani! Grab my hand!" Mayor Huey exclaimed, leaning over the edge of the roof with his hand outstretched. His other free hand was clamped around the cut on his neck. He didn't seem worried over Charlie's presence next to him.

Instead of attacking Mayor Huey, Charlie stood where he was. He stared at me, his expression confused but vacant. He wobbled when he blinked.

"Fuck," he murmured.

His body tipped over the edge.

I shrieked as he fell past me. The muffled thud his body made once it hit the ground was final amongst the cacophony of the city's nightlife. I refused to look down. I knew that if I did I'd fall.

"Grab my hand!" Mayor Huey called again, straining his hand. His red stained fingers glistened like melted rubies in the moonlight. I shook my head and concentrated, lifting my free hand to reach him. There was about a foot between our fingers. It was utter agony to reach any further. I couldn't do it.

Lift yourself up, Phani!

"It...hurts," I cried, tears leaking.

The pain in my shoulders was burning into a crescendo.

"You can do it. You have to!" Mayor Huey reassured desperately.

Phani!

Fuck!

I made one last ditch effort to lift myself up using what little energy my upper body possessed with my free arm. If it hadn't been for Catalina controlling the muscles in my other one, I would have fallen for sure. The extra effort I added seemed futile, but it was enough for Mayor Huey to grip my hand tightly.

Despite his gallant help, Mayor Huey's face worried me. He looked extremely pale in the moonlight as beads of sweat rolled down his forehead. He was panting as if he'd run a mile. He was going to bleed out if he kept this up!

To my surprise, Mr. Lucrum's freckled face, sans spectacles, peered over the edge next to Mayor Huey. With his help, both men were able to pull me back up to safety.

"Oh thank God!" I sniffed, my body shaking from the cold, the pain, and my near-death experience. My arms burned, and my knees still ached. I wiped the tears from my eyes as my teeth chattered.

Despite the roughened-up state he was in, Mayor Huey saw my tears and handed me the folded handkerchief from his blazer pocket. Only half of it was soaked in blood. I smiled my thanks just as he apologized. Mr. Lucrum rolled his eyes in response. He shrugged out of his jacket before placing it over my shoulders. Because his warmth lingered in the fabric, I found I could breathe easier.

After dabbing my eyes, I turned to peek over the roof.

Charlie lay sprawled face-first on the ground, limbs splayed and bent unnaturally. A red flower bloomed from the center of his white catering jacket. He didn't move. I swallowed, feeling nothing but a languorous reprieve now that the threat he presented was over.

Katie hovered in the air a few stories above Charlie's body, not quite going to him, but not removing herself from the area. She wasn't crying anymore, nor did she look saddened by his death. Instead, Katie appeared calm, as if she were waiting. Waiting for his spirit to rise.

I looked away.

"Phani, are you alright?" Mr. Lucrum asked as he tucked the gun used to off Charlie into its shoulder holster. When he spoke, I noticed his voice sounded familiar. Catalina heard it too.

"Darling?" she said.

Mr. Lucrum smirked before lifting a hand to rip the flesh off his face. My eyes widened as Aedes's recognizable face came into view once he had gotten rid of the freckled silicone covering his nose and face.

Unlike my flabbergasted expression, Mayor Huey wasn't shocked by Aedes's big reveal. In fact, judging by the way he greeted the other with warm camaraderie, it appeared Mayor Huey had known it was him the whole time.

What the fuck?

"What took you so long, Eric?" Mayor Huey asked, stepping away from me to put a hand against his bleeding neck. "I thought Phani and I were goners."

My face slackened.

Eric? Did he just say Eric? Aedes's real name was Eric?

What were you expecting? Catalina responded.

I stared at the two men as they conversed with each other, Aedes taking out a roll of gauze from his pocket and patching Mayor Huey's neck. For some reason, the revelation of Aedes's first name was a bit... anticlimactic. It reduced the mystique and enigma that made him a tall, menacing figure of dubious authority. Despite my crushed expectations, I was glad this next stage to our forced acquaintance-ship meant I wouldn't have to quake in fear every time I heard his voice.

I looked up and noticed Burngemear was still present. A gasp from Katie had me turning in time to see Charlie's pale spirit rise above the edge of the roof. His jacket was stained red, his legs and arms broken and angled awkwardly. They rippled for a moment like a reflection in a pool of water before appearing normal, as though Charlie had never fallen off the roof and been shot at in the first place. He looked to be in a daze, snapping to attention when his sister gently touched his shoulder.

Suddenly I felt Catalina split herself from me. My back arched. My body was weightless for a split second before gravity slapped it down. I gasped, desperately gulping air as the sudden loss of her presence became similar to shucking off a warm sweater.

Catalina took a menacing step towards Charlie when she remate-rialized, her gaze so intense it blazed. The curls floating around her oval-shaped face made her look like a wrathful angel ready to commit violence. Her barely contained fury was a terrible beauty.

Charlie, unaware of Catalina stalking him like prey, inspected his body, turning this way and that before glancing at his sister. He cried out in fear and anguish when he saw the burn wounds Katie sustained prior to her death. Charlie knelt and wept with dry eyes.

"I'm sorry," he choked between sobs. "I'm so sorry. I'm sorry this is how we ended up. I should have been a better brother, I should have tried harder in school, I should have been quicker, smarter, more cautious. I should have paid more attention to you."

His unhappiness permeated the air, creating heavy pressure on my chest and stomach. Tears pricked my eyes. It was so jarring to see him vulnerable. Even when he had been with me, the polite gentleness he exuded felt guarded.

Katie didn't say a word in response. Instead she crouched and touched his cheek with one hand, a content smile gracing her lips as her face rippled to normal. Charlie looked up, his expression a wrinkled mess. I could practically see the imaginary tears and snot that would have adorned his features had he been alive.

"Thank you," she said at last. "For trying your best. I wish things had turned out differently for us too, but that's okay. It's over now. We can stop struggling."

He smiled slowly, eyes relieved.

Charlie's attention was snagged from Katie when Catalina approached him. His form wasn't as solid as hers, but it was still visible enough that I could see fear creep into his jewel-like eyes.

"Well, look what death dragged in," Catalina mocked, scarlet lips curved. "Karma's a bitch, 'ain't she Dawson?"

"La Patrona, I—!"

Catalina cut him off when she lunged at him. She grabbed his throat with a gloved talon-like hand. Despite his struggle against her grip, Catalina's energy was stronger and more dominant. She didn't buckle under his aura of desperation.

"Ya done *fucked up*, Charlie," she snarled. "*Now you suffer.*"

Catalina looked ready to rip into him with gleeful pleasure. That's when I saw it.

Her brown eyes glowed a vibrant red, bleeding into the scleras until she appeared almost demonic. Her curls became fluffier, her stance taller, even her teeth resembled sharp blades in the pale moonlight. She was simply...otherworldly.

Charlie gasped at the startling transformation. She ignored his pleas and pierced his throat with her sharp nails. I knew hurting him wasn't physically possible, but Catalina seemed like a real threat right now. Could she hurt him as a ghost? Because any more pressure and the man would lose an Adam's apple.

"Catalina, wait!" I cried, causing Aedes and Mayor Huey to look at me as I struggled to get up. I didn't notice the mayor help me nor Aedes scold his injured friend for moving so freely.

"No! Stop, please! Patrona!" Charlie choked out.

"Catalina!" I said again, alarmed by the change taking over. "Please stop! Don't do whatever it is you're going to do! Yes, Charlie deserves it, but that doesn't mean you should do it!"

"Why not?" Catalina demanded, eyes flickering from red to brown with each blink. "I want to destroy him just like he destroyed my life. I can make him disappear, you know. Charlon Dawson could cease to be. *Forever*."

What? What the hell was Catalina talking about? Spirits can't disappear forever; they're already dead! The worst that could happen to them was ending up in Tenebris. Oh God, what was happening to her? Why were her eyes red? That's never happened before to any spirit I've seen. This almost demonic version of her, that wasn't normal.

I swallowed, suddenly apprehensive.

"It's not your place to judge or hurt him. He's already dead, remember?"

"He should pay. It wouldn't take much effort."

"Please."

Catalina laughed, canine teeth sharp. "No. I don't think I will."

Something odd was happening to Charlie. The edges of his figure began to fray. They were being pulled in Catalina's direction as if she were some vacuum. Katie shrieked as Charlie began to lose energy, his frightened eyes drooping.

"Stop it, please! Stop it!" Katie cried, rushing at Catalina and banging on some invisible force field that prevented her from getting any closer. She wailed and screamed as Charlie's figure began to fade. Catalina laughed.

It took me a second, but I soon realized that Catalina was

consuming his energy. His spiritual essence. She was going to devour Charlie until he literally ceased to be.

"*STOP IT.*" I shrieked angrily, running to the edge of the roof. Someone grabbed the sash of my dress, preventing me from toppling over again.

Catalina turned her head and looked at me, a feral snarl forming on her plump red lips.

"*DROP HIM.*"

She practically growled in fury before throwing Charlie away. He groaned, a quarter of his transparent figure missing. Katie rushed to his side and enveloped him in a protective hug. Catalina sneered at them. Her eyes flickered from red to brown as she tried calming herself down, exhaling and inhaling sharply.

"You have some *nerve*," she snapped, turning around to face me. "*HE DESERVES CONSEQUENCES!*"

"And he will," I said, my voice back to its soft volume. I didn't have to be loud for Catalina to hear me. "But he will answer to *him*."

Catalina whirled around when she saw me glance at Burngemear. She swallowed before looking at me once again. This time her eyes remained brown. I exhaled in relief.

"...Phani," Charlie whispered, his figure now disintegrating in a familiar way instead of fraying. He looked up and stared at me. "Thanatos is still out there. He's livid and he wants revenge. Be careful."

Before I could ask him to elaborate, Charlie's human form was no more. A glowing sky-blue butterfly with a torn wing took his place, tinkling faintly like a fairy as it fluttered here and there.

Katie began to disintegrate as well, but before succumbing entirely, she turned and smiled at me, her charred features transfiguring into normalcy before bowing her head.

"Thank you. I don't know if his judgment will be merciful, but now I can live in peace."

Her glowing fragments curled into another small glowing butterfly. Together, Katie and Charlie's souls soared towards Burngemear until they disappeared into his dark depth.

"Phani, enough gawking at the sky and talking to yourself," Aedes remarked, reaching to turn my face to his unimpressed visage.

Reality came crashing and I blanched in embarrassment. Have I been speaking to Catalina and Charlie in front of Aedes and Mayor Huey this whole time? Oh God, what must Mayor Huey think of me? *Especially* after fighting against Charlie and speaking to his sister beforehand. If I had been hoping for them to see me as normal, it was over now.

"—what's been done about the bomb?" Aedes finished, eyeing me with expectation.

I blinked.

Oh shit, the bomb!

Mayor Huey and I raced to where he had placed the bomb earlier. When I came near and glanced at the timer, my blood turned cold. We had exactly eighty seconds before the bomb detonated.

"We better run now," I said to them.

"Damn it," Mayor Huey cursed. "She's right. I can't throw the bomb now. My other arm won't function properly."

"You shouldn't have bothered in the first place," Aedes snapped, pushing me away from the bomb and dragging Mayor Huey away.

I stared at them, torn as instinct warred with logic.

Burngemear still hovered over the roof, rainbow butterflies swirling around him. As if sensing my gaze, he turned his head away from the city skyline and stared at me. He and I both knew we'd never make it off this roof in time. I clenched my fists as a wild, desperate idea formed.

Cursing softly, I broke off from Aedes's grip and ran towards the bomb. I was out of my damn mind, but what other choice did I have?

"Phani, stop! What are you doing?!" Mayor Huey yelled.

"Phani! What are you doing?" Catalina whooshed towards me as I grabbed the home-made bomb. It weighed next to nothing in my hand, a pound at most.

Forty-five seconds left.

"What I must do," I answered her, closing my eyes.

I tried not to focus on the last thing I saw; Aedes—should I call him Eric now?—running towards me with his hand outstretched. Instead, I pictured frozen streets, thick fog, and overcast skies. I tuned out loud honking cars and shrieking ambulances until only silence and the occasional soft whispers remained. I even imagined my lungs burning from the cold air.

Please let it work, please let it work...

I opened my eyes.

Tenebris greeted me like an old friend.

I grinned.

Alone on the roof, the abandoned cityscape of Asphodel looked even more pitiful against the dark, sunless sky. The wind blew harshly, rustling my dress and hair every which way until I shook from the chill. The scent of rain and rubble blended with soil and dust. It permeated everything until it was all I could smell and taste.

The timer read thirty seconds.

I ran towards the direction of the lake and stopped until my shoe kissed the edge of the roof. I paid my new fear of falling little mind and tossed the bomb as far as I could. It arched for a second before landing unspectacularly in the withered garden below. To my relief, it didn't detonate upon impact, which meant the timer was our only threat now.

Small dark creatures made of gray, oily skin roamed the grounds below. They scattered away in surprise when the bomb landed. They eyed it with heads cocked before looking up to peer at me. They had no eyes, just bottomless bloody craters. They smiled, flashing large sharp teeth.

I turned away.

When I closed my eyes, I sent God a quick prayer asking to be returned home. If there was ever a time to have faith in my father's God, now was definitely it.

Thankfully, upon opening my eyes, I was back in the physical realm of Asphodel City. I smiled. The night time noise was obnoxious and loud, the lights bright and garish while gasoline and cold wind filled my nostrils with home's familiar grittiness. Home. I was back home!

I laughed as I ran towards Eric and Mayor Huey's slack-jawed astonished faces, tugging at their sleeves urgently in passing. I had a strong feeling we needed to move away.

"Run!" I shouted.

They eyed each other briefly before Eric grabbed me like a football and dragged Mayor Huey with him. We were past the glass dome just as an earthquake-like sensation hit. The air imploded, the wind whipping around us like a furious hurricane. The building shook. The glass panes in the dome shattered. From somewhere, people screamed.

Eric pushed us down and covered our heads until the pressure in the air and the shaking tremors abated. Once all seemed calm, we looked behind us and saw that other than a few rustling trees, broken glass, and construction materials messily scattered about, the night appeared ordinary once more.

Eric blinked twice before rubbing his eyes, looking all around us and the stillness that followed. I noticed Burngemear was gone. Catalina too. The only sounds now were the police sirens sitting in front of city hall.

With an arched brow, Eric turned to look at me.

"What the fuck?"

XXIV.
THESE GHOSTLY HANDS MEET

City Hall was surrounded by everyone: police units, SWAT teams, reporters, news vans, ambulances, city officials as well as onlookers not involved, but still curious about the whole fuss. Everywhere I turned, lights flashed, and to make matters worse, it began to drizzle.

Mayor Huey currently stood surrounded by dozens of reporters and cameras of many sizes in front of a wooden podium on the steps of City Hall. He'd been hastily patched up by the nervous paramedics hovering behind him, impatient to start performing damage control. He reassured the citizens of Asphodel City that tonight's madness was not an act of terror, but a one-time fiasco by a madman broken from grief. I was amazed by his unruffled appearance. If I hadn't been with him earlier, I never would've been able to tell the man had almost died tonight.

I also noticed no one spoke of or even mentioned the absent "Mr. Lucrum". Eric had disappeared by the time Mayor Huey and I came across the SWAT team. I was later escorted and attended to by my own medical unit before a familiar poker-faced police officer showed up. He told me he was assigned to write down my point of view of the incident, but before he could, Idrina burst in. To my surprise, the officer hadn't said a word to her about the interruption. He merely tugged his rain hood down before stepping outside the second she appeared. Ryan eyed the officer briefly before turning his attention back to Idrina and me.

As soon as Idrina and I were reunited, the dam of emotions my cousin had been holding back burst. The first thing she did was hug me so tight I yelped when her grip agitated my sore arm muscles. After making sure the paramedic had looked me over, she began to reprimand me.

Did I not know I could have almost died? That she had almost lost her favorite little cousin? That our family wouldn't have been the same without me? The rhetorical questions continued in that vein and to be honest, it was touching to hear she cared so much. Despite the chew out, I noticed I wasn't being looked at or treated like a special, broken child. This more than anything got me.

"Idrina," I interrupted. "So what you're saying is, I made the foolish, but conscious decision to stay behind, right?"

Idrina paused mid-word. "Yes? Have you not been listening to me? Of course you made stupid decisions, as opposed to…?"

"The voices in my head telling me to cause a spectacle and stay behind for the gun fight."

"Oh." Idrina hadn't been expecting that.

Ryan had been attached to Idrina the whole night, but mid-way through her scolding, he wandered off to speak to the paramedic about me. I was glad he wasn't here to hear my next few sentences.

"Yeah," I continued. "You've been insisting I find a psychiatrist, but obviously that hasn't happened. I was wondering if you thought my schizophrenia was the cause of all this."

"I didn't think so. Did any voices tell you to get involved?"

"No. That was all me. I made the conscious choice to make a scene which got me involved in the drama. No one told me to do it."

Idrina whacked my arm. "Then don't do it again! I didn't think your schizophrenia was involved. Before you came to stay with me, I studied your mental illnesses and the files *Tio* Luis said you consented to. This entire stunt didn't seem like schizophrenia or psychosis was the cause, but I admit I was worried it would screw you over against the gunmen. Of course, you're a smart girl, Phani, but next time there's danger, *patitas pa' que te quiero!* Got it?"

Little legs, how I love you. I chuckled at the saying, relieved to know where Idrina's mindset was on tonight's fiasco. I had been expecting worse.

"So, you're not going to kick me out of the apartment because I'm mentally unstable and poor?"

Idrina's expression morphed into horror.

"What?"

I ducked my head. "You kept asking if I'd found a job and a psychiatrist yet, or if I'd decided on a major. I thought maybe you wanted me to get a move on and pull my weight. Everyone else kind of handles me with kid gloves but—"

"You thought I was doing the same with you?" Idrina sighed, crossing her arms. "Phani, I'd never kick you out. We're family! Not to mention my landlord gave me a sweet deal years ago so you technically don't have to worry about rent. I've never needed it, but you seemed so motivated that I just let you do you. I'm sorry I made you feel differently. That was never my intention."

Oh. Wow, was I suddenly embarrassed. My face was hot enough to melt a candle.

"Not to mention," Idrina added, "I've always believed you were capable of making your own decisions with a sound mind. It's been years since you know what and I think you've grown from that, not to mention you've grown period."

I smiled.

"I know I come across as overbearing sometimes, but to be honest, I just didn't know how to act around you," Idrina admitted, fingers shifting against her arm. "The last time I saw you, you were a kid scared of your own shadow. I hadn't bothered to contact you when I moved away, nor had I asked about you. I was absorbed in my own little world until one day, you called me out of the blue and I realized, 'Oh! Phani's in college? And she's moving to my city? *And* wants to stay with me and help pay rent? Where did the time go?'"

I giggled. A heavy weight I hadn't realized was bothering me until then suddenly lifted from my chest. I came up to Idrina and hugged her of my own volition, the smell of roses and perfume bringing warmth and comfort.

"For what it's worth, same," I said. "I'm glad we're cousins."

Idrina ended up crying and returning my hug, stuffing my face into her ample chest. I didn't blame her. Tonight had been a close call for everyone—and some truths just had to be outed.

I was glad to know Idrina wasn't going to kick me out or declare me insane in the future. But mostly, I was just glad to know my cousin genuinely cared about me. No poverty or illness would get in the way of that.

I finally got a break from Idrina's smothering when she received a phone call from her parents—which I was sure was only a matter of time before my father got wind of what happened. He and his sister, *Tia* Gloria, liked to talk a lot. She wandered a little ways away for privacy. Ryan had returned shortly after and stayed back with me to make sure I finished getting checked out by my assigned EMT.

Now that I was free, the officer who had approached me earlier came back just as the EMTs continued their work on me before Idrina had interrupted.

Strict was the first word that came to mind when describing him. After that, handsome. That was soon followed by the intense urge to run far away so he wouldn't bite my head off. When he stared at me, it felt like I was in trouble for simply breathing. That being said, there was something very familiar about him. As if I had already spoken to him before. When he introduced himself as Officer Scrow, I internally gasped. This was the officer who had guarded the entrance of Orpheus Theater! The one who had seen my face in the red wig! Did he recognize me? If he did, the man didn't mention it.

Scrow filled the small interior of the ambulance with his hulking form before turning his attention to me. He didn't seem thrilled to be here, his expression remaining dead-panned all throughout my edited story. When I finished recounting tonight's incident, I stared at the metal floor as if it were the most fascinating surface.

"So, let me get this straight: you and Mayor Warringson went up to the roof to get away from the shooter. Didn't it occur to you to just keep running toward the City Hall exit? Half of the city's police force was bunking down there."

I shrugged. "I wasn't thinking. Mayor H—I mean, Warringson followed after me to make sure I was safe."

Scrow's corn-flower blue eyes kept their piercing sharpness when I made the mistake of glancing up. His frown didn't soften either. The silence stretched. Beside me, Ryan glared at Scrow as though seeing him ruined his night.

I swallowed. Did Scrow not believe me? Was he onto me?

"Alright. Why did you yell fire earlier this evening when there wasn't a fire? You caused a disruption and lots of physical harm. People were trampled in their rush to leave. Witnesses even reported seeing you outside shortly before everything went down later in—"

"Excuse me, but it sounds like you're accusing my client of something," Ryan snapped, scowling at the larger man.

I blinked. Whoa, whoa. Client? Since when? Did I need to be? And why was Ryan getting antsy with the man? Sure, Scrow's questioning was becoming uncomfortable, but that hardly warranted Ryan's lawyer mode.

"I'm not accusing her of anything," Scrow answered patiently. "I'm just trying to make sure what I'm hearing is correct."

"Um," I began. "I went outside to get some fresh air. I suspected something wasn't right when I saw the shooter with a gun. I didn't want him going off prematurely, so I tried to evacuate everyone without making him suspect anything."

"Why not just notify the officers on duty at the gala?"

"As if she could," Ryan reminded him. "The security guards present were compromised. Which, by the way, *your* department will hear about seeing as they were pre-approved by *your* captain."

"I panicked," I said, hoping that would end whatever was going on between the two of them.

Officer Scrow returned Ryan's scowl. There was tension in the air. I wondered what the cause of it was. Just when it seemed like Ryan was about to retort, Scrow finally flipped his notepad closed.

"Listen, Stryker, I'm not trying to cause a fuss—"

"Really now? Then is my client being detained?"

"No—"

"Then this interview is over, yes?"

"That wasn't—"

"Scrow!" called an officer from outside the ambulance.

Scrow wasn't too pleased by the interruption but turned around.

"What?"

"Time to retreat. GRAVE arrived. This entire incident is now under their jurisdiction. Captain's labeling it a G-1427 and leaving it in their hands," the other officer said, adjusting his rain poncho.

A vein popped out of Scrow's neck as cornflower eyes bulged.

"What? They can't! We were here first—"

"Ahem," interrupted the officer, gesturing towards me, Ryan, and the medical staff, our ears wide open. Scrow gave us an annoyed look but said nothing further.

"Just do as you're told. You're in enough trouble without defying orders," his police friend said before turning away. Scrow frowned, pocketing his pad and pen. He turned to stare at me and I hastily looked away.

"Looks like we're done here," he said, voice rumbling as he hopped off the ambulance. "Don't do anything stupid next time, Miss Carmel. Stryker."

Ryan nodded his head stiffly before the man disappeared. I turned in my seat to face him.

"What was that about?"

"Who knows."

"No, I meant him and you."

Ryan sighed, rubbing his face. "Scrow's a pain in the ass. He's one of those stubborn, idealistic detective types that keep barking until their man is behind bars. It doesn't help that I'm a lawyer that's kept a few of his perps acquitted or jail-free. The last time we worked against each other was for a client of mine a few months ago. In trying to find evidence that I couldn't claim was inadmissible in court, he broke certain rules that got him suspended."

Yikes. I was suddenly glad Ryan had been with me for the interrogation. If he hadn't, Officer Scrow might have kept digging and prodding at the holes in my edited story. And it's not like I made it up; Mayor Huey did. He insisted I stick to it.

"Trust me," he had said earlier, face pale as the blood in his shoulder continued to seep despite the pressure Eric and I added. His neck was also bleeding but thanks to the gauze tape Eric had tied earlier, he was holding on strong. "As much as I'd like to hand over this entire ordeal to the police, Eric's presence only complicates matters."

Eric, who had been supporting Mayor Huey's weight as we walked, offered us an angelic smile.

"You're welcome," he said. "Next time you host a gala, double check your security. I would hate a repeat of tonight. And Phani, try not to date the enemy next time either."

I flushed at the memory, his mocking words said in the sweetest of tones. He disappeared shortly after. Probably to gather his remaining men and escape without getting caught. Mayor Huey and I were found by the SWAT team a few minutes later.

I came back to the present and returned my attention back to Ryan.

"Thanks Ryan," I said, smiling. "I appreciate your help."

"No problem, Phani," he said with a smile of his own, ruffling my hair affectionately. "If you come across him again, just mention my name. That should make him back off."

Something about the way he said it made it seem like the hostility went further back than just the usual workplace rivalry.

"Now stay put. I gotta find Idrina and make a few phone calls myself." Ryan waved before stepping outside the ambulance.

With a blanket over my head, I suddenly felt drained and overwhelmed now that the adrenaline from earlier was over. I was in the middle of some breathing exercises when I spotted Catalina standing under a tree not too far from me. My concentration flew out the window. I looked around. Since the EMTs were busy with other victims and Idrina was still busy who knows where, I snuck away, shock blanket wrapped around me burrito style. When I got near, I was glad to see the tree Catalina stood under blocked most of the rain.

"Hey," I greeted, happy she appeared alright.

When she disappeared with Burngemear earlier, I worried I wouldn't be able to see her again. Even though I've only known Catalina for about two weeks, I nearly sacrificed my life for her dying request. Money or no money. And if there was something I should get from her for my troubles, it was friendship. Or at least an acknowledgment of one.

Catalina smirked. "Glad to see you're still in one piece, Huey and Darling included."

I laughed, the ominous weight of our mission finally lifted from my shoulders. I could breathe easy now, no longer stressed or anxious. The freedom and carefree atmosphere surrounding me was both heady and strangely deceptive. I was a little paranoid that someone at any moment would jump out and shout "just kidding!" and force me to endure Catalina's stressful mission all over again.

Thank God that wasn't happening.

"It's over," Catalina said. "It's finally over. We found my killer and stopped him."

I could hear the astonishment in her voice. Her expression crumbled before she could turn away and hide the pain. Despite her claims to the contraire, I knew Catalina was still upset by her untimely demise, and I don't blame her. She had been a vibrant young woman who believed herself to be the master of her fate. For it to be snuffed out so abruptly, it was the worst insult ever slung her way. But then, taking away young life before it even had a chance to shine was always a tragedy in and of itself.

I took a deep breath before hovering a gentle hand over her shoulder. Catalina glanced at me, eyes almost glistening from the police lights. After a minute of understanding silence, we both smiled.

"It was bound to happen," I told her. "What comes around goes around, right?"

Catalina frowned, but eventually nodded. Was she thinking about the demon aura that nearly possessed her earlier? She had been angry to have been thwarted from tearing Charlie a new one, but the way Charlie almost disappeared, to be *consumed* by Catalina was still scary. Hopefully it was only her anger that made her act that way.

Catalina sighed before stretching her head, finally meeting my eyes with relaxed brown irises. She looked peaceful. I knew then that she had finally accepted her death.

Never had Catalina appeared more courageous to me then in that moment.

"To be honest," Catalina said, tilting her head to stare at the night sky. "I was starting to doubt it. But I'm glad Darling and Huey are safe."

"So you got nearly everything you wanted in the end."

Catalina smiled sheepishly. "Not entirely. I never did get my cute husband and adorable baby. But I suppose one can't have everything. Do me a favor, though?"

"Mm?"

"Don't settle, Phani, and don't hide. It's tragic to live your life wasting away. You only get one shot so live the way *you* want to. Find your purpose, know yourself, and do what makes you happy. Fuck what anyone says. If it's finding your own cute husband and having an adorable child, I won't complain. Cause if you do, I *will* be living vicariously through you."

I half-laughed, half-gasped, mouth opening and closing like a fish.

"Whoa there, girl. Let me find a better job and finish college before we cross that bridge, okay?"

"Fine. But remember what I said. And *don't* wait too long or else someone will steal your man."

I was about to mutter "what man?" when I sensed someone behind me. To my surprise, it was Eric. He approached us, bundled up in a slick raincoat, his face exposed to the elements. It still amazed me what a difference a bit of putty can make.

"Nice face," I said.

Eric smirked, inclining his head in thanks.

"You know everything you saw tonight is confidential, right? If you talk, you disappear," he threatened with a friendly smile.

Catalina laughed. I huffed in response.

"I know, I wasn't going to say anything. Believe it or not, I know how to keep a secret."

"Good," he said. He turned to look at the media frenzy surrounding Mayor Huey. "Listen. If I didn't already believe in the supernatural, I would have thought someone had slipped me some acid when I wasn't looking."

Shit. Almost forgot about that.

When I briefly left for Tenebris to remove the bomb, I didn't think to wonder whether my body would still be in the physical world. Frankly, I was too relieved about successfully transporting the bomb to even care. If Huey or Eric saw me disappear with the bomb and come back without it, they would be crazy not to be suspicious of me. Especially since the bomb never went off in the real world. Neither man mentioned a thing about it though.

Huey probably chalked it off as hallucinations caused by blood loss, but Eric? I should have known he would interrogate me at the first opportunity. It was starting to become his *modus operandi*, along with kidnapping me.

"What did you see?" I asked, dread pooling inside my belly.

Eric ran a hand through his hair, regarding me with a cool expression. He smiled before I could stew in my thoughts for too long.

"Something very shocking," he said at last.

Catalina grinned. "He's just messing with you. When you left for Tenebris, your body became transparent before vanishing. It lasted a few seconds, but Burngemear left and forced me to disappear before you returned. Thankfully I was dumped in the Aether Realm, so I was able to come back."

"I'm glad. I was worried you'd be gone forever."

Oh wait.

Catalina's smile faded, her eyes dimming. She looked away.

Eric watched as I talked to myself, saying nothing, no judgment of any kind on his pretty face. He did eye the air across from me with a scary intensity though. If I wasn't so worried about Catalina, I would have asked him to look elsewhere.

"Catalina? What's wrong?" I asked.

Eric spoke up, his voice animated. "Catalina? She's here?"

Catalina faced him, lifting a hand until it touched his cheek lightly. Eric turned his head to look at her, sensing her unusually cool touch despite the chill in the air. They were at eye level. It was almost as though he could see her.

"I feel you," he said. "Very softly."

"I'm so glad you're alright," she said, eyes shining. If she could blush or cry, she would have done so already. "This entire case was killing me inside."

"She's glad you're safe," I told him. "This was hard for her."

He scoffed, but a smile peeked from behind the fist he hid his lips with.

"Catalina, you wouldn't have had to worry if you'd stayed out of the way. But you never do listen, not when you think you can make it right."

She laughed. "As if I could stay away! This was *my* case just as much as it was yours. I'm not your right-hand for nothing, you know! I—the fuck?"

I gasped, covering my mouth. Eric tensed, his hand hovering over the gun holster under his jacket.

"What's wrong?" he asked.

If it wasn't so damn cold, I was sure the tears would have been flowing down my cheeks. Right now, they stung as they stayed put.

"Catalina. She's fading away," I whispered.

Catalina glanced at her hands, surprised. Her fingertips were dissipating into the damp night like pixie dust. She looked up, determination etched in her eyes.

"*Bueno.* It's time."

"Catalina," Eric said, his voice faltering.

He lifted his hand to touch the one on his cheek. That's when I became a witness to Eric's vulnerable side. His eyes betrayed him just as his other hand opened and closed in helplessness. This was a man about to lose his best friend. One connection, one bond, one lifetime of trust. Severed by mortality's natural course.

It was painful to watch.

"I'm sorry. Sorry for letting you down like this," he murmured at a volume not above a whisper. He let his hand drop. "This wasn't how it was supposed to end."

"I know," Catalina smiled sadly.

"When I asked you to work with me, to help me, I naively thought we'd be safe. Even after several close scrapes, we always made it out. It infuriates me that you died because of my carelessness." His voice hardened. Eric glared at the ground, fist clenched. "God, I'm so pathetic! I failed you! I tried to give you everything, but like always, I can never make *anything* right!"

"No! You tried very hard! I've always believed in you!" Catalina argued desperately, touching his cheek again with her missing fingertips. Her feet were gone. She looked at me. "Tell him, Phani!"

"You didn't fail her," I said, hesitant. Eric looked at me. "She knows how hard you tried. Catalina's always believed in you."

"From the moment you became my friend in that pomegranate field, I knew I would dedicate my life to you. You are worthy, and it made me very happy living my life knowing you were there. Not to mention there was never a dull moment between us." Catalina gave him a wide grin. "No matter what, you'll always be my best friend, Darling. I love you."

Eric didn't say a word after I relayed the message. His eyes were dry as he stared at the weeping sky. The atmosphere between them felt tangible; years of memories, friendships and feelings still solid and thick between them.

I sighed with envy. What a beautiful thing, to have a connection with someone like Eric and Catalina had with each other. Maybe that's why I allowed myself to care for Charlie so fast. What would such trust and love feel like?

"Phani, can I possess your body for a quick minute?" Catalina asked. "I'd like to give Eric a little something, just so he can't say I never did anything for him as his wingman."

By now her knees were gone, as was the ends of her long hair that used to brush the small of her back. I didn't have the heart to deny her so I nodded. She wasted no time phasing into me, her familiar presence settling in as if I'd submerged myself in water. She was in control now as she lowered the blanket from my shoulders and took a step towards Eric.

"Darling dearest?"

Eric flickered a glance my way, obviously confused.

"Catalina? What are you doing?"

Catalina moved me until I was leaning against Eric, my head tilted as a seductive smile graced my lips. She placed my hands against his chest until it slipped behind his neck, forcing him to bend down and meet me at eye level. I was mentally freaking out.

What was Catalina thinking? This was too intimate!

I closed my eyes the minute our lips touched. An electric zing coursed through me, raising the small hairs on my body as a fiery warmth scorched my skin. Despite this oddness, the hot flesh of his lips was a delicious contrast against the icy wet backdrop of the night. They were firm, but plush and tasted of peppermint and vanilla. I shivered when his warm hands found themselves on my hips.

Suddenly, a series of images came to the forefront of my mind. One of withered flower crowns, a flooded abandoned cathedral, twilight peeking through eternal gray skies, and the echoing laughter of a man and woman. I could feel prickly grass beneath my soles and fog coating my skin, the smell of rain and dirt, crushed petals of lily and lavender. Nostalgia, longing, and sadness filled me until the images and emotions dissipated as quickly as they had come.

I blinked. What just happened?

Those images, memories...had they been Catalina's?

Our peck was less than twelve seconds long. To me however, it had lasted a lifetime. Backing up, I saw that Eric had closed his eyes too. When he opened them, he was swift in using the leverage of our parting to put space between us.

"What was that?" he asked. He was staring at me oddly. A strange gleam entered his ash colored eyes before it was hastily shuttered away, replaced instead by a polite neutral expression.

Catalina twisted my lips into a smirk.

"A thank you," she said.

He raised a brow. "Catalina or Phani?"

"You wish," she laughed before abruptly pausing. The mood became somber when she had me look up at him once more. "I thought I should let you know, I know about your secret plan."

Eric suddenly tensed. His smile returned with charm.

"What? Stop kidding around Catalina."

She rolled my eyes and smacked Eric's chest. "I'm not just saying this to jerk your chain, Darling. I don't think what you're up to is a good idea. In fact, it's a horrible idea. But I only want you to be happy and if your plan helps with that, then I'll support you. I just hope you don't regret it later."

Eric stood there, rendered speechless. He took an unsteady step back, his cheeks flushed for once. His reaction was comical, but curiosity got to me. What secret plan did Eric have to make him so flustered and mute at the mere mention of it? I thought about asking, but I knew that neither Eric nor Catalina would reveal a thing to me. I stayed quiet instead. It was a good thing, too, since Catalina's presence began to weaken, and I knew she still had a couple of things left to say to me.

Phani, she began. *Despite dragging you into this mess, thank you for not giving up on me halfway. You have major cojones, mija. You... you're a good friend.*

I raised a hand to make sure the tears didn't fall. Eric remained where he was but looked away to allow me some privacy.

Stay strong, okay Phani? Weird shit happens in Asphodel City so watch yourself. If you ever need help, find my allies; Clawbra and, I can't believe I'm including her, but BB as well. Tell them I fucking insist.

"Thank you," I whispered before frowning. "I'll miss you. You were the first friend I made here."

Catalina laughed.

You need to find better friends. But thanks, babe, that means a lot. I normal—oh shit! My secret stash! Your reward!

I shook my head, smiling. "Don't bother. I finally found a job. It's not glamorous but it'll pay the bills and that's what counts."

Fucking finally! I hope it's nothing pathetic or else I'm going to be thoroughly disappointed in you.

"It's definitely not a bland nine to five."

Eh, my money is better, but if you insist, I won't shove my cash down your throat. Hasta luego, kid.

And then, she was gone. For good.

I felt her spirit leave me. A ball of white light phased through my chest before gradually taking the shape of a black butterfly. It grazed the skin of my cheek before fluttering over to Eric's for a quick peck. I tightened the blanket around my shoulders, feeling a lot emptier now that I knew Catalina had moved on. She flapped towards the lake where Burngemear lingered.

I blinked several times, surprised to see he was still around. Wisps of multicolored souls swirled around him, all shining bright against the inky darkness. I was half tempted to ask him if Catalina would be alright wherever she was going. From where I stood, however, I could see no animation or emotion behind the demon-like skull. Just thinking about being in his presence made me shudder, fear suffocating me in a vise-like grip.

I turned away.

Eric escorted me back to civilization before disappearing into the night.

XXV.

LAST RITES

TEN DAYS HAD PASSED since Catalina's funeral.

Eric—who for some reason acted as intrusively involved in my life as Catalina had once been—told me that she'd been buried at the exclusive and private Elysium No. 3 Cemetery in Vanit Town. Only those with trust funds even knew of its existence. To my surprise, Eric had been most generous in handing me a visitor's pass. I was free to use it if I ever wanted to stop by. When I finally decided to pay my respects to Catalina a few days later, my somber mood manifested into rain, slushing the streets of Asphodel City into a muddy, murky mess.

With an umbrella in hand, the clammy chill did little to discourage me, however.

Tucked away into the dense forest surrounding Vanit Town, the cemetery was a quiet neatly trimmed place with marble tombs and granite plaques. Vibrant multicolored bushels of flowers dotted each grave, all freshly picked. Some had roses and daffodils with a couple of baby's breaths while others sported orchids and carnations. One even had a bonsai tree.

While my offering wasn't as ostentatious, I acquired some wolfs-bane for Catalina from one of the greenhouses I had scoped out during my first week in Asphodel. It wasn't normal placing poisonous plants on one's grave, but I knew Catalina would be thrilled by the gesture.

Her tombstone was located far from the main section. It was near the back, away from civilians and enclosed in a separate gated area. Two weeping angel monuments with swords pointed skyward guarded her. I ignored the sighs and whispers of broken spirits as I walked past them, their faint manifestation lingering stubbornly. It was an unpleasant sight but at least it wasn't noisy and haunting like other cemeteries I'd seen around the city.

I stopped walking.

Someone's gaze was boring into my back with a frightening intensity that increased the longer I ignored it. An indistinguishable harsh whisper sounded, followed by a maniacal cackle. The small hairs on my neck rose. I whirled around in fear, expecting some dark demon or mean spirit hovering behind. There was no one around. The spirits that had been present in the area a few minutes ago were gone. I was completely alone.

The cemetery felt eerie and unnatural in the stillness of the afternoon. The rain did little to brighten the atmosphere. My grip on the umbrella handle tightened.

"Hello? Anyone out there?"

No response.

It remained that way for a few minutes. Eventually, that ominous feeling I sensed disappeared. I exhaled shakily, searching the cemetery for anyone or anything that might have been cause the of the scare. Just as before, I found no one. Had it all been in my head?

Feeling paranoid, I shook my head and continued walking. It was probably another atmospheric haunting.

Upon locating Catalina's ceramic marker, I saw there was a long epitaph in stone above her name. I knelt to read the inscription, careful not to let the wet grass dampen my pants.

A LOYAL BEST FRIEND
ALWAYS, ETERNAL, FOREVER

Terror You Bring
Standing Guard,
You Sing
Believing in Him
A Hades they See
Conquer your New
Underworld

~

Catalina Beatrice Patron
November 13, 1988 – October 9, 2015

"I hope you conquer," I said. "Wherever it is you are."

I arranged the wolfsbane with care using gloved fingers. Once I fixed the scarlet ribbon so it wouldn't appear crushed, I took out a small laminated card from my pocket and placed it against the bouquet. I hoped the words WARNING: POISONOUS PLANT. DO NOT TOUCH CARELESSLY. USE GLOVES did the trick in letting the caretakers and other mourners know not to touch the wolfsbane recklessly.

I frowned when I heard hoarse breathing between the pitter patter of rain. That wasn't me, was it? I looked up.

Burngemear stood behind Catalina's gravestone, looking like he'd always been there when that certainly hadn't been the case. I shrieked, falling ungracefully on the wet grass in terror. I hadn't sensed or heard him approach at all! I hastily got up and backed away, tightening my grip on the umbrella handle further. I couldn't see his eyes, but I knew he was staring at me. I could feel it. I swallowed.

"What do you want?" I asked. If I listened closely and ignored the heavy beat of the rain, I could hear Burngemear's faint raspy breaths.

Time is running out, he said. *Tenebris needs a ruler.*

I shuddered as suspicion crept like a hideous spider.

"Surely you don't mean me?"

He must return to the throne, to take my place. You must oversee this...

Spare me. Why was Burngemear so chatty all of a sudden? What was he even talking about? Who is even this 'he' that he's referring to? As far as I knew, Tenebris didn't have a ruler. Who but the devil would want to rule such a domain?

I blinked. Wait.

Don't tell me Burngemear wants me to find the *actual* devil?

Tirisha and I had spoken of Tenebris's origins, but I don't think she ever mentioned someone overseeing the place. If anything, I assumed it was Burngemear who ruled. But if he wasn't in charge, then who...?

Dread filled my veins like liquid poison.

"H-How am I supposed to find your replacement?" I asked. Catalina's face came to mind, lending me courage to look at my tormentor head on. "And if I did find him, I don't work for free."

Burngemear stared at me for a long time, tilting his head to one side. Neither of us said a thing after that. I exhaled. We've reached an impasse. No way was I going to be bullied or intimidated into doing his bidding, no matter how terrified I was.

How may I serve? He said at last.

I blinked, amazed he would agree to hear me out. Glancing at Catalina's headstone, I noticed her engraved name overflowing with rain water. It looked as if it were weeping.

"Catalina," I said. "Wherever she is, I want you to make sure she's not suffering."

Burngemear lifted his hand to stroke the incisors of his mask— vein-like scarlet streaks glowed prominently against his inky skin. Sharpened fingertips touched smooth bone.

How curious, his deep voice rumbled. *You needn't worry, however. This request has already been asked of me.*

What? Who could have asked this of Burngemear? Had Catalina struck a deal with him already? At least that's one less thing to worry about. Now I just have to deal with Burngemear's ridiculous request; I wonder if I could dissuade him of it somehow.

"I don't think I'm qualified to carry out such an important task," I tell him.

His chuckle raised the hairs on my arms. I took another step back.

No one is more qualified. Tenebris's ruler, he will be obvious to find. Your real task is to convince him to return home.

Obvious? The only obvious candidate I can think of is Erebus and though he makes complete sense, I'm hoping it wasn't him. I really can't with the mafia right now, not after what I just dealt with a few days ago. I was banking on not returning to that life anytime soon.

If you should fail, Burngemear continued, *all of Asphodel, and the world beyond, will sink into a realm so black that even demons will flee in droves to the gates of Heaven...*

"What? No!"

... if the throne is finally filled and the crown bestowed, all will be right. If not, you will be forced to take the mantle and remain in Tenebris. Forever.

"NO!"

Burngemear dispersed just as Eric's familiar figure walked through the billowing black smoke as though birthed from the frigid abyss. His heavy footsteps broke the uniformity of the monotonous sound of rain. I blinked in surprise for a few seconds before a smile broke. I've never been so happy to see his face before!

"Phani?" he said, surprised to see me. He glanced at the wolfsbanes I placed on Catalina's grave. Thanks to my outburst, they had wilted. Their delicate violet petals crinkled like burned paper. Eric didn't comment on their appearance. Instead he shrugged out of his large dark coat and placed it around my hunched shoulders.

"Oh, um, you didn't have to," I mumbled, glad for the lingering warmth on the heavy material. Soap, sandalwood, and some obscure cologne teased my nose with its pleasant and surprisingly comforting scent.

Though I'll never admit it, I was glad for his presence as it helped me calm down until my racing heart steadied to a normal rhythm. I knew I was going to have to see Tirisha again about Burngemear and his crazy request if I was to keep my sanity intact. I can't go through another stressful situation. I barely made it out of the first one alive.

"It's the least I could do," said Eric. "Were you visiting Catalina?"

I nodded. "I thought I would pay my respects and see where her new haunt was."

He laughed. "She would accept no less than Vanit Town for the location. I wanted something simple for her gravestone, but I knew her coffin had to be made of the most expensive materials; the finest cherry wood, breathable silk lining, gold calligraphy for her name. I even had it stowed away in a large stone tomb underneath our feet to discourage any grave robbers."

"Grave robbers?"

"I had her bulletproof choker buried with her."

"Oh."

"I had rumors circulate that Erebus threw it into the ocean in a fit of rage. And another that he had it melted and remade into a cameo of her where he keeps it hidden in his vacation house somewhere in the South Pacific."

I blinked. "That's quite a goose chase. Was Erebus pleased with your rumors?"

He grinned. "He suggested it."

"Does anyone know she's buried here?"

"Only Erebus and I. Her family is under the impression they have her real body. I sent a decoy."

That wasn't nice, but I suppose it would be safer for them considering all the enemies Catalina had amassed as a crime boss. Eric checked his watch.

"I thought you should know I managed to uncover more information regarding Charlie."

That's a name I hoped to never hear again.

"His past doesn't justify his actions," I said.

Eric smiled. "Couldn't have said it better myself. But seeing as he had ties to Thanatos, I had to be thorough on Erebus's behalf. Charlon Dawson had a sister named Kaitlon, Katie for short. After much digging, I discovered they both lost their parents in a car accident when they were young. Orphaned, they were taken in by the state and put into foster care. He had a record of several misdemeanors and one arrest of attempted battery before he came into Erebus's employ."

"Why'd Erebus take him in? He sounds a bit sketchy."

I gave Catalina's grave a parting glance before Eric and I walked away.

"One of the younger members saw Charlie in action," Eric explained. "When I was made aware, I paid the young man a visit and saw his skill for myself. I soon told Erebus and before we knew it, he was recruited as a newbie member shortly after. He looked like a kid who simply needed a chance. With his talent and street smarts, he made it into Erebus's Inner Circle as a Fifth-Tier inductee in less than three years."

We passed by a forlorn angel, face upturned to the weeping heavens.

"What about his sister?"

"Ironically enough, Katie turned out to be an upstanding citizen. Graduated high school with stellar grades, accepted into Asphodel U on a scholarship. Even volunteered at a homeless shelter in South Coast."

I knew where this was headed.

"When the turf war broke out, Katie had been inside the building when it got bombed."

I grimaced. "What about Timothy? Who's he?"

"That part gets tricky," Eric said, guiding me away from a flooded pathway. "Rumors circulated from their old haunts that Katie had been assaulted. A few of their acquaintances swore she had been pregnant at one point. But with no baby or hospital records of a reported incident for anything, there was no evidence I could find to confirm my findings."

Assaulted? I winced. I knew then who Timothy could have been. Katie suddenly earned my new-found respect for coming out as strong as she did. To even face the sun and think of others when you've been hurt so deeply, that's hard and very brave.

I sighed, taking care to stay underneath my umbrella. It was clear that Charlie had taken his responsibilities as an older brother seriously, though it was a shame he chose to live the way he did after her death. Katie obviously hadn't approved of his new path.

"I wonder what Thanatos told Charlie to make him turn against Erebus."

Eric frowned. "That is worrying, but more so that Thanatos is still alive. Last I knew, he had left Asphodel due to a medical problem. But if he's back, Erebus needs to be on high alert. The attack against Mayor Warringson was daring. It cannot be allowed to happen again. Further investigation on the matter revealed that Mr. Rotley had been working with Thanatos the whole time."

Whoa. "Seriously? Him? But why?"

"When I, uh, *talked* with him one-on-one, he said he and his family had been threatened by Thanatos to hire the extra security without properly screening them. That's how Charlie was able to sneak the henchmen in, along with their weapons. Mr. Rotley hadn't known the men would attack the way they did."

Oh man. I could just picture the plump, once-stern man trembling as he made the preparations that would make it easier for Charlie to terrorize everyone. Despite his actions, I hoped his family was okay.

"What'll happen to Mr. Rotley?"

"Haven't you heard? He turned himself in to the police and confessed to organizing the whole attack."

"What?" I gaped.

Eric smirked. "It was a wise choice. I told him I'd keep his family safe but there was no guarantee he himself would be. Thanatos has a habit of disposing loose ends. Behind the bars of the ACPD, he'll escape certain death."

I scratched my head. "But why say he was the sole organizer? Why not admit to being manipulated? He could've gotten a lighter sentence."

Eric chuckled, as if what I'd said was funny. I frowned.

"What?"

"Phani, if one is ever involved in a fight between Thanatos and Erebus, it's prudent to keep quiet. If one values their life and sanity, that is. Once you start mentioning their names to the media, nothing good comes out of it. Trust me. Why do you think Mayor Warringson is doing the best he can to minimize the crisis without mentioning what really happened?"

Huh. I didn't entirely understand what he meant, but I suppose he did have a point. Best not to speak of complicated things and get others involved in underworld business.

I blinked. Whoa. I sounded like Catalina just now.

Speaking of Warringson, I wondered how Mayor Huey was doing. After the attempt on his life and that of City Hall, unlike Eric, I didn't get the chance to see him again. He seemed to be alright now, reports from the media letting everyone know that his injuries hadn't been life-threatening. I thought of asking Eric about him but decided against it. Wouldn't want him thinking I was after the man romantically.

"Out of curiosity," I said. "What does your boss think of my involvement in all this?"

Eric tilted his head as he pushed back the strands that fell forward.

"Well, he wasn't pleased to hear a civilian had involved herself in underworld business. He thought about making you disappear."

I gulped, horrified by the revelation. Eric smiled and wagged a finger at me, doing little to assuage my sudden fear.

"Don't be scared," Eric continued. "It was a brief thought. Especially when he discovered you didn't actually kill his most prized crime boss."

"That's reassuring," I said dryly. "Did you tell him I can see, you know, ghosts?"

Eric winked at me, gesturing that his lips were sealed. I blinked in surprise.

"Really?"

"Of course. It's obvious you don't want people to know. And you should have at least one person in your corner. Someone to make sure you don't get into any more trouble."

I wasn't sure what to say. My ears and neck became flooded with heat. I've got to stop being moved by every kind gesture someone does on my behalf. In this case, however, getting a dangerous mob boss off my back was a blessing.

"Thanks," I mumbled, embarrassed.

The wind blew and with it the rain became uncoordinated. Eric readjusted his umbrella, blocking his handsome face from the dreary weather. I realized we were standing a little too close.

"I should head back," I said, turning away to take his coat off.

"No, keep that. I have plenty. Actually Phani, I'm glad I caught you here. I was going to stop by your cousin's apartment to deliver this."

"Deliver what—"

I stopped talking when I saw Eric take out a small crème envelope. I arched a brow when he offered it to me. It felt light in my hands. When I peered inside, I nearly swooned.

"I can't—"

"You never cashed in the check I gave you last time so I can only assume you threw it away," he said with a smile. "So, I found Catalina's 'secret' stash and deposited the whole thing. This is what she owed you for your services. Take it."

"B-But—"

"Take it, Phani. It's what was agreed upon. I understand refusing the check I gave you, but this is the one you earned. An agreement made is an agreement to be honored. That is the way of the underworld."

Well, when he put it like that, he did have a point. So, I took it. I earned the right and I knew exactly what I was going to do with the hundred thousand.

"Alright," I began with a smile as I approached him. "Now I can finally pay back my debt. Here's my thanks for your thoughtfulness."

"Debt?" Eric echoed in confusion. "What d—"

I tugged at his lapel and made him lean down until I gave his cheek a soft kiss. He smelled even better up close, and in this weather, his body heat was hypnotic. At the same time, I slipped the envelope inside his jacket pocket. When I released him, Eric looked surprised, his cheeks reddened. I giggled. Score one for me!

"Phani?"

"There. Debt repaid," I said with a smile. "I owed you for the dress and accessories Catalina charged to your account."

Eric blinked and touched his cheek in wonder. "Phani, I wasn't going to hold that against you. Catalina does that all the time. It's fine. I have plenty of money."

I shrugged. "It wouldn't sit right with me regardless. Yeah, I wanted the hundred thousand, but I feel like the last two weeks changed me. I'll come up with the money some other way. A more legit way."

"But you only owe me a little over eight thousand. What about the rest?"

I smiled. "I'm glad you asked. There's this charity I was hoping you'd do me the honor of donating to: The Leda Sanctuary. They help victims of sexual assault, domestic violence, and homelessness in the Massachusetts area. They also bring in resources for foster kids and give them fun activities to do around their communities. I figured this was the least I can do for Katie's memory. She'd want to prevent others from going through what she went through and what Charlie ended up becoming."

Eric looked at me as if he'd never seen me before. He blinked before shaking off the stupor and gracing me with his usual smile.

"Very well, then. Consider it granted. Not too eager to quit your dream job of holding up signs in this wet, winter weather, huh?"

I flushed in embarrassment before turning away. How did he even know about that? I certainly hadn't told him!

"It's a respectable job, you stalker!"

Eric grinned—no doubt glad to have the upper hand—before following after me. The cement walkway under us was soaked, reflecting our dark blurry figures like a speckled mirror. I stepped on a puddle, the water harmless against my rain boots.

"Never said it wasn't," Eric reassured me, fixing his lapel. "But if you'd like a warm and dry job this winter, I do know of one that's currently available. Room and board included."

I stopped walking and faced him like a gullible sucker, waiting for more. Damn if that didn't sound tempting. But this was Eric, aka

Aedes, aka Orcus, I was talking to. He had to be pulling a fast one on me, preying on my vulnerability like the manipulative person he was. The whole Mr. Lucrum act only intensified my paranoia, though I took comfort in the fact that my instincts knew something had been off about him from the start.

Still, it couldn't hurt to find out what the details were. If the job was legit, that is.

"What's the job?"

"An assistant to an assistant," he replied vaguely. "An office type environment."

That didn't sound so bad.

"How much does it pay?"

"Triple what you'll be earning, per hour," he added.

Sold.

"Who's the employer?" I asked.

My smile soon turned into a frown when I saw Eric Van Darlington grace me with the most handsome and gentlest smile I ever saw. His gray eyes glinted in the pale afternoon light. Not a good sign.

Turns out, my stay in Asphodel City was going to be a lot more life changing than I originally thought.

FEELING IS TRUTH

WHEN THICK SOOTY lashes opened to reveal caramel eyes, it took Catalina a few minutes to realize she was staring at an overcast sky. It threatened her with thunder and rain. As if to make sure she wasn't mistaken, an icy breeze whipped harshly past her.

Blinking several times, Catalina's sculpted brows furrowed when she saw herself sprawled on damp asphalt in the middle of a deserted street. A familiar deserted street. She was at the intersection of Franklin and Crenshaw, two blocks from her downtown apartment. While she preferred staying in her Vanit Town townhouse, her apartment inside the heart of the city was convenient for its easy distance to her office.

Everywhere she looked, thick fog greeted her. It tasted of stale ice and prevented her from seeing anything past a few yards. Catalina noted she was alone.

She shivered, goosebumps rising along her skin as the frigid wind numbed her fingers. She could barely move her joints without feeling stiff. A sudden thought occurred to her. She rolled one opera glove down and touched the small hairs on her arm. They stood at attention. How odd. She hadn't felt cold since the night she died.

When Catalina stood up, the first step she took was obscenely loud to her ears. Her heels made a sharp clack against the asphalt, the sound echoing through the fog.

Past the gray wall, tall dark blobs came into view. There was no face or definitive shape to any of them from what she could see. They steadily grew in size and appeared solid as they approached her, their color a muddy black without texture. One continued forward as the others stopped by the edge of the clearing. It now stood a few feet away from her.

Catalina could hear her heart beating. It felt odd to feel it thumping in her chest when it was usually dead in the physical realm. A small kernel of fear and anxiety settled inside her. She swallowed. She noticed the tall blobs beginning to flank her all around the intersection, blocking any chance of escape.

Fury seized her as she clenched her fists. The audacity! She'd be damned before she'd allow these shadow-looking Cousin Itts to intimidate *her*. She was Erebus's most prized crime boss for Pete's sake!

Catalina was a conqueror, a woman who bowed to no one and did as she pleased. She would not let a thing like death swallow her, not like she almost did to Charlie. She had a purpose, born for something more. Catalina felt this so strongly she could almost feel it in her soul, could almost taste the conviction of her belief.

She didn't know how, but Catalina would prove herself.

"Lárgate." Get out of my way.

A deformed smile appeared on the stomach of the brave blob. Catalina cracked her neck. It was on.

She dashed forward, her sharpened nails slicing the body of the shapeless figure. She had expected her hand to phase through—she was weak here after all, just a pitiful spirit finally judged and sentenced. Catalina was fully prepared to be at the very bottom of the chain of command before she could even attempt to claw her way up or survive eternity—she was unsure how the rules worked around here.

So imagine her surprise, and the creature's, when black liquid sprayed the air, smelling of old blood. The blob screamed like a boiling tea kettle, rows of square white teeth exposed. Its damaged solid body soon vanished from existence, black congealed ink plopping to the ground. It was the only evidence left that her opponent had existed.

There was a small puddle of water near Catalina's feet. She almost paid it no mind, but her reflection caught her attention.

Her eyes...*they were glowing.*

Ruby red bled past the iris and seeped into the scleras. She gasped. The canine teeth in her mouth looked sharp enough to cut diamonds. Was this Hell's doing? Was her eternal damnation starting already? It took Catalina years to find her signature look—hair long and curled just so, make-up flawlessly applied, body shapely but toned, teeth straight instead of crooked—and she hated anyone who messed with her self-esteem. Was the distortion of her good looks her punishment then?

Way to hit below the belt, she thought angrily.

When Catalina lifted her blazing gaze, the remaining blob creatures hissed like deflating balloons. They retreated into the fog, disappearing as if they too had never been. Suddenly, Catalina was alone once more. Or so she thought.

When she turned around, she jumped in fright upon catching sight of Burngemear.

Big as an air balloon with a cloak so bottomless it rivaled the ocean floor, the creature that haunted Phani hovered over the asphalt as black smoke intermingled with the fog around them. The mask skull he wore looked foreboding. Darkness filled the empty sockets of his missing eyes. His presence was so stifling Catalina felt as if she were being buried alive.

She swallowed, taking a fearful step back.

"W-What—What do you want?"

His response surprised her.

A loyal companion you have been, living your role as designed. You were given a chance to escape and be something else, but you came back, he said, voice deep and penetrating as it vibrated against her chilled skin.

Catalina turned as he moved, circling her, staring. She wasn't about to lose sight of him and give him a chance to attack her unawares. His words confused her though. She didn't know what he meant. Was he always this cryptic?

"What are you talking about?" she demanded.

Burngemear pointed an ashen finger at her forehead. Nothing happened at first. Suddenly, her skin burned and prickled until the sensation spread throughout her body like wildfire. Needles stabbed every inch of her skin, muscles, organs, bones. Scraping and scraping and scraping until the pain touched her sanity, fragile as glass. It would shatter. It would shatter!

But she would not let it!

Catalina grit her teeth, swallowing her screams with irrational rage. She bit her bottom lip, tearing tender skin until it split and bled, oozing scarlet blood down her chin. Her nails stabbed against the cloth of her gloves, the force almost ripping the delicate fabric. Catalina scrunched her eyes shut.

Now this was starting to feel more like hell, she thought.

The pain continued, and it burned, clearing her mind until it was the only thing she knew.

How long has it been already? Hours? Days? Weeks? Time became endless in her mind. She was just one hot second away from howling in agonizing pain and releasing her insanity when Burngemear spoke and immediately ceased the pain. She gasped.

Such a good girl, the devil praised, lowering his hand. *I see humanity has not weakened your spirit.*

"W-What are you—What are you going to do to me?" she wheezed, feeling groggy and drained now that the onslaught of burning pain receded like a whiplash.

I have been tasked with making sure you do not suffer.

"Then what the fuck was that?"

A test. You cannot stand beside your Master if you cannot handle a little pain. Now come. Tenebris will experience a change like never before. It will need your assistance in maintaining order if it is to remain in one piece until the Master returns.

Suspicion trickled.

"Master?"

The true ruler of this realm.

Alarm bells went off. As Catalina stood there staring at him with wide eyes, face tilted, she realized Asphodel City and all its inhabitants were going to be in for a rude awakening, possibly even the world. She clenched her bruised fists.

"Why do you need me? What will I do?"

Burngemear chuckled as he allowed the black smoke to swallow the woman whole. Catalina did not protest, mainly because her mind was suddenly flooded with old forgotten memories, familiar volatile emotions, pleasure, anger, sorrow, love, loyalty. Even her prized skills and forgotten powers bestowed to her since she was created came rushing back like a tidal wave.

Yes. She understood now. It was back, it was all back. *She* was back and ready to conquer.

Catalina Patron was a fond chapter now over.

It is time, Burngemear said, *to return to your rightful place as Cerberus, the Guardian Hound of Tenebris.*

ACKNOWLEDGMENTS

Inferos Edge has been through some wild times and lots of revisions. I'm forever grateful to Miss Jessica, an editor who was assigned to me back when Eight Little Pages was still a thing. They may be gone, but Jessica's brilliant influence at shaping the overall story structure will live on. I heartily apologize you had to call me out so many times. Like, my face was red every time I read the highlighted sections that pointed out obvious mistakes.

Sorry, lovely!

Second, I want to shine the spotlight on my roommates, the FADS. They've been around since the conception of my book. Even after the writing, the editing, the drafting, and the capricious decision of whether I should traditionally publish Inferos Edge or just self-publish. You have all been a witness and wonderful support for me during the most stressful of times.

Seriously, without Cheeky Nando (the roomie, not the UK restaurant food chain), Catalina's name wouldn't have been an intimidating Spanish bombshell. Without Sarah, this story would have been a disorganized mess and Aedes's name wouldn't have sounded cool at all. And Alarcon, midnight fast-food buddy, thanks for being listening to me talk about whatever. I enjoyed our mid-night therapy sessions.

Also, I want to thank *mi familia*. Despite this novel not being up their alley, my parents have always been in my corner since hearing about the disappointing news of my desire to become an author. The same goes for my grandparents, *Abuela* Ana Maria and the recently late *Abuelo* Juan Hulse, who were most enthusiastic about my book despite its content *definitely* not being up their alley. Honestly, their support, prayers and goodwill meant far more to me than they will ever know.

A nod of acknowledgement must also go to the little brothers. Havi, I appreciated your feedback. Keep it real with me always. Danimals, stay creative and do you. I see great things in your future!

And lastly, more thanks go out to my beautiful and saint-like critique partner, Miss Katie Hudson. The fact that you even wanted to be my CP during the first edition of this book made me cry like an emotional mess. Not to mention your critiques and opinions of my novel have been invaluable. Looking forward to your own published novel in the future because I will so be the first to pre-order!

Until next time!

LIST OF TRIGGER WARNINGS

This book includes sensitive material of the following:

- Gore
- Death
- Violence
- Massacre
- Kidnapping
- Implied suicide
- Mentions of bigotry
- Mentions of mental illness
- Mentions of supernatural figures

Remember to pace yourself, practice self-care before, during, and after reading. If you feel you cannot tolerate the sensitive material in this book, prioritize yourself first and do not continue to read.

TURN THE PAGE FOR
A SNEAK PEEK OF...

AVERNUS WITHIN

THE FALLEN PANTHEON

BOOK TWO

Coming Soon...

AN ILLUSION IS BUT A LIE

THE FIRST CHURCH OF ASPHODEL had been a witness to many odd happenings in Asphodel City since its conception during the mid 1600s.

Witch hangings, raging fires, religious persecutions, secret town hall meetings, interracial and classist clandestine love affairs, illegitimate births from said clandestine love affairs, and revolutionary war battles. As time crept forward, the original purpose for the Asphodel church fell by the wayside, especially when the Van Darlington family came to town.

Building their own impressive chapel for public use, it far outclassed the modest termite tainted, wooden structure the First Church of Asphodel was built with. It could never hope to entice parishioners away from marble floors, stained-glass windows, fragrant candles, and sturdy bullet hole free walls. They even had pews with cotton cushions on them. The splintering cracked benches of the old FCA could never compare—not to mention, the First Church of Asphodel was barely larger than four horse stalls, even with the added annexation over the years.

Sadly, the place didn't inspire much alms from even the most devout of Christians.

As a result, and to keep from being demolished, the First Church of Asphodel had been used for many occasions and events. Some legally questionable. It's even been used as a make-shift morgue on more than one occasion; a storage shed for guns and livestock, a jail of several means for suspicious criminals, underground railroad rest stops for those fleeing to Canada, and a crime scene reenactment for house parties.

Eventually, the owners of the church sold it to Asphodel City around the 1900's and it has since been classified as a historical landmark in the 50's. No one besides the Historical Upkeep Society ever steps foot inside anymore—even they barely do more than check to make sure the support beams weren't rotted before neglecting to inspect it for another decade or so.

But then one day, a curious stranger broke inside.

Quiet as the wind, they purposefully left behind a glimmering gold disk. It was riddled with carved markings on both sides and weighed a solid two hundred pounds—supposedly. Placed underneath the hollow podium, it has since remained. It was the most valuable item the First Church of Asphodel had ever received in all its years. It cradled and hid the precious disk like a mother caring for a child.

For once, the structure had purpose. It felt...important.

Then, the stranger returned twenty years later and took back the disk like a hideous thief, snatching it away without so much as a whisper. The First Church of Asphodel didn't even have time to mourn its loss because that same night, several hours later, the padlocked front doors were broken in with such force the hinges broke.

"Fuck! I told you to use the battering ram carefully!"

Several men rushed inside, guns raised and pointed every which way. They scouted and inspected each corner and crevice the church had to offer. It wasn't much. Eventually, a petite svelte woman stepped inside, gun drawn. She cut an imposing but striking figure in a purple accented white power suit.

"Well?" she demanded. "Status report!"

"Clear."

She lifted her wrist to her lips. Her sleeve drew back to reveal a slim watch. "Ya hear that, Orcus?"

"Loud and clear," he answered from behind her.

Scowling, the woman turned to glare at her charge. Standing unapologetic at the entrance of the First Church of Asphodel was the most charming but contradicting man she had ever been acquainted with.

"Seriously? I told you to stay behind and wait for my signal! How the hell am I supposed to function as a bodyguard if you keep doing stupid shit like that?"

Orcus rolled his gray eyes. "That vacation really did a number on you."

The glare intensified. "How could I relax when you threw yourself at a bomb the minute baby cousin Huey does the same?"

"You work too hard, Miss Nishay. How about I buy you a large gift basket from your favorite cosmetic store?" Orcus bribed as he looked around the small space. The floorboards underneath his loafers creaked.

The woman glared harder in return. "It's Nox."

After a moment she contemplated the offer. "It better be worth over two grand. *Minimum.* And if I see any shades paler than coco, I'm fucking you up. And *not* in the good way."

Orcus grinned in response. "So close! Deal then. I'll even add a large fruit basket with plenty of pomegranates from my family's farm."

Nox wilted further, crumbling under the carefree, rascally charm only Eric Van Darlington was capable of. She sighed, her stress meter lowering.

"Fine. Just go search whatever it was you were looking for."

"Roger that. Anyone find a solid gold disk?" Orcus asked aloud as the men continued to search the perimeter. An owl hooted in the distance.

"None so far, sir." Cyrus, Nox's second-in-command, approached. "It doesn't look like this place has anything inside at all."

"Are you sure your source was correct? No one's touched this place for years it seems," Nox observed, her nose wrinkling at the sight of dust clinging to the hem of her pants.

Orcus ambled around, gray eyes cooling as they surveyed each inconspicuous surface. He closed his eyes for a moment. Nox studied his face intensely, eyes greedy for a sign.

When Orcus opened his eyes, he flickered a glance at Nox and smiled.

"I know you're skeptical that my homeless contact was telling me the truth, but he's never lied to me before and he wouldn't start now. The disk is here." His eyes glanced at the empty podium. "It just wouldn't be out in the open."

Cyrus looked at the podium. "We checked there. Four times in fact. There aren't many places to hide things in here."

Orcus chuckled, walking forward.

"You guys just have to look underneath," he kicked the flimsy wooden structure. It resisted at first, but after three solid whacks, it fell back, "the underneath."

It crashed to the floor with heavy fanfare. Dust clouds rose. Underneath the podium was a heavy circular indentation. Its center was free of dust as wood cracked and split away from the weight of the object that once resided there. A folded note was taped in its place.

Nox whistled. "Well, I'll be! I guess you *can* hide something in here."

"But it's gone," Cyrus pointed out. "And what's with the note?"

Orcus plucked the note and unfolded it. He was quiet as he read the parting message.

Nox was about to address Orcus when her mouth stilled, the words on her tongue evaporating under the quelling fury rising in his gaze. Gentle gray clouds became blazing pools of liquid steel. The light atmosphere inside the First Church of Asphodel dropped so hard the building's foundations rattled at the slightest November breeze.

No one said a word.

At last, Nox swallowed.

"Orcus?"

The wooden podium shattered into splinters from the kick Orcus delivered. No one visibly flinched, but their hearts did accelerate when Orcus turned away, stalking briskly to the exit.

"We're done."

Nox turned to her men and nodded at the door. "Pack it up."

Two minutes later, the First Church of Asphodel was empty and closed once again. To say the last ten minutes had been bizarre was an understatement.

Orcus was bent over a tombstone rumored to belong to the original pastor of the church. His grip was tight, knuckles white, tendons popping under the force of his fury. His breath came out in heavy pants, broad shoulders rising and falling.

Nox stood several feet away, hands to her side. She eyed him for several minutes before looking away. She wasn't sure what to say to cajole him out of his mood. Nox could count the number of times she'd seen Orcus unhinged on one hand. Even then, Catalina was usually around to calm him down. She used to be the only person he would listen to seriously. With her gone, Orcus was like an untethered helium balloon ready to float away. And something told her once Orcus floated to his highest limit and popped, Bad Things would follow.

"Nox," he gritted out after a moment.

"Yes?"

"This area was surveyed for how long before I arrived?"

"Two hours. We had a camera planted before that so technically three."

Orcus exhaled, seeming to put himself back together by sheer force of will.

Nox glanced at the fist where the note was crumpled.

"What did the note say? Who's it from?"

Orcus laughed before turning around and placing a hand over his face.

"Fucking *Thanatos*. He got here first. He knew I figured out where he hid one of the disks but moved it to a different location at the last minute. *HE'S FUCKING TOYING WITH ME.*"

In a fit of rage, Orcus grabbed his gun and shot the tree beside him five times. The old oak remained steady, but its remaining yellow leaves fell with a sigh. Nox flicked the wood chips from her shoulder.

"If Thanatos thinks he can beat me, he is *sorely* mistaken," Orcus hissed through clenched teeth. "*I always win.*"

Just when it seemed like he was getting ready to pick up steam, his phone rang. Orcus and Nox paused before eyeing each other briefly. That was a different ring tone. Nox had never heard that ring tone before. Orcus turned away quickly and answered.

"Hello?" Nox could hear a voice, but she couldn't make out the words. The man's attention was fastened to the call though. His expression changed, his shoulders relaxing, tension shrinking to something minor, manageable. Who was he speaking to? Araminta possibly?

"Where are you exactly?" Orcus spoke. He began to pace. "Stay put. I'm coming to pick you up." Once he hung up, he stared at Nox with the most pitiful eyes she'd ever seen. Goosebumps rose on her skin. "I have to go. It's Phani."

Of course. His ex girlfriend Araminta would be crazy to call him again after the stunt she pulled last time. Only naïve baby-faced Estephanie with a penchant for sticking her nose where it didn't belong would get caught in trouble once again. But why call Orcus? Nox thought the girl didn't like him.

"What about her?"

"I need to get her," he said, rushing a few steps away before turning around in a panic and repeating the steps a few seconds later. "Are there blankets in the car? Anything hot? Agh! Doesn't matter. I'll get one of the boys to do it. Shit, I drove here. Tell Bucky he's driving me tonight."

His thought process became consumed. Nox blinked at the change in personality. Since when has Orcus ever looked unsure of himself?

The note he had been clutching earlier fell at his feet. Just as he walked away for sure this time, Orcus looked back, eyes wide.

"Oh and Nox? Before you head home, do me a favor?"

Nox sighed. "What is it?"

Orcus's smile turned gentle. "Burn the fucking church down."

Nox didn't blink. "Consider it done."

He stepped away from the church ground at a brisk pace, gravel crunching under his polished shoes with each retreating step. Nox watched him leave until he was gone. She bent to pick up the fallen note and frowned at the message.

TOO LATE!

I TOOK IT BACK!

ROT IN HELL WHORESON!

I'D SOONER SEE THIS CITY BURN

THEN GIVE YOU BACK WHAT YOU WANT.

DID I MENTION YOU MIGHT GET A

FRIEND JOINING YOU IN THE

UNDERWORLD SOON?

A TIT FOR TAT, AFTER ALL.

"What cheek," Nox said aloud, folding the note before tucking it away inside her suit. "Now why would Thanatos toy around with Orcus like that? That's gonna bite him in the ass later."

Turning around, Nox called for Cyrus. He appeared from the church's shadows, ever patient, ever ready.

"You heard the man, burn this place. Leave no trace behind."

Cyrus briefly eyed the church. "Are you sure? It *is* a historical landmark."

Nox smirked. "Perfect. The flames will send a message then. Make it quick though. It'll snow soon."

ABOUT THE AUTHOR

ALEJ MCKINLEY is a short, but fierce Honduran immigrant living in the US with a penchant for drama, mystery, fantasy, and romance. Living vicariously through her characters, she is a hopeless romantic and lover of good fight scenes. When not writing, Alej is a jaded but optimistic digital artist, a closet Central American nerd, and collector of pink shoes. She hopes to one day call the UK home.

Stay connected with Alej McKinley on Twitter, TikTok, and Instagram (@alejishere) or join the AM Fam mailing list through her website, alejmckinley.com, where she talks all things bookish updates, writing craft, and storytelling related.